ALSO BY AMBER LEE

CALL IT SERIES

Call It Hope

Call It Fair Game

CALL IT FAIR GAME

AMBER LEE

Copyright © 2025 by Amber Lee

All rights reserved.

No part of this publication may be reproduced, distributed, or transmitted in any form or by any means, including photocopying, recording, or other electronic or mechanical methods, without the prior written permission of the publisher, except as permitted by U.S. copyright law. For permission requests, contact Amber Lee.

The story, all names, characters, and incidents portrayed in this production are fictitious. No identification with actual persons (living or deceased), places, buildings, and products is intended or should be inferred.

Book Cover by Books and Moods

Editing by Tormented Author Services

Formatting by Amber Lee

This one's for the ones who fight, flirt, and fall anyway. To everyone who's done playing nice—Let the games begin... and may the best heartbreaker win.

CONTENT WARNING

This book contains explicit sexual content, strong language, depictions of parental trauma, and other mature themes that may be triggering or sensitive for some readers.

PLAYLIST

CALL IT FAIR GAME

1. Nothing Matters—The Last Dinner Party

2. Chihiro—Billie Eilish

3. Killshot— Magdalena Bay

4. Give Me Everything— Pitbull, Afrojack, & Ne-Yo

5. Starboy (feat. Daft Punk)— The Weeknd

6. Midnight Sky— Miley Cyrus

7. Fire for You— Cannons

8. Still With You— Jung Kook

9. Void— Melanie Martinez

PROLOGUE

"I'm leaving!" I heard my mother yell at my father from downstairs. Wrapping myself in my blanket, I kneeled closely against the door and placed my right ear on it. They hadn't known I was awake and listening; if they had known, they probably wouldn't have said all the things they did. Deep down, I knew it was wrong of me to eavesdrop, but I simply couldn't find it in me to stop.

"You can't just leave me alone with our son! He is just a little boy who needs his mother!" my father screamed; I flinched at his harsh tone. My heart beat ferociously in my chest; I felt as if it would burst out at any moment.

"He doesn't need me! How could something I never loved ever need me?!" There was a sudden silence after her grating words. I didn't know when I started crying, but my tears drenched my face, my chest desperately heaving as I struggled to breathe. Panic overwhelmed me. I'd never felt this way before and felt as if I would die at any moment.

"You don't mean that, you love Micheal," I could hear the tremor in my father's voice; it was despairing. It wasn't him, not the strict father he showed me every day of my life. "What? You're leaving for good?"

"Yes. I'm leaving for the states and never coming back. Don't waste your time believing or even hoping that I'll come back, because I won't. I'm sick of this life, I'm sick of this place, and I'm sick of you." My mother's voice was cold as ice. She showed no emotion; she was a completely different person.

"Evelyn, please, I can't do this by myself. The three of us can leave Korea together," my father weakly suggested. I knew he was running out of ideas and ways to keep my mother from leaving.

"You don't get it. I said I don't want to be with you or Micheal. I want to live my life without stress or depression! You both are the reason I'm like this!" The sound of her suitcase handle being pulled open sprung my legs into action. I sprinted down the stairs like my life depended on it. I thought maybe if she saw me, maybe if she heard my cries for her, maybe if she realized how much I loved her, she would stay and try to love me back.

Right as I reached the last step on the stairs, I tripped and fell on my face. My parents rapidly turned toward me; the look of terror written on their faces was unforgettable. For a split second, I saw my mother's eyes water, and I felt a spring of hope in me. Without warning, she turned away and walked out the front door.

I couldn't bear to see her leave, not when I knew she wouldn't come back. "Ma!" I yelled as tears rolled down my face. "Ma! Please!" I wept and wept. My knee hurt from my fall, but I still forced myself to stand and run after her. The desperation in me was hopeless, but I had to try; I had to stop her from leaving me. My hand was inches away from the door when my father wrapped his arms around me and held me tightly.

"Let me go!" I screamed, "I need to go after her!" My father's chest heaved on my back as he cried his own tears. I didn't understand how he could hold us back; why wasn't he going after her?

I placed both of my palms against the door and looked outside the glass, watching the car drive off with my mother inside it. Once it was gone, my legs gave out, and I fell to the floor with my father behind me. We had spent that entire night on the floor crying together.

This isn't fair, none of this is fair. Is the only thing I constantly kept telling myself that night and I never forgot it. How could a mother do this to her son? How could a wife do this to her husband? Women are evil; they're not nurturing, loving humans; they only bring pain and suffering.

In that moment, I vowed to never love another woman, never let another woman in my heart ever again.

CHAPTER 1
MICHEAL

EIGHT MONTHS EARLIER...

I INHALE DEEPLY, WELCOMING THE SMELL OF GASOLINE AND rubber before sliding my helmet on and mounting my motorcycle. Shifting my weight onto my left leg, I kicked my right leg back and then up and over the bike. Once I straddled the engine, I sat down and acquainted myself with the controls. Revving my engine, I made sure that the brakes worked before riding.

I recently invested in my Triumph Bonneville a few months ago to get my way around the Big Apple without having to deal with New Yorkers on the subway or overpriced cabs. It's by far the best decision I'd made.

Back home in Korea, transportation was never a problem. It was affordable and efficient, much like New York. But when I moved to the city for college, I finally bought my dream bike. Sure, public transit was convenient, but it was nothing compared to the freedom of riding my own bike.

Clutching the lever, I shifted my bike in first gear. My favorite part was warming up the engine. There's a sense of thrill that rushes over me the moment I feel the engine's vibrations.

It's like bungee jumping. Your heart races before jumping because you are excited for the thrill that was coming. I placed my right foot on the center stand and made sure it was flush on the ground, then pushed my bike forward. I heard the click of the kickstand pop up.

Pressing the shifter down from first gear, I released the clutch slowly, and gently twisted the throttle. As the bike gained momentum, I pulled both of my feet on the pegs, accelerating forward, steering away from the cabs driving on the street.

I instantly felt the adrenaline rush that comes from riding; the exhilaration that stimulates the release of dopamine. There's nothing better than this. There's no better feeling once you jump off the cliff; it's almost as if you're flying.

It's freeing.

I'm on my way to Avenue nightclub, New York's most popular scene. It was almost impossible to get a spot on the list, especially on nights like tonight. They're throwing a Halloween party and I only had a ticket thanks to a friend. Dylan Cruz, owner of Cruz Fine Art, has quite the reputation, and let's just say, he could get in anywhere he wanted at whatever time he wanted.

When he gave me the invitation, I couldn't turn it down. I, myself, couldn't get a pass in. Working in finance didn't provide me with much of a reputation that would gain their attention. I had been to Avenue once for my birthday; my good friend Adam Pearson arranged it for me. He owns Pearson Book Group, one of the biggest publishing firms in the entire industry.

I convinced him to come tonight, which was a total surprise. He hates big scenery and large crowds. Convincing him to go was like convincing the grass to turn blue. Nearly impossible, but I did it.

Avenue wasn't a far drive, especially on my bike; it was about two miles away. As much as I'd like to continue to feel the wind against me, it ended quickly. I pulled into a parking area on the side of the street across from the club with the bright red neon lights that spelled the word 'Avenue' in all capital letters. Turning off the ignition, I put the kickstand down before taking off my helmet. I shrugged out of my leather jacket, revealing my joker costume beneath. I hadn't had time to pick a less common costume, so I had to wear last year's costume. It fit tight around my arms and chest, but I wasn't complaining.

I folded my leather jacket the best I could and put it in my saddlebag. After I secured everything, I made my way to the main entrance that was packed with people lined up, waiting to enter. As I walked up, I saw a variety of costumes. Barbies, superheroes, zombies, and about five jokers. I continued walking and grimaced at the jokers I passed by until I came up to the front of the velvet rope protected by security. The bouncer, with a tablet in hand, looked like he'd rather be anywhere else. His jaw was set, his brows were furrowed, and he sharply exhaled when the guy ahead of me fumbled with his ID; his patience already wearing thin.

"Name," he said flatly, eyes glued to the tablet.

"Micheal Zhang," I responded. He barely flicked his finger down the list before shaking his head. "You're not on the list." His tone was clipped, already moving on.

"What? I'm on it," I argued. "You didn't even look through the entire list."

His grip tightened around the tablet. "Are you telling me how to do my job?" His gaze finally snapped to mine, daring me to push it further. He was looking for a fight; hell, it's obvious that he'd been in a foul mood long before I even walked up. I noticed his name tag labeled 'Lev' and I suddenly didn't blame him. I'd be pissed at the world if my name was Lev, too. God, his parents had to hate him.

"Listen, man, I'm on the list under Dylan Cruz," I explained, certain that it would clear this misunderstanding. He curled a brow, mildly impressed by my words.

"Dylan Cruz? Should I know who the fuck you are?" He looked like he was about to laugh, like this was all some kind of joke. If he did, I wasn't sure I could stop myself from reacting. That was the one thing that always got under my skin—being laughed at. It was a minimal action, sure, but in moments like this, it ticked me off.

I clenched my fist, ready to throw the first punch right to his nose until a heavy hand landed on my left shoulder. "Micheal," a light Spanish accent spoke. I turned to see a tall brunette standing behind me in a Top Gun costume with his glasses on. It was Dylan Cruz.

"What's up man," I greeted him, relieved he came while I was standing outside. "This guy is giving me a hard time; he says my name is not on the list," I explained to him.

"I see," he said, as he adjusted his glasses. "Our names are on the list. Micheal Zhang and Dylan Cruz. If you do not see it on your tablet, I can give Diego a quick call to confirm." Diego was the current owner of Avenue. The security guard checked the list one last time with a smug look on his face. After his second scroll, he seemed to find it because his smile dropped faster than it had appeared.

He didn't mutter a word as he unhooked the red velvet rope, letting us in. I flashed him a smile as I walked past him. The music got louder the more we walked in; I could feel the beat in the music matching my heartbeat.

I took in the decorations surrounding the venue once we got on the dance floor. Spider webs covered the ceiling and the bar, and dark red and purple lights filled the space. Skulls and spider decorations were scattered around the room. I'd never seen a venue so dedicated to its theme, but again, there was a reason Avenue was the best.

I looked around the building and suddenly felt an urge to drink. It's been a long week since my father has been hounding me to visit him in Korea. You could say that he and I have a rough relationship. If I could skip those visits, I would, but he had made it a condition—every two years, I had to see him. In return, he'd continue my monthly allowance. It wasn't much, at least not by his standards, but just enough for me to survive. Very few knew I came from wealth; the Zhang's name was well-known in Korea, but here in America, I was just another face in the crowd.

My father owned a medical center in Seoul; it was like the Mayo Clinic of Korea, but probably bigger. So, yes, he was rich, which made our family name prominent, but I'd never looked at it like my money; it was always his.

I knew deep down that if I took ownership and became in charge of our family business, I would be in debt with my life. It was simple; if I wanted that amount of money, then I'd have to pay with my soul; never living the life that I *wanted* and never making the choices I *wanted*. No amount of money was worth that. I would rather struggle to make ends meet, and with the extra cash I received from my once every two-year visit, I was comfortable.

Before I knew it, I was at the bar standing next to a blonde in a Barbie costume who was ordering six shots of tequila. Shaking my head, I tried to get in the game. This was a party, drinks, attractive women... I should be enjoying myself. I glanced over my shoulder, catching a glimpse of Dylan across the room, already chatting up some brunette in a tight dress. Typical. I scooted closer to the blonde and noticed the diamonds attached to her pink jeans.

"Excuse me, I couldn't help but notice how beautiful you are, and it would've bothered me all night if I didn't come over to say hello." I extended my hand to her along with my signature charming smile. "Hi," I added. She smiled at me; her eyes wandered to my costume all the way down to my shoes.

"Hi," she greeted back with a smile. She slightly bit her

bottom lip, and I instantly knew I had her right where I wanted her. "What's a handsome guy like you doing here alone?"

"Isn't it obvious? I was looking for you," I prompted and took another step closer to her. It was easy to flirt with women when you gave them the right compliment. They were like plants; you gave them the right amount of water and they'd come to life.

"Is that so?" she asked playfully. I slowly nodded and took a quick glance back at the dance floor, noticing Dylan had already found a dance partner. An idea sprung to my mind as the bartender handed Barbie her shots.

"How about this? You take these back to your friends and you meet me on the dance floor," I suggested, eager to find out who this girl dancing with Dylan was. He wasn't the easiest human to approach.

"Okay," she blushed, grabbing the tray with both of her hands. I gave her a wink before she walked away. Right as she left my eyesight, I headed out to the dance floor.

As I approached Dylan and his mystery girl, I saw that another woman came into view. She had straight jet-black hair that reached down to her hips, which only made her hip movements look more hypnotizing. While dancing, she twirled with the other woman, laughing and smiling. She was wearing a black corset and a black miniskirt that hugged her curves. I'd never been so allured to a woman before. Tempted, yes, allured to the point where I couldn't control where my legs took me; no.

In a matter of seconds, I was behind her, smelling her perfume like a creep. She smelled like citrus and cinnamon, the strangest combination, and yet, it was perfection. It was the type of scent you wanted to snuggle up against next to a warm fire.

She twirled once more until she bumped into me and made me stumble backwards. I grabbed her wrist and saved her from a fall. As I was about to speak, dying to know more about this mystery woman, she beat me to it.

"Watch it," she growled. I chuckled to myself. She's got claws; I liked that in a woman. There wasn't a fake 'sorry' or a fake laugh, which only made me more intrigued and amused.

"You're the one who bumped into me." I smiled, wanting to know where this was going; If she'd back down or continue standing her ground. Which, frankly, never happens with other women.

"Didn't your parents teach you to stay away from the devil?" she replied, annoyance filled her voice. *The devil? That was her costume?* Sue me, but it didn't look anything like it. But then, I noticed the devil horns on her head, the small amount of blood poured over her cleavage. How defined her brows were.

"Yeah but, I'd always been a sinful child. Maybe you could help me with that?" I teased. I knew it was only going to feed the monster waiting to emerge from inside her, and god dammit, I wanted to see it.

"Go to hell," she snarled at me, and I couldn't help but grin.

"Only if you're there. Then I'd go happily." I winked at her. She seemed fed up with me; right when I thought she'd break loose, she surprised me. She looked back at her friend and walked away shortly after. Disappointment crept up inside me, and I was even more surprised at this feeling she left me with.

"Who was that?" I asked Dylan, feeling my checks hurting. I had a huge smile plastered on my face as I watched her go. For some reason, watching her leave was my favorite thing yet. Her walk, the way her hips swayed to the music without her trying; it was so damn satisfying.

What the fuck was wrong with me? Why was I getting so worked up over a chick I met minutes ago? One who clearly wanted to kill me.

"That's my friend, Celeste," her friend clarified. I'd never met a Celeste before, and I'd met plenty of women in my lifetime. Even her name was different, unique.

"Easy Micheal, I don't think that's a smart choice," Dylan advised me. Oh, I knew that, but it only made me want it more.

"Yeah, but I love the game," I replied, sure of my answer. The moment Celeste made it out of my eyesight, I looked around until my eyes rested on Adam. "Dude! You made it." I greeted him, glad to see he stuck to his word.

"You didn't give me much of a choice, did you?" he replied. "Cruz, was it?" He added in a dangerous tone I'd only heard twice in my years of knowing him. Once, when someone threatened to take over his top student position at Harvard business school and another time when he spoke to his uncle.

Dylan gave him a firm nod before he looked down at where his hand held the woman's wrist. I instantly watched Adam's face transform into a maddening look.

"Your hands. Off," he demanded. Dylan didn't miss a beat letting go. Adam stepped closer to her and slowly took her away. Dylan was left standing beside me, shocked. It took me a moment to realize what had happened.

Of course, Adam came for her. I chuckled deeply as I connected the dots.

"What the hell was that?" Dylan asked, swiftly becoming irritated.

"You know what it was," I told him, quickly becoming bored with the situation. Suddenly, a light hand rested on my right shoulder and I turned around to find Barbie smiling. I didn't know why I was expecting Celeste when I had just seen her storm off because of me.

"Hey!" Barbie said flirtatiously. I didn't even bother to ask for her name, and I had no genuine interest in finding out.

"Ah Barbie, how about I get you a drink, huh?" I asked her; I wanted to get away to see if I could find Celeste in the crowd. Her smile dropped as she looked around the club with me.

"Are you looking for someone?" she asked, annoyance seeped into her tone.

Jesus, I needed to get away from this crazy blonde. She was just… easy. There wasn't any fun in that.

"I was checking which bar had the best liquor for you," I said as an excuse.

"Oh," she giggled, her cheeks turned pink.

See? Easy.

"Yeah, if you could excuse me," I walked past her, headed toward the bar, and gave the impression that I was getting a drink. I made my way through the crowd until I was out of her eyeshot.

I squeezed between two people standing at the front of the bar and noticed a woman took over as bartender. She was kneeling on the floor, reaching for a fresh bottle of liquor. Excitement ran through my blood the minute she stood up from the floor.

It was her.

Celeste smiled as she lifted the bottle for everyone surrounding the bar to see; they whistled and clapped, excited to see that there was indeed more liquor. She made drinks faster than they were ordered, mixing liquor, adding ice, and pouring it into the cups. She moved swiftly through all the different types of liquor and picked them without having to look at the name; it was impressive.

She didn't miss a beat as she handed the customers their drinks, lost in her own world, completely unaware of me. I whistled louder than everyone at the bar and caught her quick glance. Her eyes rapidly narrowed, and that was when I knew she saw me.

Finally.

"What do you want?" she asked without looking me in the eye. She was going to be a hard one, but those are the best ones once you've earned them.

"Let's stick with the theme, yeah? I'll take a cosmopolitan." I answered her. She didn't respond, instead she made it. Somehow, she managed to make it in a matter of three seconds. She slid the drink across the bar; it stopped exactly an inch from me.

That was hot, I'll admit it.

"Hey!" I yelled to get her attention above the loud music. She looked back at me and rolled her eyes.

"What's wrong with the drink?" She was annoyed with me yet again.

"It's not a drink, it's my phone," I answered. She looked at me, confused, like I was an idiot.

"What?"

"Yeah, look," I handed over my phone, ready for her to type her information in. "It doesn't have your number. Seriously, I don't think it'll work without it," I smirked at her. This was the part where I expected her to smile and put her number in.

"Can't you see I'm working? The world doesn't stop for you." She spoke to me like a child that didn't understand the meaning of the word no. But to be fair, she hasn't said no yet.

"The world won't, but will you?" I asked, proud of my quick save. She didn't seem the least bit impressed, which was killing me. How could she be this stubborn?

"No. Can you move? I've got other drinks to make," she stated firmly.

Alright, I could take a hint.

I raised my hands up in surrender and took a step back. When I turned around, I was face to face with Malibu Barbie again.

Fuck me, I should've known the costume was a sign of crazy.

"I was waiting for you on the dance floor," she said, pouting. God, there was nothing I hated more than a woman who pouted like a baby. It was not cute at all.

"Can I get you a drink?" Celeste yelled to Barbie.

What the actual fuck? I had to yell and basically hover over the bar to get her attention.

"He got me a drink; no thanks," she answered and looked

back at me. Celeste huffed behind the bar and suddenly, I'm amused with why. So, I stood back and waited for it to unravel.

"He did?" She prompted and raised her left eyebrow.

Such perfect eyebrows.

"Yes…" she answered.

"Huh, no kidding. He's not your boyfriend, is he?" Celeste finally looked me in the eye; she was searching me with a smug look like she had found out a dirty secret that I didn't have.

"He's here with me–" I cut off Barbie.

"Why do you care?" I pushed, wanting some type of response.

"You're right; it's none of my business."

"It's not," I assured her.

"Alright."

"Are you and her–" Barbie uttered, but Celeste interrupted her. I almost wanted to laugh at the way she was getting so bothered by a stranger.

"I'm sorry, were you not just asking for my number?" Celeste asked abruptly.

"I apologize; didn't you say that you *didn't want* to give me your number?" I teased her yet again; I knew damn well I caught her red-handed.

"What?" Barbie questioned.

"No," Celeste answered defensively. Barbie grabbed my drink out of my hand and threw it directly at my face. I'm stunned, completely still and silent. I had only met that nut job literally twenty minutes ago!

"Jerk," she announced and walked away. I was trying to comprehend what had just happened when I was sprayed down with beer.

"I agree," Celeste added and put the beer spray gun down. She had a big smile on her face and before I knew it, security was behind me.

"What, from the bottom of my heart, the fuck?!" I exclaimed.

"Oh, did you get wet? My mistake." She sprayed my face again and gave me an evil smirk. "Oops," she muttered and covered her mouth. She made one right choice tonight, and it was choosing a costume that fit her just right. Because she was the fucking devil.

"Sir," security prompted behind me.

"Yeah, I get it. I'll be out." I didn't make a bigger scene than I'd like to because I'd much rather be escorted out of this place once than be completely blacklisted from the club. Looking at Celeste one last time with hatred in my eyes, I told myself I hated that woman. What the hell did I see in her?

I walked out of the club pissed and drenched in beer. Once the doors slammed closed behind me, I remembered that I rode my bike here. My helmet, my bike... they'd smell like beer by the time I got home.

"Damn it!" I yelled outside; a couple walking past me scurried away from me. They probably think I was a psychopath in a joker costume yelling in the middle of the street on Halloween. For one, I knew I made one good choice tonight. Dressing up as a joker because tonight turned out to be a total joke.

God, what the hell is wrong with me? Why am I allowing that woman to get me all riled up? If I ever saw her again, she'd seriously regret it. I clenched my jaw and exhaled sharply, forcing myself to shake it off. One night. One woman. It didn't mean a damn thing. I wouldn't let it. I yanked my helmet off my bike and shoved it on, gripping the handlebars so tightly my knuckles turned white.

Get it fucking together Micheal. This will *never* happen again.

CHAPTER 2
CELESTE

PRESENT...

"Wʜᴇɴ ʏᴏᴜ'ʀᴇ ᴘᴀɪɴᴛɪɴɢ ᴀ ᴍᴀɴ'ѕ ᴍᴀɴʜᴏᴏᴅ, ʏᴏᴜ ᴍᴜѕᴛ ѕᴛʀᴏᴋᴇ your brush upwards to get a nice, pleasing flow of the paint. Beautiful, isn't it? When you eliminate clothing, it makes it more timeless. Looking at Renaissance art, you'll realize they look like us. Our bodies are timeless, everywhere within history," Professor Ellis Farwell spoke to the class. Everyone sat in their own individual station with our wooden drafting easels and metal chairs in the large concrete classroom that smelled of paint and dust.

Every class acquired their own model, due to how long someone stood at the center with a hot, bright production light aimed directly at them. Today's lesson was to capture a human in all their forms, painting them nude. Though, I noticed that every time a new person came in, scattering across the floor onto the worn wooden platform, they avoided eye contact with all the artists gathered there. Except this model is different; he winked at every woman he saw.

I rolled my eyes in annoyance at how arrogant men could be.

When they had a decent penis, they thought they were the king of the world. But I ignored it and focused on putting paint on this canvas correctly for a passing grade. I had been in art school for about three years now, constantly learning about color theory, which annoyed the hell out of me. Everyone knows the primary colors are red, blue, and yellow. But they needed to quiz you on it every other week.

Whatever, I only have until the end of this month left before I begin working at my dream job in creating and selling art at the Laurosse Gallery. I began their internship program this April, which was beyond exciting; I had been itching to start ever since I took my tour last year.

"Celeste, I believe your measurements are a bit too small," my professor spoke behind me as she studied my painting. She was trying to say that I was painting this guy's penis too small. To be fair, she said to capture the humans in their truest form. This man might have a decent penis but he most definitely, without a doubt, has small dick energy. Plus, I'd seen better.

"Oh, I didn't realize; it must be the lighting." I tried to use it as an excuse to substitute for the real reason why I painted it this way. The professor tilted her head as she stared at the model, trying to make sense of what I said.

"That's all right, just do heavy strokes downwards to add the extra length. Then add the details afterwards," she advised me before moving to the next student. Great. Now I had to waste more paint to create a "perfect penis" on a pathetic excuse of a man.

It is for a passing grade, Celeste. You are almost finished...

That was what I constantly kept telling myself. Sometimes it helped me get through it and sometimes it just pissed me off. Nobody ever informed me about how expensive art school was. You had to invest in your own supplies, brushes and painting knives, canvas and panels, oil, acrylic, watercolor and spray paint of all colors, pen, pencils, and markers. I could go on and on and the list would continue.

How did I manage to pay for all of this? Let's just say I was in debt; debt that kept growing with each class I attended.

But, the great news was that I will get paid well. Good enough to pay off my debts and pay for things I enjoy while living comfortably. Suddenly, I heard giggling from across the room, completely distracting me. An artist who had her blonde hair up in a bun looked at our model with hearts in her eyes. Our model, on the other side, was constantly winking and flirting with her.

"Ugh, pathetic," I said under my breath to myself as I picked up my soft bristle brush to blend with smooth strokes.

I better receive a good ass grade for this.

I was dying for this class to end, which isn't a common feeling for me. Usually, I was always in the zone and so focused that time passed without me realizing it. That was what it was like to paint, to leave this world and enter a completely different one. One that was still and quiet, slow, and peaceful. It was addicting and I couldn't seem to find the feeling anywhere else.

Yet today, I was completely over it. I was over playing Jack in the movie Titanic, painting his French girls; except I was painting an idiot with an ego that shot up through the roof and into space. Did I mention I hated men like that? No? Well, I do. More than I should. Most women would find it attractive. I found it…well, repulsive.

I've grown to like making men feel intimidated; to stare into their eyes as if they were the only person in the room. If a man broke eye contact or could not look you in the eye, there was a sense of power that only women held. It was a sense of dominance and control that no man could resist once you've learned to master it. Nowadays, that power is handed to the men. Not many women truly used their ability to take control, and it was incredibly aggravating. But it didn't stop me from flirting with men. In fact, I did it more than I should. I liked to sting first, get them nervous before they could do it to me.

"Okay, class, finish your last details before heading out. You have five minutes," our professor announced.

Crap.

I wasn't done; I needed to blend the paint to create a vibrant scenery for the background. As is, I could turn it in without finishing, still ensuring a passing grade, but I was an artist and this was my art. Leaving it undone was unacceptable to me. Quickly, I blended the paint as well as I could, attempting to make it look nice rather than messy.

In the process, I spilled more paint on my overalls. I'd worn the same overalls since high school and I had a dab of red from back then to prove it. I'd been told multiple times by one of my best friends, Elaina, that I should strive to make a different fashion choice. Truth is, you couldn't wear anything fashionable while painting, unless you wanted it to be a part of the art. Also, I liked my overalls; I thought they were cute.

Paint had a way of finding its way into my hair as well. But, this time, I thanked God I pulled my hair up into a messy bun. If I didn't, it would have been horrible. Removing acrylic paint from curly hair was extremely complicated, and I unfortunately know this from experience.

"Paint brushes down, please. You may display your canvas in the back to dry. Excellent job today everyone!" Every student stood from their station and dropped their canvas in the back as instructed. They scattered out of the classroom like a bunch of rats, leaving nothing but silence behind. "That includes you, Ms. Castillo," my professor called out. She only used my last name when she was serious.

"I know; I was waiting for everyone to leave so I can place my canvas in the spot that I want." It was much easier to move other people's work around to make space for my art. That was the advantage of being the last to leave.

"Goodbye Ms. Castillo," she pushed as I settled my art on the top of the drying rack.

"Bye Professor, see you tomorrow." It was a Wednesday afternoon, and I had planned a wine night days ago with the girls. I hurriedly grabbed my bag and walked out of the studio.

I sighed as I heard the doors closed behind me. Man, I wished I had my own studio where I could stay for hours without having to worry about closing time. A space where I could freely express myself without having to deal with others. Instantly, I missed the smell of paint the moment I stepped outside into the New York air.

My apartment was only a ten-minute walk from the studio, and it was the main reason why I chose to live there. Sure, the building wasn't the prettiest nor safest place in town, but it had everything I needed. It was right in the middle of everything: my school, my job, and my favorite convenience store, The Haj Spot.

God, how I loved that convenience store. It never failed to have the right snack to match my current mood, and right about now, my exhausted mood was craving some chips. It wasn't until I saw a sign spelling out 'The Haj Spot' in bright red neon lights that I felt relieved. I swung the door open, letting the ring of the bell announce my presence.

Bo, the owner, was always the first to welcome me with a smile at the register. Hell, I'd be happy to see myself if I were him with how much time and money I spend here. I was practically keeping this place open.

"Celeste, long time no see," Bo greeted me and adjusted his cap. I'd only seen Bo take off his cap once, when he had thought he was alone. Maybe he was uncomfortable with going bald at the top of his head? I was always confused about why he always wore his cap, but now I knew he wore it to hide his balding head.

"Long time indeed," I replied, knowing that I was just here

yesterday at three in the morning because of a powdered donut craving I had.

"What can I get for you this time?" He asked with a crooked smile. I hummed, pretending to think.

"Chips. Pizza and... caramel flavored?" I questioned, wondering if he had my craving this time. No matter how crazy the craving was, Bo always seemed to have it.

"Of course!" Bo pointed at me humorously. He ran to the back, only to return with a cardboard box still closed with tape. Settling the box on the counter, he pulled out his pocket knife and sliced the lids open. I peeked over his shoulder and saw several blue bags of chips. Of course, he had a box of pizza and caramel flavored chips just lying in the back. "Ta-Da!" he exclaimed.

"Bo, teach me your ways," I said, staring at the chips with hearts in my eyes.

"No can do; I'd lose my most valuable customer." He handed me two bags and walked back to the register.

"Yeah, yeah. I'm bound to find out one day, Bo." He chuckled as he scanned both bags.

"Four dollars and thirty cents." Digging in my bag, I found a crumpled up five-dollar bill.

I should really invest in a wallet... I thought, while I quickly straightened it out on the counter, handing it to him.

"Keep the change." I winked at him, taking the chips out the door with me. Once I exited out, I checked the time on my phone and made sure I was still on time to wine night.

Right on time.

As I went down the subway stairs, I dug for my white headphones and played my go to song; Nothing Matters by The Last Dinner Party. I walked up to the gates, swiped my transportation card and entered, realizing that the train I was supposed to hop on was about to close its doors. *Crap.* If I didn't get on this train, I was going to be late.

As the doors slid closed, I ran and turned my body vertically, barely squeezing through the doors. Tripping over my feet, I hit the dirty ground the moment I got past those doors. Everyone surrounding me glanced in my direction, and glanced away, not bothering to help me up.

I cleared my throat, slightly embarrassed, and picked myself up.

The wine tonight better be strong, because hell... I need it.

I gripped the pole closest to me and rocked along the ride. The ride ended quickly; the first stop was where I got off.

Exiting through the doors, I headed up the stairs to the street. I was welcomed by a cold breeze that made me shiver in response. We were at the end of March, which meant the cold was coming to an end as well. Thank God, because the New York cold showed no mercy.

Elaina's building was a short walk from the subway; I'd say it was about a seven-minute distance. As I turned a corner, I came face to face with the facade of Elaina's building.

I strolled into the building and headed toward the elevator, pressed the button, and waited for two minutes. The elevator doors remained closed, so I pressed the button again rapidly. I wasn't the most patient person known to man; I think cavemen were more patient than me... The light blinks on and off, not able to hold on to my request.

Alright, forget this.

Giving up waiting, I pointed myself to the nearest staircase and climbed the two-flights of stairs to reach Elaina's floor. I slowly lost my breath in the process and thought I needed to start working out more; stairs always defeated me.

Nevertheless, I made it to the door with the numbers 223. I gave a hard knock before stepping back. I heard a few ruckuses from behind the door before Elaina opened with a smile and rosy cheeks.

"Finally," she chuckled. Elaina never chuckled freely without having some…I gasped loudly.

"You guys started drinking without me?!" I barged in, setting my bag on the floor. "How dare you?!" My friend Katherine was sitting on the couch with an empty glass in her hand. I could see the remnants of red wine in the bottom of the glass, proving she had a glass, or possibly more.

"It's not what you think…" Katherine tried to reason.

"Really? Cause it looks exactly like what I'm thinking." I crossed my arms and raised my right brow. No one could handle the raise of my brow.

"Okay, yes… but it was for a good reason!" She declared and rose from her seat.

"What could possibly be a good enough reason?" I asked, willing to hear them out. "Valery wouldn't have done this to me," I added. Our friend Valery was back in Barcelona, finishing up her culinary studies.

"Celeste…" a British accent announced from a phone. I scanned the room until my eyes landed on the iPhone set on the coffee table.

"No way," I started, accepting the low blow. Valery was on FaceTime with her own cup of wine from her apartment. "Seriously?"

"We were celebrating while we waited for you," Katherine explained. "Adam got chosen for an award at the CEO ceremony. It's an event they plan for the CEOs from known companies; they all come together and vote for the CEO of the year."

Adam was the CEO of The Pearson Group, one of the biggest publishing firms in the literature industry, also known as Katherine's attractive boyfriend and business partner. They met a few months ago, when I basically swiped his business card during one of my Avenue night shifts.

The thought of having a huge opportunity just waltzing around the club in the form of a man preyed on my mind. I felt as if I owed Katherine this chance. It was my way of repaying her for the loyalty she'd given me all these years. She was a grand friend and still is; she deserves everything and more.

In the end, it all worked out for the greater good. They were both happy, successful and in love; something I doubt I'd ever feel.

"That's great for him, but I don't see why you couldn't wait twenty minutes for my arrival," I voiced. Elaina rubbed my right shoulder, attempting to comfort me.

"You're right, we should have waited. The excitement got to us," Katherine said. "Let me make up for it," she adds.

"You could try..." I could be bribed into forgetting this... I took a seat beside Katherine on the couch and reached for the clean wine glass on the coffee table. "First, I'd like to catch up to where you guys left off," I spoke sarcastically. "How many glasses?"

"That's not important; have your first glass," Katherine suggested. Elaina shied away from my question, practically answering it.

"That many, huh? Am I going to find an empty bottle lying around the apartment?" I looked around, sensing Elaina's nervous energy.

"Ha! Of course not!" She exclaimed as she picked up her glass and took a generous sip.

"Right..." I sassed.

"Okay, back to what I was going to say. The CEO ceremony is next Saturday..." Katherine said; I hummed in response.

"Again, great, but what does that have to do with me?" I asked, unable to understand where this was going.

"I was going to tell you before you interrupted me. Let me talk, yes?" She cautiously leaned forward and placed her glass on the floor. I nodded as she turned back to me. "Adam gave me an extra ticket, knowing how much I'd love to have one of you guys by my side."

"Very considerate of him," I admitted. Seriously, what didn't this guy do for Katherine? It just proved how obsessed he was with her. I bet that extra ticket was pricey, but then again, Adam would spend whatever it took to see Katherine smile; this wouldn't be the first costly purchase he'd made for her.

"I was going to ask if you could come with me," Katherine clarified. I sat before her, speechless. She couldn't possibly think I would be the right choice for that event. *Me? In a cocktail dress?* I barely wore anything other than my painted overalls. Elaina, though? She would be a good choice.

"You're joking, right? You can't be serious," I declared. Katherine only gave me a confused look. She seemed baffled by my response. I didn't mean to sound ungrateful; I really don't think I'd be the best option. Imagining being in a room filled with billionaires as an artist fresh out of school wasn't the best feeling in the world.

"I am most certainly serious; I wouldn't want anybody else by my side," she assured me.

"Why not Elaina?" I asked as I glanced at Elaina sitting on the chair across from the couch.

"I'm assisting a fashion show that Saturday. Plus, I think this could be a nice change of scenery for you. You're always locked up in that studio, painting," Elaina blurted after being silent for most of the conversation. I gave her a skeptical look. "Listen, I'm not saying there's anything *wrong* with that. I'm saying it wouldn't hurt to crawl out of the hole for a day. You used to go out all the time, now you've stopped!" She exclaimed. I could ignore what she said, but I couldn't ignore the fact that she was right.

I sighed as I took in her words on a deeper level.

It was true; I was the type of person someone relied on when they needed a night out, the person who was always in the search for fun, who could *guarantee* you fun. Within these past few months, I had become devoted to my art. I was told that the last year of art school was intense, and man, were they right...

Finding myself as an artist, trying to create something that was deemed good enough, has made me lose myself. I tried so hard to make sure everything was perfect and in the end; I was never truly satisfied... Maybe I should go.

After a moment of silence, I came to my senses, downed my glass, and answered. "Fine, I'll go," I breathed.

"Ah! For real?!" Katherine energetically jumped from the couch and threw her hands in the air. Elaina stood from her chair, slightly wobbling from side to side. I buried my face in my hands and shook my head repeatedly. I couldn't believe I gave in so easily.

Really held your ground there, C.

"Yes, but I'm going into hibernation at the studio for the rest of this week! I need to finish and turn in my last piece before graduation next Monday," I added.

"Done!" Katherine yelled, with a smile plastered on her face. Instantly, the decision felt less dreadful.

"Cheers!" Valery's voice breaks up with the bad Wi-Fi.

"I'll drink to that!" Elaina shrieked. I winced at her high-pitched tone. Elaina raised the bottle of wine in the air before refilling our glasses.

"Cheers," I muttered.

CHAPTER 3
MICHEAL

I was woken up by an insufferable headache, unable to remember what happened last night, swiftly tossing around in a bed that didn't quite feel like mine. Rolling over, I knew I had to check the time. Last night before heading to the club, I had set an alarm for eight in the morning to ensure that I would get to work on time. Sometimes I needed it, and sometimes I didn't.

Though, this morning it seemed that I didn't need it after all. I stretched beneath the covers, groaning as I reached for what I thought was my phone on the nightstand closest to me. My hand grabbed hold of an incredibly small iPhone and I forced myself to open my eyes. Squinting, I noticed a pink phone case with daisies and turned it over to check the time.

The screen lit up to a photo of a blonde woman who held a white dog that could easily be mistaken for a rat. The time on the clock was 9:00 am. I rubbed my eyes and looked at the time once again.

9:01 am.

Fuck! I was late. Springing off the bed, I searched for my clothes around the unfamiliar room. I found my underwear and pants on the floor next to the door and my shirt thrown over a vanity mirror. Quietly, I changed into my clothes, careful not to wake up the mystery woman sleeping on the bed. Once I was fully dressed, I looked for my shoes around the room.

I groaned as I realized my pair of Jordans were on the floor beside where the woman slept. Slowly, I tip-toed toward my shoes, trying not to make a sound. I was an inch away from finally reaching my shoes when the floor creaked under my weight.

"Crap," I whispered under my breath. I froze before the woman and strongly gripped my shoes, pausing for a moment before swiftly moving again. Two steps away from the door, I heard the bed squeak. *So close.* I did an eighty degree turn to face the woman who was now wide awake, stretching out her arms as she took me in. "Hey *you*." I greeted her.

"Leaving already?" she teased and sat up, crossing her legs.

"Ah... I'm late for work." It wasn't exactly a lie; I was on time, but on the verge of being late. I had to be in the office in thirty minutes.

"You don't want a coffee? I can make you one quickly," she offered.

"Man, I'd kill for a coffee. I'm sure your coffee is *fantastic*, but like I said, I'm late." Trying my best to kindly decline the offer. I couldn't wait to run out of her apartment.

"Okay." She grinned. "I had a great time last night, Micheal. A *really* great time," she emphasized, checking me out. I reached for the doorknob and placed one foot out the door.

I paused for a second, trying to recall her name. Nothing popped into my mind. Not even a hint.

Did she say it started with a J? I think she did. Jules? Jennifer? Jenna? She definitely looked like a Jenna...

"Likewise, Jenna." I winked at her as I sprinted out the door, not sparing her another look and not asking for her number.

"It's Jessica!" she yelled as I slammed her apartment door shut. I stepped into the hallway, feeling a sudden twinge of confusion. I couldn't even remember how I even got here last night.

I hurried down the stairs and out into the parking lot, my mind still reeling. The place was practically deserted, just a handful of cars scattered around. I scanned the lot, searching for my bike.

Finally, I spotted it, leaning against a lamppost near the far end of the lot. I made my way over, relieved to find it still there, but my brain was still trying to piece together the rest of the night.

Well, no hard feelings. I rarely remembered the names of the women I'd slept with, nor could I tell you the number of women I slept with; I lost count when I turned twenty-four. Now, I am twenty-seven and working a nine-to-five job in finance at Hanson Wealth Management.

A real dream, if you ask me.

I went to business school for two years at Harvard to get my MBA, only to waste it on a job like this. Originally, it wasn't my first choice; I wanted to be an entrepreneur coming fresh out of high school, but my father thought it was ridiculous. He said it was an option for those who couldn't afford an education.

My father raised me as a single parent. My mother had left us when I was six; she continued living her life and didn't spare me another thought. Her career was more important than her own son and she wanted nothing to do with me. Growing up, I spent every mother's day knowing that other families had what I wanted. I went to school knowing I didn't have a mom who would volunteer for school field trips, help me with my homework, or to simply just be there for me when moments between my father and I got rough.

My entire life consisted of moments like those. My father is Korean; he's from Seoul. His way of parenting is stricter than others. My mother, on the other hand, is half-American, half-Korean. My father never speaks of her; it's a taboo topic for us and I didn't blame him. I didn't want to know about the woman who willingly left her family. Women aren't givers, they're takers. They take what they can and leave, just like my mother did.

My mood instantly lightened the moment I placed a hand on my motorcycle. Who said money couldn't buy happiness?

"Good morning sweetheart, how I missed you," I gently said to my bike as I took out my leather jacket from the pouch. I normally had a one-sided conversation with my bike. Many thought it was weird, but I didn't. I never felt ashamed of showing my bike a little love. If anything, it felt as if speaking to it made it run smoother.

Call me crazy, but every time I did, I felt the difference.

I patted my pockets as I got ready to leave, suddenly realizing something. Where was my phone? Double-checking my jacket, then my pants. After a moment of fumbling, I found it in the front pocket of my jeans, thank God.

I checked the time on my phone, 9:20 am, and I had to be at the office in ten minutes if I wanted to avoid another complaint from my supervisor. He'd been watching me plenty; he was like an itch I hadn't been able to scratch.

"Alright, sweetheart, let's get you warmed up," I muttered as I put on my helmet. I got onto the bike and turned on the ignition. Once I felt the motor's vibrations, I gave it a slight push to start.

I passed several cars that were stuck in traffic before arriving at the office, saving myself a good thirty minutes with this bike. That was why I was so fond of it; it constantly saved my ass and was a joy to ride as well.

I parked my bike across from the building, took off my jacket, revealing my white cashmere long-sleeved shirt. I rolled up my sleeves and fixed my pitch black hair after taking the helmet off. After securing everything, I made my way to the front lobby.

"Morning Micheal," the security guard greets me from the front desk as I emerge through the doors.

"Morning, Dave," I answered, walking toward the elevator and pressing the 'up' button. The doors opened, and I got on. I pushed the button to the fifth floor and waited patiently against the wall. The doors slid open, showing the entire office in a hectic manner.

I exited off the elevator and quickly made my way to my desk. Cubicles filled the entire floor and the employees with higher positions got their own private office with a door. Unlike mine, my cube is in the center of all the chaos.

I took a seat in my chair, the only thing I liked about my mini cubicle. I paid about three hundred for this exact chair; it was a modern fully reclining adjustable *leather* chair. The cushions felt like heaven, worth every damn penny.

To be honest, I wasn't about to waste that amount of money on a chair, but after sitting my ass on it, I knew I had to have it. I saw it as an investment; I sat in that damn chair all day planning budgets, performing audits, monitoring transactions, and preparing invoices. Basically, I stared at my computer like those obsessive bird watchers.

As I logged into my computer, I'm interrupted by my colleague, Ryan.

"Hey man, I need your help to prepare this invoice for Aaron Pearson," he explained, peeking through the office dividers. I rolled my eyes, annoyed that he'd asked for my "help" on another invoice. This guy couldn't work on his own for an entire day, even if his life depended on it.

"Listen, man–" the sudden call of my name cut me off.

"Mr. Zhang. My office, now," my boss ordered from his office across the room. Ryan looked back at me with a cheeky expression.

Dipshit.

"Got it, boss," I responded as I rose from my seat. Before leaving my desk, I logged off my computer, not wanting Ryan or anyone else in the office to get any funny ideas, like going through my computer. They would do that here; they couldn't help but be in each other's business; constantly on the lookout for whoever had success coming their way. They were like vultures; whatever got left behind or un-done, they would fly right in to eat the rest.

I made my way in strides, coming closer and closer to my boss's office. I hadn't been called to his office personally before, not for the last three years I'd been working for this company. Walking into the room, I shut the door behind me and took the seat across from his desk.

"Just to refresh my memory, you've been working here for three years now?" he began by asking. I stared at him with a bored expression.

"Yes sir," I replied.

"And you've been using that computer the entire time of your employment?" He asked. I scrunched my brows together, not able to follow.

"Yeah... I'm confused about why I'm here," I admitted, wanting answers. Sure, I might not love my job, but I was good at it. I was persistent and dedicated. Even though I felt like a damn zombie that constantly needed to visit a club with drinks to feel the tiniest bit alive.

He didn't answer me, instead he pulled up documents on his laptop and redirected his screen to me. "Read," he demanded. I chuckled to myself at his sudden order. *Fucking dick.* Nevertheless, I scanned the document.

The top of the document was labeled "Breach Confidentiality," explaining that I'd exposed sensitive information of a client that isn't even mine. What the fuck was this? This was bullshit. I hadn't exposed or released any type of information that belonged to my clients, much less someone else's.

"I didn't do this," I argued, not about taking the blame for something I didn't do.

"We found the files on your computer and we traced their destination; it led back to you," he explained as he locked his hands on his desk. "Mishandling this kind of information can lead to legal repercussions from the client. This breach also affects our client's careers, and we have no other choice but to face the consequences. Unfortunately, this means you're fired effective immediately."

"Fuck that," I spat out by mistake. The words fell out of my mouth with anger. "Sorry, I meant to ask why? Don't you need to go under investigation if it's sensitive information that's being leaked?" I asked, trying to find a loophole.

"You're fired Mr. Zhang. Pack up your desk and leave." My boss left me in shock in my seat. I didn't know what the hell he was talking about; I didn't know where he found the files and how it got traced back to me. Three years I spent in this office doing everything right, only to get fired over some bullshit I didn't do, when I should be employee of the month.

I got up from my seat and walked out of his office to take the walk of shame back to my desk to pack my things. I only had a notebook, basic office supplies such as pens and staples, and my files; it wasn't much.

"Since you're leaving, does that mean I can have your chair?" Ryan asked, obviously enjoying this.

"Fuck off, Ryan, I'll come back for my chair. You better not sit your dirty ass on my chair; I'll know if you did, you fucker," I responded before grabbing my box of belongings and heading to the elevator. At that moment, I realized I no longer had a stable income. I had to pay rent next month, and I didn't have any money saved since I lived paycheck to paycheck.

My mind rapidly searched for solutions as I rode the elevator down to the main floor. I reached the lobby and walked out the doors to the streets. Hopping on my bike, I rode all the way back to my apartment. The ride was long and intolerable as I held the box of my belongings with my right hand and the bike handle with my left.

What the hell was I going to do now? I had bills to pay with no job, no form of income. Those assholes didn't even give me a two-week notice. That has got to be illegal, right? Even if it was, who was I kidding? I couldn't afford a lawyer; I couldn't even pay my rent.

Think Micheal, use your brain for once.

The only realistic options I had were contacting my father or asking Adam or Dylan to give me a job. The first option was unacceptable; my father would most likely see this as an opportunity to take even more control over my life.

The shame I would feel even accepting a dollar from him would be insufferable. I wanted to be rich. Filthy rich, like the television show Crazy Rich Asians type of rich, but because of my own hard work. It would solve every single one of my problems and anyone who disagrees is full of shit. Money is power, and power is everything. Just ask my father.

My father wanted me to work in the medical field, but I was always hesitant about it. While I tried, I fucking hated it. I couldn't bear the idea of being in a hospital for most of my life, so I convinced my father to agree to business school. It wasn't going to make me the second generation Dr. Zhang, but it was going to get me a respectable career.

I wanted to have something of my own… my money, my business, my name, and I didn't want to depend on my father's money. If I did, I would forever be in debt to him. He wanted control over my life, and he was obsessed with shaping it into what he considered being "perfect."

I couldn't disagree more. I would rather work my ass off and be a free man than to be his little project.

As I arrived in front of my building, my phone buzzed in my pants pocket. "Damn," I said to myself. I was unnecessarily famous today for the wrong reasons. People just couldn't leave me alone; it wasn't even afternoon yet, and I had experienced enough to call it a day.

I dug for my phone in my pockets while trying to hold the box of items with one arm. Finally, I gripped my phone and pulled it out of my pocket, and the box slipped from my hold and fell to the ground. My items scattered across the street.

This is the cherry on top.

I let out a harsh, irritated groan. This day really had it out for me. I ignored the text and parked my bike. Swiftly, I picked up the items from the ground and threw them back into the box. My phone buzzed yet again, and I knew I couldn't ignore it much longer. This better be fucking worth it; if it's a spam text, I'm going to lose my shit.

> Adam: Call me when you have the chance.

> Adam: It's urgent.

"Now what?" I whispered to myself as I contemplated whether I should call him or not. Carrying my box through the door of my building, I walked to the elevator, pressed the call button, and dialed Adam on my cell. He picked up three rings later; at the same time, the elevator doors dinged open.

"Micheal," Adam greeted. He was never the type of person who greeted someone warmly, nor courteously. But I had gotten used to the fact that he was a grump throughout the years.

"What's up, man?" I asked as I walked into the elevator. I pressed my floor number and waited for his response.

"I have an event coming up, The CEO Ceremony, and I was going to ask if you would like to join me?" he suggested in a firm tone. "It's being held at Azure Grand over at Fifth Avenue.

It's one of the most exclusive venues in the city. You'll want to dress up for the occasion."

"Must you always be so formal, Adam?" I joked; I could hear his exaggerated sigh over the phone. "Why the invite? Are you not taking your girlfriend?" I exited the elevator and headed toward my door.

"Obviously she's coming; I'm inviting you because Katherine is bringing a friend. I found it fitting for you to keep her friend company," he admitted.

"So, she doesn't feel like she's third-wheeling, even though she is," I corrected.

"Yes," he said.

"So, basically, you're forcing me to go on a date with a woman I don't know for the entire night?" I curled a brow as I held my phone between my ear and shoulder while I dug for my apartment keys in my back pocket.

"Yes?" he added, sounding more concerned than the last response.

"Is she attractive?" I unlocked my door and kicked it open. I walked in, dropping the box at the entrance and flicking the light switch on.

"I can't answer that," he said defensively.

"Ah, she is, isn't she?" I prompted.

"That's for you to find out," he stated firmly. I loved messing with Adam; I found it incredibly satisfying whenever I broke through his icy exterior.

"Oh, she definitely is. Sweet."

"Why are you like this?" he asked, clearly annoyed with me. I chuckled in response, slightly proud of myself.

"You love me," I added. I shut the door closed harder than I expected.

"Was that a door? Are you not at the office working?" I winced at his question. I didn't want to answer him and I didn't want others to know I got fired just yet. Adam was the type of person that would try to take matters into his own hands by offering me a job, or lending me money. It would be impossible for me to accept it; it would feel more like a debt than help. I knew he would be doing it out of the tiniest bit of kindness he had buried deep in his heart, but even then... It just wouldn't feel right.

"No, I left early." I gave him half an answer, afraid I wouldn't be able to follow through with a made-up story. He hummed softly, making me nervous. My palms began to sweat, and I couldn't breathe as easily.

Adam knew me too well, more than my other friends do, which was why I felt nervous that he could sniff out my lie. I was ashamed and embarrassed that my career had ended quicker than the blink of an eye. How could I let this happen to me? I had to have the craziest amount of karma outweighing the luck in my life.

God, won't this call end sooner?

"Alright, well, Saturday at 8:00 pm. Don't be late," he states, forgetting his suspicions and automatically assuming my attendance. I sighed, feeling an immense amount of relief washing over me.

"I didn't say yes," I chuckled, knowing I was going to show up, anyway.

"Wear a suit." He ends the call.

Okay then... Goodbye to you too.

I slipped my phone back in my pocket, locked the door, and headed toward the kitchen, completely ignoring all my belongings from work on the floor.

Should I just throw everything away?

They weren't important things; they only reminded me of the fact that I now had no form of income; a reminder that I was now broke until I found a solution.

But how many available solutions did I have? I served myself a glass of water and paced around the apartment, sipping and thinking of options. It took me circling my apartment four times and an empty cup to come up with an idea. I worked at a successful firm. I had my own clients who chose to work with the company because of me.

My clients were all making a yearly income of over a million dollars, and most of them owned the company that produced this money. Who says I couldn't reach out to them now and ask for a job? I could work with them and earn their trust, which could potentially allow me to make the same amount they do. That was it... my ticket to financial freedom!

Straight away, I retrieved my work notebook from the box and searched through the pages, hoping to find someone who would likely take my resume. Thank God I didn't throw this notebook away; I had it all in here.

I came across a page with a list that contained all my clients. In total, I had about seven clients that weren't provided by Hanson Wealth Management and chose to work with *me*. First on the list is Diego Ford, owner of Avenue nightclub. I would call him, but that guy gave me the creeps. There was something off about him; for now I'd skip his name on the list.

Okay... going down this list was a bit concerning for me. I stopped on Dylan Cruz; he had become a friend of mine while working with him. I invited him to Avenue for my birthday last year and I could confidently say we were on good terms. Dylan Cruz had inherited Cruz Fine Art, a family business. They house only the finest collections of art, the type of art that has a similar price to what a private jet would cost.

His family had built this business not long ago in Spain; they were what you would call 'new blood' but don't let that fool you; Dylan Cruz never seemed like new blood. In fact, he seemed as if his family had been generating this amount of money for generations. He knew how to strategize and how to run a company. I could tell by the numbers, and the numbers never lie. I briefly became friends with Dylan after working two months with him but quit working with my firm the moment his numbers had a drastic increase, and I never got to know where he was getting the extra money; he didn't give anyone the chance to find out.

The more I thought about it,, he was the perfect person to reach out to. I was going to find a way to get into his circle, whether he liked it or not.

CHAPTER 4
CELESTE

For six hours, I've been in the university's art studio trying to finish my final piece before turning it in to Professor Ellis Farwell. This art studio has become my home for the past year; I was the first one to enter and the last to leave. Most people wouldn't spend their Thursday night working on an art project, but most people didn't rely on art to physically live. It was inevitable; it was like breathing for me.

Starting next week, I will no longer depend on this studio. I would no longer have a place to go whenever I needed to release bottled up emotions. To be honest, I had never thought about what I would lose in the process of gaining something else. Don't get me wrong, I was thrilled about the internship at Laurosse Gallery. I adored the atmosphere it had, the emotions and energy that vibrated off the walls. But I couldn't help but feel...

I chose to work there my first year of art school. It was the only place that made me feel anything, really, whether it was happiness, curiosity, confusion, sadness, or anger. I can say I have experienced all of the above.

There was nothing wrong with the gallery itself, just that it wouldn't have a studio for me to paint. When I graduate, I will no longer have access to this magical place. For some artists, such as myself, the aura that flows out of the painting has to do with not only the artist's emotion, but the location that the artist is in. These places can trigger inspiration and emotions.

I would miss the smell of wood, the smell of paint and dust, the dimmed lights that made the room feel more relaxing... It took the pressure off of me from stressful situations in my life. It would loosen the tightness I felt. The stool felt familiar and the air in the room was different from the air we'd breathe outdoors; it was somehow fresher. One day, I'd have my own studio and I would never, ever leave.

Unfortunately, my time was running out quicker than I'd like it to. The studio usually closed at 10:00 pm and it was currently 9:45. I had fifteen minutes to blend the additional colors on the canvas, but I couldn't rush the process otherwise, it would end up looking like shit.

"Finishing up C?" a deep voice spoke, breaking my concentration.

"Trying to Oliver," I admitted, heavily sighing at the canvas. I had completely lost my train of thought and couldn't seem to retrieve my idea. *So close, yet so far.*

"Oh, I interrupted, didn't I?" Oliver winces at me. Oliver was a close friend of mine; I had met him my first year of art school. We had gotten close our second year, and I noticed he had developed a crush on me. He thinks I haven't got a clue and preferably, I'd like to keep it that way.

We'd always greeted each other, including the nicknames we gave each other; C was mine and Ollie was his. I only ever used his real name when I felt bothered, which was clearly the case right now.

"I don't know, did you?" I questioned in a fiery tone. Oliver bows small with his hands tucked behind his back; I then realized that he had them hidden since he entered. I became curious about what it was he was hiding.

"I apologize for the mistake, but I came bearing gifts." He pulled out a greasy paper bag of empanadas and smiled. My stomach instantly betrayed me as it loudly growled. That slick bastard knew that I would never turn down food, especially after having spent the entire day at the studio.

"Fine. I'll eat them," I mumbled, slightly annoyed that I had given in so quickly. "Thank you," I added.

"You are very welcome." He winked as he set the greasy bag on the empty table across the room. I abandoned my station and took a seat on the stool that was inches away from the food. Oliver reached for the nearest stool and scooted it closer to me. "The painting seems to be coming along nicely," he commented, nodding toward my canvas.

I glanced back at it, taking in the streaks of deep oranges and soft purples blending into the horizon. A bonfire flickered at the center, casting a golden glow on the sand, with silhouettes of people gathered around, their laughter almost tangible in the brushstrokes. The waves rolled gently in the background, reflecting the fire's light like scattered stars on the water.

"You think?" I looked over my shoulder at my unfinished work.

"Definitely. It'll be ready in no time," he said, and smiled. That was who Oliver was; the sweetest person you'll meet. He always had the right words to say and the right amount of support to give. I'd be lying if I said I had never thought about giving Oliver a chance. He was a great guy, handsome, talented, and kind. He had great hair for a redhead and his brunette eyes were nice, but I didn't have a crazy attraction toward him. The type of crazy that has you thinking about it 24/7. He'd never kept me on my toes or made things more exciting. Plus, he wasn't my usual type.

I was drawn to men with an effortless confidence, a sharp

mind, and a little edge. Someone who carried himself with quiet intensity, like the kind you see in a man who doesn't need to say much to command attention. Strong jawlines, dark eyes that held a story, and a presence that made the air shift when they walked into a room. But that wasn't him.

"You've been here for a while C; you should give yourself a free day." This wasn't the first time Oliver told me this. I was simply a stubborn person; I liked things done my way. But, this time, a certain person convinced me, and her name started with a K.

"I have an event this Saturday with Katherine; it's supposed to be a fancy ceremony," I said, as I took a bite of my chicken empanada.

"Really?" he asked, shocked. He stared at me, as if he was trying to figure out which lie I was telling him. Luckily for me, I was telling the truth.

"Yes, is that so hard to believe?" I glanced at him, daring him to speak his mind. Just for once to tell me off.

"No, of course not. I can believe it." He chewed his food while looking around the room. See? A little too sweet. It's not that being too sweet is a bad thing, just that it gets sort of boring from time to time. At least for me, I was too fiery.

Oliver was like a marshmallow, and I was a fire. I'd burn the poor marshmallow till it turned into nothing but ash. What I needed was someone who offered wood; something that would fuel my fire and maintain it. Someone who accepted the fire and would do anything and everything to keep it alive. I wanted someone who needed and craved the warmth I offered. Was that too much to ask for? Perhaps it was; that's why it was so easy to stick to flings and casual dates. I think Oliver knows it deep down, and wouldn't take the risk of ruining our friendship, which I appreciated.

"Have you thought about adding white for the bonfire?" Oliver asked as he studied my painting.

"What?" I mumbled, completely out of it.

"White, it could be what you're missing," he repeated. I stared at the canvas, mentally layering the color over my work. My breath caught as I realized what he meant.

I had played around with every shade imaginable, deep oranges, rich blues, soft purples, but I had completely skimmed past white. It wasn't just an absence of color; it was contrast, highlight, movement.

"Ollie, you're a genius!" I jumped up from the stool and reached for my brush. I dipped it into the white paint and began adding gentle streaks along the waves, where the fire's glow reflected on the water. Then I touched up the bonfire itself, brightening the center so it looked like it truly flickered against the night. Finally, I added a few specks, stars barely visible in the dusky sky, a soft mist rising from where the sea met the shore.

By the time 10:00 pm came, I was cleaning up the edges and added the final touches, feeling extremely satisfied with the outcome. It was subtle, but it changed everything.

"I have nothing to wear," I said as I scanned my closet. It was Friday afternoon, and I had Elaina and Katherine come over to help me choose a dress for the event that was in less than twenty-four hours.

"Don't you have a cocktail dress?" Elaina asked, standing at the door of my bedroom. Katherine sat quietly on my bed as she observed the current situation.

"Don't be ridiculous. Of course I have a cocktail dress." I rolled my eyes away from Elaina and continued to search through hangers. I was getting irritated with this entire situation; I wished it would just disappear.

"Then?" she asked, shrugging it off.

"Then, what? I have a cocktail dress for the club, not for a *billionaire ceremony.*" I pointed at my closet aggressively. Any minute now, and I'd storm out of my bedroom and forget this whole thing.

Just breathe and get it done, was what I told myself to keep calm.

"I know this can feel overwhelming, but the event might not be what you think," Elaina said, scanning my closet again. Elaina always seemed to understand how another person felt by how they spoke; she sensed my nerves almost immediately. "If you want to be a successful artist, selling art for a fortune, these are the types of crowds you'll find yourself in. Perhaps not this specific crowd, but a similar one. It's best if you get a little taste of it now." I didn't want to admit it, but she was right.

Taking a deep breath, I allowed Elaina's words to make sense in my troubled mind. Taking a step back from my closet, I slumped onto the edge of my bed next to Katherine. She met my eyes and gave me a soft, reassuring smile. That was Katherine's power; she was able to share her calming energy with someone with just a look. "You're going to look beautiful, don't worry," Katherine added.

"A beautiful third-wheel," I said, dreading the fact that I'd be alone most of the time.

"Actually..." Katherine whispered as her smile grew bigger. Elaina took a black, floor length cocktail dress from my closet and laid it out on the bed.

"What...?" I waited.

"Adam is bringing a good friend of his; I heard he's pretty handsome," she voiced louder with confidence. "So, you won't be third-wheeling in this situation."

"Really? Wow, a date, how exciting, no?" Elaina added, clapping her hands in celebration.

"Great, so we'll be fourth wheeling," I summarized, certain that this wasn't going to be a date, because I didn't want it to be. I had zero interest in dating anyone right now, but deep down, the thought of not being alone didn't suck that much... Just as long as the other person knew it wasn't a date.

"Oh, come on, did you miss the part where I said he was handsome? You got really excited for me when you found out Adam was good looking, and he was my boss," Katherine argued.

"Yeah, but that's different. You liked him, it was written all over your face. You couldn't keep a straight face when he was mentioned," I explained.

"It's not that different," Elaina said, she straightened the dress out on the bed. "This is the dress. I'm going to cut the tiniest bit of the material at the bottom; I'll create a small slit on the right side, and I'm going to get rid of the long sleeves. It'll be perfect," she explained the vision she had in her head, while me and Katherine tilted our heads trying to envision it. "You'll wear a pair of long earrings I got from a previous fashion show and some black stilettos. Also, you'll wear your hair curly; it'll tie the entire outfit together,"

"You want me to wear my natural hair?" I asked, hesitant about her decision. I'd never doubt her; she was a professional in this field, even if she was waiting to get discovered by the industry. Truth is, it's hard to get recognized in any big industry, but it doesn't take away the amount of worth your talent has. But, still, as a curly head, I was always taught to straighten my hair for important events. It was a sign of professionalism, seriousness, and beauty.

"Yes, trust me, you'll look like a goddess with your coily curly hair," she said, sounding confident in her fashion advice.

"How are you going to finish all of that tonight?" Katherine warily asked.

"I'm altering it, not making it from scratch. It'll take around three hours to finish if I focus." Elaina grabbed the dress and walked out of the room. We both followed her to the living room, where she dug in her purse for tools. She miraculously pulls a sewing kit filled with pins, scissors, hand-sewing needles, a tape measure, and marking tools.

"Who travels with a sewing kit?" I asked, completely taken aback in surprise.

"Me, your friend who's about to save your life." She handed me the dress. "Now, I need to take your measurements before I cut anything. I need a glass of wine, walnuts, a cleared out coffee table for my tools, and for you to change into this, pronto," she said so effortlessly, like a surgeon demanding specific tools to use next in their procedure. I gulped, realizing that we were going to be here a lot longer than three hours. Especially with those incredibly small hand-sewing needles.

"I'll get the wine!" Katherine exclaimed as she headed toward the kitchen.

"I'll be right back." I marched off to my bedroom once again, mentally preparing myself to feel tiny needles pinch my skin. "It'll be worth it, definitely." I quietly winced to myself as I changed into the cocktail dress.

CHAPTER 5
CELESTE

Saturday night came faster than I expected, and here I was, getting dolled up for this event. Earlier this morning, I had tried to escape to the studio for at least a few hours. But unfortunately, it didn't work out. I couldn't help but feel jittery as Katherine curled certain parts of my hair. My hair was already curly, but Katherine suggested a more voluminous hairstyle. I, on the other hand, was finishing my makeup and decided on a smokey eye, though it's been a while since I'd done such a bold look; it seemed like the perfect occasion for it.

"Nervous?" Katherine asked as she released my hair from the curling iron. Ignoring her questions, I kept staring at my reflection in my bathroom mirror. I wished I was in my painted overalls, glancing at my canvas in different positions, wondering what was missing and what could be added.

"Volià!" Elaina exclaims as she walks into the bathroom with my dress in her hands. She had spent the last few hours adding the last details to the dress. It was absolutely breathtaking; the black shimmery gems she sewed on the sleeves, the slit she added on the right end, made it look like a completely new dress.

Perfectly done. Of course, I couldn't show my excitement too much; I was still in a rebellious state of mind.

Katherine's jaw dropped to the floor the moment she laid her eyes on the dress. "Oh, Elaina, it's spectacular," she said. Elaina, with a proud look on her face, smiled. She took a few steps back and squinted her eyes as she took me in.

"Your hair looks beautiful," Elaina complemented. "Love the dark look." I anxiously shook my hands and smiled.

"Yeah, well, I was aiming for that," I said. My stomach growled as I put my last layer of mascara on. I didn't understand the nerves I was feeling; the angst, the nausea. It's like my body knows something I don't. Should I mentally prepare myself for this? No, how could I?

"The event starts in an hour; you should start thinking about getting into this dress," Katherine added as she handed me the black fabric. I nodded, received the dress, and began changing. Katherine had been ready since she arrived; she came in a shimmery gold metallic dress, her hair straightened, and makeup freshly done.

Once I slipped into the dress, I turned my back to Elaina so she could zip me. I hadn't seen how the dress looked yet, but it felt amazing. It hugged every one of my curves, giving me a secured feeling. Gasps filled the room as I turned and faced them. "What? Is something wrong?" I asked, concerned if the gasps were good ones or not.

"Nothing. There's absolutely nothing wrong, everything is perfect," Katherine admitted, with a huge smile plastered on her face. I quickly made my way toward the long mirror to see the finished look. As I came into frame, I let out the tiniest gasp. It was me but...enhanced to an extreme amount. This dress, my hair, my face, the jewelry.

It's me.

I was at a loss for words; I felt like a duchess. No, a queen.

Katherine and Elaina smiled behind me as they admired the

look on my face. Katherine quickly checks her phone and yelps. "We're going to be late! We had to leave like five minutes ago." She grabbed her clutch and my wrist and ran out the door, dragging me down to the garage. Elaina ran behind us, holding our dresses so we wouldn't trip. We were like Cinderella after the ball, except we ran to get there instead of running to leave.

We arrived at the event just in time. The limo came to a stop right in front of the building holding the event, where Adam stood outside waiting for us. The building was beautiful, its facade clad in sleek glass and steel; a towering skyscraper dominating the skyline. The rest of the city lights reflected off the building, almost like a mirror. Adam opened the door for the both of us to shuffle out of the limo.

"You look beautiful, Angel," Adam complimented Katherine with hearts in his eyes. She smiled stupidly as she grabbed a hold of his forearm. They looked so in love, the type of love you only see in movies. "Celeste, you clean up well," Adam said with a friendly smile.

"Oh, thanks. I rarely get dressed up for these types of things," I answered. "Congratulations on getting invited to an event like this."

"Thank you. It's not my first CEO award," he responded.

Jesus, humble much?

"Though it is my first with the real prize on my arm." He looked down at Katherine.

Okay, now I'm getting the feeling that I'm going to be a third wheel.

Once their little moment was over, Adam spoke. "Shall we?"

"Yes." I smiled and followed behind them. As we walked in through the double doors, I was in shock. Whoever designed this building has a mind of gold; the modern luxury interior design was the die for. Simplistic, clean lines, and high-quality materials characterized the entire space; a perfectly fresh and contemporary take on elegance. It was only the lobby that I'd seen; I couldn't imagine how extravagant the event itself would be.

"I have invited my good friend, Micheal, to join us tonight; I didn't want you to feel alone, so I hoped you'd both enjoy each other's company," Adam suddenly spoke as we entered the insanely clean elevator.

Why does it smell like lavender and chocolate here? Amazing.

"Oh," I responded.

"I thought it was a great idea; he reminds me of you," Katherine added.

This sounds more and more like a blind date...

"Hm, he does?"

A male version of me doesn't exist; I'm far too great for a man to match. Not to be sexist or anything, but all men have disappointed me, including my father. I wouldn't say I'm a man hater, but I would say that I would prefer to distance myself until I feel like there's something worth taking a chance on. What's so wrong with that?

"I think you'd really like him," Katherine said. Keeping my mouth shut, I didn't say another word; I didn't want to if I was being honest. A blind date is not what I came here for; I came here to support my friend.

The elevator dinged open on the thirtieth floor. I had been so lost in thought, I hadn't realized how quick we'd gotten there. We walked off the elevator and headed towards the event. They had reserved the entire floor for this private event; there were a good amount of servers walking around with champagne glasses and little appetizers on their silver round trays. I held myself back from grabbing food so early; that wouldn't be very ladylike of me.

I must be mindful, demure, elegant, and sophisticated.

The lights were dimmed to a perfect level, the music classical, the overall vibe of this event felt far too luxurious for someone who didn't live this lifestyle. It was beautiful, but I don't think I could do this often.

Without realizing it, I had wandered off without Adam and Katherine, finding a small gallery with lovely paintings and sculptures; I suddenly didn't feel like I stuck out like a sore thumb. I came face to face with a vintage painting I studied at my university. It was called *Water Lillies*, a 1919 painting by Claude Monet. It depicts a scene in Monet's French pond, showing light reflecting off the water, with water lilies on the surface. The yellow, green, pink, red, the pinch of white and orange was a masterpiece. It was so magical to see in person, I almost couldn't believe it; you could see the direction his brush was flowing and the minor details he added... the colors that he mixed... This is history.

How could they have such a prized possession here at this event? How is it not guarded enough? I can't see any security around this room unless they're in disguise.

"Beautiful, isn't it?" a dark, Latin accent spoke. I briskly turned to the man in a plain suit and black glasses. "It's one of my best collections," he admits.

"Your collection?"

There was no way in hell a man his age could be in possession of this world-wide famous art piece. He seemed too young for that–late-twenties at most.

"Yes," he answered. "I have only the best pieces of art in the industry. If you're interested in a painting, I'd be more than glad to help you. Here's my card." He dug in his coat and handed me a card.

Without saying another word, he left the room. The material of this paper is strong, it's almost unbreakable. *Dylan Cruz, Cruz Fine Art.* I chuckled to myself that he thought a person like me would talk business with him.

Me? Purchase a multi million-dollar painting? Yeah, no. Wow," I whispered to myself.

There's so much money in the art world, it's not even funny. That'd be my dream; to open my own gallery with amazing art pieces such as this one.

I glanced at the water lilies once more before taking my leave. Katherine is probably wondering where I went. If I didn't leave now, I would never make it out, so I forced my legs to move.

Okay, time to go. I marched out of the room with firm steps, rushed out the double door, and suddenly bumped into someone.

Losing my balance, I slipped backwards. I tightly shut my eyes, bracing myself for the fall, until a pair of arms wrapped around my waist and cradled the back of my head. I squinted open an eye to peek at this person who caught me. Black straight hair, skin pale but clear as glass skin, double eyelids, slim nose, full lips, small face. He was incredibly handsome, and he looked like he walked straight out of a rom-com as the lead male.

"Are you alright?" he asked in the smoothest voice. I recognized it from somewhere; I couldn't figure out where, but it was on the tip of my tongue. He helped me regain my balance as I stood on both legs and out of his arms.

Unfortunately...

"Yeah, I'm fine," I answered, suddenly feeling nervous. I forced myself to make eye contact and remember my strategy: *Intimidate him before he does to you.* Looking into those brown eyes, they fully captivated me. How could someone be this handsome? It should be illegal with how close he was to my ideal dream man; looks wise, that is.

God, his eyes were to die for.

Dark, almond-shaped, and impossibly deep, they hold a quiet intensity that makes you feel like he sees right through you. They have a way of lingering, of holding your gaze a little too long, as if searching for something unspoken. His brows, thick and naturally arched, add to his expressive face. I'd bet they furrow slightly when he's deep in thought and lift in amusement when he's teasing... His jawline seemed like the Gods themselves sculpted it, effortlessly defined, as if carved by careful hands. His cheekbones are high, subtly casting shadows that emphasize his aristocratic features.

His hair is jet black, thick, and perfectly tousled, with just the right amount of volume. The strands fall naturally, slightly covering his forehead, never messy, always as if he just ran a hand through it without a second thought. It has a soft shine under the light, hinting at silkiness, the kind you'd instinctively want to run your fingers through.

He's tall and lean, he seems like the type of person who doesn't have to try too hard to stay fit. His arms are toned and strong, his biceps defined but not overdone, just enough to make it noticeable under his suit. His shoulders are broad, his chest is firm, his body lean but athletic; he carries himself with effortless confidence, moving with smooth, controlled motions.

"I know you from somewhere," he admitted, pointing his finger at me as he tries to remember.

"You do?" I asked, curious about how, since I can't help but feel like I've met him before as well. "Do you live around here?"

"Brooklyn," he answered. "You?"

"Midtown." His eyes squinted as he smiled... Such a breathtaking smile. When he smiles, it's not immediate—it starts slowly, tugging at the corner of his lips before blooming into something dazzling.

"Got to hate the traffic there every morning, huh?" he joked. I nodded; I didn't know what to say without sounding stupid.

"It's not so bad. My job and university are close to my apartment."

"Where do you work?" he asked.

"Avenue. I'm a bartender." There was an unexpected pause

as we both looked at each other. Suddenly, I connected the pieces and realized where I knew him from. *No...* I get the impression I'm right because his entire facial expression changed. The flirtatious atmosphere completely dissolved into a dark vibe.

"You're that crazy ass bartender who sprayed beer at me!" He furiously narrowed his eyebrows. "You owe me a new helmet! Do you have any idea how horrible it is to get your hair drenched in beer and then have to wear your BRAND NEW EXPENSIVE HELMET?!" he exclaimed. People around us began whispering, but I didn't care; I screamed back even louder.

"CAN YOU BLAME ME?! YOU ACTED LIKE A CREEP!" I argued. It was a lie; I was actually really attracted to him, but I was playing hard to get because I wanted him to chase me. But, admittedly, I lost my shit when I realized that not only was he flirting with me, but he was flirting with another woman.

"A creep?! I was fucking charming!" he said in a lower tone, almost as if my calling him a creep insulted him. But, truly, the best word to describe him would be wynorrific. Something being both beautiful and pleasurable, but horrific at the same time.

"Not to me. Thanks for nothing, asshole." I turned my back to him and strode to find Adam and Katherine inside the event.

"Thanks for nothing is crazy; I *literally* saved you." I heard him say as I kept walking away.

What a disappointment.

He was too good to be true; way too handsome to be perfect. Walking into the space that held the event, I noticed multiple round white tables around the room, with chairs and nametags. I scanned the room, looking for Katherine, until I found her sitting with a glass of champagne in her hand, as Adam approached her, standing by her side.

I left her alone for so long.

The voice kept repeating in my mind as I got closer to her. I felt like a horrible friend. Well, I'm sure she'd understand once I tell her about my encounter with *Mr. Too-Good-To-Be-True* back there.

"Kat," I called her name as I approached the table.

"Hey! Where were you? I thought I lost you," she said as she patted the chair next to hers with my name tag on it.

"I'm sorry, I got a little caught up with the art gallery they had. Also, I lost track of time talking to this guy I met." Her eyes widened at my words.

"A guy?" she asked excitedly, wanting more details.

Oh Katherine, how let down you'll be when you hear this...

"Yeah, but it's nothing to be excited about; he ended up being an asshole I met before at Avenue," I explained to her as I grabbed a glass of champagne off of a waiter's tray who walked past us and took a seat.

"Oh no," she said.

"I know. Far too handsome for that soul. He would've been perfect if he was anyone else with that same face." I shrugged as I took a gulp of my champagne.

"Oh, well, don't worry about that. You still have another shot tonight with Micheal, you haven't met him yet," she added, and winked at me. I guess she was right, maybe Micheal is more handsome and charming than Mr. Asshole.

"Oh, and here he comes now." I drank the last drop of champagne from my glass before turning to meet this mystery man.

"Micheal, meet Celeste, Katherine's friend," Adam announced before moving out of the way. Once I saw his face, let's just say...my jaw couldn't have dropped faster.

CHAPTER 6
MICHEAL

I shook off the horrible encounter with the devil woman and continued on with my plan. Adam had invited me to the CEO award ceremony to keep Katherine's friend company. I agreed because I simply couldn't turn down a suitable date. But, it wasn't until I found out that someone I had been trying to pin down got invited to this ceremony. Dylan Cruz hosted a yearly annual gallery at these events; rich people go crazy over the pieces his company sold. The plan was to find Dylan and speak to him; Katherine's friend could wait a few minutes.

Straightening my tie, I made my way inside the gallery. Out of the corner of my eye, I saw him speaking to a man in front of a green painting. I took a deep breath, building the courage to speak to him.

Alright Micheal, time to get that bag.

As I approached him, the man who he was having a conversation with left, leaving the perfect opening for me.

"Dylan Cruz, long time no see, brother," I greeted him with a smile. He turned his attention toward me and lent his hand out to me.

"Micheal Zhang, pleasure seeing you here. How's the

company holding up?" he asked me, as if it was my company. Little does he know, I'm newly unemployed.

A man's best dream...

"Well, I wouldn't know; I left a little while back," I responded, taking this chance to request for any job openings. I'm almost positive his firm had to have some type of position open. What type of multi-billion dollar company doesn't? "Actually, I'm glad you asked because I was hoping that you had a job opening." I shot my shot, praying that he would say yes.

"At Cruz Fine Arts? I'm sorry, but we're not taking any new employees. We're actually cutting people out as of now," he said; my hopes had dropped in a matter of seconds.

Fuck. What was I supposed to do now?

"That's a shame; I understand, though. No worries, my man." I turned on my heels, preparing to leave until his voice stopped me.

"If you're really interested in finding a job that pays good money, I might be able to help you out," he suggested, as he discreetly looked around the room, like he didn't want anyone else listening in on the conversation.

"Yeah? That'd be awesome. I'll take it!" I said without giving it much thought. All I needed to hear was the job pays good money, and that's it. Dylan gave me a tense smile as he fixed his glasses.

"I didn't even tell you what the job was, the risks," he explained.

"I'll take it, regardless; not taking it would be a risk for myself." Dylan sighed at my words.

"Alright, how about this? On Monday, we'll meet at my office to speak more about it. I'll explain the risks and the rest of the details you would need before taking this job. If you agree, we'll begin right away," he said. I gave him a firm nod, knowing that whatever it was, I was going to take it.

"Sounds good," I agreed wholeheartedly. I was relieved that

my freedom was right around the corner. Some risks? I could do it. Good pay? I could most definitely do it.

Try me.

"Monday, 9:00 am, don't be late." Was the last thing he said to me before he walked up to the next person analyzing the paintings. Feeling victorious, I took my leave and headed toward the CEO award ceremony a few doors down. This night was starting to feel extremely lucky for me. I basically secured myself a job and I'm about to meet my hot date that I'll possibly be going home with tonight.

As I entered the room, Adam's hand landed on my shoulder. "Trouble finding the Ceremony? I'm about to claim my award," he said, his voice firm and confident.

"How do you know it's your award?" I chuckled, scanning the room for my mystery women.

"Because it simply is." He shared a smug smile.

"You cocky bastard, you might just win," I answered, knowing deep down that the award was his, too. Adam patted my shoulder before heading toward our table.

"I'd like to introduce you to Katherine's friend," Adam voiced as he passed the following white tables until we reached ours. "Micheal, meet Celeste, Katherine's friend." He briefly moved to the side so I could meet the beautiful… devil woman.

I locked eyes with the woman of my literal nightmares. Of course, it had to be her. Though I could tell she was just as shocked and disappointed as me. I was offended by her reaction towards me, or else I'd have been impressed at the speed with which her jaw dropped.

"You again." Her voice bled with pure hatred. Christ, I disliked this woman as much as she did me, but that 'you again' sounded far too personal.

"Me again," I added with a certain charm. I couldn't help myself but push her over the edge even more. It's only fair after she almost ruined my night.

"You two know each other?" Adam asked, confused as Katherine looked at Celeste, concerned.

"It seems that we do, small world, isn't it, Celeste?" I knew that she was cursing me with everything she had on the inside.

"Why are you here?" she asked with disgust.

Not so smart, I see.

"Probably the same as you, to get some. I can obviously see that's not going to happen," I responded, knowing it would only get her pissed.

"You're pathetic; that's nowhere near the same reason I'm here," she argued defensively. Katherine's mouth opened a few inches. I'm sure it was her plan to get us together, and she now realized just how horrible of an idea that was. "God, you have to be my karma."

"Your karma? Ha! If anything, you're mine, sweetheart. You owe me a new helmet and a new pair of shoes. You dirtied mine when I saved you from your ridiculous fall." I could feel my anger building. I was getting way too affected by this conversation. It was supposed to be all fun and games, but I was weirdly feeling enraged by her.

"Ridiculous? What?! You expect people to not make one clumsy mistake?" She crossed her arms with a large amount of sass.

What a drama queen. I feel bad for the bastard that'll end up with her.

"You're absolutely right, I apologize. Not everyone can be perfect like me." I bowed sarcastically.

"Why, you arrogant ass–"

"Okay! How nice of you to join us Micheal, you can take my seat beside Adam and I can take yours beside Celeste," Katherine interrupted her lunatic friend before she made a bigger scene.

"Thank you," I accepted, as I reached for her seat, happy to get as far as I can from that crazy woman.

"No, you don't have to do that. We'll be fine." Celeste surprised me with her sudden response.

Is she nuts? Why does she want to be next to me? I mean, I get it, I'm handsome. But come on?

"You came to be with Adam, not to deal with this; I'm sorry, I'll dial it down a bit as long as Coccydynia over here leaves me alone."

I'm sorry, Coccydynia?!

"I promise," she voiced in such a sincere tone, I almost believed her.

"Okay," Katherine hesitantly agreed before taking the seat I was so close to having.

Why, why me?

It's such a shame too. Celeste is a breathtaking woman; she has a flowerlike face and a moonlike figure. But I can't get ahead of myself. It's said that even the devil was the most beautiful human of them all. I think the best way to describe her after meeting her twice is beauty and chaos intertwined. Like a deadly nightshade or an aconite–a beautiful plant that secretly has enough poison to kill you.

I ignored the sudden thought that crept its way into my mind. Instead, I reached for a sandwich that was placed in the middle of the table. My fingers lightly grazed over the savory white bread, until a cruel, long nailed hand swatted my hand away. I almost cracked my neck with how drastically I turned my head.

"What the *fuck*?" I questioned Celeste.

"Are you seriously reaching for food now? They just started," she whispers as she points to the stage, where there was, in fact, a man speaking. I sighed heavily as I leaned back in my chair.

"So?" I asked.

"So? It's rude," she stated as a fact.

"Oh yeah? Says who?" I quirked my brow at her, certain that she probably pulled this crap out of her bare ass just to spite me.

"Brazing Magazine." I almost spit in her face with the outrageous laugh I wanted to let out.

Is this chick serious? No, there's no way.

"Brazing Magazine?" I repeat, unable to keep my chuckle to myself.

"Aww, does the poor, childish adult not know how to read? It's okay." She pats my arm three times like someone would have to a child. I only smiled, because if I gave any reaction, I'd cause a scene. "Oh, the lip bite, you're not angry are you?" she asked, sounding satisfied with herself.

"Lip bite? Staring at my lips Luci?" She looked both confused and disgusted. To be honest, getting stared at by a woman like her can feel intimidating in a way. It felt like trying to hide your sins from the devil.

"Luci?"

"Lucifer. I think it suits you perfectly, if you ask me." I crossed my arms, ended the conversation, and completely ignored her. The corner of my lip lifted an inch when I saw her face shift into a horrified expression. I was mentally preparing myself to ignore her if she tried speaking to me again, but to my surprise, she didn't try. It probably shocked her; the nickname.

"The Award for CEO of the year goes to Adam Peasron, CEO of Pearson Book Group," the speaker announced. Adam rose from his seat and made his way toward the stage. The entire room stood and applauded as Adam claimed his award. I clapped and whistled loudly as he stood in front of the microphone. For a second, I found myself lost and couldn't understand how I missed the beginning of the ceremony. Has she distracted me that much? If so, that's gotta be witchcraft.

She really was evil...

"I want to express my deepest gratitude to the incredible woman who made all of this possible, Katherine, my partner in both life and business. Your unwavering support and dedication have been the cornerstone of all our achievements. I also want to extend my heartfelt thanks to my exceptional team and family at our company. Your tireless efforts and commitment, day in and day out, are the driving force behind our success. Thank you all for this honor. Enjoy the rest of your evening!" Adam walked off stage while the crowd applauded him again.

"Congrats, man," I exclaimed as he returned to our table. "That was... a very emotional speech." I teased him, knowing that this was the first time he accepted an award with such a profound speech. Adam wasn't the type to say more than two words when claiming an award. He's softer now, and we all know it's because of Katherine.

Love is something I can respect, though that doesn't mean that I believe it'll happen to me. Not to that extent, at least, but I know who I am; I'm someone who's broken, but someone who isn't interested in being put back together, either. I've been solo with a little company here and there, but that's pretty much it. It might sound depressing or boring to most people, but I promise it's not. Ever heard of the term me myself and I? Yup, that right there was my life motto.

I should tattoo it on myself one day.

Katherine appeared beside Adam, smiling warmly as she leaned in to kiss his cheek. "You were amazing up there," she said softly; her pride was obvious in her voice. "It was a beautiful speech."

Adam chuckled, shaking his head. "Thank you, angel." He glanced down at the award in his hands, turning it slightly as if he still couldn't believe it. "But this one feels weirdly special." His smile was genuine, something I hadn't seen in a long time.

I smirked, watching them. "Thanks for coming, even if it didn't work out with Celeste," Adam added, his tone teasing.

"You owe me for that, by the way. Getting reunited with Lucifer wasn't what I had in mind for tonight," I answered, looking to my right to make sure she wasn't there.

So what if she was there? I already called her Lucifer to her face.

But she was gone.

"Was she really that bad? To be honest, I've never seen you get so riled up because of a woman." He chuckled like it was funny.

"That's not a woman, that's the devil!" I confessed confidently.

"Right… However, I'm glad you came." Adam smiled and left to find Katherine. The event had just started, but I wasn't going to stick around for much longer. I came and got what I needed; now I could leave satisfied with *most* of my night.

I shrugged out of my jacket and rolled up my white sleeves. I immediately made my way towards the exit, but for a split second, I felt the need to turn. The moment I turned, my eyes instantly met Celeste's. Dark, alluring like a siren, a promise of hell. For a moment, we stared at each other before I took it upon myself to break eye contact and waltzed out the door.

The most random interaction I had with someone that I utterly despised.

CHAPTER 7
MICHEAL

Monday morning came, and at 9:00 am, I was sitting in the waiting area of Dylan's office, waiting for him to call me in. His office was located in a luxury building… *no surprise.* Though, I did expect it to be more artsy, since that was his entire business. The building's interior consisted of grays, whites, and beige colors. The only color present in the office was the pastel orange couch I was currently sitting on.

"Mr. Cruz will see you now," a lady with a blonde ponytail and a black jumpsuit said to me. I rose from my seat and followed behind her. She walked down a narrow hallway and didn't stop until we reached the very end, which I thought would be a deadend. Only it wasn't; it was Dylan's main office. His door looked like it was part of the wall, no doorknobs visible. There was only a keypad.

The woman typed six numbers into the keypad and pushed the door open with force, leading us through. As we entered, I realized that we had just walked into a library; bookshelves lining the walls. The space was fucking insane; you could host an event of one hundred people here with no problem. I'm quickly confused, because the only thing this library didn't have was a desk or an actual office.

"This way please," the lady spoke again as she magically appeared across the room. She must have walked there while I was distracted by the monstrosity of this place. The vibe in the room wasn't airy or open. It seemed heavy and dark; it kind of reminded me of a dungeon. Someone could be sentenced to life reading books here.

I continued walking behind the woman until she stopped in front of a black door. "This is it. You can go on in; Mr. Cruz is already expecting you," she said to me before walking out.

"What in the world..." I said to myself as I wrapped my hand around the black door knob. Is this guy a freaking vampire? Hiding this well away from the sun? I turned the knob and walked in. Yup, just like I thought; no windows.

What is it with this guy?

"Micheal," Dylan greeted me with a smile. I marched over to him to shake his hand. He rose from his desk and walked around the desk and met me halfway.

"Dylan, how are you?" I asked politely.

"I'm well, thank you. Please, take a seat." He motioned toward the chair in front of his desk.

"What's with the dungeon and no windows?" My curiosity got the best of me. There was no way that I could sit through this entire meeting without asking. Dylan chuckled as he stared at the floor.

"I work better in closed off spaces," he answered truthfully. I took a seat as Dylan made his way back around his desk and sat down. "Now, let's talk business, yes?"

"Please do." I nodded as I got comfortable.

"This job that I mentioned... it's not as easy as you probably think it is." He rested his hands on the desk with a concerned look on his face. He kept choosing to prevaricate every time I asked for the truth.

"To be fair, no job is really that easy, is it?" I responded.

Why did he look disturbed? Is he worried I'll turn down the job? What is it?

"True, but this is something out of your comfort zone," he stated as a fact, as if he already knew my limits and the type of lines I wouldn't cross. He probably thinks I'm someone who has a guilty conscience. To his luck, I'm the complete opposite. I'll do anything, except kill someone. That, I won't do.

"Go on," I tempted him. He kept beating around the bush and I wanted him to get on with it; to tell me what I was going to be dealing with.

"This is a side business I created with my good pal, Fernando, not long ago. Basically, we get customers who want a specific painting we do not have. We look into art pieces and the gallery that holds those pieces. We gather a fair amount of information before making our move and taking the pieces. After we secure the art, we sell it to that loyal customer, and of course, the customer is aware of how we came to have possession of the art," he explained.

"You're robbing art from other galleries to sell to your customers," I summarized in my own words.

"If you want to word it like that, yes," he confessed. I nodded and leaned back in my chair. Robbery. That's the job. I couldn't help but ask myself how far I really would go to live comfortably. Did my morals have the strength to deny this offer?

"How much?" I asked without another thought.

"Excuse me?" He looked at me, confused.

"I said how much? How much do you make on one of these requests?" If I was going to do this, I better be getting paid a fuck ton of money. My morals, they had a price, but for the right price, I would do it.

"The upcoming job we have, our customer is willing to pay one hundred forty-seven," he said.

"Thousand?" I asked, unimpressed, preparing to turn down the job in its entirety.

"Million, Micheal." I froze in place. Did he just say *million*?

"Come again?" I stuttered, my mind went blank and all I could see was green. Filthy green all over the place. I could legit bathe myself in green; I could use those bills as fucking wallpaper if I wanted to.

"Since you would be joining us, we would divide the price by the three of us. So, forty-nine million each."

Holy shit! I hit the fucking jackpot. Forty-nine million?!

"Count me in," I said, sure of my answer. Who was I kidding? Where else could I find a job that could guarantee me forty-nine million in an instant? Nowhere.

"Are you positive Micheal? There's no going back once you sign the contract." He took out the document and set it in front of me with a black feather pen. Do I look like I want to go back? Hell no. This would allow me to have my life planned out; I could finally do the investments I had wanted to do, and I could easily turn those forty-nine million dollars into hundreds of millions of dollars.

I didn't respond; instead, I grabbed the pen and dragged the paper closer to me. With a swift movement of my hand, I signed my signature in black ink at the bottom of the page. It was official; I was going to rob a painting from a gallery and get forty-nine million dollars for it. I kept repeating the phrase in my mind until I believed it.

Placing the pen down, I pushed the document back to Dylan. He glanced at the signature before putting it away in a file. "Now I can share the details of this request." Dylan pulled out another file from his drawer and passed it to me. I opened it and found a picture, name, and a copy of the art wanted.

"This is our customer, Richardo Brock. He's going to gift the painting to his granddaughter, who recently became an art fanatic for her birthday, which is in July," he explained. "The piece is called *The Kiss* by Gustav Klimt. If you know anything about art, you'll know that this piece is quite popular; one of the most desired art pieces in the industry. The name of the gallery it is in is Laurosse. It's quite popular. We'll need to get extra information on this gallery. Security, employees, store system, owners, everything."

"When do we start?" I scanned the file quickly before setting it down on the desk.

"As soon as possible. I would recommend going tomorrow; count the amount of cameras you see, try to count and remember where each alarm is. Speak to an employee, a woman, if you can," he suggested as he took the file back.

"A woman?" I asked, as I leaned closer to him.

"For a handsome guy such as yourself, I would hope you know how to seduce a woman. Use your good looks for our benefit. The closer you get to her, the better."

"Understood." My phone rang in my pocket. I dug into my pants to retrieve it, and I sighed as I looked at the screen. *"Incoming call: Father"* the banner said. "I have to take this," I told Dylan as I stood from my seat.

"Of course, I'll give you some privacy," he said before leaving the room. I answered as soon as I heard the door shut.

"안녕하세요 *Annyeonghaseyo—Hello—*" I greeted my father over the line. My father preferred speaking Korean because he wasn't fully comfortable with his English.

"Your two years are up. When will you be coming to Korea?" he asked; I sighed while looking up at the ceiling.

"*Abeoji*, I'm busy with work; I can't come right now," I answered, hoping that this time he would respect that.

"Our deal was every two years. On this date, it has now been exactly two years. Find a time to schedule a two-week trip to Seoul," he said arrogantly. Of course, he wouldn't change his mind; it was his way or the highway.

That arrogant bastard.

"Fine, I'll try to figure it out, but I'm at work and I cannot speak to you right now." I could feel his judgment over the phone.

"You are a Zhang! You do not need to work like a pitiful employee when you have a family business to run!" he yelled over the phone. I covered the phone with my hand as I groaned in frustration. This is why I moved across the world; I couldn't bear his constant jabs. He is, what I would describe to be, a fussy cat with claws; someone who wasn't afraid to draw blood if you didn't comply with his wishes.

"I already told you, I want nothing to do with it! But I will try to find a flight and a date; until then, stop calling me. I will inform you once I have the tickets." I was ready to end the call until he yelled one last thing.

"Better not come back alone once again!" With that, he hung up. Not come back alone? Now he wanted me to bring someone else? You've got to be kidding me. Seriously, what was his deal? Did he enjoy randomly popping into my life at the worst times?

"Finished with your call?" Dylan stepped back into the room the exact time my father ended the call.

"Yes, thank you. Tomorrow, I'll check out the Gallery and make those notes," I said, gathering my thoughts before taking my leave.

"I'm excited for us to work together. I have a good feeling about this."

Oh, I do too.

"Likewise." I shook his hand and left the office.

CHAPTER 8
CELESTE

"Congratulations!" Confetti sparked in the air. My graduation day came, and I felt like I was opening a brand new chapter in my life. I had goosebumps just thinking that now, anything can happen in my life, but the main thing I thought about was my internship at Laurosse. I would be professionally working at a popular gallery. It was a dream come true, and I couldn't wait to start.

"We're so proud of you, C!" Katherine said and handed me a bouquet of flowers.

"You did it!" Elaina said as she hugged me from behind. The only person missing this experience was Valery, but like always, she was virtually present.

"Happy Graduation CC!" she announced through the phone.

"Thanks, but when are you actually going to congratulate me in person? I firmly believe I deserve a five course meal cooked by one the best," I said to her.

"Hey, believe me, no one wants me there more than myself. Being the last person to graduate sucks," she confessed with a pouty face. Valery was the youngest out of the four of us, hence the reason she's always the last to finish things.

"C!" Ollie yelled from across the yard. The ceremony was outdoors, and the weather couldn't have been better than it was today. Flowers blossomed and leaves danced along the gentle breeze. I excused myself from the girls and marched over to where Ollie stood. "Feels weird that graduation is finally here, right?" he asked as he handed me a bouquet of red roses.

"This is for me? I thought they were yours," I said as I accepted them. He simply shrugged as he smirked to himself.

"They're for you. I would give you so much more if I could. You deserve only the best Celeste," he admits with a subtle blush on his cheeks. Oliver was never subtle about his minor crush on me. I continue to ignore it because I dreaded hurting him. Oliver was a brother to me, nothing more, nothing less.

"Thank you Ollie, you deserve the best too." I smiled and gave him a hug. "This is where our lives truly begin," I whispered into his ear before letting go. "Take care; I'll see you around," I said, heading back to my girls.

"You better, or I'll hunt you down myself!" I heard from behind me. I only chuckled, knowing that I'd cherish this moment for as long as I could.

Joining Katherine and Elena, I was ready to leave this place in order to start the rest of my life. A part of me felt terrified. Being in school felt like walking on rope, but I knew I had a safety net underneath me to catch myself if I lost my balance. But now, heading into the real world, I felt like I was walking on that same rope, only without the safety net to guarantee my safety.

At that moment, as Katherine and Elaina held on to me on each arm, I knew that they would be my new safety net. I could jump face first into this new chapter in my life and guarantee that I would survive.

It was officially my first day as an intern at Laurosse and I was petrified, to say the least. I stood at the entrance, waiting for my mentor to meet me. Meanwhile, as I waited, I took the chance to look at everyone who worked here. They looked intelligent and lavish, like they belonged here, like they were overqualified for their positions. However, the gallery was exactly how I pictured it; spending time here could make someone feel wealthy. It had that strong of an impression.

"Celeste Castillo?" A woman called. I raised my hand like an idiot, afraid of losing her attention. The worst part is, I couldn't hide the horrified expression on my face. That had to be one of my biggest problems, not being able to hide what I felt within. I just *needed* to show others how I felt. Thankfully, my new mentor found it funny and chuckled.

"Sorry, I'm a nervous wreck. This is literally my dream job," I admitted.

"Oh, please don't apologize. I think it's cute. I'm Meredith," she said, holding the clipboard in one hand and offering her other hand to me to shake.

The name Meredith seemed to match her perfectly; she had long luscious red locks, bright green eyes, and wore a beautifully altered white jumpsuit which showed off her slender shoulders. She looked like she belonged in the gallery, and I wanted to be just like her. This is comfortable and confident.

"Nice to meet you, Meredith," I said, shaking her hand.

"The pleasure is all mine, Celeste. Let me show you around the gallery before you begin." She led me through the entrance, showing me each room and what type of art it held. We must have visited at least ten different rooms; I hadn't remembered the gallery being this big.

"Here is a clipboard that holds a description of each room and the paintings that are housed there. We expect everyone who begins here at Laurosse to memorize the contents of this clipboard. Look at it as your bible for this career. If you want to succeed, you must know this information." She handed me a thick packet with over a hundred pages. I skimmed through it and it indeed had all the history and details someone would have to know about each painting.

"Of course, I'll make sure to drill this information in." I pointed at my brain, trying to assure my dedication toward this job. Though, I hadn't realized the amount of information gallerists had to learn.

"Perfect, then you shouldn't have trouble keeping up with the rest of our employees," she said with a light smile. "Also, I forgot to mention that the position you're interning for is one that is shared amongst other fellow interns." I took a moment to process her sentence.

"Excuse me? I didn't quite understand what you meant by that," I confessed.

"You didn't think you were the only intern working this position, did you?" she asked, seeming to be amused that I would think I was chosen to intern for this position alone. "Oh, honey, no," she said in a calming tone; one that a teacher would use for a child who was mistaken. "This position is very popular amongst other art majors, such as yourself. This isn't a permanent position until you prove that you deserve it. Everyone who now works here full time had to earn their position. I was once where you are now," she explained.

"Oh," I whispered, slightly disappointed.

"You strike me as someone that wants this badly. You remind me of myself if I'm being honest. I'm betting on you to win, so don't make me lose my money." She winked as if she didn't just admit that the rest of the employees bet on other interns like a horse race. But, putting all that aside, she said she would bet on me. I couldn't help the smile that was creeping its way onto my lips. "Don't worry, there's only one intern you'd be competing with this season. We cut a bunch of other people due to them not meeting the qualifications." She walked to the very back of the gallery where staff go on break.

We entered the lunch room that held the other intern. I couldn't see his face from the back, but he reminded me of Oliver because of his ginger hair. "Oliver, I'd like you to meet our other intern, Celeste."

Wait, did she just say Oliver, or was that just me?

He turned steadily and smiled at me. Smiled. I couldn't believe my eyes; the boy I knew since my freshman year of college was now standing before me. What in the world was he doing here? He never mentioned that he got an internship at Laurosse.

"Hello Celeste, it's nice to meet you." That greeting felt like a slap to the face. Now he was pretending to not know me? Okay, he was definitely playing a dirty game.

"Alright, Celeste, today you'll be working at the front with Jasper. Make sure to keep that clipboard on you in case a customer asks for your help, you'll direct them to the art piece and wait for an employee to take over," she said to me, as my eyes stayed on Oliver like a target.

"Oliver, you'll be working at the back. We have a few paintings to unpack, and you'll be helping three other men; they will show you the process," she told him. "Alright, best of luck and if you have any questions, don't hesitate to reach out." She left me in the room with Oliver.

"What are you doing here?" I asked him, trying to keep my cool.

"Internship. I got accepted last minute, and I thought it'd be a nice surprise."

"A nice surprise?!" He was joking; he had to be. Because who in their right mind thinks that this is a nice surprise?

"Listen, I just thought it would be nice to work with someone I know," he said, trying to make it sound pleasing to me.

"We're competing for the same position; it's not nice." I left without saying another word to that *pendejo*. I needed to focus and prove that this has been my position since the very beginning.

Making my way to the front desk, I patiently waited for customers to arrive. As I waited for time to pass, I read through some of the pages on the clipboard and prayed I would get asked about a painting I recently read about.

Thirty minutes passed until I had my first customer. I didn't notice until they spoke up to catch my attention. My mind was focused on maintaining the information I had been reading.

"Excuse me, could you direct me to a painting?" he asked in an alluring tone. I redirected my sight onto him and noticed that it was no other than Micheal. This day was only getting better and better. I must have done something truly atrocious in my past life to deserve a moment such as this one.

"Are you serious?" I asked, laughing in frustration. His face morphed into annoyance.

Trust me, buddy, I feel the same.

"Can you just spare me the agony and show me the art I want to see?" he asked, as if it was me who whipped up this torture for fun.

"How about no?" I asked with a pleasing and welcoming smile.

"No?" He asked, baffled.

"No," I repeated. Maybe he needed a clearer sign. Perhaps I should show him the distraughtly red art piece we have in room seven, where the other paintings of despair are displayed.

"Okay, Celeste, we met on the wrong foot. I think we could get along if we started over," he suggested in an angelic tone.

Who exactly is he fooling? The same man who speaks his mind, even if it sounds disrespectful, is now saying this to me? I don't believe it. Not for one second.

"Are we speaking the same language right now? Did you get

hit on your head with a glass bottle? No," I answered him. He rolled his eyes, finally showing his true persona.

"Just show me the goddamn painting. Isn't that your job? You can't refuse me the service or pleasure of being in this gallery." As much as I hated to admit it, he was right. I couldn't kick him out, not without him making a scene.

"Fine, what painting is it?" I asked, pissed that my first customer on my first day had to be him.

He didn't answer right away. His eyes were drifting, not to the wall behind me where paintings hung, or even the little card with the artist's name, but to the corners of the ceiling. To the exit. To the desk by the register.

"Hello?" I waved a hand in front of his face.

He blinked, like he'd just remembered I was standing there. "Right. Uh…" His gaze finally flicked to the painting, then darted right back to that same corner, where one of the security cameras blinked red.

"*Tango Argentino*," he said, shying away from me. He didn't want to look me in the eye when he told me which painting. It's funny, I didn't picture his art taste to be correlated to a painting like *Tango Argentino*. I mean, don't get me wrong, it's a sensual piece, filled with sexual tension and passion. A piece that showcases love. The dance of passionate love, to say better, illustrates the scent of a woman while a man demonstrates his manly grace.

"*Tango Argentino*," I repeated, glad that he picked a painting I was familiar with instead of having to search through the clipboard for information. I actually used to come to this gallery to look at that painting, and the others that were next to it. "Right this way." I put my hands behind my back as I led him to the painting. "It's this one right here," I told him as we stood in front of the piece. "I'll get someone to help you the rest of the way." I turned to leave.

"That won't be necessary," he announced loudly.

"Okay, is there any–" I was going to be a good intern and ask if he needed anything else, but he interrupted me saying the next thing.

"No, thanks Luci," he said without sparing me a look.

Wow, what a gentleman he is. Amazing, really.

"Oh yeah, for sure. Truly a pleasure serving you," I said in a sarcastic bow. "Asshole," I whispered under my breath. His jaw tightened in anger, I presume?

"Witch," he said underneath his breath as well. As if he heard me when I mindlessly called him an asshole. "Hey, quick question. How's the security here?" He asked out of the blue.

Who asked about the security here?

"How would I know? Now, are you done here?" I asked, ready to kick him out myself. I thought I could be in the same building as him, but I can't find my focus with him here.

"Yes, Luci, I'm done," he answered, putting his hands in his pockets. "It was a pleasure seeing you again, here of all places Luci, I mean it," he said with a tight smile where his eyes squinted so much, it looked like they were practically shut.

"Oh, no, the pleasure is all mine." I bit my tongue so aggressively, I could taste the blood. "Take care now! Make sure to never come back!" I exclaimed in a cheerful tone. Why must *he* appear at important times in my life? His presence was almost a curse these days.

CHAPTER 9
MICHEAL

I told Dylan I would head straight to his office after setting foot in the Laurosse Gallery, and again, a wonderful surprise intruded into my life. The moment I saw Luci's face at the front desk, I cursed the heavens for putting me in this position. I desperately prayed for wisdom and patience from my ancestors; if they were even listening.

"Seduce the first woman you find there," he said.

Yeah right.

Of course, when I'm given a job worth forty-nine million dollars, it means I had to put up with that devil of a woman. There's no way I could do it; I couldn't stand her, and I knew for a fact that she would never give me a chance. I would get *zero* information from her; she'd be the type to report me for any minor thing I do.

As I arrived at Dylan's office, I tried to think about how I would bring up this subject.

Hey man, hate to break it to you, but our entire plan is fucked because of a woman.

What the hell are you supposed to say to that? Oh yeah,

maybe something like this, *Yo Micheal, you're fired because you suck.*

I'm painfully holding in my composure because I'll go batshit crazy if I keep replaying the encounter from earlier.

"I'm here to see Mr. Cruz," I told the same blonde that brought me to him last time.

"Do you have an appointment?" she asked with grace. I envied people like her, so calm and collected; so iced that nothing bothers them. How I wish to be like her right now.

"No, he said to meet him now," I said. I'm almost positive she saw the crazy in my eyes, because she instantly picked up the phone and dialed what I believed to be his office phone. Within a few seconds, she put down the phone and started walking. I followed behind her, assuming that he gave the okay for me to walk in.

She input the same six number code in the keypad and allowed me to go in. As I entered the familiar library, she closed the door behind me, leaving me in the room alone. I guess since I already know where his office is from here; she didn't need to escort me further.

"Dungeon date part two," I said to myself as I paced towards Dylan's office. If I owned this library, I would hold annual Halloween parties here because of its creepy vibes.

I harshly knocked three times on his door and waited for a response.

"Come in," I heard from the other side of the door., I opened it, preparing for what would be a moment to remember.

Whatever you say Micheal, sound smart.

"Micheal, what's the intake at Laurosse?" he asked straightforwardly. He didn't even allow me to take a seat first.

"To start off, I counted fifteen cameras walking through the gallery, one in every corner positioned horizontally. Each painting has an alarm set around the canvas, detecting movement and noise.

That was the only information I was able to grab with the short time I had there." I told him the minor security details I mentally noted as I walked behind Celeste. I didn't want to start by telling him the problem before telling him what he wanted to hear.

"Perfect, what else?" he prompted, leaning back in his chair.

"Yeah, about that…" I began by saying. "It seems that we have a small problem, or rather big, if we're talking about her…" His eyes narrowed with confusion.

"Pardon?" he asked.

Here we go…

"The employee I came across…" I paused to choose the right words to use without it sounding so… frank. But at least there was no way to sugarcoat it. "She is the devil," I admitted.

"You've lost me," he said. Of course he was lost; he wouldn't understand until he met her.

"Okay, allow me to further explain." Standing back, I hoped that this wouldn't be a deal breaker for the job. I explained the first time I had ever encountered her at the Halloween party at Avenue, up to our encounter today. "This woman hates me, and she works at the very front of the gallery. I don't think I'd be the right choice to be the insight of the gallery; she almost kicked me out the moment I stepped in the building!" I exclaimed, finishing my rant.

"So, to my best understanding, you two are familiar with each other?" He asked after *everything* I had told him. My eye twitched at the realization that the only thing he grasped from the entirety of my rave was that we "are familiar with each other." I sighed, annoyed that I even had to explain any of this. It's a waste of my precious time.

"I wouldn't say familiar. I would say it's unfortunate to know each other."

"Right, alright then, perfect. You will go back and slowly convince her to like the idea of being around you."

Is he deaf? Did he have a hard time comprehending what I said?

"Did you miss the part that she hates me to death?" I asked, truly in shock that he oversaw it.

"Oh no, I caught that part sublimely," he said. "But what you're missing are the facts, Micheal. This is something you could use to your advantage."

"How would I use that to my advantage?" I was intrigued by what he was getting at.

"In order for a woman to 'hate you to death,' she has to feel something for you. How do you think hate comes to be? There is a fine line between hate and love. Both require the same amount of fire and passion towards the person, and with that in mind, it's quite simple to switch that feeling of hate to love with the right amount of persistence, of course." He shrugged as if what he said was equivalent to explaining what two plus two was.

"You want me to spend even more time with her than I already had to today? Are you insane? I can't stand that woman!" I stood my ground; I'm dealing with her. Nope, not me, no, sir.

"Okay, then look at this like a challenge. If you succeed in getting her to love you and get all the information needed from Laurosse, I'll pay you five million from my shares. But you must accomplish both by July; we are currently in April, which gives you about... three months. Can you do that?" he asked.

Can I do that? Play around and show off my charm for five extra million dollars? I'm fucking Micheal fucking Zhang for fuck's sake, of course I can do that! With this face and my persistence, within three months I'll have her falling to my feet.

"Dylan, you just released a monster man. I'm in," I agreed, liking the sound of fifty-four million more than forty-nine. I felt like I was walking on water. That woman has no idea what's going to hit her.

"Excellent," Dylan announced. "It's settled; I'll write it in on the contract. I'm sure you must be heading out now, since I suppose you have quite a lot to strategize."

"Indeed, I do," I responded, knowing that this wouldn't be as easy as it sounded. The chasing game required time and energy; luckily for me, I had the right amount of experience to attack this with full confidence. In fact, I think I'll use Adam dating Katherine to my advantage. If I could convince him to set up a day where I can meet Celeste outside of the gallery with friends, it would go smoothly.

Yes, that was the plan. Part one of getting Luci to fall for me was finally in motion.

CHAPTER 10
CELESTE

"He wants me to go to a bar tonight? Why would he want to do that?" I asked Katherine over the phone, having received her call as I left work. It surprised me to hear from Katherine that Adam had planned an activity for a group rather than just the two of them. This would be the first time that we would do something like this; Elaina and I practically have to pry Katherine off of Adam to get her to spend a girls' night with us.

"He suggested that our friends meet up regularly. I think it's a wonderful idea."

Of course she thinks it's a great idea; I'm sure Adam proposed it *just* perfectly. I guess it wasn't a dreadful idea on his part, but I will admit, I am a bit taken aback.

"But so sudden? I mean, I finished work minutes ago. Does it need to be tonight? I'm too tired to go to a bar," I said, stepping into the subway. The mere idea of going anywhere but home right now sounded appalling. Today had drained every ounce of energy from me, leaving me feeling utterly spent.

The chill of the night wrapped around me like a heavy blanket, amplifying my weariness. All I wanted was to burrow beneath the covers and surrender to the comforting darkness.

Perhaps the idea could have been more appealing to me if it were any night apart from tonight.

"I know, I know, I completely understand if you can't come tonight. It won't be the same without you…" There she goes again with her dramatic sigh. Damnit, she knows exactly how to get me to feel guilty. Since I've started working at Laurosse, I haven't been able to spend any quality time with the girls.

"You know what, maybe sparing an hour won't be so bad…" I couldn't believe I had surrendered so easily; the thought of going home had been etched in my mind. Yet, the idea of disappointing my friends weighed heavily on me. I couldn't find peace in leaving them behind, cursing my loyalty, the one weakness that had always held me captive.

"Really?!" she squealed. Shaking my head, I knew that what I had said was irreversible. I could tell she was practically glowing with excitement; there's no going back from here. "I'll text you the address! See you in fifteen minutes!" she exclaims.

"Fifteen?" I asked, confused.

How would she know the exact amount of time it would take me to arrive?

"The bar is fifteen minutes away from Laurosse, and you said you just left. So, you couldn't have gone further than five minutes. See you then!" A short beep comes across the phone once she hangs up.

Surely, it took exactly sixteen minutes for me to arrive at Tito's Bar, a cozy, dimly lit pool bar with a rustic vibe. Vintage posters and string lights adorned the walls, creating a warm, inviting atmosphere. The sound of clinking glasses and lively chatter filled the air, and as I entered, I immediately felt the buzz of energy. In the back corner, my group of friends were gathered around a pool table, their laughter echoing throughout the bar.

As I approached them, I could see Adam leaning against the table, cue stick in hand, animatedly recounting a hilarious story from last weekend to his brother, Aaron. Katherine was beside him sitting on a barstool, her head thrown back in laughter, and a bright smile lighting up her face as she listened to Adam's story. Her eyes shifted to me, and her face changed to a welcoming smile.

"You made it! Elaina couldn't make it tonight; you were the last person we were waiting on. Let me introduce you to Jess; she's actually the one who designed my book cover." Katherine introduces me to Jess, who was beside her sipping a drink, shaking her head in mock disbelief at some guy's bravado, clearly enjoying the banter. "Sorry to interrupt, but this is one of my best friends, Celeste."

Jess turns around and allows a perfect view of the man she was speaking to. "Hi, I'm Jess," she smiles as she lends out her hand. I wasn't able to greet her correctly because the man beside her was the only man that ticks me off by just being alive. Of course he was here, shooting down a shot at the bar. Katherine nudged at my shoulder, bringing me back to reality.

"Sorry, yes, hi, I'm Celeste. It's nice to meet you." That was a lie; I didn't even care to meet her. It's a shame Elaina couldn't make it; it would've been less awkward with her constant comments.

"And you've met Micheal already," Katherine said, emphasizing Micheal's name to get his attention.

"Yes, I have... Unfortunately," I spat, Micheal twisted his body halfway to give me a look. Deep down in those brown eyes, I could see resentment. I was sure he would greet me with some low insult that could easily get confused as a joke. He and I both knew that wasn't the case; he meant it with his entire being. But truly, what surprised me was what he chose to say.

"Want a drink?" he offered, and I snickered to myself.

Him buy me a drink? What did he want to do? Throw it at my face to get revenge for that time I sprayed beer at him?

I couldn't figure out what game he was playing, but I felt like I needed to be on my toes.

"Why, you want to slip something into my drink? You look like the type to do that." I insulted him; I thought that's all it would take for him to go back to his normal self.

"Really? I do, huh?" He leaned in closer toward me. "You and I both know that's not what you really think." I leaned away from him, seeking to keep him out of my personal space.

"What is wrong with you? Never heard of someone's personal bubble? You're centimeters away from popping mine; back off." He chuckled, as if what I said was funny. Did I just walk into an alternate world where this man was trying to flirt with me? He hated me like five minutes ago…

"You know how to play?" he asked out of the blue.

So much for the conversation being over….

I turned to look into his eyes, searching, hoping to find out whatever his plan was, but I found nothing. They seemed sincere, like there was absolutely no malice behind them.

Strange…

"Know how to play what?" His eyes lowered down to the floor as he shook his head. I may have heard wrong, but I could have sworn he called me a dumbass under his breath. Scratch that, knowing him, I probably heard right. Within seconds, he picks his head back up with the fakest, yet most charming smile known to humankind.

"Pool." He nudges his head towards a pool table under a dimly lit spotlight. The sound of balls clacking and soft music in the background.

"Right, I knew what you meant," I stated as a fact; his eyes only narrowed with disbelief and I took a moment to regain my thoughts.

"So do you?" he asked again. I wanted so badly to ignore

him, but that would probably only make it worse since he was the type of idiot to stir a hornet's nest. I don't know if I would consider it bravery or stupidity.

Stupidity for sure.

"Who doesn't?" I answered confidently.

Actually, I used to play pool with my father when I was younger, before he passed away when I was seven. He died in a car crash and I hadn't thought about him in such a long time. I buried those emotions along with my father at his grave. My mother wasn't in the picture, so my grandmother was my parent for most of my childhood.

"Careful there Luci, it sounds like you're quite cocky about it," he taunted.

I forced myself to push all of those depressing feelings down and focus on what was going on in front of me. It's unfortunate, though, that it's him that's in front of me.

"I would call it confidence. Why? Are you insecure and hate the thought of a woman being better than you at something?"

"Are you challenging me?" he questioned.

I couldn't help but roll my eyes and cross my arms over my chest in annoyance.

Could he be any more annoying?

With a deep breath, I leaned in close, flipping my hair to the side, knowing that it drives men crazy, and gave him my best sultry, sparkling eyes.

"Nah, not interested," I whispered, inches away from his face.

What better way to exit a conversation with a man than shamelessly flirt with him? It's like dangling candy in front of a baby, and god, I enjoy the disappointed face that comes with it.

Turning my back to him, I walked back to the pool table, where Adam was finishing his game with Aaron. With a smooth stroke, he sinks the 8-ball into the corner pocket, winning the game.

"Great match, you closed it out beautifully," Aaron said to Adam as they shook hands.

"Good game," Adam replied as Katherine clapped cheerfully behind him.

Just as I was about to clap for Adam's victory, a large hand wrapped around my wrist, pulling me around. Micheal grips my wrist tighter as I come face to face with him.

What the fuck was his problem?!

Resisting against his hold, I glared daggers at him.

"Play with me," he said. I looked at him, astonished. The audacity of this man.

"No," I said flatly, trying to pull my wrist free of his grip.

"You just love being difficult, don't you?" He smiles, clenching his jaw so tightly, his jawline could cut glass.

Why did it bother him so much? What did he want from me?

He took a breather before suggesting the next thing. "How about a friendly bet?" I slip out of his grip and stand back.

"I'm listening." A bet... the first thing that came to mind was money.

"If you win, I'll leave you alone for good; I'll never bother you again after tonight." I take his offer into consideration; it was good, but not good enough.

"I like the sound of that, but it needs something else. If I win, you'll leave me alone for good AND pay off my student loans." His eyes widened at the last part of my suggestion. "If you disagree, I'm not interested. And by the way you're acting, I'm guessing what you want from me is important." He huffed, which proved I was right.

"No, not important. But fine." He said, smiling to himself. I blinked, surprised that he agreed to my terms without knowing exactly how much I owe. "Don't you want to ask what I want if I win?" he asked, putting his hand out for me to shake. I took his hand and agreed; a deal with the devil.

"No," I said confidently. "I'm going to win regardless; therefore, I don't need to know what you want." He nodded, walking straight past me.

We made our way towards an empty pool table and Micheal grabbed a cue from the wall and leaned against the table, waiting for me. I grabbed a random cue that was left on another table. Putting my hair up in a bun, I eyed the table with determination, when in the corner of my eye, I could see Micheal chalking his cue with a confident grin. Possibly one of the hottest things I'd seen in a long time, and I despised him for it.

"What's going on here?" Adam asked with a surprised smile plastered on his face. "A friendly one-on-one?" Katherine comes up beside him, shocked by what she was seeing.

"Adam, this is anything but friendly. My student loans are on the line," I said, looking at the table, creating a game plan for myself.

Micheal has to be good at pool if he agreed to a bet that meant paying for my loans. I knew he would underestimate me because I'm a woman, but I would use it to pull the rug out from right under him.

As the first break is about to happen, the anticipation builds, and our friends lean in closer, eager to see who will take the first shot. As they gathered around the table, Micheal glanced at me, a playful challenge in his eyes.

"Ready to lose, or are you just here to keep me entertained?" he asked. I wanted nothing more than to wipe the grin off his face.

"Dream on! You're going down, and I'll make sure of it," I replied. Adam, unable to resist, interjected with a laugh. The air was thick with anticipation and the room suddenly got quieter.

I started the game by breaking the rack, slamming the cue ball into the triangle with aggression. Balls scatter, and the 8-ball teeters near the edge of a pocket but doesn't fall. Micheal snickers loudly; I added so much force, but no balls pocketed.

Shoot! I'm already off to a terrible start.

"Nice," he commented; the tension was palpable as I gave him a death glare.

Now that it was his turn, he stepped up, eyes narrowed, and selected the solids. Lining up his shot, he sunk the 1-ball. He smirked at me, rubbing it in my face that he made the first shot. Our rivalry continues to heat up, and I easily become annoyed and aim for the stripes. I pocketed the 9-ball, then gave Micheal a pointed look.

Take that asshole.

He raised both of his hands and smiled. Nothing made me angrier than someone smiling in such a serious situation such as this one.

"That's a solid shot, I'll admit," he said, but the tension was thick as I stared Micheal down.

"Your words mean nothing to me; you could shove them right up your *royal arse*." Adam chuckled in the corner, clearly enjoying this. Katherine and Jess watched with full concentration.

We were now mid-game, and I tried a tricky shot on the 4-ball, sure that I would make it. But, I missed; the cue ball narrowly missed the side pocket.

"Crap!" I exclaimed, frustrated. Of course, I went for the flashy play and paid for it. That miss might haunt me for the rest of my life...

Micheal moved in to capitalize, lining up a shot on the 11-ball. No! That asshole better not, I swear... He makes his move and sinks it with a smirk.

"Nice try, Luci."

Oh, I could snap his neck right here, right now! Breathe Celeste, there's still time; it's only mid-game.

"Oh, the shade! Micheal's clearly enjoying this," Aaron chuckled, as he sipped his beer.

That, for whatever reason, got me even more upset. The

tension builds, and my frustration is getting out of hand. I clenched my jaw and went for the 3-ball but missed again.

Dammit! I can't afford another slip-up.

Micheal, seeing the opportunity, took the aim at the 14-ball. He sunk it again and added, "Guess you need to practice more. All that cockiness for this?" This wasn't a regular pool game anymore, no... this was war. Psychological warfare is in full swing.

At the climax, this was my last chance. I tried to shake off the pressure and focused on the 7-ball. It looked like my only choice. I went for it and sank it but grimaced at Micheal. It's about time I finally found my rhythm, but could I turn the tide? I'd have to keep this momentum until the very end. For my student loans, I'll be the rightful soldier for this. I won't lose!

Micheal lined up for the 8-ball, his eyes locked on it. He took a deep breath and made the shot, but the cue ball rattled around the pocket.

"Don't make it in, don't make it in, don't make it in," I chanted under my breath as my heart pounded at the same rhythm the ball rattled. I must be a witch because it rattled its way out of the pocket hole.

Thank god...

My turn came and Micheal had given me an opportunity. With the ball in hand, I positioned the cue ball carefully for the 5-ball. I sank it easily and gave Micheal a smug grin. I felt like jumping around the table with joy, but I needed to keep my cool. My celebration will wait for when I win this game.

"Celeste is back in the game!" Adam commented.

I could tell Micheal was getting desperate; he attempted to regain control, aiming for the 10-ball. Surprisingly, he sinks it.

Aiming for the 8-ball, I made my shot but hopelessly missed the hole by an inch. I accidentally nudged the 8-ball closer to the side pocket, a perfect win for Micheal. My face dropped instantly.

No... No!

The finale was finally here; in this phase, we would determine who would win or lose. Micheal eyes the 8-ball, a wicked smile on his face.

"No," I said desperately, as his smile only grew. He took the shot, and with a perfect stroke, sank the 8-ball. "No!" I yelled.

"Micheal takes the win!" Aaron exclaimed as he and Adam made their way to congratulate Micheal.

I had despairingly, dejectedly, despondently lost to Micheal, who still had a smug grin plastered on his face. He might have won, but this rivalry was far from over.

Katherine and Jess comforted me; I received a pitiful pat on my shoulder and loser back rubs. This couldn't get worse... Micheal made his way around the table until he reached me. He gave me his hand to shake.

"Good game," he said sarcastically.

"Shut it," I said, already grabbing my purse and planning my exit. I dreaded hearing what Micheal wanted from me. Maybe if I sneak out right this second, he won't realize it. I'm practically inches from the exit until I hear the most alarming voice in my entire life.

"Hey, hey, where do you think you're going?" he called out to me.

Dear Lord, why me?

CHAPTER 11
CELESTE

"Hey, hey, where do you think you're going?" he called out to me. "You owe me a bet, Luci; don't you want to know what it is?"

The dread settled in as soon as I realized there was no way out. That stupid bet. Why hadn't I just said no? Now, whatever came out of his mouth, I had to go along with. No one to blame but myself. Why did I have to be so competitive, so prideful? Staying in my seat at the bar with a cold beer seemed like the smarter choice. Somewhere, in another world, a version of me was probably doing just that.

"What do you want? For me to get a lousy tattoo I'll regret for the rest of my life? Dye or cut my hair in a ridiculous hairstyle? Wear a lousy costume around New York? WHAT?!" I yelled. He didn't react, he only smiled charmingly. His face quickly became insanely punchable...

"Those are all tempting, but no," he said, pointing to his chin. He purposely thought to himself, dragging on the torture of waiting. Once he decided, his eyes widened, and he snapped his fingers like it was the greatest plan in history. "I want seven dates," he said, pointing his finger straight at me.

"Come again?" I asked.

Did I hear him right? Seven dates? Like *dating* dates? Sounds like complete torture; cruel and unusual punishment if you ask me... All that effort to win, and this is his prize? No, I don't believe it for a second; there has to be a catch. I call BULL! *Bullshitttt!*

"Seven dates. The time, date, and location are of my choice, and you have to give me a real shot," he clarified.

Is he playing with me right now?

"You're hilarious; seriously. Talk about confusing me! Ha ha!" I dramatically laughed out loud. "Alright, you had your fun; what do you really want?"

"That is what I want. Why's that so hard to believe?" I crossed my arms, giving him the most unconvinced face. He coughed and chuckled. "Sure, you're a difficult woman, but who doesn't enjoy a challenge?" he asked.

"You should be a comedian," I replied. "I'm not going out with you, not on one date, and you can bet on *that* for the rest of your life." I pushed him back and continued walking toward the exit.

"If I'd known you were an unfair player, I would've never played with you. Unfortunately, you're stuck paying back the debt," he voiced behind me. I gave him a 'talk to the hand' gesture, tuning him out entirely.

"Not gonna happen!" The door of Tito's Bar swung open, letting out a blast of music and laughter that spilled into the chilly night. Stepping outside, my cheeks flushed from the warmth inside. I wrapped my arms around myself, the cool air hitting me like a splash of cold water. "That bastard must be out of his mind!" I said to myself.

"Taxi!" I whistled, calling a get away cab while I still had the chance. As if the universe listened, a cab pulled over.

Thank god.

"Hold on!" A voice sliced through the night, and I turned to see Micheal running after me. He most definitely is out of his goddamn mind. He looked ridiculous, but that was nothing new. I hurriedly put my hand on the door handle to open, desperate to get in. Within seconds, he shuts the door and yells to the taxi driver. "Give me five minutes sir."

"Again? My gosh, you want a prize that's completely ridiculous!" I exclaimed, tired of dealing with him.

"Oh, but it sure would've been perfectly fine if I had to pay off your student debt!" he yelled back. It was as if we were arguing like children on a playground; each exchange more exasperating than the last. I turned to walk away again, but he stepped in front of me, blocking my path, and I raised my brow, unimpressed. "I'll pick you up after work tomorrow night for dinner," he said, and I blinked.

"Dinner? You're joking."

"Dead serious." My heart raced at his words, but I shook my head, struggling to maintain my composure.

"Are you deaf? Do you have trouble with social skills or something? Because there's no way," I fought back. He stepped closer, lowering his voice as if the night itself might conspire against him.

"You owe me whatever I want, and what I *want* is seven dates." Did he mean that like a threat? I hesitated, caught between annoyance and intrigue. I didn't want to admit it, but there was a thrill in our back-and-forth that had stirred something in me.

"Hey lady, you getting in?" The driver yelled. Looking up at the night sky, I contemplated my choices. If I didn't agree now, he would make it his life's mission to bother me; he would come to my job, bother my friends... I had a strong feeling the chase would never end; not that easily, at least. The New York traffic sound of honking and drilling brought me back.

"You're insufferable, fine." I agreed. A lopsided grin broke through his face; I knew he wasn't going to give up. "But don't think this means I'm suddenly your biggest fan."

"Wouldn't dream of it," he said, the spark in his eyes promised mischief and something more. The way he looked at me, a mix of challenge and disingenuous, made my pulse quicken. I crossed my arms, trying to maintain my cool demeanor.

How can a person you hate that much make you feel this way?

"She'll be leaving now sir, thank you," Micheal said to the driver as he reopened the door for me. "After you." He winked.

God, what did I get myself into?

"Jeez, what a true gentleman," I replied sarcastically and climbed into the cab. As the door slammed closed, I released a breath I wasn't aware I was holding in. I couldn't help but feel worried and... excited? No, definitely not excitement... More like nausea. I had to keep my guard up at all times; I don't know what devious tricks he would pull out of his sleeve. Overall, I couldn't believe I gave in... I had shoved myself in an even deeper hole than I was already in.

The ride to my apartment was unbearable. Every moment felt drawn out, my mind unwilling to let go of the memory of our conversation. I couldn't stop replaying it, particularly that damn pool table. My heart raced as my thoughts wandered, imagining his hands on me, his lips trailing along my neck, his breath hot against my skin as he slid my legs apart, taking control, daring me to surrender.

I exhaled sharply, forcing the thought away before it went any further. *No.* I couldn't let him have that kind of power over me. But damn it, my body was already betraying me.

It wasn't until I saw Oliver waiting in front of my building that I finally snapped my mind out of the gutter. I checked my phone; it was well past midnight. What on earth could he want at this hour?

I pull out my wallet to pay the cab, only for the driver to decline my cash. "The ride was already paid for, miss," he said. My eyes narrowed as I tried to remember paying for the ride, and I couldn't recall doing that.

"I don't think I did; you're mistaken," I answered, not wanting to take advantage of his confusion and get a free cab ride. Karma was real, and I definitely did not want to pay for it another way in the future.

"Miss, the man you were with paid for it. Unless you want me to drive you somewhere else, get out," he said, kicking me out of his car. Micheal had paid for my cab tonight as well? Tonight had to be the most bizarre night of my life.

Taking the hint, I climbed out of the cab. I shut the car door and caught Oliver's attention; he turned and anxiously waved at me with a quirky smile. I made my way up the steps to the door of my building and stopped before Oliver.

"Hey Ollie, what's wrong?" I asked, wanting him to get right to it. Tonight wore me out, and I wanted nothing more than to fall face first onto my bed. I was so tired, I wasn't planning on changing out of my clothes.

"I thought you were in your apartment sleeping. I honestly wasn't expecting you to show up," he admitted. He seemed nervous, swaying left and right, only looking into my eyes every five seconds.

"Okay, were you going to call me or…?" I dug for a response, trying to seek clarity. Did he need help and feel ashamed to ask for it? Was he just looking for a friend to talk to? I couldn't put my finger on it, and I couldn't sense what it was.

"Ah, no, I wasn't…" he said in a soft-spoken voice. "I don't know why I'm here," he added, scratching the back of his neck while looking down at the floor.

"Alright… Well, would you like to come in? Drink tea maybe?" I asked. I couldn't leave him out here knowing he was anxious. Plus, he didn't exactly live near my apartment building. He sighed heavily, looking up at the night sky.

"Actually, I lied. I know exactly why I'm here," he said, sure of his answer.

"Okay." I sat down on the top step, ready to hear his reasons.

"Celeste, we've been friends since freshman year of college," he started off by saying. I nodded and quietly waited for him to continue. "And I've been hiding something from you since sophomore year." He cleared his throat, trying to find the right words. I could tell he was beating around the bush, unable to come out with it. My first thought was, maybe he was coming out of the closet? That would be a shocker, because I never sensed the vibe from him.

"Whatever it is, I'll support and accept you. You should never be ashamed or nervous to say what or who you like; sexuality doesn't define a person," I said, trying to ease the pressure. Oliver was like my little brother; it worried me to know he struggled to tell me something.

"Jesus, I'm not gay, Celeste," he said defensively. "Did you think I was?!" he asked, sounding extremely offended, which was not what I was aiming for.

"No! Absolutely not! I just didn't know what else you'd hide from me since sophomore year," I tried explaining, hoping to redeem myself. "I do not think you're gay, I promise." He looked at me warily.

"Good, because that would suck. Especially with that I was trying to tell you," he said, cracking his knuckles. "I wasn't going to tell you anything at all, but I came all the way over here to walk back and forth in front of your building. I stared at your window for the past two hours, thinking of ways I could tell you this." As I listened to him speak, I suddenly knew what he was trying to say, what he was feeling.

"When we graduated, I didn't think I'd see you consistently. But then we got the same internship, and I knew I couldn't keep this in for long. I came here and didn't think you'd show up; I took it as a sign. Celeste, I'm in love with you; I have been since sophomore year and I haven't been able to stop thinking about you." My heart dropped at his words; I felt my heart breaking for him. It hurt me to know that I would need to turn him down and possibly lose him as a friend... I felt nothing more than brotherly love for him.

"Oliver..." I silently spoke, scared of hurting his feelings.

"Don't say my name like that; it sounds like you're going to reject me." He chuckled, trying to find humor in this situation. "Please, don't say it. I know, no, I can feel what you're going to say."

Now it was my turn to sigh, and I tried to hold in my tears. This news woke me up quicker than I thought it would.

"I love you, I do, but not in the way you want. It's a sisterly love; I just don't see us ever getting to that point. I do love you, and I really don't want to lose you," my voice cracked as tears rolled down my cheek. This felt like a goodbye, and I didn't want it to get to this point, ever. "I'm so sorry; I wish I felt differently."

"I know." His tears rolled down his cheeks as well, and I knew I hit him where it hurt. "But I can't continue being a close friend. It's painful knowing that you'll never feel the same for me. I think I just need some space until I can move on from you. Afterwards, maybe we can be friends again," he says, now hitting me where it hurts. He held my hand and squeezed it tightly before letting it go and standing up. He gave me a small smile and walked down the stairs.

"Ollie–" I called after him, unable to catch my breath between cries. My breathing hitched, and I tried to stifle the sobs that threatened to escape.

"I won't give up my internship because it's a big opportunity, but try to ignore me when you show up to work, and I'll do the same. I'm sorry, I wish you the best Celeste; I really do," he said, leaving my building. All I could do was stare at his back until he disappeared into the night... not once did he look back or wave goodbye. My back pressed against the cool concrete, my knees drawn up to my chest.

The soft hum of the city around me felt distant, almost like a muffled soundtrack to my sadness. I blinked back the tears, but they betrayed me, spilling out repeatedly. The moon cast a light over me, reminding me of the conversation that ended our friendship; the words that had lingered long after they were said. I never wanted to lose him; I honestly never thought I would. It's naïve to think a friendship like that lasts forever, but it still stung.

New York was awake, but here, in my little bubble of despair, it felt like everything was sleeping; my tears, the lullaby for the world. After a while, I wiped my eyes, hoping that those tears would be the last to fall. With a shuddering breath, I finally rose from the steps and headed inside my building.

The moment I entered my apartment, my body had automatically found its way to the bedroom. I collapsed onto my pillow, feeling its softness envelop me. The noise of the world drifted away, each sound dripping off like water, until I was left in nothing but silence. I shut my eyes, surrounding myself with stillness, and for the first time that day, I felt a sense of tranquility wash over me.

CHAPTER 12
MICHEAL

It was here, the night I would take Celeste out for a date. I dreaded her response the moment the words slipped out of my mouth. I was practically biting my tongue when I suggested we go on a date; in fact, I bit down so hard I drew blood. It was all to benefit me in the long run… but I had an agonizing feeling that taking Luci out on seven dates would feel like experiencing all seven deadly sins in one person.

The problem I was dealing with now was where I was going to take this woman on our first date. As much as I loathed the idea of spending extra time with her, I needed her knowledge on the gallery even more. Would I say fifty-four million dollars was enough to go out with this woman? I'm not sure, but I'd find out today.

What's the one thing that would impress a girl on the first date? A guy who goes all out, showing how determined he was to win her over. But it can't be done with money; it needs to be done with care. For example, making a home cooked meal rather than taking her out to a restaurant, or setting up a picnic rather than having her sit on your couch for Netflix and chill. Those are the things that drive women crazy; it's what grabs their interest.

Most of the time, I don't need to use that method, but in this case... I do.

Suddenly, I had the brilliant idea of setting up a dinner for two on the rooftop of my apartment building. It has a large, spacious area, and it overlooks the city's lights. It's refreshing and aesthetically pleasing. What better way to spend a first date?

I'm a genius.

I'm hoping this plays out exactly how I want it to. If not, I'd have to throw her off the building. Oops, a little mistake.

I'm joking... partly.

I had told Celeste I would pick her up after work, which would be around 11:00 tonight. I have the opening and closing hours of the gallery memorized. During the weekends they closed later, during weekdays the closing time was 9:00 pm. It was currently 9:30, which meant I had about an hour and a half to prepare everything. Thankfully, I already had everything I needed.

I steadily carried various things to help me set the mood of the space with me up the stairs to the rooftop, and once I made it to the top, I dropped the things on the floor. Taking a step back, I analyzed the space and what I could do with it. The city laid beneath a blanket of darkness, allowing the lights that were dotting the skyline to look like stars scattered across a vast canvas. I began getting busy, transforming the space into an intimate haven.

I had set up a small round table, draped in a soft, white tablecloth that caught the gentle night breeze. It was the perfect temperature outside for dinner. Once I finished setting up, I stood by the door to take in the final scene. Mismatched purple plates gleamed under the soft glow of candlelight, while polished silverware sparkled like tiny constellations beside them.

The table sat between four sturdy poles at each corner. I'd strung up bright fairy lights, their warm bulbs twinkling overhead, winding along the railing and creating a space that felt brighter, almost magical. I admired the effect, the soft glow casting a serene, almost enchanting light over the table. But somehow, it still felt off. Something about this... felt like a task. Like something I *had* to do, rather than something I *wanted* to do.

I ran a hand through my hair, the memory of my mother's departure still sharp, even after all these years. I'd sworn to myself I'd never let another woman get close after that. Every woman I'd tried to care about had been a reminder of that ache. They came, they left, and the emptiness they left behind never seemed to heal.

A small sigh escaped me. This whole setup, this effort, it felt like I was trying to convince myself I could give someone what they needed. But the truth? I was still too scared. And honestly, if there was any other reason I'd be doing this, the effort would be pointless. What was the point, anyway? She'd leave, just like the others.

My last task was cooking the meal. I could take the easy way out and order takeout, make it seem like I made it. But, for whatever reason, I felt like she'd know. I was already spending a good amount of energy preparing this; cooking a dish should be easy work. I'd like to think I'm quite the chef. Many who've had the pleasure of tasting my food would say the same.

I hurried back to my apartment and began cooking. My mind whirled as I considered my options. I didn't want to overdo it, but I still wanted something that would show I cared. So, I settled on grilled chicken with roasted vegetables, simple yet satisfying. The pan sizzled as I placed the chicken on the stove, the sound instantly making my mouth water.

The aroma of garlic and rosemary mixed with the heat of the skillet, sending a wave of comfort through me. On the other burner, I'd tossed sweet potatoes and brussels sprouts into a smaller pan with olive oil, salt and pepper. The vegetables crackled as they roasted; the edges crisping up perfectly while the chicken cooked on the larger stove. I moved between the two pans, flipping the chicken carefully, making sure the golden brown crust formed before checking the vegetables to see if they were caramelizing just the right amount.

I hummed lightly under my breath, a rhythm I couldn't help but follow as I focused on the cooking. The scent of garlic and herbs filled the apartment, making the entire place feel warm and inviting. My knife sliced through the potatoes with a satisfying crunch as I cut them into threads with a touch of butter and a sprinkle of parsley. Perfect.

Once satisfied with the outcome, I covered the pans, letting everything rest as I checked the time. My stomach dropped when I glanced at my watch. *Shit.* I wouldn't have enough time to head down to Laurosse and pick her up now. I'd pushed everything too close. But I wasn't going to let the meal be ruined for a few minutes. She could wait. She could always wait.

Suddenly, I remembered I have her number thanks to Katherine. I basically harassed her for it, and wouldn't stop asking until she gave in; my persistence works for me in many ways. I type away on my phone, sending her my address. I knew I was supposed to pick her up, but that plan had gone to shit. Now, I could only hope she'd still keep her end of the bargain and show up. It was a gamble, but what else was new?

> Micheal: 21 India St, Brooklyn, NY 11222. Head straight to the rooftop. I'll be here waiting for you. Don't forget, you owe me.
> Micheal.

Alright, now all I had to do was wait. I grabbed the chilled red wine from the fridge on my way out, making sure it was perfectly cooled. The meal was still hot; the tender marinated chicken and roasted vegetables nestled carefully in their pans. I carefully balanced everything, wine in one hand, dishes in the other, before making my way to the rooftop.

Entering the space I created amazed me. It looked even better than I thought it would; maybe the lights shone brighter because it got darker? I wasn't sure, but I was more than pleased with it. I quickly redirected my attention to the empty plates, begging to be filled. As I served each plate, the savory aroma of garlic and herbs filled the air.

With everything set, I poured two glasses of chilled red wine; the liquid catching the light from the fairy lights.

How much longer is she going to take?

Honestly, I wouldn't be surprised if she decided to ghost me, given that I was supposed to pick her up, but it would obviously be the wrong decision.

To my surprise, the door swung open, revealing Celeste in her work clothes. A fitted, tailored black blazer that accentuated the waist she was hiding, paired with a black silk blouse that draped charmingly. Beneath, sleek high waisted-pants in a deep charcoal clung to her curves without being overly tight, still allowing ease of movement. She had her hair tied up in a ponytail, and a minimalist leather crossbody bag slung casually over her right shoulder. Seeing her like this brought me back to the first night I met her on Halloween.

Déjà vu at its finest.

When she stepped onto the rooftop, her gaze swept over the setup, and her lips curled into a smirk.

"Wow Micheal. Trying to impress me? Or are you planning to throw me off the building to get rid of me?" I forced a laugh, a brittle sound that didn't reach my eyes.

"Ah, you never know," I replied, but the tension that followed made it clear I'd misspoke. Nevertheless, she took her seat; her smile faded as she processed my words.

"Right," she said, her tone flat. "Great start."

The vibe shifted instantly. I could feel the irritation coiling in my stomach, twisting and turning. She was everything I loathed —overly enthusiastic and annoyingly talkative; this girl had no filter whatsoever. I cursed myself for agreeing to this ridiculous arrangement. I'd been determined to get what I needed from her, but now I was itching to escape; itching to tell her off and kick her out.

But I remained equanimous during this mental crisis; I'm grateful that she can't hear my thoughts. She's not stupid though, and I'm sure she can sense how I'm feeling, but I have to keep myself calm and remember why I'm doing this.

"So," I said, breaking the silence with forced cheer. "How's the job treating you?"

"Wouldn't you like to know?" She fidgeted with her fork, playing with the food I prepared for her ungrateful ass. I leaned back, crossing my arms.

"That terrible, huh?" I asked, watching her expression change from curiosity to indignation.

"No, it's going quite well. I can see myself working there long term," she said defensively, dropping her fork and reaching for the glass of wine. *Should've poisoned it, but I'm too good looking to spend the rest of my life in prison.* "You wouldn't understand; you know nothing of the industry I'm in," she added, her voice rising slightly, a spark of irritation lighting up her eyes. That hate, that fire...

"I think I know enough," I replied confidently. "Truthfully, I think the whole thing's a mess. Too many abstract pieces and not enough talent. Nowadays, you see paint splattered on a canvas and people call it art. There's no true meaning in art anymore." Her eyes widened; I could tell I just pushed a button.

"You can't be serious. Paint splattered on a canvas isn't the only form of art we have. We have history, real art. There's a real vision there!" she argued.

"Vision?" I echoed, leaning forward with a challenge. "It looks like a bunch of toddlers' artwork that mommy and daddy stick on the fridge. But hey, I'm sure it appeals to your—" I paused, smirking, looking her up and down, "—unique taste."

Her jaw tightened. "You wouldn't know good art if it smacked you in the face. It's about interpretation, Micheal. Maybe it's you. You're just too narrow-minded to see it."

"Or maybe I just don't want to waste my time pretending to appreciate mediocrity," I shot back, enjoying the way her eyes flashed with anger.

The air crackled with animosity and yet, there was something almost exhilarating about our back and forth. It was as if we were both stuck in a game we couldn't exit, each jab fueled by an underlying resentment that simmered just below the surface. It was the most entertaining thing I'd experienced.

As Celeste continued to argue her points, I found myself half-listening; the words blurring together as I plotted my next move. Obviously, I didn't know shit about art; I needed information. But this was turning into a battle of wills I hadn't anticipated. It's keeping me on my toes, and I don't want to mess it up and prove her right. I want her to be the sore loser, as childish as that may seem.

"I can't believe you think you're some kind of art critic," she snapped. "Just because you ride a fancy motorcycle and have a nice face doesn't mean you have good taste."

I raised an eyebrow. "Nice face, huh?" I winked; she rolled her eyes dramatically. "And just because you're an art enthusiast and working at a fancy gallery doesn't mean you're not naïve. Not everyone shares your—what was it again?—vision."

The tension deepened as we looked at each other in a silent struggle for dominance, and the charm of the rooftop faded into a stifling weight, slowly dissolving and evaporating into the night sky.

"I don't like you, you don't like me. What the hell are we doing here?" she asked, sick of this disagreement. "Why did you set this up? Why cook for me? Why?"

"Didn't I make myself clear last time? I just want to, okay? I just do."

The things I would do to kick her right out the door right now would be insane. Maybe fifty-four million dollars isn't worth seven dates with her if this is how frustrating our first one was. I felt like I was babysitting the biggest brat in the world.

She shook her head, quickly losing the only patience she had. Despite the way she was constantly testing me, I had remained phlegmatic.

"What if I don't agree to your terms, huh? What would you do? No, scratch that. What *could* you do?" She stood up, asserting her dominance, placing her hands on the table and staring me down.

She wants to play? Okay, let's play Luci.

With a sudden surge of energy, I pushed myself up from the chair; the legs scraping against the floor. My heart races as I rise, fueled by a mix of frustration and determination. I slammed both of my hands on the table, inches away from hers. The glasses of wine shook, almost tipping over with the amount of force I used.

In front of me, mere centimeters away, I noticed her throat gulp in shock, a fleeting moment of vulnerability.

Gotcha, this is where you're weak. Isn't it?

I leaned in closer, searching her eyes for a reaction. To my surprise, she didn't pull away. Instead, we held each other's gaze, our chests rising and falling in sync, the air thick with unspoken words.

The tension hung between us like a taut string, vibrating with possibility. I felt an undeniable pull, a mix of desire and urgency, as if the room had narrowed down to just the two of us. The flickering candlelight danced in her eyes, and for a moment, everything else faded away. If she came just a little closer, I'd be making some really bad decisions. I'm not in my right mind, and I know it. And yet, I'm not doing anything to avoid it.

Getting a look at her face up close and personal is captivating on a whole other level. Here we were, arguing about what real art is, and here she is, a work of art herself. The small freckles across her nose looked like small splatters of paint, her blush and her skin a rich, caramel glow. Radiant, like polished bronze. I'm almost in awe.

A vibrant pink flushed across her cheeks as she noticed the transformation of my face. I could feel my expression soften for her. Why? I have no fucking idea. This is the same devil woman I met all those other times; it's not anyone different. If she were anyone else, maybe there could have been a possibility for something between us.

Finally, as the wind wicked up, Celeste was the first to break eye contact. To be honest, I don't recall how long we stood there, lost in each other's eyes. Her looking down at her watch broke the wicked spell I seemed to be under.

"You know what? This has been… enlightening, but I think I need to call it a night. I'm not feeling great—Stomach pains," she said, a forced smile attempting to mask her irritation as she gripped her shirt.

I knew it was a lie, an excuse to get away, and I felt a surge of satisfaction.

"Sure, go ahead. Can't say I'm surprised," I said cooly, watching her gather her things with shaky hands.

As she walked away, I couldn't help but feel a strange mix of relief and lingering resentment. This was supposed to be a simple transaction, the simple part of the job. Yet here we were, caught in a web of hostility that only seemed to thicken. The night has spiraled into an unexpected confrontation. I saw her wrap her hand around the door handle, and I swiftly called her nickname. After I spent most of my night entertaining her stupidity, I wasn't going to just let her leave, let her win.

"Hey Luci." She turned, exasperated.

"Don't call me that," she spat.

"Six more dates. You owe me six more dates, don't forget it," I reminded her, but really, I was reminding myself.

If I said it out loud, then I wouldn't go insane. Her entire demeanor changed; she puffed up her chest and walked out the door, slamming it behind her. I swore the rooftop shook like a mini earthquake with her exit.

I have a bitter taste left on my tongue, like a horrible after taste. Something you couldn't get rid of easily.

What the hell was that? And I had SIX more to go? I'm fucked.

Celeste Castillo is going to be the one to kill me. If I'm going to survive this, I'm going to need to wear a cross around my neck when I'm with her; protect me from her vicious witchcraft. That's the only reason that actually makes sense in my mind; it's the only thing that explains the weird tension between us.

And here I thought she was the devil. Oh no, she's a witch.

Deal with it, Micheal. Make it short and sweet; trick her into falling for you.

Yeah, that shouldn't be hard. She got her chance to take jabs at me tonight; hopefully next date she's better. If I take her to a public area, she'll be forced to bite her tongue and keep her tone down.

Yes, perfect. That's exactly what I'll do. Hold on, Celeste, because I'm coming for you and there's nothing you can do to stop it.

CHAPTER 13
CELESTE

Last night had to be the worst date I had ever experienced, and I've had my fair share of awful dates. Not only did we spend most of the time arguing, he was a complete asshole about it. But that's not even the worst part. This man, after a mess of a date like that, after he didn't even show up to pick me up, told me I still owed him those six remaining dates! He's a fucking maniac, a lunatic!

That's not normal, is it? Despite his obvious pulchritude, the night was extremely tiresome. This date had one-hundred percent left an indelible mark on my brain and not the good kind. I honestly didn't know what I was walking into; it was terrifying. Being around Micheal was dangerous for me, he was an asshole, but he seemed like the type of asshole who could sweep you right off your feet without you realizing it. I understood that the moment I saw the setup he had done for me.

The sight of the chilled wine and candlelit dinner instantly made me resolve to stay away from alcohol. Thank goodness I did; I can only imagine what might have happened in that fleeting moment between us. His face was just a breath away, his eyes locked onto mine, our breaths mingling in perfect harmony.

The heat surged through me, and goosebumps pricked my skin as his nose brushed softly against mine.

I felt as though I were dipped in a warm bath of honey, its sweetness wrapping around me and making everything feel blissfully soft and sensual. I sighed, lost in a revery I couldn't escape from.

"Celeste," Meredith called.

S*nap out of it!*

He, out of the seven billion people in this world, could not be the one to make me feel this way. I won't permit it! Not even over my dead, rotting body. I couldn't believe I caught myself daydreaming red-handed; this was unacceptable. Especially at my job, where I couldn't afford to daydream. I turned around, focusing my attention back on her.

"Good morning Meredith," I smiled worriedly; I wanted to avoid any agonizing orders from her today. I have a gut-feeling she's going to test me, and I didn't have the strength to do that today.

"Good morning, thought I lost you there. I need you out back, clearing one of the rooms. We have new pieces coming in this week," she explained, as she walked to the very back of the gallery. I hurriedly, but silently followed behind her, taking mental notes of what she was saying. "A quick warning; the room is a complete disaster. We've used it as storage for years, now that we need the space…" She stood in front of a door that seemed to exist in its very own defiant state of entropy.

She pushes the door open, revealing a room that is a labyrinth of chaos, stacked high with random objects, papers, and fragments of half-finished projects. Old canvases lean precariously against the walls, their edges curling and cracking with age. Piles of broken frames littered the floor, some of them completely shattered, others clumsily stacked, as if there had been a hasty attempt at order that was long abandoned.

The air inside felt heavy, thick with dust that clung to every surface, suspended in the stable atmosphere like a thousand little motes of forgotten history. The only source of light was a weak and yellow light bulb, casting strange shadows that seemed to move the slightest when shifting your gaze. I stepped in, taking in the disaster I was to deal with. I steadily moved to my right and mistakenly hit a bin that overflowed with discarded art supplies.

There's a constant hum of unfinished tasks, as if the room is caught in an eternal, unyielding state of clutter, a place where the mess isn't just physical, but a kind of living, breathing presence that refuses to be contained.

"For motivation, anything you clean out is yours to keep if you want it. It's all going to the garbage, regardless." She handed me multiple trash bags and a worn out broom. I sighed heavily, trying to keep my composure. On her way out, she turned one last time. "Oh, and if you need me, you can ask Oliver, who's out front today. You both are doing a role switch today." She smiled, surely relieved to leave all the work to me.

She shut the door behind her, silence corrupting the room. I jumped right into it; complaining would only waste my time instead of helping me. I begin cleaning out the right corner of the room, where an old easel, warped and splintering, stood there, half hidden beneath a mountain of paintbrushes, dried tubes of paint, and empty bottles of turpentine. The remnants of forgotten creative bursts, waiting for someone to use them again.

As I looked through the paint brushes, I realized that most of them were vintage brushes. I couldn't believe my eyes when I saw the gray band with the words 'Reserva' on them. With a gasp, I dropped them in shock.

I just scored myself some three hundred dollar brushes in the first session of cleaning. The smell of stale oil and dried acrylic paint lingered on these tools, sharp and almost pungent. I couldn't believe it; I would make sure that these worn out art supplies reached its entelechy back at my apartment. After graduating, I haven't had enough time to search for a new studio to escape to. Hence, the need to be painting at home, which worked for a short amount of time, but I was sure that I would grow tired of it, eventually. If I'm being truthful, I was close to that breaking point.

The floor, once wood, was barely visible beneath layers of dust and the occasional smudge of dried paint. I wondered what they used this room for? I was almost positive they used it as a studio. It's incredible how everything felt suspended in time, as though someone had started a cleaning project years ago and never quite found the energy to finish it, like an endless cycle of collecting, creating, and abandoning.

"It's your lucky day; I'm going to save a lot of you," I said to the objects as if they were living beings. I opened two trash bags, one for things I'd take to the garbage, and the other for things I wanted to keep. Reaching for my phone, I played music from my most used playlist.

After cleaning up half of the room, a knock interrupted my flow. Both trash bags were filled to the brim, most things overflowing, spilling out of the bag. I was excited to bring everything back home with me, but dreaded the thought of dragging the thick, heavy trash bag filled with goodies across New York. But, whatever; I wanted them that badly.

Another knock came from the door, reminding me I had to check who it was. I walked across the room, wrapping my hand around the golden doorknob and twisted it open. Oliver's face was the first thing I saw, and I could tell he was bothered; by what, I couldn't tell.

"Oliver, hi," I greeted awkwardly. This was the first time I'd seen him after that night in front of my building when he practically dumped me as his friend. He pointed at my face, without greeting me back.

"You got dust on your face," he clarifies, looking down at the floor. I reached for my right cheek and rubbed it off.

"Oh, I didn't realize. Thanks," I said, slightly embarrassed. We've never had trouble speaking to each other; conversations were our specialty. Now it just felt like a sin, and not the kind that had your heart racing, the kind that made you feel guilty. Like you were drawing in pure despair. But nonetheless, I acted oblivious to it.

"Yeah, but I didn't come here to check on you." *Ouch, okay.* "There's a guy up front asking for you." Oliver's jaw clenched.

"A guy? Who…?" I stopped myself before I realized who he was talking about. My stomach rolled in misery, tormented by the thought of facing him. Didn't he have enough of me yesterday? "Right… I'll be right out." I smiled, deciding whether it was a good idea to see him. Knowing him, he came back here just to fuck with me.

"I'll keep the work going here while you deal with your things," he suggested, avoiding eye contact once again. I'm about to argue it, but he knows it too well by saying. "It's not a big deal, just go," he said, swapping places with me and kicking me out of the room.

The door slams in my face, stating the obvious: he desperately wanted to get rid of me. I normally wouldn't care if any other man did that to me, but because it came from him... my friend of *years* is ridiculous. All because I didn't feel the same way, didn't mean he had to be a dipshit about it.

Without much of a choice, I continued my day, determined to cross this other lousy thing off my list. I made my way toward the front, where I suddenly saw Micheal, his back to me. I stopped a few inches away from him, ready to send him out the door. He turned to look at me and I saw him holding a boba drink and a paper bag that most likely had a tasty pastry in it.

Don't give in for one of your favorites, Celeste, come on, don't sell yourself short.

I can practically taste how savory the combination of the heavenly flavors are from here.

How did he know I liked this? Loved this? Would freaking die for this right this second?

He's tempting me right now, without even speaking. He doesn't even know I'm watching him like a starved homeless person. I took a deep breath in, putting up a face of a normal person with a full stomach, not at all starving and desperate for the goodies in his hands.

"Celeste," He greeted with a teasing smile. "I brought you snacks; I figured you'd be hungry," he said, playing the role of the perfect boyfriend, when in reality I know he doesn't want any of this. It's hard to tell what's real or not sometimes with him; it's confusing as hell.

"You brought me food because you thought I'd be hungry?" I echoed, trying to understand it myself. He smiled even wider and nodded. "How did you know I liked boba and butter croissants?" I asked.

"Had a hunch," he answered. I glared at him silently. "Alright, fine. I asked Katherine what you like to eat, and she said that this was your go-to." He handed me the boba and croissant, waiting for me to take the bait.

"Did you poison it?" I asked, my tone filled with attitude. I crossed my arms, refusing to take it.

"Damn, you're right, I should've," he sarcastically replied, taking out the croissant. The buttery pastry looked soft and moist, crispy on the outside and warm on the inside. He took a bite, making my mouth water. "Mmm, too good. I can tell why you like this so much." He took a sip of the boba drink as well, squinting his eyes in delight and making a slight hum of satisfaction. My eyes followed his lips as he licked them, his eyebrows raised slightly, giving an impressed face.

"I'll have it," I spat out without thinking. I would've said anything to stop him from making any other faces or noises that would make me feel all warm and flustered. He gave me the drink and the bag without argument.

"Good choice." He winked and stood by, waiting for me to take a bite or a sip.

"Anything else?" I asked, but what I really wanted to ask was, *"Why are you still here breathing?"* He chuckled, putting his hands in his pockets. He wore a black linen shirt with black pants that looked ridiculously good. His black hair was perfectly combed back, and he smelled like expensive sandalwood with a hint of lemon.

What fragrance is that? I'd buy it and spray it over my overalls as I painted.

It's just a fragrance, not him. I'm not complimenting him, to be completely transparent. I only like the smell he's giving off. It's not the same thing, it's totally different...

"I didn't come all this way only to give you food," he implied.

"Of course not," I answered, fully aware of what his intentions were. He was like death haunting you down; you know it's inevitable.

"Our second date, I was thinking later on this week, perhaps, Wednesday?" he asked, smirking to himself, clearly not thrilled about this conversation, but determined.

"You're serious," I said, narrowing my eyes, already suspicious. "After last night, I figured we'd both stop this nonsense." I lied, hoping I would gaslight him with his decision to continue.

"After a date like that? I thought it went incredibly well," he replied.

I paused, taking in what he was saying, before letting out a dry laugh. For a split second, his smile slipped and turned to frustration. He quickly caught it and switched back into a forced smile.

"Really? Because personally, I truly believed one of us would have been thrown off the building. I'm surprised we're still here."

He rubbed his eyes in annoyance, but still tried to remain

calm. I couldn't understand; I was giving him the hardest time. Everyone who's close to me knew it was impossible to convince my intransigent self to change my mind.

What did he expect? For me to continue agreeing and end up lollygagging on dates all afternoon? I know I've done some bad things in my life, but never anything so horrendous to deserve this.

"You know, you're lucky I'm not *completely* insane. So, let me get this straight. You want me to spend an evening pretending to be interested in you, and vise-versa, for what?" I asked, wanting nothing but the truth.

"Who said I'm pretending? I have a reason for everything I do, and soon enough, you'll be able to see that." His words were supposed to feel comforting and reassuring, but it felt like a threat, a warning. His words were equivalent to a 'run away from me' sign in bright red wording. I had a qualm about trusting his words.

"What if I don't agree?" He chuckled. The sound of his chuckle ran through my body, setting off a million goosebumps.

"Then you'll have to pay off the debt in a different way," he said, leaning closer toward me. I slowly stepped back, wary of any eyes watching this encounter.

"I'm not sleeping with you." I swallowed, allowing my nerves to take over.

"No Celeste, you're not. I don't force women to sleep with me; they do that willingly. I mean, you'll literally have to pay off the debt with money, and I'm afraid it will exceed your regular budget," he said, his eyes pinning me down in place. "But if you want, you can throw in the sleeping with me part, if it were to make you happy."

He tried to ingratiate himself by purposely making me nervous. I would have sworn I had control over myself, but here I am, stuck in place by only his gaze and his voice, and I hated it.

"How do you know what I can and can't afford?" I shot back, straightening up, trying to match his cold confidence, but it didn't have the effect I was hoping for.

"Because no one I know can," he replied with a chilling calmness; his words were so simple, they felt like a slap.

The man moved in circles I couldn't even dream of. He'd been at the CEO ceremony, for God's sake—proof enough that his contacts and mine were galaxies apart. If they couldn't afford it, I sure as hell couldn't.

"So," he continued, his voice smooth, almost too casual, "What's it going to be?"

I scoffed, letting out a soft snort, masking the way my insides twisted. I forced myself to look bored, even though his words stung. "You're bluffing."

He leaned back, a small, amused smirk tugging at the corner of his lips. "The choice is yours. But don't say I didn't warn you when you realize you picked wrong."

His tone was colder now, dismissive, as if I were nothing more than an insignificant nuisance, and yet the smirk, the way he reveled in his control, sent a wave of fury surging through me. Every fiber of my being screamed at him, cursing him, wishing I could wipe that smug look off his face.

But all I could do was stand there, boiling inside, and play my part in his sick little game.

"Fine! I'll go," I spat. I stood there for a moment, processing what I had just agreed to. The words were out before I could stop them, but now they felt like an anchor, dragging me into something I wasn't ready for... Again.

"Great, I'll see you on Wednesday then." He smiled with a satisfied nod, as if everything was going exactly as he had planned. With that, he turned and walked away without another word, his figure disappearing into the labyrinth of the gallery's corridors.

I swallowed hard, the tension in my chest tightening as I

made my way back to the room I was cleaning. Once I made it to the door, I paused for a few seconds. The gallery around me suddenly seemed smaller, quieter. It felt suffocating, as if the air had thickened, saturated with the remnants of his presence. The man was up to something I couldn't fathom, and somehow, agreeing to that date, *to this game*, felt like I was stepping into a battlefield.

Shaking my head, I quickly pulled myself back together. I couldn't stand here brooding, thinking how I would survive these next six dates, especially not with Oliver in the next room. I took a deep breath and opened the door.

Oliver looked up from the floor, his sharp, indifferent eyes catching mine with an irritated glance.

"Done with your little power trip?" he asked, his voice laced with that condescending tone that made every word feel like an insult.

I bit my lip, trying to keep my frustration in check, especially with the encounter I just had with Micheal that made me feel like I could kill four men with my bare hands.

"Power trip?" What the hell are you talking about?"

He didn't flinch, only sighed as he tilted his head up to the ceiling.

"I went to check on you. You were standing out there, looking all smug and talking it up with your new boyfriend." I didn't answer immediately. Part of me wanted to snap at him, tell him to mind his business, but I knew he was hurting. I mean, it had to hurt seeing my exchange with Micheal after he confessed his feelings for me.

"It's not like that," I said, forcing myself to stay calm, trying to focus on the task at hand. "But it's really none of your business. You made it clear that you wanted nothing to do with me anymore; this shouldn't concern you."

Oliver's lips twisted into a small, almost mocking smile.

"Whatever," he begins, "But you, out of all women, know

how these guys work. They think they can have everything, control everyone and everything."

I straightened up at that, feeling a burst of heart rise in my chest.

"I'm not everyone, Oliver," I snapped. "And I'm not some damsel in distress who needs saving; I'm not an idiot that needs guiding. Also, you don't even know him. How would you know?"

His expression stayed the same, but the air in the room seemed to shift, like he was taking a mental note of something I hadn't meant to show.

"Whatever," he muttered again, clearly uninterested in engaging any further. He walked past me, without sparing me another look, and stepped out of the room as if the conversation was already forgotten. The door slammed shut behind him, leaving me with a simmering tension in my chest.

I couldn't stand the feeling of not being in control, of being overlooked as a woman. I didn't know what Micheal wanted from me and I knew exactly what Oliver wanted from me. My life had taken a sudden change, my girls being the only thing still intact.

Glancing at the clock on the wall, covered in dust, I noticed it was almost time to wrap up before lunchtime, but I still needed to finish cleaning the back room before I could leave. I didn't want to come back to this mess afterwards; I think that would be my final straw for today. With a sigh, I walked back to a stack of art supplies, grabbing a rag and some cleaner. My mind wandered back to the conversation I had with Micheal, replaying his words.

"Then you'll have to pay off the debt in a different way... What's it going to be?"

He had won once again. Men like Micheal often leverage their ability of persistence and the life they can offer to attract the women they desire; so why shouldn't women use their beauty to attract the men they want? It's a mutual exchange. Isn't that a fair exchange? I'm young, creative, and Latina. for heaven's sake!

That was the answer. If I played along, pretended to show interest in him, he would show me his true intentions; I could find out what it is he wants from me. Fighting it wasn't helping me; look where it has gotten me so far...

By the time my break came around, I had finished cleaning the entire room and was ready to head out for lunch. I took the opportunity to mentally map out exactly how I was going to approach the next date, and how I could be as convincing as possible.

Did he really think he wouldn't get karma for messing with women this way? No. No woman would be okay with this, and we don't forget. We wait, and then when they least expect it, we make them pay.

Micheal doesn't know it, but I am going to be his biggest karma yet.

CHAPTER 14
MICHEAL

"How's it going with our source? Have you made any progress?" Dylan asked, spinning lazily in his chair. It was a Tuesday afternoon, and I'd been called into his office for a rundown of the past week.

I leaned against the doorframe, trying to ignore the buzzing of the fluorescent lights overhead. Dylan's office reflected his position perfectly: sleek and minimal, with just enough personal touches to keep it from feeling sterile. Today, his usual air of casual indifference was tinged with a hint of impatience, as if he expected something from me.

"I'm getting there," I replied, crossing my arms. "Our source is still playing it close to the vest, but we're definitely getting closer. I just need a bit more time; the pieces are slowly starting to fall into place."

Dylan stopped spinning and leaned forward, the casual demeanor slipping away.

"Allow me to remind you that we don't have time for it to *slowly start falling into place*," he said, his voice sharper now.

"And allow me to remind you that you didn't quite give me the easiest person to work with. It's a miracle she agreed to a second date, and the first was horrible," I spat, losing my patience. I couldn't stand the fact that he was putting this on me. I was trying my goddamn best here; she was at fault for this.

"She's a stubborn woman, so what? In Spain, that's all you see in women," he said. The tension in the room was palpable, and it was clear Dylan was already strategizing, contemplating the point at which patience would become a liability. "Listen Micheal, if you don't bring me some type of useful information by the end of next month, you're out."

"Are you serious?" I asked, at a loss for words. There was no way in hell that this woman would cost me this opportunity. No, I wouldn't allow it.

"You won't leave me any choice but to do so. I trust you will deliver, yes?"

"Without a doubt," I lied through my teeth. "In fact, I'm taking her out tomorrow night," I said, straightening my posture.

"Is that right? Where are you taking her?" he asked. It sounded more like a suggestion than an actual question. He off the bat assumed I had a terrible idea, one that wasn't worth playing out.

"Well, that part I'm still figuring out," I admitted.

"Micheal, in order to seduce a woman, you need to at least plan an amatory date," he stated as a fact. "And in order to plan an amatory date, you have to know what it is that she likes. Did you at least obtain that piece of information?"

"She's a wanna-be artist working as an intern at an art gallery; it's not rocket science figuring that one out." I said. Dylan's lips curled into a smirk as if an idea popped in mind. "What?" I asked warily.

"Consider yourself extremely lucky Micheal, because I've got just the thing." He smiled as he reached for a drawer in his desk. He pulled out two tickets; they had shiny, metallic accents of silver that made them more visually striking. I could instantly tell their exclusive tickets to somewhere expensive. He dropped the tickets in front of him on the desk. I walked over, reeled in by the vibrant color.

I grabbed both tickets, and with a closer look I could see a clear marking, a stamp with the words "VIP Exclusive" on the front, and the back held a code. These tickets looked legit, but I had no clue what these tickets were for.

"It's for an art event we have coming up. I've partnered up with Nicolas Geneva; you've met him once at Avenue." I suddenly remembered the stuck-up prince of a small country in Europe called Ludornia. Mr. Golden Spoon Boy, first in line for daddy's throne.

He was the definition of chaos and recklessness. To be fair, he didn't need to be responsible yet; he wasn't ruling a kingdom. I'm positive his family publicist takes care of any messes the little prince makes; it's ridiculous. Allegedly, women in the U.S. were very fond of the prince; he was considered to be a ladies' man for having a title. Please, I bet I could wing more women even if he had the prince's name tag on him.

It's a fact, and I'm not jealous, just to be clear.

"Yes, I recall meeting him," I said, biting down my sarcasm.

It wasn't my choice meeting him that night. Dylan had brought him along and I was so desperate to win Dylan as a client, I would've let him bring a clown with him if he felt like it.

"Unquestionably, this is your golden ticket," Dylan said, sounding positive that this would win Celeste over.

I felt like laughing in his face; I can't speak for Celeste when I said this, but I honestly don't believe for a second that this girl can be bought out. She seemed too stubborn for that, which I respected to an extent. But again, who am I to turn down the offer he's giving me? It could work.

"Alright, I'll use them. Thank you," I replied, shoving the tickets in my back pocket.

"Thank me later when things go well." He grinned, looking

proud of himself. *Yeah, right.* I'd consider myself lucky if she even genuinely smiled at me.

"Perfect. Make sure to be on your best behavior. Keep in mind, all eyes will be on you for most of the night. I expect to hear nothing but good things."

Great, can't wait.

Round two with Celeste, here I come…

CHAPTER 15
CELESTE

GREAT, MY DATE WITH MICHEAL IS OFFICIALLY ON FOR TONIGHT, I received a text from him confirming the time for our date. It was Wednesday afternoon, around the end of April, and I was having a coffee date with the girls. They have no clue on what's truly been going on between Micheal and me. They only know we've been going out, completely oblivious to the part of him partially blackmailing me to do so. God, I want to shed a thousand tears right about now.

Throwing a tantrum on the floor like a child honestly sounded nice. I could definitely blow off some steam by kicking and slamming my legs and arms on the floor like a child. Unfortunately, I wasn't in my humble home... Everyone would be traumatized if I did.

"So, what's the deal with Micheal? You've been keeping an unreasonable amount of tea hidden from us," Elaina commented as she sat down with her coffee.

"About that–" I began by saying before Katherine cut me off.

"Can I just say I knew it?! I knew you two would hit it off. Micheal always seemed to remind me of you, even though you're both completely different." She smiled before sipping on her iced coffee.

Oh, Kat... how can I tell her now?

"Ha, definitely! But uh, the problem is—"

"Problem? There's a problem? Did you kill him and need us to help you dig a hole or something?" Elaina asked, interrupting me again. I couldn't get a damn word in with these girls. I had to fight for my life to say a full sentence.

"Why would I kill him? I'm not crazy," I responded, rolling my eyes.

"You *are* crazy when someone triggers you." Elaina wasn't fully wrong; I was known for throwing the most dramatic episodes when someone tested me. I was a calm person as long as said person didn't pick on me.

"We're getting off track; what's the problem?" Katherine asked, bringing us back to the previous conversation I was trying to have.

"Right, so the problem... I wouldn't really say it's a problem, but I would say it's a hostage situation," I answered. Elaina and Katherine's eyes widened at my words. "Okay, I'm being overly dramatic," I added before explaining the entire situation; I made sure to sugarcoat it for Katherine.

"No way, Micheal?" Katherine asked, as if the man was an angel that could do no wrong. I would be charmed by his face too, Kat, I feel you. "He must really like you to be going through this much trouble to get seven dates with you," she admitted.

"What?!" I exclaimed, confused by how she views the situation.

"Yeah, what guy would ask for seven dates as a debt for losing a game of pool? Seven dates are oddly specific, though," Elaina said. I slammed my hands on the top of my head, my fingers itched to pull on my hair.

"Yes! Thank you; seven dates aren't just oddly specific, it's suspicious!" I shouted, desperate for someone to validate my thoughts. I needed to make sure I wasn't going insane.

"Not suspicious, just oddly specific. Maybe seven is his lucky number? Hence the reasoning behind his choice to pick seven dates. It's like he's trying to get you to fall for him during it," Elaina clarified, and I almost wanted to take two on the child tantrum.

"We have a date tonight," I murmured, wanting to leave the cafe giving none of this a second thought.

"Really? Then what are you doing here? You should be getting ready at home!" Katherine's eyes sparkled with mischief. She was already mentally planning my look for the night.

"Truthfully, I think I'm just going to fake my interest in him, so it goes by faster," I said.

"Well, you could," Elaina responded, nodding. "But then again, you never know. You could fall for him while 'faking' your interest."

Yeah, not happening.

A sudden thought hit me. Letting them dress me up tonight would make my life so much easier. I could focus solely on planning how I would pretend to be interested in him. Well, part of me pretending—it was really just his personality I had to fake it for.

"Hey, do you think you guys could help me get–"

"Yes!"

"Of course!"

They both answered in unison, cutting me off yet again. I couldn't help but laugh, knowing I was in for a treat.

Four hours later, I found myself in front of the mirror, adjusting my dress one last time, smoothing down my freshly done hair. I looked like a vision of elegance and allure. Elaina had given me a sleek black Saint bodycon dress she made. It clung to my curves, covering every inch of my figure with the perfect balance of sophistication and sensuality. The dress, with its simple yet striking design, exuded understated luxury. It looked more flattering than any luxury design brand. The fabric shimmered softly under the lights, hinting at the curves that it effortlessly embraced, making every movement feel like a statement.

Katherine did my face and hair. My hair, long and straight, cascaded down to my back like a glossy silk curtain; its deep black strands contrasting against the sharp lines of my dress. The smooth, flawless finish framed my face perfectly, sealing the look together. As for my makeup, she chose a bold, inviting, and undeniably sexy look. My brows, bold and well defined to frame my face, rich, warm-toned eyeshadows, and a fine line of eyeliner, making them look sharper. As for my lips, a rich plum color that made them stand out.

I had to admit; I looked good, *really* good. But tonight wasn't about looking good for myself; it was about keeping up appearances. "Well, I guess it's time for me to go," I said, walking over to grab my purse from the dresser.

Elaina shot me a teasing smile. "Are you nervous? You know… playing a fake part?" I knew what she was really saying. *Are you nervous about going on a date with a guy you actually find attractive but don't want to admit it?*

I rolled my eyes, though my lips twitched in a half-nervous smile.

"Nope. I'm not exactly into him. Tonight, I'll be doing an easy acting gig." I leaned in conspiratorially. "I'm just going to act interested. I'm a pro at faking that, aren't all women?"

Katherine raised an eyebrow, an amused grain crossing her face. She snapped a picture of me without warning. "Valery approves," she said with a grin. "Sounds like a fun night."

I nodded, though the thought of it still felt like a challenge. I could pretend, play the part, but I wasn't sure how long I could go along with it. Micheal had a keen interest in pissing me off, I couldn't trust myself to be well behaved for most of the night. One could only hope for that.

"It's all part of the plan; he won't suspect a thing."

As I walked toward the door, I heard Katherine call after me.

"Don't forget to have *some* fun, okay?" I chuckled to myself, heading out the door with a wave.

I wasn't entirely sure on what to expect tonight, but it was bound to be interesting, nonetheless.

Thirty minutes and a cab ride later, I found myself waiting for Micheal in front of a tall building. I was feeling anxious, like how someone would feel on an actual date. I never expected it to be in a location like this one; I know what building this is.

This wouldn't be your typical gallery; it's a rented space to host art events. But it's not for anyone to rent out; only those who had a name in the art world could have the privilege to do so. I stared up at the building and suddenly heard a motorcycle pull up. I can see Micheal parking his bike across the street in a black tailored suit. He took off his helmet, his hair perfectly combed back the way I liked it, and with a little help from the wind, I could smell the scent of his cologne from where I stood.

He got off the bike and made his way toward the building. He quickly glanced over at me and looked away. Did he not recognize me? He stood there, waiting for what seemed to be me? I didn't know if he was testing me or if he was seriously oblivious to the fact that I was standing right across from him.

This is the perfect time to begin phase one of tricking Micheal.

"Excuse me sir, have you seen my date anywhere near? I can't believe he had the audacity to leave me alone for so long,"

I spoke out loud enough for him to hear. He rapidly turned around and stood back, shocked. It took him a second to respond.

"Haven't seen him, but he sounds like an ass," he finally responded. "You look amazing," he added on a serious note, his gaze lingering on me for a beat too long.

"Thanks," I replied with a casual shrug. "You clean up well yourself."

His eyes widened at my broad compliment. "Luci, did you just give me a compliment?" he asked with a teasing smile. I know he asked the question so he could hear it again; I never had anything nice to say to him until tonight.

"I did; let me know if you can't handle it," I answered in a flirty tone, while giving him a pouty look. On the outside, I kept my cool, on the inside though... I was basically shaking like a leaf in the wind.

I've done this a hundred times... why is it so hard to do it with him?

His teasing smile faltered for a moment, and I could see the wheels turning in his head. I didn't know if he was confused or just processing what was happening, but I wouldn't let it distract me. I took a slow, deliberate step forward, narrowing the distance between us, just enough to make it a little harder for him to back away from this strange moment.

Intimidate them before they intimidate you. And you're going down, fucker.

"Honestly," I continued, keeping my tone casual. "I didn't expect you to show up with that whole bad boy vibe. You've definitely got my attention." I raised an eyebrow, studying his reaction closely.

He cleared his throat, then laughed nervously, clearly caught off guard.

"Well, Luci, you've got me there. But you don't really mean it, right?" He was smiling, but there was a flicker of uncertainty in his eyes now, something I haven't seen before that gave me the green light to be completely bold.

I tilted my head, flipping my hair to the side, and held his gaze a little longer than usual. "Why wouldn't I mean it?" I asked, my tone teasing but softer, almost coaxing. "I'm not that bad at giving compliments. You should be thankful; people like you don't get praised enough." I took a pause and looked him up and down. "Maybe you get praised a little too much, especially with that face."

His expression softened slightly, and his shoulders slightly relaxed, but the tension still lingered between us. It was like he was unsure of how to handle me *genuinely* flirting, even for just a moment.

I stepped back, pretending to think. "Then again," I said, smirking, "maybe I'm just testing how well you handle compliments... or maybe I want to see you trip over your words for once."

His lips twitched, as if he was holding back another smile, but this time there was something different in his eyes, something that wasn't all playful banter anymore.

"Maybe you just like making me uncomfortable," he shot back, his voice low, but there was a hint of something else under the teasing. "Is that it?" he adds in a whisper.

I could feel my heart beating faster, but I didn't let it show. Not yet.

Phase one, remember? This was just the beginning.

"Who says I'm trying to make you uncomfortable?" I countered with a shrug, but my voice dropped just a little; something in it almost... intimate? "Maybe I'm just having fun with you."

The silence between us stretched for a second, and I couldn't help but notice how close we were now. The part of me that had been shaking on the inside was now steady, my confidence growing, but it was tempered with something I hadn't expected: a hint of vulnerability.

He leaned in slightly, lowering his voice. "Well, you've got me intrigued now. What's the endgame here, Celeste? You playing me or something?"

The way he said my name, almost like a challenge, sent a jolt of something electric through me. I swallowed, resisting the urge to look away or throw up...

"No endgame," I said slowly, letting the words hang between us. "Just playing a fair game; wouldn't you say the same?"

The tension between us shifted and became almost tangible. It was like we were both trying to play some kind of game, but neither of us fully knew the rules. And just for a moment, I wondered if *he* knew what was really going on... or if I was the one fooling myself.

Either way, I wasn't about to back down now. Not with him.

He bit his lip and looked at me like he was contemplating all of his life choices. I felt small under his gaze, like he was a starved predator, determined to make me his next meal... Dangling food in front of a wild animal will only get a chaotic response. Was I an amateur for being this bold, this quick?

Shoot, now I'm the one contemplating all of my life's choices.

Abruptly, he sighed heavily and gazed down at his shoes. He made a sharp *tsk* sound. "Let's go inside Luci," he said, grabbing me by my arm and making his way through the building until we reached the entrance of the gallery.

Micheal handed in our tickets to the security at the front and we entered the event; the halls filled with guests stationed at each art piece. As we maneuvered through the crowd, an awfully familiar painting caught my attention. I pulled my arm out of Micheal's grip and made my way towards the piece.

The Scream by Edvard Munch hung on the wall like any other regular painting. How could they have something like this here?

"What is it?" Micheal asked as he walked up behind me. He looked at the painting and let out an understanding "Oh."

"This is a famous painting, and it's here. I mean, I studied him in school. They even had us recreate his painting for an assignment, and now I'm looking at it with my own eyes. I can't believe it," I admitted. "It's so much more emotional in person; I mean the color, brush stroke technique, and the expression, wow the expression..."

Micheal chuckled at my amusement. "You had to recreate it? Please tell me you still have the assignment," he said. "Wait, let me guess, it looked like a child painted it. Did mommy hang it on the fridge?"

"And I suddenly remember how *charming* you really are," I whispered. Dammit, I didn't even make it halfway on this date and I already messed up. This wasn't as simple as I tricked myself into thinking it was. "To answer your first question, I don't. It's probably still in the studio if they haven't cleaned out all the graduate students' work," I replied. Micheal's arm brushed mine for a split second, spreading warmth down my arm. I could feel his attention—too much attention, really. "And no, mommy didn't hang it on the fridge. I don't have parents; they're dead," I admitted the dark truth like it was nothing.

"I'm sorry," he said so abruptly, probably realizing what an ass move it was.

"Don't be; I don't remember them. How could you feel grief for losing something you never really had?"

Micheal stayed silent, I'm sure at a loss for words. What woman brings up the death of her parents on her second date? And speaks on it with no emotion. Micheal coughed, suddenly changing the subject.

"Could you still get into the studio? You know, if you wanted to pick up that work?" He asked., Perhaps I could manage to sneak in if the janitor who knew me worked those late hours.

"Actually, if it's still how I remember it, I think I can. Yeah,"

I answered, loving the idea of going into the studio one last time.

"Great, let's go after the event." He decided without asking me if I wanted to go. "That way you can put it on your fridge. I don't think anyone else is going to have that hanging on their fridge." I was about to tell him off and tell him how absurd the words coming out of his mouth sounded, but I got interrupted for the millionth time today.

A man in a black tuxedo, golden blond hair and blue eyes stood in front of Micheal and me. He flashed a pearly white smile and lent his hand for me to shake.

"Good evening, I'm Nicolas Geneva and *you are* undeniably beautiful, love," he spoke in a European accent.

I couldn't figure out where his accent was from, but it sounded rich. Valery has a British accent, but it doesn't quite sound like this. It sounded as if you were being coated with warm chocolate; does that make sense? I don't know, all I know is that he is beautiful and his voice suits him perfectly.

"Celeste," I answered. I felt Micheal's posture stiffen beside me, his gaze flicking between Nicolas and me. His jaw tightened the second Nicolas grabs my hand and lands a gentle kiss on top.

"Prince Nicolas, always the charmer, aren't you? Please don't harass my date, just because you're royalty in Europe doesn't mean you can walk around America expecting the same treatment," Micheal said in a joking tone, but I could read the threat between the lines.

"Well, well, well, if it isn't the infamous ladies' man, Micheal Zhang. It's an honor to chat with you again," Nicolas said, finding Micheal's sudden comment rather amusing. "Miss Celeste is a gorgeous woman; you really outdid yourself this time. Treat her right, yes?" He winked.

It was a friendly interaction, but in between the lines it's like their silent communication was saying something entirely different from what was being said out loud. But it was obvious that Micheal was getting uncomfortable. His hand, which had been resting lightly on my back, tightened subtly.

"Ah, not to worry, your royal majesty. I've got it covered," Micheal responded in a sarcastic tone, his voice grew dark and hollow. Nicolas smiled, taking two glasses of champagne off a waiter's plate that passed us.

"And I'd expect nothing less of Mr. Zhang." He handed me one of the two glasses he held in his hands. "For you dear." As I reached for the glass, Micheal grabbed it from me.

"Trying to make my date drink now? Careful, wouldn't want another scandalous newspaper landing on your old man's desk over morning tea time." Nicolas chuckled at Micheal's rude response.

"Indeed, we would not. Will you both excuse me? I have a list of guests I still need to attend to before the night ends. But please, enjoy the beverages and the beautiful art. Feel free to place an offer on a piece that speaks to you. Goodnight." He nodded effortlessly, his movement smooth and controlled.

As Nicolas walked away, I caught the flicker of something dark in Micheal's eyes. I'd never seen it before; the look made me shiver.

"Sounds like you know each other," I spoke, breaking the sudden silence that was left by the prince.

"Friend of a friend," he simply clarified, not wanting to go deep into explanation.

"Hm," I said and wandered through the gallery, feeling Micheal two steps behind me. I stopped at every painting and gave Micheal a short history of the art and the artist behind it. As the night wore on, I grew more at ease. It wasn't so bad—this whole charade. I could pretend, I could fake it, and I was doing a damn good job of it.

As we neared the end of the exhibit, I felt a bit more relieved at the fact that it was slowly coming to an end; a little more time and I'd be done with phase one. That was until he grabbed my hand, turning me to him. The air left my lungs as my chest collapsed against his.

"Let's go, we've done enough looking," he suggested in an irritated tone.

Why?! I was so close to being done with this!

My patience was wearing thin; I hated feeling like I was walking on the tip of my toes around him.

"Actually, I'm feeling a little tired," I tried lying once again to get out of spending even more unnecessary time with him. I've done my part for tonight. Faked it and made it to the end; why would I want to torture myself more?

"I get it..." he said in an understanding tone, "If the painting is that bad, and I mean to an embarrassing point, I get it."

Shit. Why am I so bothered by those words?

He knew what he was doing; he's basically dangling bait in front of me, and dammit, it's good too. He's good. A mature adult would say no and go home; it's the smart choice. But the problem was, when Micheal became a child, I became one too. I got down to his level and fought with him.

"Bad? Alright fine, you want to see a masterpiece that will shut your stupid mouth up? Let's go." I said, marching out the doors with determination.

I could only hold out for so long... I was going to break eventually and regrettably, this was my breaking point.

CHAPTER 16
MICHEAL

THERE SHE WAS; THE REAL LUCI. SHE CAME ON OUR DATE looking and acting completely different, and I mean different to the point of being unrecognizable. It worried me; I thought she was going to kill me at some point. But I calmed down the moment she allowed her true self to join the party; I was hoping to get a bite out of one of my baits.

I know it's not the smartest thing to do, not when I'm trying to win her over, but fuck it. Messing with her and pissing her off was the highlight of my day. She was acting way too nice; it was obviously fake, though it was intriguing to see how bold she was acting. I didn't think she had it in her, to be honest.

And there was this moment of vulnerability, when she shared the tiniest piece of herself, of her childhood. It shocked me to find out she grew up without parents and I related to her. Except, the only difference between her and me is her parents had no choice. My mother chose to leave us, and my father decided to continue life without acknowledging me. Except now, he only wanted to be in my life when he started growing older. So, in a sense, I felt as if my parents were dead, too.

The need to change the subject was insufferable; she spoke about it like it didn't affect her. Which was a lie; we always feel even when we don't want to.

But don't get me started on *Prince Nicolas*. He was standing by a large abstract piece, talking to a small crowd of people. His eyes locked on Celeste almost immediately, and without hesitation, he broke away from the group and made his way toward her. I was already expecting the worst, but Christ, that was diverting. Though, I couldn't understand the dark, possessing emotion I felt toward Celeste. It was random as hell.

Perhaps I shouldn't have addressed the situation the way I did; it was stupid of me to threaten a prince, but at the moment I couldn't give a single fuck. I felt weirdly protective of Celeste, and I couldn't explain why. I didn't even like her enough to react that way. Maybe because it all happened so quickly, right after she told me her parents were dead.

However, I forgot the interaction the minute it ended; I had no interest in revisiting it. I'm guessing Celeste decided to do the same, since she continued her search through the gallery. She dragged me along to every painting there was to see, and admittedly, I grew bored with it. So, I grabbed a hold of her arm and told her that we were leaving.

"Let's go, we've done enough looking," I said, determined to get her out of here. I could see the irritation growing on her face; it was obvious she wanted no part in it.

"Actually, I'm feeling a little tired." She tried lying; it's quite easy to know when she's lying. Her eyes do this funny thing where they slightly twitch for a split second. If I wasn't paying attention, I would've missed it.

"I get it…" I said in an understanding tone, "If the painting is that bad, and I mean to an embarrassing point, I get it." I added and waited patiently for her to take the bait. Right when I spoke those words, I saw a flash of fire in her eyes and I knew I had her.

"Bad? Alright fine, you want to see a masterpiece that will shut your stupid mouth up? Let's go," she said, storming out the doors with nothing and no one stopping her.

And just like that, I got her to do the hard work for me. I casually walked out, following behind her and came to a stop. She stood in front of my motorcycle, analyzing it, and rapidly turned around.

"No," she said precipitously.

"No?" I repeated, unable to understand the big deal. Has she never rode a motorcycle?

"There's only one helmet, and I'm wearing a strappy black dress," she said as she pointed at the helmet that sat on my motorcycle and then dragged her finger and pointed it toward herself.

Without speaking, I took off my jacket and gave it to her. "Put this on, and as for the helmet, you're wearing it." I said, grabbing it.

"But–" she tried to argue, but I instantly placed the helmet over her head.

"Let me know if it's too tight," I said as I tied the straps; she looked up to the sky and rolled her eyes. Once I was done, she was wearing my oversized jacket that reached to the bottom of her hips, with a helmet far too big for her head. She looked ridiculous; it was adorable. "Flattering," I said sarcastically.

She crossed her arms, giving me a defiant glare. "You know, I could ride without this," she muttered, shifting uncomfortably under the weight of my jacket.

"Not happening." I smirked, crossing my own arms. "I'd rather have you look ridiculous and safe than stubborn and hurt."

She let out an exaggerated sigh and shook her head, the helmet wobbling slightly. "Fine. But if anyone sees me like this, I'm blaming you."

"Blame away," I said, stepping closer and giving the straps

one last check. "But you'll thank me when you don't break your neck." Her eyes softened for a second before she narrowed them at me again, determined not to show any weakness.

"I won't owe you anything," she snapped, but her voice lacked its usual bite.

"Sure you won't." I grinned, then turned toward the bike. "Now, get on. We're wasting time."

"I didn't realize we had a time limit; do you have somewhere you've got to be?" she questioned, and that same bite in her voice made a comeback.

"Not at all, but I would rather spend my time riding the bike instead of wasting it here, standing and waiting." I winked. Deep down, I wanted to get any piece of information I could. I figured my chances of retaining some at said studio would be higher than here. "Hold on tight," I said, revving the engine.

She hesitated for a second before reluctantly wrapping her arms around my waist. The warmth of her touch sent a flicker of something unfamiliar through me, but I shook off.

We sped off; the wind whipping past us. I felt her grip tighten as I made a sharp turn around a corner. She stuck to me like glue; I could hear the little gasps escaping from her as I picked up the speed. The adrenaline of riding alone is one thing, but the adrenaline of riding and having her behind me is addicting. She's trusting me with her life right now, and the thought seemed bizarre to me.

"How are you holding up back there?" I yelled as I drove past a honking taxi.

"Oh, like a champ," she screamed back. "Hey, I didn't give you the address. How are you going the right way?" she asked as we came to a red light.

I cleared my throat and pretended I didn't hear her question. I'm stalling so I could come up with an answer that won't give me away. Of course I know where she went to school; it's in her record, which Dylan made me study before 'pursuing her.'

The traffic light turned green, and I hurriedly sped through the street. I wouldn't be able to hear her throughout the rest of the ride. As I came to a stop in front of the studio, I knew that I couldn't run away from her questions.

"I asked you a question!" she yelled as I parked the bike. I took a deep breath, keeping my hands firmly on the handlebars, hoping to stall for just a few more seconds.

"Yeah, I heard you," I said, swinging my leg over the bike and standing up. "Just, you know, traffic and all." I turned to face her, trying to look casual, but her expression was anything but amused. She got off the bike and crossed her arms, still wearing that oversized jacket and the helmet that looked like it would slide right off her head.

"Well?" she pressed, narrowing her eyes. "How did you know where I needed to go?" I rubbed the back of my head, trying to think of a lie that wouldn't make me sound suspicious.

"Lucky guess," I said firmly, forcing a grin, but I knew she wasn't going to buy it.

"Lucky guess?" she repeated incredulously, her voice dripping with skepticism. "You just happened to guess the exact location of my school out of all the other art schools in the city?"

I cleared my throat, trying to appear nonchalant. "Your friend mentioned it once," I said quickly, hoping to dodge any further questions. Her gaze lingered on me, skeptical but less pressing. She rolled her eyes, finally dropping the subject.

"Right..." Without another word, she shrugged out of my jacket and took off the helmet. Once she placed both items on my bike, she walked toward the door of the studio, glancing over her shoulder once to make sure I was following.

As soon as we reached the entrance, she paused, looking around as if making sure no one was watching. "What are you waiting for?" I whispered, glancing at the locked door. She flashed me a mischievous smile and pulled out a small pin from her hair. The strand of hair that was being held from the pin fell forward, drowning me in that sweet scent of hers.

"When I forgot my keys, I would use a hairpin or a pocket knife to get back in. The idea of going back to my apartment pained me. You could say I'm an expert," she joked, her voice playful. It sounded real, like she wasn't faking it. Like she didn't completely hate the idea of being here with me.

I raised an eyebrow, watching as she expertly slid the pin into the lock. "An expert, huh? Should I be concerned?" I asked, leaning more into her scent.

Tonight she smelled like a mix of paint and jasmine, with a faint trace of something warm, like cinnamon or vanilla, lingering in the air. It was subtle, but unmistakable... an oddly comforting contrast to the bold, chaotic energy she carried.

"Perhaps... I'm quite dangerous when I'm messed with. Even pretty boys such as yourself will get cut." She grinned as the lock clicked, and she pushed the door open. "After you, sir." She gestured to me to get in.

"I believe the right term is ladies first," I replied, standing still.

She shook her head with a small smile. "Oh no, see, you're the fall guy. If anyone's in there, you'll be the first face they see. Therefore, after you."

With a small shrug, I slipped inside, Celeste following behind me. The dim light of the street fading as the door closed behind us. The studio smelled faintly of paint and old wood, the silence heavy around us. Canvases leaned against the walls, and sculptures stood half-finished on pedestals, casting eerie shadows in the faint light.

"So this is where the infamous Luci worked on the astonishing remake of 'The Scream.'" I teased, looking around the room. As I waited for her to respond, there was silence. I turned around to find her standing behind a racket, searching through paintings. "Celeste?" I called after her, regaining her attention.

She looked up from the racket, waving the painting in her hand back and forth.

"I found it," she said, slightly biting her lip. "Though I must warn you, it's far above average. Especially for a refrigerator." She smiled as she walked back with me, the sound of her heels clicking the floor matching my heart beat.

I raised an eyebrow, smirking at her dramatic presentation of the painting.

"Far above average, huh? I guess I should prepare myself for greatness."

She stopped in front of me, holding the canvas close to her chest, her eyes sparkling with mischief.

"Oh, it's nothing short of a masterpiece. But, like I said, it's more suited for, you know, kitchen decor."

I crossed my arms, trying to suppress a grin.

"Well, let's see this legendary piece of art, then. Don't leave me in suspense."

With a flourish, she spun the canvas around, revealing a chaotic splash of colors; abstract and vibrant, with bold strokes that somehow felt like the perfect description of human emotion. Personally, it's better than the original painting; I could *feel* this painting, and no artist has earned this type of response from me. She did it with a simple recreation of an original. But I wouldn't dare flare up her ego by admitting that.

As she held up the painting, her grin faded slightly, as if she wasn't sure how I'd react. I looked at it for a long moment, taking in the messy, wild style, the way the colors seemed to clash yet complement each other all at once. It was bold, intense… just like her.

"Well?" she asked, a little edge creeping into her voice. "Are you going to make fun of it, or are you too speechless?"

Shit, I'm being too obvious.

I smirked, meeting her eyes.

Chill the hell out, you're overdoing it and for what? For a woman you can't stand?

"I'm not sure whether to call it a masterpiece or a warning sign."

Her lips twitched, but she didn't back down.

"Careful. I told you before, I'm dangerous when messed with."

"Is that a threat?" I teased, stepping closer, just enough to see the flicker of something in her eyes... defiance, curiosity, maybe something more.

"A promise." She lifted her chin slightly, her gaze never wavering. I took another step, the air between us charged with a tension that had been building since the moment we met. "You know, you've been threatening me since day one. But here we are, sneaking into an art studio to steal your painting like partners in crime."

She rolled her eyes, trying to hold on to her tough exterior, but I could see the cracks.

"I'm only here because I need someone to take the fall if things go south."

"Right," I murmured, leaning in just enough to close the gap between us, the scent of jasmine and paint hitting my nose, making a comeback even stronger than last time.

For a second, neither of us moved, the tension thick, the silence louder than any words. Then, almost reluctantly, she broke eye contact, looking away with a quiet laugh.

"You really don't know when to stop, do you?"

I smiled, stepping back, but not too far.

"Maybe I just get a kick out of pushing your buttons."

She looked up at me, her smirk returning.

"Keep testing your luck, and you might find out I bite harder than I bark."

"Really? Cause as far as I know, it's all been bark and no bite," I replied.

"Maybe I just haven't decided if you're worth biting." This time, the threat felt different; less about distance, and more like a challenge I was ready to accept.

As we stood there, her painting still in hand, I reached out to take a closer look at one of the brushes perched on a nearby easel. Before I knew it, the brush slipped from my fingers, knocking over a smaller jar of paint. A splash of bright red shot across the canvas- and splattered right onto Celeste's chest and face.

"Oh, crap!" she exclaimed, looking down at herself in disbelief. Her once serious expressions dissolved into a mixture of shock and laughter. "You've got to be kidding me. This is just perfect, no, fantastic."

I froze for a moment, staring at the vivid streak of red painting across her cheek dripping onto her collarbone. But instead of apologizing, I found myself smiling.

"Hey, I improved your masterpiece."

She shot me a look of playful irritation, trying to wipe the paint off, but only smearing it further.

"Yeah, right. More like you ruined it."

I couldn't stop grinning.

"You know, I think red suits you."

It looked incredibly sexy on her.

She huffed and took a step back, wiping at the smear with the back of her hand, but it only spread more. I stepped in closer, my fingers instinctively reaching up to gently swipe the paint from her cheek. Her breathing hitched as I touched her, and for a second, neither of us moved. My thumb brushed across her bottom lip. Slow and deliberate, and I could feel the heat radiating between us.

Her eyes flickered up to meet mine, and for a split moment, everything else disappeared; time itself stopped just for us. The studio, the paintings, the mess... none of it mattered. It was her and me.

Her chest rose and fell a little faster, her lips parting as she looked up at me and down at my lips. The space between us seemed to vanish. The hatred, the anger, the fighting... it was fuel for this exact moment.

I leaned in, close enough to feel the warmth radiating from her skin, close enough to hear every faint breath she took. My heart was racing, and I could tell hers was too.

Just as my lips hovered inches from hers, she suddenly stepped back, breaking the moment.

"It's... it's getting late," she said, her voice a little shaky as she brushed her hands down her paint-smeared dress. "I should, uh, go."

I blinked, the intensity of the moment shattering, replaced by the awkwardness of the situation. I forced a laugh, stepping back as well, trying to shake off the tension that still hung in the air.

"Yeah, right. Of course."

She turned quickly, grabbing her painting and slipped in under her arm, avoiding my gaze as she headed for the door.

"Good-good night." Was the last thing she said before I heard the door shut behind her.

Just like that, the moment was over. But I couldn't shake the feeling that this was far from the end. What the hell was I getting myself into? What I'm feeling for her is lust and nothing more. Sure, I might hate her guts and everything about her, but she's attractive. It wouldn't be human of me to ignore that.

It's fine Micheal, just don't fall for it again.

After Celeste left, the studio felt impossibly quiet. The smell of paint and wood lingered, her scent no longer overpowering the spaced. Without her presence, the place seemed larger, emptier. I ran my hand through my hair, trying to shake off the weight of that moment, but my thoughts kept drifting back to her... the way her breathing hitched when I touched her, how quickly she'd pulled away.

I glanced around the room, half-thinking I should leave too, but something kept me there. The easels, the canvases, the half-finished sculptures all seemed to hold pieces of her. There was an energy in the space, something raw and personal; it was the closest thing I could get to being inside her mind.

As I wandered further into the studio, something caught my eye. A leather-bound notebook, half-hidden beneath a stack of sketch papers on a cluttered desk. It didn't look like it belonged there, tucked away as if it was lost and forgotten. My curiosity got the better of me, and I flipped it open.

The pages were filled with Celeste's sketches-rough drafts of paintings, notes on color palettes, and tiny scrawled reminders. But as I turned further, something more interesting appeared: detailed notes about an upcoming art gallery; Laurosse. Dates, contacts, ID information, passcodes… everything was meticulously listed.

This is it.

I knew I should stop reading, but I couldn't. It was everything Dylan had tasked me with finding, all laid out in front of me, hidden away in Celeste's notebook, and she had no idea I was looking for it. To be honest, I didn't expect to find it.

She must have forgotten it on her graduation day. How could she be so careless with this? A pang of ugly guilt shot through me, but I pushed it down. This was what I came for. This was my job. It's not my fault that she forgot the notebook and left it behind. Celeste… she was just an unexpected complication. I couldn't afford to let myself get distracted.

Without another thought, I took my phone out and captured pictures of the pages. I then snapped the notebook shut, slipping it back where I found it, taking a mental note of the details. I wouldn't take it with me, it would be too risky. But I had most of what I needed now.

The weight of what I had to do pressed heavily on my chest

as I glanced around the studio one last time. The temptation to linger, to try to make sense of the strange pull I felt toward Celeste, was strong. But I couldn't let her get in the way of the mission; she wasn't my problem to deal with.

After all, I might not need her anymore after this.

CHAPTER 17
MICHEAL

My father's name flashed on the screen, and a familiar sense of dread washed over me. I had been dreading his call recently and have been using the excuse that I was busy. But I know I could no longer keep using this same excuse. So, I took a deep breath and accepted my fate, swiping right to answer with the brightest tone I could muster.

"*Abeoji,*" *Father,* I said.

"Micheal! It's time for you to fly to Korea," he declared in our native language, his voice booming with authority.

I winced and rolled my eyes.

"Yeah, about that. I've got a lot going on right now. Can't I push it back another month?"

"Absolutely not," he replied, the steeliness in his tone leaving no room for negotiation. "You haven't visited in two years. I expect you to be here next week." Next week would be the beginning of May; I couldn't leave right in the middle of everything.

"Next week?" I protested, feeling the pressure rise in my chest. "I can't just drop everything, I have work commitments that—"

"Your work can wait," he interrupted, his voice firm. "Family comes first. You know this. You will come to Korea and see me. This is important."

I sighed, frustration bubbling beneath the surface. "I understand that, but–"

"No excuses," he snapped. "I'll have someone pick you up from the airport. You need to learn to prioritize your family over your work. Learn to work the family business and you won't have this problem."

I clenched my jaw, knowing it was pointless to argue.

"Fine. I'll make the arrangements," I conceded, though I felt a knot tightening in my stomach.

"Good. I expect you to behave like a proper son," he added, his tone softening slightly but still commanding. "We have much to discuss, and it's time you learn about the responsibilities that come with being a Zhang."

"Yeah, sure. I have to go," I said, feeling a mix of resentment and obligation. As I hung up, I stared at my phone, the weight of the conversation sinking in. I had to inform Dylan about this last-minute trip, and I knew he wouldn't be pleased.

I stood outside Dylan's office, feeling the weight of what I was about to face. I'd been pouring myself into gathering intel about the gallery and that elusive painting, but now it was time to report back. Taking a deep breath, I pushed the door open and stepped inside.

"Micheal! Come in," Dylan said, his eyes lighting up as he gestured for me to take a seat. His energy seemed more welcoming today; it's obvious that he approved of the progress I was making. "I've been reviewing the details you provided. Excellent work. We're almost ready to move."

"Thanks," I replied, trying to mask the unease twisting in my stomach. "But I need to let you know... I have to visit my dad in Korea soon. I can't keep putting it off; he expects me every two years." I explained the situation to him.

Dylan's brow furrowed, and I could see the gears turning in his head.

"I understand family obligations, but we're on the brink of something big here. You can't just leave in the middle of this mission. Time's crunching."

"I know," I said, running a hand through my hair. "But it's my dad. He's stubborn... and very invasive. He'd have his team look into me if I don't comply, and I can't let him find out about any of this. I can't afford to skip out on him now."

Dylan leaned back, an irritated expression on his face.

"Look, I think you can go. You've gathered a ton of information about the gallery. All you need to do now is get specifics on that painting."

"Okay, but–"

"While you're there, I have a suggestion. Take the woman... What was her name?"

"Celeste," I said, the name catching on my tongue.

"Yes, Celeste. Take her with you."

"Why would I do that?"

Dylan's expression turned shrewd. "Think about it. A trip to Seoul is exciting. It'll keep her engaged, and you still need her for more information."

I crossed my arms, feeling the tension rise.

"Are you serious? Taking her sounds like trouble, and correct me if I'm wrong, but you just said the information I brought you was perfect."

"I did, yes. But that doesn't mean your work is done here. Do you truly believe it's trouble? Or an opportunity?" Dylan countered, leaning forward, his intensity ramping up. "You need her to feel invested, and nothing brings that out like a little adventure."

The thought of taking Celeste on the trip to meet my family made my stomach churn. I hated her attitude, the way she challenged me at every turn. Yet, I couldn't shake the memory of those unexpected moments…the heat that surged between us whenever we were close. I hated that most; all logic flies out the window when I'm alone with her for too long.

"Look," Dylan said, sensing my hesitation. "You can either make this mission a success or let it fall apart. It's your choice. Oh, and Celeste, she's your only ticket out. If she doesn't go, you can't."

I clenched my jaw, the truth settling in. I couldn't back out now. We were so close to securing everything, and I needed to see this through. I'll be damned if I let all the time I spent with her go to waste. I'm claiming my cash at the end of this and that's that.

"Fine. I'll ask her to come."

Dylan grinned, clearly pleased with himself.

"Great! Just remember, you need to play your part well. If things go sideways, you're out."

"Yeah, I get it," I muttered, already bracing myself for the next conversation ahead.

As I left Dylan's office, the reality of what I had to do hit me like a freight train. I had to convince Celeste to join me on this trip, and the prospect of facing whatever sparks might ignite between us was more daunting than the mission itself.

Hate had nothing to do with the physical chemistry we had; there was no denying that.

"You're what?!" Adam asked, shocked by the words coming out of my mouth. "What do you mean, you're leaving for Seoul and taking Celeste with you?"

"Exactly that," I answered. I decided to have a drink with

Adam and Aaron Pearson. They were like the brothers I never had, and I could rely on them when I needed to talk. "I think it could be great." I added, lying through my teeth, shooting back a glass of tequila, followed by sucking on a wedge of lime.

"You do? How long have you known this chick? Last time I saw you both together, I could've sworn you'd both kill each other over a game of pool." Aaron spoke up.

"Micheal, I don't know what you're trying to pull with Celeste, but allow me to remind you that she's connected to Katherine. You hurt her, and it hurts Katherine, therefore I'll need to hurt you," Adam threatened before taking another sip of his regular drink; a bourbon with ice. I knew it bothered him deep down, knowing I was going out with one of Katherine's friends.

"It's not like that," I replied, shaking my head. "We're just going to Seoul for a bit of fun. It'll be good to get away, you know?" Actually, the thought was killing me; I was dying to escape my fate.

"Fun?" Adam raised an eyebrow, clearly not buying my act. "You think this is just some vacation? What's really going on? If you don't tell me now, I'll find out, eventually."

I shrugged, playing it off.

"Just a chance to bond. You know how it is. Maybe I can show her the sights, and who knows? It might be good for both of us."

Aaron leaned forward, skepticism painted across his face.

"Yeah, right. You're not fooling us, Micheal. You two are known to butt heads, and you are not the kind of guy who takes girls on spontaneous trips. What's changed?"

"Nothing's changed," I insisted, a little too quickly. "I'm just being smart about this. A trip can bring people closer together, and I think it could work in our favor. Plus, I really…" I choked on half a cough before finishing the sentence. "I, uh, really like her."

"Wow, what passion," Aaron commented with a lazy expression.

Adam narrowed his eyes, clearly still not convinced.

"Just remember, if this goes south, you're going to have a lot of people on your back—including me. You've always got to tread carefully when it comes to Katherine's friends."

"Noted," I said, rolling my eyes. "I can handle it. It's not like we're getting *super* serious or anything. It's something chill."

"This sounds like a recipe for disaster," Aaron scoffed, shaking his head.

"I promise it's nothing like that. Just a little adventure. No big deal."

"Alright, if you say so," Adam said, still looking skeptical. "But be careful. I don't want to see you getting into something you can't handle."

"You say it like she's a starved wild animal that'll kill me," I laughed, only to find their faces serious, not an ounce of humor written anywhere in their expressions.

"Sure…" Aaron replied.

I clicked my glass against theirs, suppressing the knot tightening in my stomach.

"To adventures, then. What could go wrong?"

As I drowned the drink, I felt a flicker of doubt. I knew I was lying to them, but I had to keep my focus on the mission. The last thing I wanted was for this trip to spiral into complications I wasn't ready to face, especially with Celeste.

"So, how should I convince her?" I asked them. They both stared at me with wide eyes.

"Dude, are you fucking with us? You've been telling us for the last fifteen minutes of your trip with Celeste and she knows nothing of it?" Aaron asked hysterically.

"Manifesting it, isn't that what you always say, Adam?" I winked, knowing I sounded crazy right now. Adam shook his head, proving my thoughts right.

"Right... Suggestions?" I asked one last time. They both sighed, giving each other the look before giving me their suggestions.

"Just tell her it's a free vacation," Aaron slurred, leaning back in his chair. "No girl says no to a free trip. At least when it comes to me."

Ah, yes. Mr. handsome bachelor of New York City, of course it does.

Adam shot him a look.

"That's the dumbest thing you've ever said, and you've said a lot of dumb shit."

"Really? Like you haven't. Shall I list them?" He pulled out his phone, going through his notes.

Brothers.

I leaned forward, rubbing my hands over my face.

"This is gonna blow up in my face. I already know it," I said out loud, without much thought.

"You're just overthinking it," Aaron said, a little too confidently for someone who'd barely offered any decent advice. "Get her to come along, make it seem like something beneficial, and maybe—if you're lucky—she won't hate your guts by the end of it."

I scoffed. "Yeah, because nothing says 'trust me' like dragging her halfway across the world for our next date."

"You'll figure it out," Adam said, standing up and throwing some cash on the table for drinks.

"But right now, I have to head back to my woman. She's at home waiting for me and I'm here still talking to you idiots. Enough drinking; you're not going to come up with a reason on how to convince anyone of anything like this."

I glanced at my watch. It was late, and the buzz of alcohol was slowly kicking in, leaving me with nothing but a blurry mind.

"Yeah, I should head out."

Aaron waved a hand lazily, already sinking deeper into his chair.

"Good luck. Don't get killed by her during it."

I gave a half-hearted laugh and stood up, the room spinning slightly as I steadied myself.

"Thanks, I'll keep that in mind."

As I walked out of the bar into the cool night air, the reality of what I was about to do hit me once again. Convincing Celeste wasn't going to be easy, especially when I had to lie about the reason. I needed to think about this thoroughly. What could convince her? What would be beneficial to her?

I took a deep breath, the city lights blurring slightly in my vision. Tomorrow, I'll figure it out. Somehow. For now, I just needed to survive this mess I'd created.

CHAPTER 18
CELESTE

Waking up later than usual, I hurried down to the convenience store for my coffee. The moment between Micheal and me at the studio replayed in my mind over and over, making it impossible to escape. As a result, I'd lost most of my beauty sleep, tossing and turning in bed. Honestly, it was a miracle I got out of bed this morning. I made a quick stop at my favorite convenience store 'The Haj Spot,' next to my building to grab my coffee. Quick, hot, and tasty. I found it to be tastier and cheaper than Starbucks coffee.

As I opened the door, the bell rang, announcing my presence as usual. The familiar aroma of fresh coffee enveloped me as I stepped inside. The Haj Spot should sell coffee at all hours of the day, not only mornings. I tried to convince Bo of it, but he's totally against it for some reason.

I headed straight to the counter, where Bo greeted me with a warm smile.

"Well, will you look at that? The famous artist. I was convinced you forgot about me," he said as he turned his cap backwards. I haven't had the time to stop by since I began my internship.

"Forget about you, Bo? When you practically sell magic here? No way," I answered, playing along.

"So I take it you want the usual?" he asked, already reaching for the cup.

I nodded, suddenly lost in thought about the moment with Micheal. I could still feel the weight of his gaze, the way it lingered just a heartbeat too long. It was disarming, to say the least.

"Here you go," Bo said, placing the cup in front of me. "You look a bit out of it today. Everything okay?"

I forced a smile, taking the cup into my hands, the warmth a welcome distraction.

"Didn't sleep much. You know how it is."

"Ah, the artist's life, huh?" he said with a knowing nod. "You'll be alright, there are always your favorite comfort snacks here."

"You sold me," I replied, turning to leave out the door. Right as I'm about to make my exit, the bell jingled, slicing through the air like a cue in a dramatic play. I froze, my heart racing anew. Micheal, of all people, stepped through the threshold, and time seemed to slow.

As Micheal stepped inside The Haj Spot, my heart raced, and I ran behind a display of snacks and ducked. I could see him through the shelves, his tall frame cutting through the cozy atmosphere of the store. The last thing I wanted was for him to spot me after the whirlwind of emotions from our last encounter.

I couldn't believe he came to this place, and I couldn't believe I had caught him here.

"Hey Bo!" he called, and I held my breath, pressing myself against a stack of chips.

This is ridiculous; now I'm hiding from him, in a place I qualify as MINE!

"Morning, Micheal! The usual?" Bo replied, his voice cheerful.

I watched as Micheal moved to the counter, his attention fixed on Bo, completely oblivious to my presence. He smiled as Bo prepared his coffee, and I felt a mix of admiration and panic. He was so effortlessly charming, and the thought of facing him made my stomach twist.

I carefully peeked around the edge of the snack display. He was now checking out the pastries. I had to resist the urge to reach out and grab one of my favorites, but I couldn't risk him seeing me. Instead, I focused on a bag of pretzels trying to act casual.

"Got any muffins today?" he asked, glancing over the selection.

"Sure do! Blueberry or chocolate chip?" Bo responded.

"Blueberry please," he said, and I watched as he leaned casually against the counter, chatting with Bo like they were old friends. It felt oddly intimate, seeing him so at ease. I circled around the aisle, carefully avoiding his line of sight. My heart sank when I realized I'd have to get past him to leave. I just needed to wait until he paid and headed out.

As I watched him pull out his wallet, I silently willed him to hurry up. As if he heard me, he slowly turned his head toward the display I hid behind, and he quietly walked towards me.

Shit, if he finds me hiding from him, I'll die of embarrassment. It'll definitely give the wrong message, like if he intimidated me or scared me. Which is not even remotely true. I tightly shut my eyes as I heard the crumpling sound of a bag of chips.

I could hear him slowly circling around the display of snacks, and he could easily find me if he didn't leave now. In a moment of panic, I spilled hot coffee over my black blouse. I hissed and instantly covered my mouth with my hand.

His footsteps stopped, and I knew that he heard me. I prayed to the heavens for something to save me. I ducked further behind the snacks, hoping he wouldn't glance my way.

"You're all set Micheal," Bo called out. He paused for a

second before walking back to the register. He collected his items and left.

"I'll see you tomorrow, Bo!" he called out as he stepped outside.

I let out a sigh of relief, peeking out to ensure he was gone.

Thank you, universe, for not being a complete asshole to me today.

I stood up straight and stepped out from behind the snacks.

"Celeste!" Bo exclaimed as he saw me stand up. "Have you been hiding there the whole time?" he asked with a worried expression on his face.

"Me? Hiding? No, no. You're confused; I was actually looking through these bags of chips, thinking that it'd be a good idea to take some to work. But I just changed my mind. I have to head out now if I want to get to work on time. Alright, take care Bo!" I spoke quickly, wanting to escape before he saw right through my rushed words.

"You spilled your coffee; here, take some napkins and let me make you another," he suggested as he noticed my wet blouse.

"No, really, it's fine. I need to cut out the coffee anyway, so yeah, I'll just be on my way. Bye!" I answered as I took the napkins and ran out the door. Once I made it outside, I let out another sigh of relief.

Only then did I realize that my blouse was far from saving. I couldn't possibly show up to work in a blouse drenched in coffee. But if I didn't show, I would be late.

Damn it!

It was either one or the other and showing up as a mess instead of not showing up at all was better.

It'll be fine; I don't think anyone would be able to notice. The wind will dry up my shirt and it won't look so wet and noticeable. It is a *black* blouse, after all.

Yeah, I can work with that. Focus, Celeste.

After taking a steady breath, I marched toward the gallery,

praying the coffee stains wouldn't be as obvious under the dim lights.

By the time I got to work, my shirt had mostly dried, but a faint coffee smell lingered. I forced myself to ignore it, sliding behind a display and pretending nothing was amiss. Things were going smoothly, or so I thought, until I caught a sight of a familiar figure strolling into the gallery.

Micheal. I froze, a wave of irritation bubbling up at the sight of him for the second time today.

So the universe did have it out for me today, huh? Okay, fine. Let's see what you got, universe!

I took another deep breath, and smiled, welcoming a guest who I very much want gone. He walked in, completely oblivious to the quiet, respectful atmosphere of the gallery, moving toward me with his usual infuriating swagger. I silently begged him to go away, but of course, Micheal wasn't one to take hints.

"Pack your bags, honey," he said, his voice carrying a little too well in the echoing space.

Turning slowly, I tried to keep my composure.

"I'm sorry, do you not see the sign that says 'Silence' or can you just not read?" I pointed to the sign I had put up at the beginning of my shift.

He ignored me, his smirk widening.

"We're going to Korea tomorrow. Make sure you're ready."

"Korea?" I repeated, incredulous. "Why on earth would I go to Korea with you?"

"Oh, come on, honey. Don't be like this, after I worked so hard to surprise you?" he asked in a sappy tone.

"Stop being fucking ridiculous!" I hissed at him. His face softened into a small smile. "I ask again, why would I?"

"Oh, I don't know, maybe because it's worth five dates," he

replied with a smug grin. "So once we're back, you can be done with me. If you choose…"

The words rang a bell in my head. Worth five dates? Done with him when I returned? I'd be lying if I said it wasn't a tempting offer, but even I knew it sounded somewhat suspicious.

I let out a sharp laugh.

"You think you can cram five dates into one trip? That's cheating, even for you."

"Already spoke to your boss about it. She practically threw a parade at the idea of you getting out of town with me," he said, sounding way too pleased with himself. He kept speaking, ignoring my response. "I don't think I've ever seen a boss so excited to release an employee for vacation. Guess she thought you needed a break," he whispered, leaning closer to me.

My mouth dropped open.

"You spoke to Meredith? You planned this *in advance*?" He's an actual psycho.

He shrugged, clearly delighted by my reaction.

"No. Absolutely not! This is messed up even for you? What gives you the right to speak to my boss and plan things in my life —which, may I add—is very busy and important right now!" I whispered-shouted. I could feel my ears and face turning red; I was about to explode in front of this man.

"Come on Luci, it's only for two weeks. Who says no to a free trip?" He asked with a smile, still not giving up.

"Me." I replied dryly, with a straight face.

"By the end of this trip, you'll be charmed. Think of it as an immersive experience." He added, thinking it would help everything sound more appealing.

I rolled my eyes.

"Immersive experience? You're out of your mind if you think I'm going to tell you anything, and I'm definitely not going anywhere with you."

"Oh, yes you are," he replied with another wink, his smirk growing as he started to head toward the door. "You don't have an excuse to stay behind, as I fixed and arranged all of it for you. There's no getting out of this one, Luci."

I clenched my jaw, watching him leave, counting to ten in my head so I wouldn't go bat shit crazy on this man.

∼

"He wants to take you on a free trip to Korea and you don't want to go. Did I get that right?" Katherine asked as she poured wine into my cup. I instantly called the girls to come to my apartment for an emergency meeting, with Valery virtually present.

"Yes, you heard right," I answered, sipping the much needed alcohol for today.

"Why don't you go? It's a free trip, after all. You're not wasting a dime," Valery suggested. I rolled my eyes, tired of nobody understanding where I'm coming from. Maybe because they don't hate Micheal Zhang like I do; maybe then they would understand.

"Let me further explain it so you can understand it, yes? A, I don't like him and B, I don't like him." I said.

"Is there an option C?" Elaina interjected, putting her cup down on the coffee table.

"I'm afraid it contains the same response as A and B," I responded.

"That certainly sounds nice," Valery added with a slight chuckle. "Perhaps going on this trip can not only give you the break that you need, but also give you an out to all of this once you return," she explained. I had told the girls that going on this trip would be worth five dates, which is the time I had left with Micheal. The thought of not having to stress about this felt so freeing.

Katherine leaned in, her eyes gleaming with mischief.

"Look, if you go, think of all the incredible food, the shopping, the new experiences... and if you're really clever, you can make Micheal pay for everything. You owe it to yourself to at least *enjoy* it."

Elaina grinned, reaching for her cup.

"And think of all the Insta stories! You'd have so much content for weeks. Plus, by the end of the trip, maybe you'll find a way to finally shut down his ridiculous advances." I chuckled at Elena's 'influencers' way of seeing the situation.

Valery nodded.

"Exactly. Use this as an opportunity to set some boundaries and wrap things up on your terms. You might actually come back feeling liberated."

I paused, considering it. They were all right, of course. A week away from everything, with the power to control the narrative? It was exactly what I needed.

"Alright fine," I sighed, unable to hide my smirk. "I'll definitely keep an open mind about it."

Katherine squealed, clinking her glass against mine.

"That's the spirit! Milk this for all it's worth. Make it the ultimate 'goodbye, Micheal' trip."

Elaina laughed.

"Just thinking of it as a strategic retreat, not a date. Go there, have fun, and maybe find a cute local guy to flirt with while Micheal watches."

"Oh, that's genius." Valery chimed in, eyes sparkling on the screen. "He'll be so focused on trying to win you over, he'll be too distracted to realize you're miles ahead of him."

I bit my lip, finally letting myself envision it—the chance to enjoy a city I'd always wanted to visit, to soak in the culture, all while keeping Micheal in his place. It wasn't exactly the peaceful vacation I'd imagined, but the idea of having control, of being the one to set the tone, was oddly thrilling.

"Okay, okay," I relented, a slow smile breaking out. "I'll go. But I'm doing this my way."

The girls cheered, Katherine raising her glass.

"To taking back your power and getting a killer vacation out of it."

We toasted, laughter filling my apartment, and I felt a flicker of excitement bubbling up. Maybe this wasn't such a bad idea after all. I went ahead and sent a text to Micheal, confirming.

> Celeste: I'm in.

> Micheal: I knew you would be, sugar ;) Airport tomorrow at nine.

> Celeste: Don't call me sugar.

> Micheal: Back to honey?

> Celeste: Don't make me take it back.

> Micheal: Okay, Luci, I can take a hint.

Okay, I'm doing this. No turning back now.

CHAPTER 19
MICHEAL

By some miracle, I got Celeste to agree to join me on the trip. I mean, I was practically shitting bricks while speaking to her at the gallery; I thought it would all blow up in my face.

Now, I'm standing at the front of the airport, waiting for her to arrive. I've been here long enough to feel the sharp bite of impatience, checking my watch every few minutes and glancing at the arrivals. I told Celeste she could ride with me after all; it's been more convenient for the both of us to show up to our flights at the same time. But she shot that offer down faster than I could finish saying it.

Honestly, her stubbornness is on another level. The moment I suggest something, she finds a reason to do the opposite, even if it would make her life easier. It's like she's wired to resist anything that involves being near me longer than necessary. Maybe I've given her a few reasons to keep her guard up, but this back-and-forth is exhausting. I'm just trying to finish this job and claim my fifty-four million.

I sighed and leaned against a pole, deciding I'll let "future me" worry about how to deal with her constant pushback. Right now, all I want is to get over this part of traveling. Flying all the way across the world seemed to exhaust me more than excite me.

Finally, after about five more minutes, a bright yellow taxi pulls up in front of me. The back door swung open, and out stepped Celeste, dressed in that effortlessly casual sweat wear, with sunglasses perched on her head and an unmistakable air of defiance. She glanced around, as if expecting to see anyone else but me standing there.

"Could've just saved yourself the fare," I called out, trying to keep my tone light. "But I guess independence comes at a price."

She gave me a look that could curdle milk, reaching into her bag to pay the driver without a word in my direction. Her refusal to even acknowledge my presence amused me more than it probably should.

When she finally faced me, she took a deep breath.

"Thanks for the offer," she said, her voice dripping with sarcasm, "But I like a bit of personal space."

"Right," I replied, stifling a smirk. "That explains the cramped cab instead of the spacious, air-conditioned car I rode in."

She ignored me, busying herself with her suitcase handle. I watched her struggle for a second before taking it from her hand. She protests, of course, but I just rolled my eyes.

"Relax, Celeste. I'm not holding your luggage hostage; I'm just trying to get to our gate before our flight leaves us both here."

She released her hold with a huff and followed me into the airport, muttering under her breath the entire way.

"We need to check in and get our tickets," I said as I walked with a suitcase in each hand. I looked back to Celeste, who seemed displeased by the entire situation. "You don't have to look like I'm dragging you to a fate worse than death," I told her as we got to our gate.

"Try not to embarrass me in front of the entire country, and maybe we'll see," she replied, shooting me a pointed look.

I chuckled, shaking my head as I set our luggage to the side.

"Me? I could never do that to you." She groaned in misery, following behind me.

Celeste's shoulders stiffened as we approached the check-in counters.

"You're going to have to get your own ticket, Luci," I said, noticing she still had her purse slung over her shoulder. I motioned for her to join me at the counter.

She frowned, raising an eyebrow as if I had suggested we walk to South Korea.

"You can't just handle everything for me, Micheal. I'm not your assistant."

"Just get your passport and ID ready, and we can breeze through this. You have it, right?" I raised an eyebrow, half-expecting her to say she'd forgotten it.

"I'm not that clueless," she snapped back, pulling out her wallet and holding up her passport. She let out a sigh, walking toward her own check-in counter. I watched her fumble with her bag a little, pulling out her ticket from a tiny pocket in her purse.

While she was handling her paperwork, I moved our bags onto the conveyor belt. The attendant at the counter scanned both our tickets and IDs, ensuring no issues with baggage. Her eyes flicked toward me for a moment noticing my name, Zhang, but then she nodded and continued. I didn't miss the skeptical glance Celeste threw my way, but she was distracted with her own ticketing ordeal to make much of a comment.

She went through security next, like everyone else, putting her belongings in a bin: her purse, phone, and a few small items she'd forgotten to pack away properly. She had headphones hanging loosely from her neck; the wires tangled like she hadn't used them in a while. I didn't ask her about it; it wasn't any of my business. The security process was quick, though there were a few moments where the line stretched a little long as people fumbled with their pockets.

Once we cleared security and customs, I led Celeste to our gate. She leaned against the wall, fiddling with the strap of her purse before pulling the headphones from around her neck, finally plugging them in to drown out the noise.

Two seconds later, they announced our flight on the speakers. Passengers began to create a line with their tickets in their hands for boarding.

"Alright Luci, that's us," I said as I took her by the hand and headed toward our door. "Before we get on, I want to warn you about something."

"Oh no," she said, as her expression turned pale. "What now?" I handed my tickets to the flight attendant to scan.

"Enjoy your flight, Mr. Zhang," the lady said before allowing us to pass through and board the flight.

"Back to what I was saying. Our seats, they're in first class," I said; her eyes widened slightly as she took in my words. "The reason I fly first class every time I go back home is because I'm a Zhang—"

"Wait, pause. First class?" she asked again, as if it was the only thing she could grasp.

"Yes, because I'm a Zhang. Before you cut me off, I was going to explain that the name Zhang is like... royalty, in a sense? I don't know how to explain it right but, I thought it'd be smart to tell you now." I wasn't going to tell her this yet, but I knew she'd grow suspicious and ask questions and I wanted to avoid that the entire flight.

"You're hilarious; now can we get to our seats?" she asked, not believing anything I'm telling her.

"Right this way, Mr. Zhang," the next flight attendant said, and we followed her through the first-class cabin, with Celeste moving like she was in some kind of alternate reality. Her eyes were glued to every little detail; the oversized seats, the soft blankets, and the complimentary glasses of champagne being passed around.

Finally, we reached our seats, and she just stood there, staring at the plush leather as if it might bite.

"Are you kidding me?" she muttered under her breath, looking over at me in disbelief. "We're really flying in... first class?"

I smirked, slipping into my seat.

"Yes, first class, like I said."

She scoffed, still hovering beside her seat like it might explode.

"You think you're some kind of king now?"

"Not a king. But, royalty, yes," I said, grinning as I stretched out and took the drink the flight attendant handed me. "It's a thing back home, okay? Try not to be weird about it."

She finally dropped into her seat, crossing her arms and huffing.

"You're ridiculous. This whole thing is ridiculous. Who needs this much space on a plane?"

"People with class, obviously," I said, shooting her a sidelong glance as I took a sip of my drink. "Also, people who don't enjoy acting like the economy's sardines. Oh, and let's not forget that this flight is fifteen hours long."

"Of course you're one to say that." She rolled her eyes. She put on her noise-canceling headphones, flipped through her in-flight magazine, and settled in with an expression that clearly said: *I don't know him, don't talk to me, and don't even think of looking in my direction.*

From the moment we boarded, I knew Celeste was going to make this trip as difficult as possible. She barely looked in my direction, marched ahead to her seat in first class, and practically created a fortress of solitude around herself.

So, naturally, I leaned in to mess with her.

"Excuse me," I whispered to the flight attendant with a sympathetic smile, nodding toward Celeste. She glanced at me from the corner of her eye and popped out an ear to listen. "My friend here has a bit of a, uh, how do I put this nicely? Stomach issue. Yes, and it's an extremely sensitive topic for her, so if she's darting to the bathroom a lot, just know it's... well, a condition."

"Oh, I see. Would she like a tea? To help relax her upset stomach?" she asked, looking toward Celeste.

Celeste shook her head with a soft smile. As the flight attendant moved on to the next passenger, she shot me a glare that could melt plane windows.

She yanked off her headphones and leaned toward me, her voice barely above a whisper but dripping with venom.

"What is *wrong* with you?"

"Oh, I'm just trying to be considerate," I said with a grin, watching as she slumped down in her seat, her face flushed as she noticed a few passengers glancing her way.

She avoided eye contact with everyone, fuming quietly and pressing her lips together in that annoyed way she does when she's two seconds away from losing it; and just to keep things interesting, every time she glanced in the direction of the bathroom, I'd raise my eyebrows and gesture helpfully toward the back of the plane.

"I hate you," she muttered under her breath, pulling her blanket up over her face to hide from the world.

I hid a smirk, knowing I had successfully rattled her, and leaned back in my seat to enjoy the rest of the flight. As I shut my eyes, I felt an aggravating pain in my right arm. I opened my eyes to find Celeste's magazine rolled up in her hand.

Did she just hit me? No, she wouldn't be stupid enough to do that.

"Sorry, I thought there was a nasty bug on you; for all I

know, it could have been poisonous. Wouldn't want any accidents on this flight," she said sweetly, but I could taste the venom behind her fake tone.

"Oh, it's no problem; thank you, really," I said through gritted teeth. "I'm just glad I could make the whole bathroom situation on a fifteen hour flight easy for you." I smiled, knowing she would hold it in.

"You, my friend, have a death wish," she said, her knuckles whitening with how tight of a grip she had on the magazine.

Poor magazine.

"One, perhaps I do have a death wish, but definitely later in life. Two, your friend? I thought you hated me. That was certainly quick, Luci." I grinned as she scoffed and looked outside the window.

Yup, best flight ever.

As soon as we landed in Tokyo for our layover and made it to the connecting terminal, Celeste was off the plane like it was on fire, sprinting toward the bathrooms before I could even catch up.

I have to say; I enjoyed the image more than I thought I would. She couldn't bother me on the flight because she was too busy trying to hold it in. I should've taken a picture.

When she finally reappeared, she gave me a death glare that I felt from ten feet away.

"You're lucky you're surrounded by people," she demanded, as she headed toward the gate for our second flight. "You're the worst travel companion in the history of travel companions."

"Oh, come on," I said, unable to hide my amusement. "It's a layover; you're fine. Besides, I promised I'd choose a different topic for this flight."

Celeste just narrowed her eyes, and I saw the wheels turning as she gave me a look that could only mean one thing: revenge. I shrugged it off, figuring whatever she had in mind couldn't top my performance on the first leg.

∼

I was wrong. I forgot the woman I was dealing with was crazy and it bit me right in the ass.

We boarded our second flight, and just as I settled in, Celeste rose to her feet, facing the aisle with a mischievous smile. She raised her voice loud enough for the entire cabin to hear.

"Excuse me, everyone," she announced with that innocent smile plastered on her face. "I just want to apologize in advance for my friend here, Micheal. You see, he has this... rare condition. He sometimes talks in his sleep. Very loudly. And the things he says can be... well, embarrassing." She shot me a mischievous glance, then continued, "Last time, he kept repeating, 'I'm scared of the dark,' over and over, so I just thought I'd warn you all. If you hear him mumbling about his 'special blankie', please don't worry."

A few passengers were already chuckling, whispering to each other, and I could feel heat rising up to my face as everyone's eyes darted to me.

I leaned over, hissing at Celeste in a low voice.

"What the hell was that?"

"Just doing my civic duty," she said sweetly, settling back into her seat as if she just tried to get me back with my same joke of humiliating me in front of the entire plane. Except I didn't stand up and announce it like the biggest news on the planet.

"Unbelievable," I muttered, as a flight attendant passed by, giving me a sympathetic look that only made me feel worse.

"Oh, and I almost forgot!" she announced again just as I thought it was over and enough for her. "Micheal also suffers from a major digestive issue. He tries to manage it, but sometimes things just... slip out. So if you catch a strange odor, it's not the baby, it's all him," she said, pointing at the little infant in the arms of a mother a few lanes down.

Celeste stifled a laugh, giving me a wink.

"Sweet dreams, Micheal. Don't be afraid of the dark now and don't worry, everyone understands your situation."

I gritted my teeth, making a mental note to come up with a counterattack. The war wasn't over yet.

The passengers' eyes widened in surprise as a ripple of chuckles spread through the cabin. My face burned, and I shot her a look, but she just tossed me an innocent look and sauntered toward her seat as if she hadn't just humiliated me in front of everyone.

I took a deep breath, trying to keep my cool, but I could feel eyes on me from every direction. I couldn't possibly let her get away with it. No way in a million years was I going to let her have *two* revenge comebacks. No, no… she was in for a treat.

An eye for an eye, as they say.

I got up from my seat and walked all the way back to economy and stopped in front of a woman sitting next to a mother and her baby. I decided to pick someone out of economy and switch tickets with Celeste just to spite her, and I choose this woman right here.

"Excuse me, miss, would you switch seats with a friend of mine in first class? She wants economic experience." Her eyes lit up at the offer.

"Yes, of course," she said with a smile. Her blonde, frizzled hair bounced as she got up from her seat. It was obvious she was a foreigner visiting Korea; she wasn't as good looking at Celeste, but she gave me the impression that she would shut up and take the offer.

"I figured, right this way,.." I said, bringing her back up with me, and we both stood in front of Celeste.

As soon as the flight attendant came by, I seized my chance.

"Excuse me," I said, leaning over with a long-suffering sigh.

"There's been a bit of confusion here. The woman beside me seems to think she belongs in first class, but I think she just... wandered up here by mistake. Started speaking nonsense to the entire plane, which is not true."

The flight attendant looked back and forth between us, a slight frown on her face. Celeste's smile faltered, and I could see the realization dawning in her eyes.

"Oh, don't worry," I added, giving the attendant a sympathetic smile. "She won't make a fuss about it. She's very understanding."

Celeste's jaw dropped as they politely escorted her out of first class, directing her back to economy, next to the baby, who was now crying and wailing at full volume. I watched her shoulders slump as she glanced over at me one last time, fury and disbelief flickering in her eyes.

I smirked, settling comfortably into my seat as she disappeared down the aisle. Sure, I knew I'd pay for this later, but for now? The satisfaction of having the last word was worth every second.

All because of my brilliant plan, the rest of the flight passed in absolute peace and quiet on my end. I enjoyed my gourmet meal and caught a movie, while Celeste texted me furious messages from the back about the babies screaming and how she was plotting my downfall the second we landed.

As the plane began its descent, I shot her one last text.

> Micheal: See you at the gate. And don't forget to thank me for the accommodations ;)

> Celeste: Fuck you.

> Micheal: Luci, there's a child beside you. Keep those dirty thoughts to yourself. Also, I'll think about it; it's a very tempting offer.

I could practically feel her eyes roll through the screen. She'll be fine; this flight was about four hours. She'll survive.

Oh, but this was far from over. As we touched down in Seoul, I felt a strange flicker of excitement. The game was on, and Celeste was about to find out that I wasn't backing down anytime soon.

CHAPTER 20
MICHEAL

We arrived in Seoul at ten in the morning, Korean Standard Time. As we got off the plane, Celeste walked out with the darkest under-eye bags known to humanity. Yeah, maybe I was a bit rough with picking the seat right next to the crying baby. However, I still strongly believe that she learned her lesson —never try to get back at someone with their own joke.

We moved through the terminal, following the signs toward immigration. The line at customs was long, but moved steadily. Celeste, still half-asleep, shuffled forward like a zombie while I handled most of the talking. When it was her turn, she blinked at the officer, barely processing his questions until I nudged her.

"Reason for travel?" the officer asked.

"Work," she mumbled, rubbing her temple.

I shot her a look, stepping in.

"Business and leisure," I corrected. "Short stay."

The officer gave us both a look but stamped our passports with little hassle. We grabbed our checked luggage from baggage claim and made our way toward the exit, the weight of the trip finally hitting us.

"Have I mentioned that you're on my list?" Celeste muttered

as she walked past me, heading straight to the only coffee shop near our gate.

"Aww, I'm on your naughty list?" I teased, following behind her with our luggages in hand.

"My hit list," she answered with hatred in her voice.

"A hit list. Wow, impressive. Can I see the rest of the list? I have a feeling it's good." She stood in front of the register, ignoring me while waiting for someone to come and take her order.

"Actually, it's a short list, considering you're the only one on it." *Ouch.* I know I should feel somewhat offended, but I couldn't stop the grin growing on my face. The idea of Celeste having a list just for me ... should I feel special? I feel special, even if it's a death wish. "Aren't they supposed to have someone up front?" she asked as she realized no one was going to show.

"You see those big sized tablets to your right?" I leaned down, my lips inches away from Celeste's right ear. "That's where you order. Here, you'll see a lot of them, especially at coffee shops." I spoke to her like a toddler, slow and clear.

"I know what they are," she stated defensively. "But I'd rather have genuine human interaction," she said, heading toward the first tablet. As she pressed on the screen, the menu appeared in Korean. She stared at it like it was the hardest math equation she'd ever seen.

"Need help?" I asked in a cheeky tone, knowing she would have to ask for my help. I suddenly realized that she would need to depend on me during this trip more than ever. It's a different culture, different language, it's a whole other world. The best part? It was my world. I liked that feeling; it was my golden ticket to get her to like me.

"Nope, that's what translator apps are for," she responded, pulling out her phone.

"Yeah, about that..." She aggressively smacked the phone

screen and groaned. "You just landed, so you'll have to let your cell update to KST first. If you'd like, the human—up to date—translator can help you until your apps can. Last time I checked, it's more convenient to have a national Korean help you with this part," I told her, stepping back to give her the space she needed. I wasn't trying to end up like her poor phone, taking unnecessary hits.

"Ok then, do it!" she spat, irritated.

I smacked my lips together, slightly shaking my head.

"This human translator works with a special password. Maybe you heard of it? It starts with a 'P' and ends with a 'with a cherry on top.'" She looked at me like she was cutting out her new favorite board to throw darts at with the words 'die Micheal, die' on them.

"Micheal, God help me... I am quickly running out of patience. I had ZERO hours of sleep on that damn plane because of *you* and I'm about to die if I don't get caffeine in my system right now," she said with a startled expression.

"Well, I hate to be the one to tell you this... but it's gonna take longer than 'now' for your coffee to get to you. I'm afraid you're a lost cause at this point—"

"Micheal!" she yelled.

"I can feel the 'cherry on top' on the tip of your tongue," I urged the words to spill from her lips. She dramatically rolled her eyes, about to give in.

"Fine! Please with a cherry—that I hope you choke on—top!" she bursts out, struggling to contain her annoyance.

"Okay, alright, I'll help you. Don't gotta be so desperate about it," I answered, a smile pulling at the corners of my lips. I pressed the 'language' button on the top and switched it to English for her. I stepped back, allowing her to choose her order.

"Seriously?" she asked, in disbelief, how quick and simple she could have solved the problem herself. In my defense, it was quite easy, considering that they had the speech bubbles filled with different alphabets and symbols.

"Correct me if I'm wrong, but the first words that should have come out of your mouth are 'Thank you,'" I said, watching her tap around on the screen, customizing her drink. I waited for her to respond, but instantly got humbled by silence. "How generous," I added, looking around the airport.

Being here at this airport felt like a fever dream. I seriously didn't think I would be here; two years ago I thought I'd never have to be forced to come back. Past Micheal was so sure he had everything figured out, but here I am, back to square one.

Honestly, a part of me wanted to fully focus on Celeste as a distraction from how I really feel about being back home. I'm not sure what word I could use to describe my family other than just... complicated. I'm not looking forward to meeting my father face to face; the sound of his voice alone was enough to bring something I hated out of me.

Not long after, Celeste got her coffee and followed behind me. We got onto the moving escalators, heading toward arrivals. As we went down, I scanned the crowd, searching for the familiar face of our family driver; Jiho. Just as we reached the bottom, my eyes caught a glimpse of a tailored suit in the midst of travelers hurriedly making their way around.

Jiho stood confidently, a sign with the name 'Zhang' in crisp lettering held high. He spotted me as I approached him, a professional and warm smile played on his lips. Celeste grabbed a hold of my arm, lost in her own world as she looked around every corner as if it were a whole other universe.

"Mr. Zhang. Welcome home," he said, bowing.

Celeste seemed to get her attention back, as she eyed my driver suspiciously.

"You have a driver here? Did he just bow to you? You're seriously royalty?" she asked, genuinely confused.

"Hello Jiho, it's good to be back home." I bowed back out of respect. Celeste only stood motionless as she tried to figure it out herself. "This young lady beside me is Celeste Castillo; she will be staying with us," I told Jiho; he bowed and said hello.

"In Korean culture, bowing is a traditional gesture of respect, greeting, and gratitude. It's considered rude or poor manners if you don't," I explained in a low voice as Jiho happily took our luggage. Celeste dramatically bowed back with a tight smile; her bow looked like she was trying to pick up something off the floor with her arms extended out to her sides. Almost as if she was closing a ballet show.

"Not exactly like that..." I commented as Jiho chuckled and continued to walk us out of the airport.

Jiho led us out to where the car was parked, a BMW 7 series, its dark paint shimmering. He opened the door for Celeste and me.

Celeste eyed me with a wary glance, her incredulity showing.

"What the hell is this? I'm only finding out you're this crazy right now?!" she exclaimed as she climbed into the back seat.

"Why? Would you have pretended to like me more?" I asked her as I got into my seat next to hers. She rolled her eyes, looking out the window.

"Micheal Zhang, not even money can make me like you," she said, her tone laced with sarcasm.

I couldn't help but smirk, but inside I felt a twinge of challenge.

"Then what would it take?" I countered, leaning slightly closer. Her silence spoke volumes, and I could sense the tension building between us.

"If your big idea was to bring me here to impress me, you're wrong. I can't be bought out," she said, looking me straight in the eyes, not breaking eye contact.

"I never said you could be," I softly spoke, leaning in just a tad closer. The atmosphere turned heavy, similar to the moment we had in the studio. Her tough expression quickly faltered as she realized.

Jiho closed the door with a soft thud, the faint sound being enough to break up whatever the hell was happening here. Celeste coughed, turning her body toward her door and away from me.

Jiho slid into the front, his demeanor calm and assured. He took a quick glance to the back and sensed the weird energy between us, quickly turning on the radio for some music. He smoothly merged into the flow of the traffic, navigating the city with ease. Through the tinted windows, I could see the world pass by: signs in my native language, faces of actors and idols plastered on every advertising board. The streets are busy as always, with numerous cafes and boutiques, and mountains in the distance.

Seoul was like New York City in a weird sense, except it was much more beautiful. The vibes were simply calmer, not as rushed as New York. We were in mid May, which in Seoul, cherry blossoms fluttered in the breeze, adding splashes of pink to the scene, while traditional Hanok houses peeked out between sleek high-rises, creating a stunning juxtaposition.

I subtly glanced at Celeste, studying her profile as she gazed out the window. Her features were illuminated by the soft glow of the city lights, and I could see the mix of curiosity and skepticism etched on her face. She seemed lost in thought, her brow slightly furrowed.

Looking at her from this angle seemed different in a way; I'm not sure how to describe what I was feeling. Confused? Perhaps that was part of it, but there was something deeper stirring beneath the surface.

The car makes a harsh turn into the parking garage of our luxury building, cutting off the beautiful sights the city had to offer and bringing me right back to my personal hell. Jiho stopped in front of the elevator, slid out of the car and came around to open the door.

"I will bring up your bags, Mr. Zhang. Your father is waiting for you," he said, looking at me with empathy.

Can't wait.

Celeste and I climbed out of the car and headed toward the elevator, security standing on the side. He pressed the button for us and welcomed us in. As we stepped onto the elevator, my heart began to beat faster, the familiar weight of anticipation and anxiety settling in.

The atmosphere was thick with unspoken words. I stole a glance at Celeste, her expression unreadable as she leaned against the wall, arms crossed. The soft hum of the elevator felt almost too loud in the silence, amplifying the tension between us. Should I warn her of what's coming? I should, preparing her would be the best option.

"Listen to what I have to say very closely," I began. "My father isn't the easiest person to get to know; he's cold and distant, often more focused on business than family. He has high expectations, and he doesn't tolerate mistakes. It's important you understand that," I explained to her. She listened to me with an impressive amount of focus.

I expected her to share her blunt opinion, to challenge me with her usual bravado. But she's quiet for a few seconds, probably thinking about how absurd this entire situation was. She then breaks the silence with a sudden question that had me thinking about everything twice.

"Why did you bring me here Micheal?"

The weight of her question hung in the air, catching me off guard and I opened my mouth to respond, but no words came. I had thought I was being strategic, but now I was questioning my motives. I didn't think I'd have to bring her here to meet my father, bringing her into the world I so desperately wanted to get away from. This was supposed to be a simple job, quick and easy. Yet, here we were.

"I told you, I thought it would be fun. Worth five dates, remember?" I quickly recovered, not wanting to leave room for any more introspection.

"This isn't even remotely fun. I'm about to meet your father and you make it sound like he'll have my head on a plate for simply being myself. This is a horrible start," she said as we kept passing floors, two floors away from reaching the penthouse.

"Smile and don't speak; keep it short and sweet," I said as the doors dinged open, revealing the luxury penthouse I lived in for half of my childhood.

She took a deep breath, her eyes darting over the opulent decor as we stepped into the penthouse.

"Short and sweet? Got it. Just pretend I'm a polite robot?"

The entryway was vast, adorned with expensive art pieces and a view of the city skyline that was breathtaking.

"Wow," she whispered, momentarily distracted from her nerves.

"Don't be fooled, living here isn't the fairytale you're probably thinking," I said, walking through a hallway of haunted memories, remembering the days coming here after school, dreaming of simply escaping. My family pretended to be perfect, like there was nothing wrong; smiles plastered on their faces hiding the cracks beneath.

I began to search for my father throughout the penthouse, hoping to find him before he found us. It would make me feel prepared for whatever he had up his sleeves. Also, he had no clue I was bringing Celeste along. He wanted me to come with someone, but I know he expected me to be alone..

Celeste quietly walks behind me, looking around my childhood home like it was a palace. Constantly hearing her soft gasps and awe for the place that didn't deserve to be praised.

"Why are we tip-toeing around the place like we're robbers?" she whispered behind me.

"I'm trying to find my father. You don't have to follow me. Just go back to the entrance," I answered, dismissing her away with my hand. She gave me a curious glance, and I knew she couldn't back down so easily.

"And miss all the fun? No way. I want to see what all the fuss is about." She smiled, keeping her stance.

I scoffed, rolling my eyes in annoyance.

"Why are you the way you are?" I muttered through gritted teeth.

"Hey, you're the one who brought me," she said, moving along. She wasn't wrong, but what she doesn't know is it was my last choice. Actually, it wasn't even a choice in my books.

I ignored Celeste's obvious presence behind me and continued the search for my father. I noticed the rooms were swapped around since the last time I visited, but perhaps his study was still the same. The only room upstairs, overlooking the city. He wouldn't change his spot for the world. He had this weird fetish of feeling like he ruled the city, even the country.

With that in mind, I headed upstairs but was stopped by a familiar voice.

"Mr. Micheal," our housekeeper, Min-Soo, called after me. Her voice sounded hesitant, unsure if it was really me. Celeste and I came to a sudden halt, turning to the woman. Her eyes gleamed with adoration. "Micheal, it is you. Welcome home. I'll go ahead and announce your arrival to Mr. Zhang."

Fuck.

This was exactly what I was trying to avoid; now he had the time to prepare whatever he had coming. I loved Min-Soo; she was a mother figure to me when my birth mother had left. But there was nothing more appealing than showing her out of the penthouse.

"Right," I coughed, my head pointing back to the entrance.

"Come along now; we want to look like we're good guests," I said, feeling nauseated.

Not long after, my father decided to show himself. He walked down the stairs with ease and confidence, his polished shoes echoing against the marble floor. Dressed in an impeccably tailored suit, he looked every bit the powerful figure I remembered, yet there was an unsettling glint in his eyes.

"Adeul, bihaeng-gineun jal osnayo? *Son, I hope your flight was well,*" he said in Korean as he approached us. "You brought along a guest; I never thought I'd see the day," he said, switching to English to communicate with Celeste.

"This is Celeste Castillo; she's a close friend of mine," I introduced her, and he looked her up and down, already judging her.

"You are very beautiful; it's nice to meet you." He bowed, with a friendly smile on his face, but I saw right through it. "Just a friend?" he asked as he moved over to me.

"Yes," I answered, quickly becoming irritated by the conversation.

"Good," he responded. "Geunyeoneun hanguk-in-i anieyo. *She's not Korean.*" he added, looking away from her with a soft smile, knowing that Celeste couldn't understand.

"Geuge yojeom-ieyo. *That's the whole point.*"

My father wanted me to marry a nice Korean girl; it's what he deemed sensible. The day my mother left us, I don't think he wanted to see another American again, or any woman of a different ethnicity, for that matter. However, I do not agree with this. I don't have a type, but I'm open to everything. If that person makes me feel the things I never thought I'd feel, I couldn't care less about where she came from. Plus, deep down, I wanted to avoid women of my own ethnicity just to piss him off.

"Well," he added with a tight nod, knowing I'd pissed him off. "We must invite the family over for dinner, and welcome my son and his new friend back home," he suggested, looking back at Min-Soo. "Begin preparation for dinner tonight and tell Hyunwoo to invite everyone." Hyunwoo was his personal assistant. The poor bastard followed him around, hoping to get a piece of the Zhang fortune. Spoiler alert, that wasn't happening.

"Wonderful. We should have a nice night ahead of us. Min-Soo, why don't you show Celeste to the guest room while I catch up with my son." He smiled at Celeste, and she warily grabbed her luggage, following behind Min-Soo. She took a quick glance back at me with an apologetic expression. It was the first time I'd seen her look at me with an expression other than hatred. It made me hate being here even more.

Once she made it out of earshot, my father began his interrogation.

"How is the junky life in New York treating you?" He switched back to Korean. "I know you got let go at Hanson Wealth Management."

"Oh, I'm living the dream. It is the city of dreams, after all," I answered sarcastically. "As for Hanson Wealth, I'm building something for myself now–"

"Of course you are," he interrupted me, sighing heavily. "When are you going to wake up? You're in your late twenties and refuse to move back here and take over the business."

"How many times do I have to tell you I'm not taking over the family business? I want no part of being a Zhang; I'd much rather be Micheal in New York." I spat, becoming incredibly frustrated with the same topic. What is it going to take for him to get it through his thick skull? I left, moved to the states, completely cutting off all the money that came from having my last name.

"You're not going back Micheal; you're staying and that's final," he ordered, and I chuckled in his face.

"What am I? A teenager? I'm an adult; you can't keep me here. There's nothing holding me back." I stepped closer to him.

"I want no part of this and mark my words, this is the last time I'm visiting." It was horrible for the family image, but I didn't give a shit anymore.

"Why don't you settle into your room? Min-Soo cleaned it out, and it's ready for you. We have guests coming over tonight." He smiled, walking away and cutting the conversation like always. My jaw clenched, my hand tightening around my luggage.

Oh, how I love to be back home...

CHAPTER 21
CELESTE

The guest room exudes elegance, with soft, ambient lighting that creates a warm and inviting atmosphere. A big, plush, king-sized bed draped in high thread count linens inviting me to sink in and relax. Richly textured fabrics adorn the upholstered headboard and curtains, while a carefully curated selection of artwork adorns the walls.

A cozy sitting area features a pair of designer armchairs and a small, polished coffee table, perfect for enjoying morning coffee or reading a book. A large window offers stunning views, framed by elegant drapes that can be drawn for privacy or opened to let in natural light.

The guest room could easily be mistaken for the master bedroom, and it only made me curious about how Micheal's father's room might look like. This wasn't a room for guests, it was a room for royalty. Someone like me didn't stay in rooms like these. I mean, the room itself was about the same size as my apartment.

I ran across the room and landed on the bed, the shape of body molding into the mattress. I sighed and took in the enormous space as my own. A soft knock interrupted my thoughts, and I instantly got up and raced toward the door in soft steps. I swung the door open, revealing Min-Soo holding a dress.

"Hello, Miss Castillo," she greeted me with a heavy accent.

"Please, call me C." She looked at me, confused.

"Okay, Miss C," she tried again. I shook my head and chuckled.

"No, just 'C.' No need for the formal Miss," I told her, welcoming her into the room. "This bedroom is incredible; I've never seen anything like it." She kindly nodded, placing the purple Saint dress on the bed.

"Dress, you wear," she tried to explain while pointing at the breathtaking clothing spread out on the covers.

"Oh, this is beautiful, but I have clothes. See?" I pointed toward my luggage with a smile. She softly shook her head, pointing back to the dress.

"Zhang dress, very nice," she answered. *Ouch*, did she suggest I didn't have nice clothes? I mean, I have my airport comfort wear. Or maybe she was trying to look out for me; she would know what to wear at dinners and events the Zhangs hosted. After all, she practically lived here.

"Okay," I said softly. "I'll wear the dress," I added, sitting on the bed.

"Dinner at six," she said before stepping out of the room, leaving me alone with my thoughts. The last few hours have been a complete shock; I had never expected all of this. From flying in first class to learning that Micheal came from a powerful, respected family. It was hard to reconcile the image of him I knew with the reality of his family. What are the odds of this happening?

Dinner at six... What did that even mean in this new context? Would it be a simple meal, or a display of wealth and status that I would have to navigate carefully?

I didn't know, but I was about to find out.

At dinner time I tried to find my way to the dining room, and it wasn't as simple as I thought it would be. I wound up in a vast hallway with multiple paintings hung on the walls. The difference between them was extremely refreshing; most art lovers settle for one type of painting technique. But here, hung on these walls, were impressionist landscapes, abstract geometric composition, minimalist monochrome, and modern figurative art.

This hallway was the only spot in the entire penthouse that had vivid colors; there was more life in this space. I continued to walk down the hall, slowly forgetting my task of finding the dining room on time. I stopped in front of a self-portrait of a little boy with his two parents. The little boy sat in his mother's lap, looking up at her with admiration, while she had her gaze set on the father, who looked directly at the painter.

They looked happy, but something about it seemed sad to me. This painting laid at the very end of the hallway, no other paintings came after it.

"Are you lost?" a soft, melodic voice asked. I instantly turned around, stumbling backward as if I had been caught doing something bad.

"Hi, um... I was trying to find the dining room, but wound up here in this hallway instead. I'm sorry, it's just this place is a maze," I responded, moving closer to her. Her black hair fell in a silky cascade down her back. Her skin was flawless, a luminous porcelain with a soft glow that seemed to come from within, as if untouched by time or stress.

Her style was understated, yet undeniably luxurious. She wore a tailored, silk blouse in a deep shade of ivory that accentuated her slender figure, paired with high-waisted trousers that skimmed her hips with impeccable precision. Around her neck rested a delicate diamond pendant, understated yet catching the eye with every slight movement.

She carried an air of calm authority, a quiet but unmistakable presence that commanded attention without a word. I knew without a doubt that she was a Zhang; she had it written all over her.

"I understand; I get lost at times as well. No matter how many times you've visited, you'll always be surprised by the space capacity." She smiled gently, allowing me to feel more at ease. I released the tension on my shoulders and relaxed. "I'm Nari, but my American name is Lily." She offered her hand for me to shake.

"I'm Celeste," I replied, taking her hand.

"Yes, I know. Micheal's friend from New York; you are quite the topic tonight," she said.

"That sounds awful," I replied, releasing her hand.

"Yes, well, it's not always the best feeling to be the main topic at the Zhang table. I should know." She rested her hand on my shoulder and began walking. "Come now, I'll show you to the dining room. If you have any questions, please don't hesitate to ask."

"To Micheal you're...?" I asked, allowing her to finish my question.

"Micheal hasn't told you about me? I must say that it burns somewhat. I'm Micheal's best and favorite cousin in the entire family. We're the only ones that truly understand each other. Considering how intense this family can be," she answered as we made our way through the kitchen. The air was filled with the rich aroma of spices and roasted meat, mingling with the faint sweetness of fresh bread. The clinking of silverware and soft hum of conversation drifted from the grand dining room up ahead, growing louder with each step.

When we entered, the dining room was everything one would expect of the family's opulent lifestyle. The long table, polished to a mirror-like shine, stretched almost the entire length of the room, decorated with silver candelabras and intricate floral arrangements.

Micheal's father sat at the head of the table, his stern gaze flicking up briefly as he noticed our arrival. The table was long and elegantly set, with the silver candelabras casting a warm glow over floral arrangements. Relatives were seated along each side, their murmured conversations halting as they took note of us. Micheal, however, was still nowhere to be seen.

I slipped into my seat, feeling the weight of their gazes, each pair of eyes quietly assessing me, measuring my worth and place among them. Just when the silence was becoming unbearable, the doors creaked open, and Micheal stepped in. His expression was distant, his gaze drifting across the room before it finally settled on me. For a brief moment, his eyes softened, but then the mask of indifference slipped back into place. Without a word, he took his seat across from me and the air grew thicker, tension pressing in as everyone sensed his unease.

"Had trouble finding your way?" Micheal's father asked, sarcasm bleeding through his voice as he cast a disapproving glance in his son's direction.

"No, actually," Micheal replied smoothly, "I kept circling around the halls." His tone was light, but there was an edge to it, subtle and sharp, that seemed to ripple through the table. The table was silent for a few seconds until Nari broke the silence with a question.

"How is New York? I just *have* to hear the things you've been up to," she asked. The woman and man sitting across from her gave her a dead stare, leading me to assume they were her parents. They both resembled her, but it's clear she carried the beauty each of them offered.

Micheal's mouth slightly opened, as he's about to answer Nari's question, but quickly shuts it back closed as his father answers for him.

"Micheal is back home, and he's going to take over the

Zhang business. Which is why I invited all of you here tonight." Micheal's jaw clenched as the rest of the family breaks out in gasps and interjections.

"You can't be serious, Eun-woo!" Nari's father exclaimed. "That boy knows nothing to run a medical franchise! He simply can not take over."

"It's been decided," Micheal's father answered. I glanced over at Micheal to find him practically fuming. He looked like he was about to burst at any moment.

"Decided? By whom? I never agreed to any of it," Micheal finally burst out.

Eun-woo's eyes narrowed, his voice calm but laced with an undeniable edge.

"You may not have agreed, Micheal, but you don't need to. This is your duty. You're a Zhang, and that comes with responsibilities you cannot simply ignore."

Micheal's fists clenched on the table, knuckles white. He took a slow, controlled breath, his gaze unwavering as he looked directly at his father.

"I'm not some pawn you can just move around, Father. I've spent years building my own path, and I have no interest in being forced into yours."

A tense silence settled over the table. Nari looked between Micheal and Eun-woo, her own expression a mix of curiosity and concern. She finally spoke, her voice gentle but firm.

"Maybe Micheal deserves a choice, Eun-woo. He's worked hard for his career in New York."

Eun-woo's lips curled into a tight smile.

"What has that career given him, Nari? Independence? Vanity? The Zhang family doesn't have the luxury of chasing whims. We're a legacy."

Micheal opened his mouth to retort, but before he could, Nari's mother spoke up, her voice surprisingly strong.

"Eun-woo, forcing him into something he doesn't want could harm your relationship. It's not wise to disregard his feelings."

Eun-woo cast her a dismissive look, as though her words meant nothing. He turned back to Micheal, eyes piercing.

"You're coming to the office tomorrow, Micheal. We'll start with an introduction to the business."

Micheal's jaw tightened, and he pushed his chair back, rising to his feet.

"If you won't listen to me, maybe I should find someone who will," he said, voice low but filled with defiance. He turned and strode out of the room, leaving a heavy silence in his wake.

Nari bit her lip, watching him go. Then she looked back at Eun-woo, a determined glint in her eyes.

"You might be losing your son, Eun-woo. Just think about that."

Eun-woo's expression hardened, but he said nothing as the door closed behind Micheal.

"I—I should go check on him. Excuse me," I said softly, rising from my seat and giving a polite nod to the table. All eyes followed me as I slipped away, the tension thick enough to feel against my skin.

I found Micheal just down the hallway, leaning against the wall, his shoulders tense and his head lowered as if he were trying to gather himself. He didn't seem to notice me at first, so I took a quiet breath before speaking.

"Micheal?" I called out gently.

He looked up, his expression caught between anger and exhaustion. For a moment, his guard dropped, and I saw the vulnerable man beneath the hardened exterior.

"Did I really think I could come back without him trying to control everything?" His voice was barely a whisper, but the bitterness in it was unmistakable. I took a step closer.

"You don't have to do anything you don't want to. Not for him. Not for anyone."

Micheal let out a short, humorless laugh.

"Easy to say when you're not the one constantly weighed down by family expectations."

I bit my lip, trying to find the right words.

"Maybe, but I do understand the feeling of being pulled in directions that don't feel right. It doesn't make it any easier, but you don't have to face it alone."

Micheal nodded.

"Maybe. For now, I just need some air."

I hesitated.

"Mind if I join you?"

He looked at me, and for a moment, something unspoken passed between us.

"Yeah," he replied quietly.

We talked out onto the rooftop, the city lights of Seoul sparkling like a bunch of stars in the sky, possibly brighter than New York. It was a different type of air; the mountains guarded the city from the outside world, leaving this treasure apart from anywhere else.

"I know I'm probably the last person you want to talk to. I mean, you're the last person I thought I'd be standing here with, but if you feel the need to let off some steam…"

His left brow slightly rose as he looked down at me. I instantly knew what went through his mind with my innocent offering.

"Wipe off that look; that's not what I meant." He chuckled softly.

"I know Luci, relax. You get riled up so easily," he replied, looking out to the city.

I rolled my eyes, crossing my arms as I leaned against the railing beside him.

"I'm just trying to help. Not everything I say has a hidden meaning, you know."

Micheal let out a sigh, but there was a softness to it, like he was letting go of some of the weight he'd been carrying.

"Sorry," he murmured, his gaze fixed on the skyline. "I guess I'm not used to people... being here like this."

I tilted my head, studying him. There was something about the way he looked out at the city, lost yet somehow determined, like he was trying to make sense of things he didn't want to say out loud.

"Being back here must be harder than you let on."

He gave a slight nod, running a hand through his hair.

"New York is... was my escape. I built something there—something that felt like mine, you know? Coming back here, it's like stepping back into a cage I thought I'd escaped."

I glanced up at him, the hurt in his voice tugging at something inside me.

"You're not that same person anymore, Micheal. You've built something real, even if it's halfway across the world, and you don't have to give it all up just because your father says so."

He turned to look at me, his expression softening as he searched my face.

"You really believe that?"

"Of course I do," I replied firmly. "You have a right to decide your own future, Micheal. No one else can live your life for you—not even him."

A hint of a smile touched his lips, and he let out a deep breath, as if releasing some of the tension that had been knotted inside him.

"Thanks, Luci," he said quietly. "I didn't expect you to be the voice of reason tonight."

I shrugged, trying to keep it light.

"I'm full of surprises. But if you tell anyone I said anything remotely nice to you, you're done for."

He chuckled, shaking his head.

"There's the Luci I despise. For a second there, I thought you were trying to be nice, like some last-minute mercy, before tossing me off the roof without warning."

I smirked, crossing my arms.

"Like I said, tell anyone, and I just might."

He laughed, the sound low and a little more relaxed.

"Noted. Besides, I'll need you for tomorrow. Nari's supposed to be taking us for a ride around town. She's pretty much the only down-to-earth person in the family, so it should be better than tonight."

I raised a brow, trying to hide a grin.

"It better be. Or I'll hop back on the next flight to New York without you."

"Alright, let's not be dramatic," he teased. "Just... loosen up."

"I have a feeling nothing about this trip will 'loosen me up,'" I replied, tilting my head up to the sky, hoping the stars might somehow lend me patience.

"Maybe, but maybe not. Either way, it's best if we just hide out for the rest of the night in our rooms," he said as he walked toward the exit door. "Within a few minutes, the rest of the guests will probably circle around this area."

He paused at the door, glancing back at me with a slight smirk.

"But I'll see you tomorrow, yes? Get a long rest. For one, you're going to walk your legs off, so you'll need the energy, and two, you really need the beauty part in 'beauty sleep.'"

I immediately slipped off my sandal and aimed it at him, narrowing my eyes. He held up his hands in surrender, laughing.

"I'm joking, I'm joking! You look nice tonight, Luci. Really." His expression softened, just for a moment. "Good night."

"Good night," I replied, rolling my eyes but unable to stop a small smile from creeping in.

As the door clicked shut behind him, I stood there for a moment longer, a smile unconsciously creeping onto my face.

Realizing it, I shook my head and gave myself a light smack on the cheek.

"What is wrong with me? You will not smile like an idiot for that disaster of a man, Celeste. Get a grip."

I took a steadying breath, hoping the cool night air would clear my head. Micheal was... well, he was infuriating, and that wasn't going to change just because he'd decided to show a hint of kindness. I wouldn't let myself fall for it.

Straightening my shoulders, I slipped my sandal back on, muttering under my breath,

"Tomorrow, you're staying as far away from him as possible." But even as I told myself that, I knew it would be harder than it sounded.

CHAPTER 22
CELESTE

The following day, I went hiking down the streets of Seoul along with Nari and Micheal. They both dressed in nice clothes as I dressed for an exhibition. I was used to walking because of living in the busiest city in America, but for some strange reason, it feels harder to do so here. After thirty minutes of walking, I was already starving.

Micheal rolled out of bed perfectly fixed and ready to go, forgetting breakfast all together. He dragged me along and it's safe to say that I didn't get the chance to get a word in about it. We've been walking for the past five hours, not stopping for breaks.

"Hey, I love the view and all but..." My stomach growled, speaking for itself. Micheal and Nari turned around at the abrupt sound.

"Hungry, Luci?" Micheal asked.

"No, I just like making my stomach growl from starvation because it's satisfying. Yes, I'm hungry!" I spat, coming dangerously close to exploding.

"No worries, we're heading to the Gwangjang Market," Nari added, continuing to walk down the street. "I think you'll like it. It has good food for great prices," she said, turning a corner.

Walking into Gwangjang Market felt like stepping into another world. The moment I entered, I was hit by a wave of scents: spicy, savory, a hint of sesame oil, and the warmth of fried food. It was packed, people bustling everywhere, chatting, laughing, bargaining.

The food stalls were mesmerizing. I saw vendors rolling *mayak kimbap* with practiced hands, each piece perfectly tiny and bite-sized, ready to dip in that sweet and spicy mustard sauce. Right next to them, giant steaming vats of *tteokbokki* bubbled away, the bright red sauce practically daring me to try its spicy goodness. I could feel my mouth watering just looking at it.

As I walked further, I reached the fabric section. I saw people running their hands over rolls of beautiful silk and satin in every color imaginable. It was a quieter area, with shoppers examining materials for *hanbok*, the traditional Korean clothing. I could see the pride in the eyes of some elderly vendors as they displayed their meticulously crafted fabrics and intricate patterns.

Everywhere I turned, there was something new to discover. The energy was infectious; people gathered around tiny tables, squeezed together, sharing bowls of *bibimbap* and chatting as if they'd known each other forever. It was a place where every sense came alive: sights, sounds, smells, tastes, all blending together in a way that felt unique. As the day started to fade, the market glowed with neon signs, the sounds of laughter and sizzling food echoing all around. It felt like I'd found a little piece of Seoul's heart right there in Gwangjang Market.

Narrow aisles led me deeper in, past rows of food stalls where vendors expertly flipped *bindaetteok*, those crispy mung bean pancakes filling the air with that irresistible sizzle. I couldn't resist trying one. I walked over to the stand, the vendor only speaking to me in Korean.

"One *bindaetteok*," I said, holding my finger up, so he knew how many I wanted. He nodded and handed me a napkin.

"How do you know about *bindaetteok*?" Micheal asked as he stood beside me, handing the vendor wons, paying for my snack. I took a bite before responding to Micheal, it was golden and crispy on the outside, soft and earthy on the inside, and so fresh I could barely wait for it to cool.

"Mmm," I hummed as I savored the flavors exploding in my mouth. I loved street food, in New York and here. "I actually know a lot about Korean cuisine; there is a restaurant back in the city that sells food that's to die for," I answered his question.

"Really?" he asked, impressed and surprised.

"Yeah, after this I want to go across and get some *tteokbokki*," I said, finishing the last bite of my *bindaetteok*.

"You got it," he chuckled as he followed me to the next food station. We ended up visiting every station and getting one of everything. We grabbed a table in the middle of all the chaos and dug into all the delightful treats this street market had to offer.

Everyone at the table was silent, busy eating their food. I thought we would go on like this for a while longer until Nari broke the silence with a question.

"So I was thinking, what does your nickname mean?" she asked, curiosity taking over.

"Nickname?" I questioned, confused by what she meant.

"Yeah, Luci," Nari clarified as Micheal choked on his water, coughing for air.

"Well, why don't you ask him?" I said, looking over at a nervous Micheal.

No one knew our arrangement; the bet or seven dates. I'm sure someone like him would like to hide that fact from anyone, and I was going to enjoy hearing whatever he makes up in his head. I raised my brow, mentally pressuring him into speaking.

Nari turned her head to Micheal and waited patiently for his answer. He took a sip of water before speaking.

"Luci is a feminine name of Latin origin that means 'light.' I thought it would match Celeste perfectly since she is so full of *energy.*" The last part sounded like it pained him to say it.

Overall, I was pissed he found out so quickly. I was expecting to see him crack under pressure, but he flew by smoothly. I hated it.

"Oh, that's beautiful," Nari said, smiling as she took a bite of her *mayak kimbap*.

"That is very well thought, Micheal," I gritted through my teeth, and he winked back at me, only making me more frustrated. Two Micheal—One Celeste, I began keeping score boards since the flight.

What? Don't judge me. Anyone would do it if they were in my shoes.

We were finishing the last bites of our food, the table quiet except for the occasional satisfied sighs. I thought we'd stay like this until we parted ways—until Micheal decided to drop a bomb.

"Nari, thanks for coming out with us today," he said casually, setting down his chopsticks. "But I'd like to spend the rest of the day alone with Celeste."

I froze mid-bite, eyes snapping up to him. Did I just hear that right?

Nari's eyes widened, but she quickly covered her surprise with a warm smile.

"Oh, sure, Micheal! Of course. I've got some errands to run, anyway." She gave me a quick, curious glance and a wink before standing up, tossing me a look that said, *What's going on here?* I had no answer for her, and honestly, I was still processing.

I waited until Nari left before turning to Micheal, voice low.

"What are you doing?"

He didn't miss a beat, leaning back with that infuriatingly calm expression.

"What do you think I'm doing?"

"Making it look like you can't get enough of me." I raised a brow, hoping to rattle him a little. "That'll ruin your whole *aloof, unbothered* persona, you know."

He just shrugged, meeting my gaze without flinching.

"Maybe I changed my mind."

The words caught me off guard, and I struggled to mask my surprise. I was about to fire back when he leaned in, his eyes dancing with a hint of mischief.

"Or maybe I just wanted to see if you'd get all worked up."

I rolled my eyes, trying to act unaffected, though the truth was my pulse was racing. The worst part? I couldn't even figure out why.

"Keep dreaming, Micheal. You couldn't rattle me if you tried."

"Challenge accepted," he replied, and his smirk was positively maddening.

With one last defiant glare, I pushed my chair back and stood, determined to keep my cool.

"Fine. Let's go then."

As I walked ahead, I could feel his gaze on me, and a thrill ran up my spine. Somewhere between the teasing and the quiet challenge in his voice, this entire game had changed whether I was ready for it or not.

CHAPTER 23
MICHEAL

I ditched Nari in order to have Celeste to myself this afternoon. It wasn't my finest moment, kicking my cousin out like that, but I needed time alone with Celeste if I wanted to make a difference with where we stood in our relationship. She was still wary of me, never truly giving in or trusting me. I didn't blame her; I don't think I'd trust myself either, especially since her intuition is right on.

"So, where are you planning on taking me?" she asked as we walked down the road.

"I'm taking you to the one place I always seemed to run away to as a teen to seek peace. I think you'll get why once we get there," I explained, taking in the views of my beautiful country.

The place that I wanted to take Celeste was the Han River in Seoul. It was my favorite spot to watch the sunset, always with a warm cup of noodles in hand. A quiet little tradition I'd kept to myself—until now. It was special to me, and I knew, somehow, it would be special to her too.

"Are we getting close to this *special* place?" she asked, crossing her arms against the soft breeze.

We reached the banks of the Han River as the sun began its descent, casting a warm, golden light over the water. The world seemed to slow down here, the sounds of the city falling away into the quiet rhythm of waves lapping against the shore. I gestured to the famous steps overlooking the water.

"Relax Luci, we're here," I replied, walking forward to claim the bench before anyone else did. Placing my hand on the wooden surface, I called over Celeste and gestured for her to sit. She hesitated, then sat, her gaze fixed on the horizon.

"It's beautiful," she whispered, almost to herself. The light reflected off her eyes, giving them a soft glow that took my breath away.

"It is, but there's something missing," I told her as I looked around for the convenience store nearby. As I scanned around the area, my gaze landed on the Seven Eleven I always went to get the best noodles in the country. "I'll be right back," I said, planning to leave her watching the view.

I began making my way toward the store until I heard Celeste catching up with me.

"Are you crazy? Planning to ditch me?" she asked, her chest heaving as she walked twice as fast as me to keep up with my normal pace.

"No, but that sure is a nice thought," I teased. "I couldn't possibly do such a horrendous thing," I shrugged, arriving at the store.

"Oh, I wouldn't put it behind you." She opened the door, walking in and shutting it right in my face.

I stood back behind the glass door and took a deep breath. I slightly chuckled at the fact that she was getting under my skin so quickly. I'm usually always the one to accomplish that, but this time around, it's been her non-stop.

Once I regained my calm, I opened the door, walking in. She was already at the shelf, scanning the ramen options, her eyebrows raised in what I assumed was a mix of curiosity and judgment.

"So," she said, grabbing a bag of Buldak spicy ramen and a cup. "This is part of your ritual? You have a nice cup of noodles, sit by the river and sacrifice whatever poor animal comes across your path?"

I leaned in closer to her, slightly pushing her back into the shelf of ramen. I kept my eyes on her as I reached up, so close I could hear her breathing hitch. My hand brushed past her hair, just barely, as I grabbed the pack of Shin Ramen from the shelf above her shoulder. For a second, she didn't move, and neither did I.

"Careful, that's a time-honored tradition you're making fun of," I whispered against her lips.

"Touchy, aren't we?" she murmured, though her voice had a faint tremor that betrayed her usual bravado. Her gaze flickered to my lips, just for a heartbeat, before snapping back up to my eyes.

"Just making sure you understand the significance of the ritual," I replied, keeping my voice low.

Her scent, a hint of citrus and cinnamon, filled the small space between us, making it harder to keep my cool. It had brought me right back to that night I met her, before I decided that I despised her and couldn't possibly fall for her.

She smirked, but I noticed her cheeks blush slightly.

"You're so intense over a cup of noodles," she said, though there was something softer in her tone, something that almost felt like… intrigue.

We stood like that, neither of us willing to break first. There was a spark in her eyes that hadn't been there before, and in that moment, I knew she was feeling it, too. That sudden closeness, the pull. Just as quickly, though, she turned away, snapping out of whatever had held us there.

"Alright, Mr. Noodles. Let's see what this 'ritual' of yours is really about," she said, her voice carefully light as she grabbed a second cup and strode to the register.

I watched her walk off, a grin tugging at the corner of my mouth. Grabbing a four-egg carton, I quickly followed behind her. As her hair swung side to side, I thought to myself—this was new territory for me. And maybe, just maybe, I liked it.

There could be a chance she did too...

As we paid and stepped back out into the cool night, the silence between us felt heavier, charged with something unspoken. She walked a little ahead of me, as if trying to keep some distance, but every so often, she'd glance back, checking if I was still there.

Outside the convenience store, I led her over to the ramen station, where the hum of machines and the smell of broth filled the air. She followed, watching me carefully as I prepared our cups of noodles, peeling off the lids and setting each one under the machine to fill with hot water.

"So," she began by saying. "What animal are you planning on sacrificing tonight? A sweet little puppy?" she asked, leaning against the counter and watching the water fill our cups.

"I'm afraid we're skipping the sacrifice tonight," I answered sarcastically, focusing on our ramen, watching it with all my might.

"You really are intense over noodles," she teased, laughing in my face.

"The timing's everything," I replied, switching my gaze to her. "You get it wrong, and they are either mushy or too chewy. The perfect cup of noodles is an art form, you know?"

She raised an eyebrow, trying to keep her usual smirk, but I could tell she was intrigued.

"Never thought I'd see you this serious about anything."

"Hey, ramen deserves respect," I said, mock-offended, as I placed the cups to the side, waiting for them to cook. "Besides, it's not *just* noodles. It's the most important part of this ritual. If the noodles are bad, the whole vibe will be off, therefore, ruining our entire night." Opening the pack of eggs, I cracked two in each cup.

I took a step back, leaning against the counter next to her, the proximity making the small space between us feel even smaller. Her shoulder brushed mine as she shifted slightly, and I could feel her presence, the warmth that somehow made everything else fade.

"Right..." she said.

We watched the noodles soften; the steam rising in gentle wisps, filling the air with a warmth that felt... comfortable. She glanced over at me, catching my eye in the reflection on the glass door of the machine, and her expression softened, just for a second, enough to give me hope that she was seeing something more.

"So, you really came here all the time?" she asked, her voice quieter now.

"Yeah," I replied, turning to face her fully. "When things got too loud, this was the one place where it all made sense. It's simple, nothing fancy—but it's mine."

She looked down, like she was turning the thought over in her mind.

"I get it," she murmured, surprising me. "Sometimes, when things get too complicated, you just need something that's... yours."

I watched her for a second, the usual fire in her eyes replaced by something softer, something I didn't see often. She glanced up and caught me staring, her cheeks flushing slightly before she looked away, pretending to focus on the noodles.

The machine beeped, signaling the noodles were done. I reached for her cup, but she beat me to it, her hand brushing against mine, lingering for just a moment longer than necessary. She cleared her throat, her eyes not quite meeting mine as she stepped back, slightly caressing her arm for comfort.

"Let's see if all this hype is worth it," she said, her voice back to its usual challenge, though her gaze showed a flicker of something else. We grabbed our cups, and we walked back out to the bench.

As we made it back to our spot, the noodles were still steaming in their cups. Once we sat down, I could tell she was trying to maintain her usual cool, but there was a slight unease in the way she adjusted her position, the way her lips curved downward in concentration as she took her first bite.

I watched, trying not to smile at the determination on her face. It only lasted for a second.

"Agh!" Celeste's voice was a sharp gasp as she suddenly jolted, her eyes wide with surprise. She immediately reached for her water, but it was already too late. Her hand went to her mouth, and she winced. "Hot, hot, hot!"

I couldn't help but laugh softly at her reaction.

"You're supposed to wait for it to cool down," I laughed even harder as she stuck out her tongue.

"You didn't tell me that!" she replied, still fanning her mouth dramatically.

Without thinking, I grabbed her cup and set it down beside mine, my hand brushing hers as I moved closer.

"You okay?" I asked, my voice softer than usual.

She shot me an incredulous look.

"No. I just burned my entire mouth off." Her eyes narrowed in playful annoyance. "This is your fault."

I leaned in slightly, watching her closely.

"You're right, I'm sorry," I said, my voice dropping low. "Let me help." She gave me a confused look, but before she could protest, I blew gently across her lips—a light puff of air to help cool her down.

She froze, blinking up at me. For a split second, the entire world seemed to pause, just long enough for both of us to realize how close we were. My breath mingled with hers for a heartbeat, and I could feel her body stiffen as she processed the moment.

"Better?" I asked, my eyes locked on hers, unsure of whether she was still mad at the noodles or if something else had changed.

Her lips parted, but she didn't immediately respond, and I could see her working through the unexpected closeness, her mind whirring.

"You—" She cleared her throat, trying to regain some composure. "You didn't have to do that."

I shrugged, leaning back just a little, though I couldn't stop the grin tugging at my lips.

"I couldn't let you suffer," I said lightly, my voice returning to its usual teasing tone.

"No, I mean, you really didn't have to do that. It didn't help for shit." She shook her head, her gaze flickering to her noodles again as if avoiding the moment, slightly chuckling. "Next time," she said, her voice quieter, "I'm waiting longer before I dive in."

"Smart choice," I agreed, though I didn't move my gaze from her. I could feel the heat between us, not from the noodles, but from something else.

I took a deep breath, my eyes drifting to the horizon as the sun dipped lower, casting the river in a soft, golden hue. The evening was falling quiet, save for the occasional rustle of trees in the breeze, and it felt... peaceful. But there was something I had to say, something I couldn't keep buried any longer.

"I used to come here a lot," I said, my voice quieter now. Celeste glanced over at me, sensing the shift.

"You've said that," she replied, her tone gentle, as if waiting for me to explain further.

I nodded, setting my cup aside and running a hand through my hair.

"It wasn't just about the noodles," I continued, the words

coming slower now. "It was... my place to think. To be alone. To forget for a while."

Celeste didn't interrupt, her gaze softening as she leaned in slightly, sensing the change. I swallowed, not used to letting people in, especially her, but something about tonight, about this place, made it feel like I could.

"My mom left when I was younger," I said, the words coming out almost before I could stop them. I didn't know why I was saying it now, but I knew it was something I needed to share. "She just... walked out. No explanation. One day, she was there, and the next, she wasn't."

There was a heaviness in my chest, a knot I'd carried for years that I had never been able to untangle. But here, with Celeste, I felt like maybe it could be different.

"I didn't understand why at first, and I blamed myself, you know?" I glanced over at her, hoping she wasn't seeing me as weak. "In my mind, I figured there must have been something wrong with me. Something that made her leave."

Celeste's eyes softened, and she shifted closer, her voice quiet as she spoke.

"Micheal..."

But I shook my head, cutting her off before she could say anything more.

"It wasn't until I started coming here that I even began to heal. This spot by the river—watching the sunset, sitting with my thoughts—there was something about it that made the pain a little less sharp. The quiet... It lets me breathe again. And little by little, I stopped blaming myself."

She was silent for a moment, the only sound the gentle lapping of the water against the shore. I could feel her presence beside me, the way she was absorbing my words without judgment.

"I know how you're feeling," she said, her voice steady and surprisingly understanding. "When my parents died, it felt like the entire world was out to get me. It all felt so goddamn personal, targeted toward me. I know I said that it didn't hurt me at all, but it did."

There was something about her words that struck a chord deep within me. Something I hadn't expected, but welcomed all the same. I turned to face her, meeting her eyes for the first time since I'd started speaking. Her expression was open; no judgment, no pity, just a quiet understanding that made my chest ache.

"You know, it's how I first got into painting. Back in elementary school, I dreaded the idea of coming home; it always felt so quiet and empty. One day, I found an art studio and stayed after school painting every day. It helped me forget that I was the girl whose parents died in a tragic car crash," she explained.

I was silent for a moment, absorbing her words, trying to process what she'd just shared. It wasn't the kind of thing Celeste usually opened up about, and yet, there she was, revealing something that most people would never guess about her. The quiet strength in her voice made it all the more real.

"You really think you can just forget something like that?" I asked, my voice softer now, almost questioning. I couldn't imagine a way to truly forget the pain of losing a parent, let alone both, and I already experienced losing one, but not to death.

Celeste shrugged, but there was a faint sadness in her eyes that made me want to reach out and hold her.

"Not forget, no. But painting... like this place did for you, it gave me a space to breathe. It made me feel like I could be someone else for a while. I wasn't the girl who had lost everything. I was just... a person, creating."

I could see it now, the painting, the quiet hours spent in the studio, the way art had become her escape.

"So, that's why you're so damn good at it," I said with a

smirk, trying to lighten the mood, though the weight of her words still lingered. "You've been practicing for years."

Her lips twitched into the smallest of smiles, though there was no humor in her eyes.

"Did you just compliment my art?"

"Did I?" I questioned, grabbing my cup of noodles and stuffing it in my mouth.

She raised an eyebrow, clearly amused, but there was still a hint of seriousness in her expression.

"You totally did! Oh my god, that's a first. I'll have to mark this day on my calendar."

Her teasing tone made a small smile tug at the corners of my lips, but I kept my gaze fixed on the river, pretending to be absorbed in the view. It wasn't the river that held my attention, though. It was Celeste, sitting beside me. The way the fading sunlight caught her hair and the way she relaxed into the moment, the sharp edges of her usual guardedness softening just a little.

"Hilarious," I added.

"I'm serious," she said, breaking the silence. "You should definitely mark the day. I'll be telling people for years how Micheal Zhang finally complimented my art."

I couldn't help but laugh, the sound awkward and a little unsteady, but genuine.

"Yeah, well... I guess even the worst critics can admit when something's good."

Her eyes flickered over to me then, and for the briefest moment, there was no sarcasm, no challenge, just a quiet understanding. She wasn't looking for approval, but I could tell she appreciated it, nonetheless. Her eyes locked on the river, allowing me to steal a glance.

The wind flowed effortlessly through her hair, her curls gently shifting away from her face as if the breeze itself had decided to keep her at ease. The golden sunlight bathed her in a soft, warm glow, casting delicate shadows across her features. I began doubting the hate I felt for Celeste Castillo, and if it was truly hate to begin with.

What was wrong with me? I'm beginning to look at her in a different light. I'm not sure it's even smart for me to consider this version of her. I should just stick to the version that pissed me off.

"Thank you for bringing me here, sharing this with me," she said, surprising me. "I know I'm probably the last person you want to be here with, but I see how healing this place can be, and I wanted to thank you."

"It's no problem," I replied, still in shock that Celeste had thanked me for something.

"If you tell anyone those words came out of my mouth, I'll hurt you," she added, placing things back to semi-normal.

"I figured as much." I chuckled. Deep down, I was not willing to end this day anytime soon. But as I noticed the sun disappearing, I knew I'd have no choice but to end it. "We should probably head back and rest; it's been a long, well-spent day,"

"Yeah, we should," she said, her tone showing a hint of disappointment.

"I'll call a car to pick us up," I said, taking out my phone. My fingers moved quickly over the screen, dialing our driver. I could feel her eyes on me, but I didn't look up. Not yet. The air felt heavier now, charged with whatever this was between us.

About twenty minutes later, he had sent a text saying he had arrived to pick us up.

We made our way to the car; the air grew cooler as the day slipped into night. Suddenly, I couldn't shake the feeling that something was wrong. There was a shift in the atmosphere, like the world had become just a little too quiet.

Then I felt it, the prickling sensation on the back of my neck, the one that told me someone was watching. I glanced over my shoulder, trying to dismiss the feeling, but then I saw someone. A figure, standing far behind us, just outside the reach of the fading sunlight. Too far to make out clearly, but close enough to make my heart skip. I squinted my eyes, trying to make out the figure better, but I couldn't.

I then instinctively reached for Celeste, pulling her to me as my eyes scanned the surroundings. My pulse quickened, and I turned sharply.

"Get in the car. Now," I ordered, trying to keep my voice steady.

She didn't question me, but the brief flash of confusion in her eyes made me wonder if she had noticed it, too. As we made our way to the penthouse, I couldn't shake the feeling that the man had been following us, and the unease gnawed at me. The question of who he was and why he had been following us had begun to haunt me quickly.

When we finally arrived, I quickly ushered Celeste inside, both of us moving swiftly to separate rooms without saying a word. But as I entered my room, I couldn't shake the image of that figure in my mind. That had never happened to me before; it was a first.

Someone was watching.

CHAPTER 24
CELESTE

WHAT WAS GOING ON WITH MICHEAL ZHANG? THAT WAS THE question I constantly kept asking myself the moment we arrived at the Zhang's penthouse. The day had gone by better than I could've imagined; I thought we would end up killing each other. But to my surprise, Micheal wasn't the worst company I had. He wasn't bad at all.

Admitting that to myself constantly made me want to bang my head on a wall, trying to save whatever sanity I had left. Three days ago, I couldn't stand the idea of spending the entire day with him, and now, I couldn't stand the idea of being alone the entire day. Was I officially losing it? No, this is all his doing. It has to be.

What was it about him that made everything so damn complicated? Micheal was supposed to be the forever thorn in my side, a necessary sting to remind me why I was here: to pay off my debt. But, I found myself thinking back to the way his voice softened when he spoke to me about his childhood, or the fleeting moments when his guard slipped, revealing someone I wasn't prepared to see. Someone I shouldn't see.

And I hated that with every ounce of my being.

How his eyes gazed into mine, searching for my soul, breaking down barriers I purposely put up for this exact reason... The breeze by the river made all interactions even more magical than they had to be. The smallest, stolen touches whenever our hands would cross each other's path...

It was maddening.

What was even more maddening was that I haven't seen him since our visit to the Han River. Three days. Seventy-two hours. That's how long it had been since I'd seen Micheal Zhang, despite staying under the same roof. Three days of tiptoeing around his father's ridiculously luxurious penthouse, pretending like his absence didn't bother me.

I mean, he was here, technically. But he wasn't *here*.

Every time I caught a glimpse of him, it was fleeting: him stepping into the elevator, his phone pressed to his ear, or passing through the living room with his father trailing behind him. He hadn't said a word to me.

I wasn't sure what I had expected. A conversation? A continuation of whatever unspoken thing had passed between us? Maybe even an acknowledgment of the way his presence lingered in my mind like a stubborn shadow?

But there was nothing.

I perched on the edge of the couch, pretending to scroll through my phone while my eyes darted toward the clock on the wall. 7:42 p.m. The familiar ache of annoyance settled in my chest as I imagined Micheal at some high-stakes dinner with his father, charming investors or attending yet another meeting that determined the fate of their billion-dollar empire. How could he be spending this much time with his father after he practically took an oath to hate him and his business?

Whatever, it wasn't like I cared. Not really. But a part of me, the part I desperately tried to ignore, felt foolish for even thinking we'd crossed some invisible line that night.

I sighed, tossing my phone onto the cushion beside me and

pulling my knees up to my chest. The city lights sparkled through the massive floor to ceiling windows, casting a cold glow over the room.

"Miss Celeste, dinner is ready," Min-Soo called softly from the dining room.

I didn't respond right away, letting the silence stretch as I stared at the city below. I wasn't hungry. What I wanted was something no meal could satisfy—a confrontation, a moment of clarity, an explanation.

What I wanted was Micheal Zhang.

That was the most maddening part of all.

I slumped onto the couch, kicking off my shoes and letting out a frustrated sigh. My reflection in the windows stared back at me, and I didn't like what I saw: confusion, vulnerability, and the nagging sense that maybe, just maybe, I was starting to see Micheal in a different light.

No. I shook my head, as if the motion could somehow fling the thought away. I refused to let myself go down that road. I was in Seoul, for Christ's sake; what was I doing here? Lying around and waiting like a pathetic fool for something that wasn't going to happen.

Suddenly, I remembered who I was. I was Celeste Carmen Castillo, a woman who doesn't sit around moping or much less *waiting*. I never waited or moped, and I mean *never*.

Just like that, I stood up, my legs moving before my brain could catch up. I refuse to spend another minute in this empty penthouse when I had an entire city out there booming with life. If Micheal wanted to play busy and avoid me after he shared the tiniest soft side he had, fine. Let him.

I made my way to the bedroom, rifling through my suitcase for something that screamed, *You're going to bite your tongue when you see me in this.* My hand landed on a purple mini-dress, the one that hugged every curve and made me feel invincible. It was bold, and everything I needed for tonight.

In this dress, I had a whirlwind of a night, bouncing from club to club in New York, and I had an entire night of free drinks and even some numbers that belonged to the top bachelors of the city. I never once underestimated this dress, and I knew for sure that it wouldn't let me down now.

Twenty minutes later, I was slipping on my heels, adjusting my makeup in the mirror. A swipe of a dark aubergine lipstick, a bold eyeliner sharp enough to cut glass. I looked in the mirror and felt proud of the reflection that stared back at me. Perfect.

I grabbed my purse and made my way to the elevator, my heart pounding with a mix of excitement and defiance. Tonight, I wasn't going to sit around feeling sorry for myself. As I pressed the button for the elevator, I glanced at my phone one last time—no messages, no missed calls. Typical.

The ding of the elevator arriving broke my thoughts, and the doors slid open to reveal a familiar face.

"Nari?" I blinked, momentarily caught off guard.

Micheal's cousin grinned back at me, dressed in a chic leather jacket over a shimmering silver top, her dark hair styled in loose waves. She looked effortlessly cool, as though she was born to walk the streets of Seoul at night.

"Well, well, if it isn't Miss Celeste," Nari teased, stepping out of the elevator before stopping in her tracks to give me a once-over. "Wow, you clean up nicely! Heading out for a night on the town?"

I hesitated for a moment, but her energy was infectious.

"Yeah, I thought I'd check out the nightlife." Nari paused, looking behind me for someone who wasn't there.

Nari's eyes sparkled with mischief.

"Alone? No way. That's not happening. You're coming with me. Girls' night!"

"I wouldn't want to impose—"

"Impose?" she cut me off with a laugh, linking her arm through mine before I could protest. "I've been dying for an excuse to blow off some steam, and you look like you need it, too. Let's go."

Before I could fully process what was happening, Nari was dragging me back into the elevator, her enthusiasm impossible to resist.

"Isn't there a reason you came here?" I asked, since her visit lasted about three seconds.

"I came by to pick up a box that was delivered to the lobby. I figured I'd stop and check on you; I thought they'd have you locked up in here. But by the looks of it, you're definitely not," she answered.

"Where are we going?" I asked, a nervous laugh escaping as the elevator descended.

"Oh, don't worry. I know the best spots in town. Trust me, by the end of the night, you'll forget all about whatever or *whomever* is bothering you," she said with a knowing smirk.

As the doors opened to the bustling lobby, I felt a flicker of gratitude. Our interaction was extremely quick; she practically swept me off my feet and didn't allow me to say no. She didn't judge me or decide to call Micheal; she treated me like I was a friend she's had for ages.

As we stepped into the cool night air, Seoul's skyline glittered in the distance, the neon signs reflecting the city's pulse, alive, chaotic, and impossibly vibrant. The streets were crowded with late-night wanderers, the hum of conversation and the rhythm of footsteps mixing with the beat of the music flowing out of every open door. It felt exhilarating, like stepping into a whole new world.

Nari led the way down the street, weaving effortlessly through the crowd.

"So, what's been going on with you? There must be a reason behind this outfit. It's screaming revenge. I should know; I'm quite the expert." Her tone was casual, but there was a curiosity about it, something more subtle.

I swallowed hard.

"Nothing really... just thinking about some things."

She raised an eyebrow, clearly not convinced.

"Uh-huh."

I sighed, my shoulders slumping slightly as we reached a sleek underground club. The name '*Treasure*' sparkled in purple as we walked closer toward the entrance. The bouncer at the door gave Nari a friendly nod as she flashed him a smile and ushered me inside. The bass hit me like a wave, the lights flashing in rhythm to the beat, making everything feel like it was pulsing with energy.

"Usual place?" I asked as Nari made her way to the bar.

"That obvious, huh?" she added as she took a seat on one of the several golden barstools.

"Quick and easy entrance, the amount of familiarity that shows in your walk like you own the place. The sudden need to pick a specific seat before someone else takes it, and of course we can't forget the gorgeous bartender that's already dropped off your first drink of the night without having to ask." My eyes tipped toward the glass cup filled with a clear liquid with an olive floating on top.

"Okay Miss City girl, you're quite the observer, aren't you?" she chuckled as she reached for her class. "I own it," she added.

"You own this place?" I asked, shocked by her casualness. She nodded with a soft smile.

"I fell in love with the place and the unique location. It's almost hidden, and those who find it will feel rewarded. It's good business, but it's not too popular, which is what I prefer."

"Wow Nari, that's amazing." I complimented, completely impressed with her.

"Thank you," she responded. "So, what will you be having? Something strong to make the conversation easier?" she asked as she called over the bartender.

"What conversation will we be having that involves me

needing a strong drink?" I asked and quickly turned my attention to the man who was about to prepare my drink. "Tequila, lemon and salt please," I winked, feeling confident with my order.

"Cute, but if you want something a bit stronger, you might want to try something else. You know, they don't say that we dominate the drinking culture for nothing," Nari added, "A soju drink for my friend here." She paused and looked over to me. "What's your favorite flavor?"

"Uh…"

"You seem like the citrus type to me, a citrus-flavored soju," she said before she let me answer.

I raised an eyebrow, intrigued by her confidence in picking my drink.

"Citrus, huh?" I said, considering her choice. "I guess I can go with that. You know me pretty well for someone I just met."

Nari flashed a playful smile.

"I'm good at reading people," she said, a teasing glint in her eyes. "Citrus is fresh, sharp, and a little unpredictable. Fits you."

The bartender nodded and grabbed a bottle of soju. With a swift motion, he shook it from underneath, creating a mini tornado inside before cracking it open. He poured the vibrant liquid into a shot glass, releasing a sharp citrus scent that filled the air. The color alone made my mouth water. When Nari saw it being served, she gave me an approving nod..

"See? You'll love it," she said as she handed me the glass.

I took the drink, savoring the cool, tangy sweetness that hit my tongue. It wasn't too strong, but it had a kick to it that made me feel a little bolder. I took another sip; the fiery burn of soju slid down my throat.

"That's actually not bad," I commented, placing the cup down.

"Trust me, go easy on it. Once you reach the end of the bottle, you'll rethink life," she chuckled, but I could see her smile dialing down slowly. "So, you want to tell me what's bothering you? I can keep secrets like no one else, you know. With the things I've kept from my family, you could call me the master," she teased, while she ordered a refill of her drink.

I hesitated for a moment, the weight of her words settling over me. Nari had that air about her, like she could handle whatever I threw her way. I glanced down at my drink, swirling the soju gently as I debated whether to open up.

Finally, I let out a deep sigh, setting the glass down.

"I'm just... confused, I guess." I ran my fingers along the rim of the glass. "I'm someone who hates being confused; it's maddening."

Nari's eyes softened, and she leaned in closer, listening intently.

"Maddening in a good way? Or maddening in a way that makes you want to throw your drink at him?"

"Try in a way of throwing pointy darts at him? Plus, I already sprayed him with a beer gun." Nari spit out a bit of her drink, allowing her laugh to fill the space.

Nari raised an eyebrow, her expression turning thoughtful.

"So, you're telling me this guy has you so riled up that you want to hurl things at him?"

I nodded, almost laughing at myself.

"Yes, and no. I'm not even sure if it's anger or... something else. I think I'm just getting tangled up in all these mixed signals he's sending."

"Typical guy stuff," Nari said with a grin, but there was an understanding in her voice. "You know what they say; when they act like they don't care, it usually means the opposite. Most times…"

"I wish it were that simple," I sighed. "I don't know if he's playing some game with me or if I'm just imagining it. The worst part is, for the last three days, I couldn't get him out of my head."

Nari swirled her drink thoughtfully, then shot me a side glance.

"You sure it's not because you want him in your head?"

The bluntness of her words caught me off guard, and for a split second, I was speechless.

"What do you mean by that?" I finally asked, frowning.

"Come on, I know a distraction when I see one. If he's on your mind that much, there's something more going on than just *confusion.*" Nari's smile was teasing, but there was a note of seriousness behind it. "You might be trying to convince yourself otherwise, but I can tell you're hooked."

I blinked at her, the sudden clarity of her words hitting harder than I expected.

"Well, that is just ridiculous," I bluntly answered, trying to hide how much her words affected me.

"I've seen the way he looks at you." She raised an eyebrow, clearly amused by her own teasing.

I grimaced, pushing her lightly.

"Don't even start."

Nari laughed, her voice rising above the music.

"Come on, I've seen the way he watches you. It's like he's obsessed with you or something."

I rolled my eyes, feeling the heat rise to my cheeks.

"He's not obsessed with me. He's just... frustrating." My voice dropped a little, the words tasting bitter. "I can't stand him. The way he acts all distant, like I'm just another problem he has to deal with, and he's the one who's leading me on for whatever reason."

Nari's face softened for a moment, sensing the frustration in my tone.

"Hey, I get it. He's not making it easy, but you've got to admit, there's something there. You can't pretend you don't feel it, and I'm not just saying this because he's my cousin, but he's not a bad guy. He's a pretty good one once you break through his tough exterior."

I hesitated, the thumping music giving me an excuse to delay my confession, but it wasn't like I had anywhere to hide. Nari was sharp, and her persistence could rival a bulldog.

"Like I said, I'm confused and in a few days I'll realize that it was just a silly phase, just like my obsession with that actor from the K-Drama True Beauty was a phase." Nari giggled at my sudden confession.

"You are just hilarious," she admitted. "Okay, let's do this. Tonight, you stop thinking about him. You forget about what's out of your control, and you *live*. You *enjoy* the night. And when you wake up tomorrow, you'll be in a better place to figure it all out."

I took a deep breath, the weight in my chest easing just a little as I looked around the club. The music, the flashing lights, the energy in the air—it was like a wave of relief. The dimly lit space packed with bodies swaying to the rhythm of the music.

"Okay, sounds good," I answered, downing the rest of my drink. My eyes squinted as I adjusted to the burning liquid churning its way to my stomach. It's a stimulant at first, slightly increasing my heart rate. I turned to go out to the dance floor, and I grabbed Nari's hand only for her to pull back.

She looked down at her phone with full concentration.

"Hold on, let me answer this text. I'll be right there. You go on!" She smiled, nudging me forward.

"Okay!" I laughed to myself, the warmth of the alcohol spreading through my veins. I was already feeling the effects, the slight buzz loosening my limbs, the tingly sensation making me feel lighter.

Nari's absence faded from my mind as the music took over. I swayed to the rhythm, letting the music guide my movements. The weight of my thoughts, the lingering confusion about

Micheal, seemed far away now. For tonight, I was going to lose myself in the rhythm and forget about everything else.

Especially about Micheal Zhang.

CHAPTER 25
MICHEAL

The image of the mystery man's silhouette stayed stitched in my mind. But now that I think about it, he gave off a youthful vibe; he didn't seem like the typical old creep following us around. Broad shoulders, slow steady walk, the kind that screamed purpose. It was like he wanted to be seen, but not caught. That familiarity felt like I knew him so well that it gnawed at me, refusing to let go. It wasn't just a passing resemblance; it was something deeper, a buried memory I couldn't quite recall.

I ran my hand through my hair, feeling exhausted. Sleep didn't come, and I couldn't feel it coming regardless of how tired I felt. It never did when my thoughts spiraled like this.

Broad shoulders. Brown hair. Average height. Familiar presence.

Did Celeste notice him, too? If she had, she didn't let on. She'd gone about her evening as though nothing was amiss; the thought of her oblivious to the potential danger made my stomach twist.

For a moment, I considered waking Celeste that night and asking her if she remembered anything, but the thought of her peaceful expression as she finally drifted off stopped me. She deserved a few hours of calm, even if I didn't.

Grabbing my phone, I scrolled through my recent calls. No one. Not a single name I could trust to make sense of this. I couldn't go to Dylan because he wouldn't know anything and I definitely couldn't go to my father and bluntly ask. If I was going to figure out who the man was and what he wanted, I'd have to do it alone.

So, for the past week, I did the most logical thing I could think of, stick by my father's side until it physically pained me. Yes, I went to numerous dinners with clients and listened to long, drawn out speeches about business and what was currently successful in the medical field.

It's easy to say that it was the worst three days of my life; it only served as a reminder of why I left and why I refused to take over the business. It was clear that I'd soon become a zombie working for something that doesn't excite me one bit. The thought petrified me.

But not as much as the idea of Celeste. That's another thing; I've been deliberately avoiding Celeste like a coward. After I opened up to her about the fucked up parts of my childhood, I couldn't find it in me to face her. How does one do that? Especially after the split moment between us, before I lost all control.

I tried to shake the thought, but it lingered like a stubborn shadow. The tiny, fragile idea that maybe, just maybe, I was starting to feel something for Celeste. It was laughable, really. Me, of all people. In the middle of all this mess, with a family business I wanted nothing to do with, and the weight of Dylan's expectations pressing down on me like an anchor, how could I possibly have the space to think about her?

But there it was, this annoying little spark every time she spoke, every time she looked at me with that knowing smile. I hated it. I hated that she understood me better than anyone else, even when I didn't want her to. She made me question everything I thought I knew about myself, about the choices I had made.

"I don't want to be here," I muttered to myself, rubbing my temples as if the pressure of the decision could somehow be eased with a simple gesture. I pushed it down, buried the idea of Celeste, and tried to focus on what I was supposed to do next.

But she was always there—quietly watching from the sidelines, her presence like a calm in the chaos.

Just stop thinking about her. I told myself.

Who was I kidding? Sitting here at this dinner, surrounded by people who only pissed me off and only have one person in mind. The amount of times I wanted to push her into a corner and beg her to let me in. Every time she walked past me, I could feel my jaw clench tight, teeth grinding as her image refused to leave my mind.

My hands clenched around the edge of my seat, knuckles white, as I fought the urge to chase after her like a maniac. If I gave in to my thoughts, I'd ruin everything.

The table buzzed with fake laughter as my father launched into another one of his stories, oblivious to the storm raging inside me. When his hand landed on my shoulder, giving me a firm, reassuring squeeze, something inside me snapped.

I shot up from my chair, the sudden motion silencing the table and drawing every pair of eyes in the restaurant toward me. Silence filled the room.

"Excuse me," I said, my voice tight, barely steady. "I have an urgent matter I need to attend to."

"Micheal," my father's sharp voice cut through the silence, his tone laced with authority.

"Not now," I snapped, my patience worn thin from the three wasted days spent chasing answers. Days spent trying to figure out if he had anything to do with our follower. It was obvious he didn't. He was too preoccupied with this lifestyle, playing the perfect host, the perfect father, to be capable of something so calculated.

I needed to get to Celeste now. I wasn't sure what I'd do when I'd get to her, but I guess I'd have to figure it out when the moment comes.

I walked out of the restaurant, the small talk reappearing as I made my way toward the exit. The drive to the penthouse was a blur. I gripped the steering wheel, the city lights streaking past like faint trails of my scattered focus. By the time I reached the penthouse, I barely remembered how I got there.

I stepped inside, the familiar scent of polished wood and faint lavender greeting me. But something was off. The silence hung heavy, too still, too empty.

"Celeste?" I called out, my voice echoing through the open space. No answer. I strode through the living room, checking the adjoining rooms, the kitchen, and even her usual spot by the floor to ceiling windows. Nothing.

"Mr. Micheal?" a soft voice interrupted my frantic search.

I turned to see Min-Soo, one of the staff members, standing at the edge of the hallway. She looked hesitant, as if she didn't want to speak, but knew she had to.

"Where is Celeste?" I asked, suddenly catching my breath.

"She left, sir," Min-Soo replied quietly. "With your cousin... Nari, I believe." Her words hit me like a punch to the gut.

I pinched the bridge of my nose, forcing myself to breathe, though the tightness in my chest wouldn't let up.

"Did they mention where they were going?" I managed to ask calmly.

Min-Soo hesitated, thinking of what she should say next.

"No, sir. Just that she was heading out with your cousin... to a club, I think."

"A club?" My jaw tightened, anger churning within me at the thought of Celeste out partying with my cousin.

"Yes, sir," she added carefully, as if trying to soften the blow.

I let out a sharp breath, dragging a hand through my hair. I hadn't expected Celeste to go out without me; I don't know why I thought she wouldn't, especially while I know the type of person she is. Bold, free, adventurous, and capable of being the very reason behind my mental breakdowns.

"Did she say which club?" I pressed.

"No, sir. Just that Nari wanted her to 'have a little fun,'" she answered.

"Right." My voice was clipped, frustration threatening to boil over. Fun? With Nari, "fun" could mean anything, and none of it sat well with me.

I strode across the room, grabbing my keys and jacket.

"If she comes back or calls, let me know immediately."

"Yes, sir," Min-Soo said, bowing slightly before stepping aside.

By the time I was in the car, I was already pulling up a list of the city's most popular clubs on my phone. If I knew Nari, and I did, there were only a handful of places she'd take Celeste. I clenched my jaw, determination hardening my resolve.

Celeste might have wanted to escape for the night, but she wasn't escaping me.

I parked my car and walked around the block, looking for a familiar underground club Nari had discovered a while ago. After she spent one night there, she decided that it was going to be her spot. After all, she was so determined for it to be 'her spot' that she bought out half of the shares and named it 'Treasure'. Of course, I was the only one in the family who knew of this. The scandal it would cause if they found out was something she and I both tried to avoid.

I didn't know what was worse, having Celeste explore the nightlife in Seoul by herself or willingly going with my cousin, who will definitely give her a night worth her while.

But what I couldn't understand was why it infuriated me so much, why I cared. So what if she parties? So what if she drinks? If she dances with a stranger that puts his hands on the curves of her body that I was dying to touch? Smell the sweet scent of her hair? Gets close enough to get a taste from the lips that seemed untouchable and sacred to me? I'll fucking kill him.

Fuck.

I was losing it, and I hadn't even stepped foot in the club yet.

Breathe Micheal, don't be a dumbass, not tonight.

I sent a text to Nari, letting her know I was stopping by.

I found the entrance tucked between two buildings, nearly invisible save for the faint purple glow of the neon sign above it. A couple stood outside, whispering in hushed tones as they smoked, and a bouncer leaned lazily against the doorframe.

The bouncer's eyes flicked over me as I approached, his posture straightening.

"Name?"

"Zhang," I said, my voice sharp. His brow furrowed, but the name did its job. Without a word, he stepped aside, pulling the door open to let me in. As I walked in, I received a text back from Nari.

> Nari: Don't you dare.

> Micheal: Too late, I'm here.

> Nari: Micheal go back home, she needs this tonight.

> Nari: I love you, but I'll have you kicked out.

> Micheal: You could, but how would the family take the news? I'm sure it's not too late to introduce a new family business.

I was blackmailing her; it was the lowest I'd go. I was definitely bluffing; I would never out her like that. Staring at my screen, I waited for her to give in.

> Nari: I understand now why one might want to shoot darts at your head.

> Nari: Fine.

I smirked as I read the text, walking deeper into the club. The music hit me first, deep and relentless, vibrating through my body as I made my way toward the bar. The air was thick with the mingling scents of sweat, alcohol, and perfume, and the dim lighting made it hard to focus on anything but the sea of moving bodies.

My eyes scanned the room, searching for her in the chaos. Nari would be easy to spot as she always sat in the VIP section. I wove my way through the crowd, ignoring the curious glances and brushes of hands as people passed me.

There she was. Nari was perched on one of the VIP couches, a drink in hand and a mischievous smirk on her lips. The moment she laid her eyes on me, she rolled them. She stood from her seat, allowing the bodyguard to unhook the velvet rope.

"You've got about five minutes to stop whatever territorial display this is and let the poor girl enjoy her night," she greeted me as she turned her eyes out to a specific spot on the dance floor. "Or are you really about to drag her out of here like some possessive caveman? Because, trust me, that won't be the brightest idea you've had."

I followed her gaze to the dancefloor, scanning the writhing crowd.

Then my eyes landed on her.

Celeste, right in the middle of the chaos and the breath I'd been holding, released all at once. She looked... stunning, her body swaying to the music. Her hair fell in loose waves around her shoulders, and the dress she wore hugged her figure in a way that made my throat tighten.

But she wasn't alone. A guy had sidled up to her, his hands resting far too casually on her hips, his face dangerously close to hers as they swayed together. Too close for my liking.

I saw red. My fists clenched at my sides, and I could barely hear the pounding bass anymore; all I could focus on was the way she was smiling, completely unaware, or worse, enjoying the company of the soon-to-be poor bastard.

"Don't do it," Nari warned, as if reading my mind. "You march out there, act like a possessive maniac when she isn't even yours, will only end badly. Trust me, Micheal, this isn't the play."

I tore my eyes away from Celeste long enough to glare at Nari.

"What's the play, then?"

Nari smirked, clearly enjoying my torment.

"You want her attention? Make her come to you."

I scowled. "I don't have time for this."

"No, but you've got time to stand here and fume while someone else has her attention?" She raised an eyebrow, sipping her drink. "Suit yourself, cousin. But if I were you, I'd either join the party or find a way to make her see she can't get you out of her head—even if she's trying to."

My jaw tightened as I looked back at Celeste, my resolve hardening. Fine. If this was a game, I wasn't about to lose. I grabbed a drink from the table, drank it, and made my way toward the crowd.

The alcohol burned down my throat, igniting something raw and reckless within me. I wasn't about to let her get away with this ridiculous stunt for attention, even if she was still oblivious to my presence. Celeste was the biggest pain in my ass, but she was the only one I've felt this way about.

Nari's words echoed in my mind as I wove through the

crowd, every step calculated, every move purposeful. If Celeste wanted a night to remember, then I'd make damn sure she wouldn't forget it.

The music throbbed louder as I closed the distance. Celeste's laughter rang out, clear and unguarded, cutting through the chaos like a blade. The sound sent a pang through my chest, half longing, half jealousy. She turned her head slightly, her eyes catching the strobe lights, and for a moment, I thought she saw me. But she didn't.

She was too focused on a complete stranger. More focused than she ever was on me.

The guy leaned in, his lips dangerously close to her ear as he said something that made her laugh again. My hands itched to rip him away, but Nari's voice rang in my head.

Make her come to you.

Okay.

I found an opening on the side of the dance floor, a group of women laughing and swaying to the music. I didn't need to say much, just a confident smile and a simple nod.

"Dance with me?" Their giggles and eager nods told me I'd picked the right group.

Walking onto the floor, I let the music take me captive. I didn't acknowledge the women around me; I barely even noticed them. My eyes kept wandering over their heads and locked on Celeste. I made sure to dance close enough for her to see me, far enough to seem unaffected.

With every beat in the music, I'd purposely dance closer and closer to her until I was about a few inches away from her. It didn't take long for her to notice. Her movements faltered for a split second, her head turning slightly in my direction.

I caught her gaze, and for a moment, the rest of the club faded away. Her eyes widened; a mix of surprise and something else, something I couldn't quite place.

I smirked, casually nodding her way. Then I turned my attention back to the women around me, acting as if Celeste's presence wasn't testing my patience. Out of the corner of my eye, I saw her lean away from the guy, her expression shifting. She was no longer laughing. No longer focused on him. She was focused on me.

Atta girl.

I continued to dance, taking the women for a small spin. I wanted her to feel the pull, the magnetic force that always seemed to draw us together no matter how much we tried to fight it. The guy must've said something to her because she shook her head, her gaze flicking back to me. She wasn't dancing or smiling anymore.

I stepped closer, not to her but to the edge of the dance floor, leaning casually against a pillar. I wanted her to make the next move, and I wanted her to come to me.

So I waited until she finally did.

Leaving the guy behind, she strode through the crowd, her steps hesitant but purposeful. Her eyes stayed locked on mine, and with every step she took, the tension between us grew, charged and electric.

Once she stood in front of me, she crossed her arms over her chest, her expression a mix of rage and confusion.

"What the hell are you doing here?"

I tilted my head, letting a lazy grin curl my lips.

"I'm enjoying my night. What about you?"

Her eyes narrowed, but there was no denying the flicker of something deeper in her gaze: curiosity, maybe even a hint of desire.

"You're following me," she accused, her voice low.

"Am I?" I asked, my tone light, teasing. "That's weird; last time I checked, I kind of own this club, so if anything, you're the one who's following me."

"That's not how that works," she huffed, clearly irritated by my words. "Nari owns it, not you," she added defensively.

"Nari bought it with the family fortune we have, so technically, it belongs to the Zhangs. Surprise, I'm a Zhang." I winked at her, speaking a bunch of gibberish. It doesn't work that way, but for the level of drunk Celeste is at, it'll be enough to shut her up.

She scoffed; the blush creeping up her neck betrayed her.

"Celeste," my voice softened as I leaned in slightly, just enough for her to hear me over the music. "Dance with me,"

Her breath hitched, and for a moment, her guard dropped. But then she straightened, her strong persona stepping back into frame.

"You have no right to be here," she said, but her words lacked conviction. Something in her voice kept deceiving her. "Not tonight."

"And yet, here I am," I replied, my voice steady, calm. "Tell me to leave, and I will."

She hesitated, her lips parted as if to speak, but no words came out.

I leaned closer, my voice soft, turning into a whisper.

"Or I could stay. Dance with me."

Her eyes searched mine, conflicted, and for a moment, I thought she might walk away. But then she surprised me.

"Fine," she said, her voice barely audible. "One dance. That's it."

I smiled, holding out my hand.

"One dance."

As her hand slipped into mine, a spark shot through me, and I knew one thing for certain... one dance wouldn't satisfy me enough. It could never be enough.

The music changed to a sultry rhythm that weaved through the air. I dragged her onto the dance floor, where the lights flickered like the heartbeat of the room. Her hand was in mine, warm and soft, her grip firm but hesitant, as if she was trying to remind herself that this was a short-term scenario.

Her body moved with precision, with a deliberate grace, swaying her hips to the rhythm with ease. Almost as if she was made to dance, instantly becoming a slave to the music. Every worry slipped away to a nonexistent world, where they no longer mattered. I matched her pace, letting her take the lead for a moment before guiding her into a turn. The flicker of surprise in her eyes as I pulled her closer told me she wasn't used to surrendering control, not even in something as simple as a dance.

"You're a natural," I murmured, my lips close to her ear. The blush that had crept up her neck earlier returned deeper now, spreading to her cheeks.

"Don't flatter yourself," she responded, though her voice wavered again. Her guard was still up, but cracks had started to form, tiny openings where I could glimpse the woman beneath the armor.

The song slowed, the tempo dipping into something more intimate. I placed a hand gently on her lower back, drawing her closer until there was barely any space between us. Her breathing quickened, and I felt it, her resolve trembling like a fragile flame in a storm.

"You're not making this easy," she said softly, her head tilted slightly downward, avoiding my gaze.

"Good," I replied, my fingers brushing over hers where they rested on my shoulder. "Nothing worth it ever is."

Her eyes flicked up to meet mine, and in them, I saw the battle she was fighting with herself. The need to hold on to her defenses clashed with the pull of something deeper, something neither of us could name yet.

"Why are you really here?" she finally asked, her voice quieter now, as though afraid of the answer.

"To be fully honest, I have no idea why," I said, my tone unwavering, "But the only thing I know is that I had to be here."

Her lips parted again, a soft intake of breath, but this time, she didn't speak. Instead, she let herself lean into me, just slightly, her movements less guarded. It was subtle, but it was everything.

The song faded, but neither of us moved. The world around us blurred into background noise, the people and lights a distant haze. Celeste's hand tightened on mine, and I wondered if she felt it too: the unspoken promise, the moment that felt like the beginning of something neither of us was ready to admit.

"Micheal..." she started, but I shook my head, cutting her off.

"Don't ruin it," I whispered. "Not tonight."

I dipped my head lower, my lips inches away from hers. My heart beat drastically in my chest, strong enough to rip out of my skin. The air between us hummed with an unspoken promise, a silent plea for something neither of us was ready to say aloud.

We both stared at each other with curiosity, confusion roaming around us. Anything could happen right now, it could do either way. She'll either stab me, or she'll kiss me.

She took a breath, her chest rising and falling in a steady rhythm, and for a moment, I wondered if she could hear the pounding of my heart. It felt like the world was holding its breath, waiting for the inevitable.

Her lips parted slightly, a soft invitation. I couldn't resist any longer. I closed the distance, brushing my lips against hers, testing the waters. It was a featherlight touch, just enough to send sparks through my veins. She didn't pull away. In fact, her hand found my chest, the touch gentle yet firm, grounding me in that moment.

Right then and there, my lips pressed against hers.

Her lips were soft and warm, like a whisper against mine. The room, the world, the mess of emotions we'd both been avoiding. It was just her and me, suspended in that perfect, fragile instant.

Her hands trailed up and grabbed at my hair, pulling me closer as if she could erase the space between us completely. The urgency in her touch matched the wild beating of my heart, and I responded in kind, deepening the kiss, letting go of everything else.

I could feel the heat radiating between us, the electric charge of every second that passed. My hands slid down her back, holding her against me, not wanting to let go, not even for a breath.

Her body molded perfectly against mine, and I felt something shift, something stronger than the desire swirling in the air.

But even as her breath quickened, and I lost myself in the press of her lips, my mind fought to stay tethered to reality. There was too much unsaid between us. Too much unspoken fear and hesitation, buried under the weight of what this moment meant.

But when her lips moved against mine again, the world seemed to dissolve, and all I could think about was the taste of her, the feel of her, and the pull that had always been there between us. It was everything I could've imagined.

The taste of cinnamon branded itself on my tongue; the shapes of her curves stayed marked in my brain, and the tension was like a taut string, pulled so tight it could snap at any given moment.

But even as the kiss deepened, there was something pulling at the edges of my mind. The knowledge that this wasn't something either of us could easily walk away from. Not once it happened. Not once she knew…

I pulled back, breathless, our foreheads resting against each other, our eyes searching the other's. Neither of us said a word.

She blinked, eyes wide, her lips trembling as if she was struggling to reconcile the touch we'd just shared with everything we'd fought over. The confusion in her eyes mirrored my own. I wanted to push her away, but there was something raw and undeniable pulling me back.

This kiss... it changed nothing, and yet it changed everything, and we both knew it.

"Don't," she whispered, her voice low, dangerous. "Don't think for a second this means anything." Her words hit me like a slap, but it didn't sting as much as I thought it would.

The denial was expected, but it didn't make the way her lips had felt against mine any less real. I swallowed hard, a knot tightening in my chest.

"I'm not the one who's confused here," I shot back, my voice sharper than I intended. "Don't pretend you didn't feel it, too."

Her jaw clenched, her gaze faltering for just a second before she steadied herself, retreating into the icy mask she wore so well.

"I don't feel anything," she lied, the words hanging between us like smoke.

"Then why are you still here?" I couldn't stop the question, even though I knew the answer. I wasn't the only one who felt the shift.

She didn't respond immediately, her chest rising and falling with every shallow breath.

"Because you're infuriating," she muttered, the slightest tremor in her voice betraying her. "Because of your stupid debt of seven dates, which I'm still trying to understand."

I didn't respond; I didn't know what to say. I couldn't tell her the truth... that I was told to do this in order to succeed with Dylan's plan.

"I'm leaving with Nari tonight," she said awkwardly, her eyes darting around the club, avoiding my gaze.

"Right." My voice was tight, my jaw clenched. "When are you going to let yourself feel something for once in your life?" I spat, the words harsh, sharper than I'd intended.

I hadn't meant to go there, but the pressure of the past two months, chasing her for this job, pushing her away and trying to get her to fall for me, was finally starting to take its toll. Now I realized it wasn't working on her; it was working on *me*. I hated the way her presence made my pulse quicken, how I kept coming back, even when I knew better.

Her eyes flickered with something… regret, maybe? I wasn't sure, and that frustrated me even more.

"Goodnight, Micheal," she said, her voice colder now, like a door slamming shut.

I watched her walk away; her hips swayed as she made her way toward my cousin. I watched them both exit through the double doors, only the music keeping me company.

I had to remind myself that this was all a game. A job. I was supposed to be gathering information, playing her like everyone else. But with every moment that passed, the lines blurred a little more. I wasn't sure where the job ended and my feelings began, and that terrified me.

CHAPTER 26
MICHEAL

The next morning, I woke up on the hard, concrete steps at Han River. My head was pounding like someone had taken a sledgehammer to it. I must've blacked out last night because I don't recall how I got here. I sat up and rubbed my temples, trying to force my brain to come into focus. Same clothes as yesterday—white linen shirt and black pants.

My phone buzzed in my pocket; I pulled it out and glanced at the screen: Dylan Cruz. I swiped to answer, holding the phone close to my ear as I leaned forward.

"Fill me in; how's it going with Celeste so far?" he asked, getting straight to the point. I deeply sighed as I looked out at the light reflecting on the water. How's it going? The question rang in my head like a bell. I would like to know that as much as he would. I didn't know where we stood after last night.

"Well, it's looking a bit complicated right now," I responded, wanting to avoid giving him a full answer. Avoiding the truth because a part of me knew that Dylan would be able to sense my feelings through my voice. I don't think I was ready for anyone to know how I was feeling, and I didn't want to accept it myself.

"Complicated? That isn't the answer I want to hear from you," he responded, his voice straining from the phone. "I expect a 'I've got her where we want' or even a simple 'good.' How do you not have her wrapped around your finger yet?" he asked, sounding frustrated.

"I kissed her last night," I admitted. Really, I wanted to keep this bit to myself, but hearing him downplay everything I've been doing annoyed me. He spoke like everything was so simple, but he didn't know what type of woman I was dealing with. Celeste wasn't like any other woman; she was tough.

"... and?" He asked, waiting for a longer response.

"What? You want me to explain to you step by step how it happened? We kissed. That's all there is to it? It's not a big deal," I answered defensively, then realizing how guilty I sounded, like I was hiding something.

"Micheal," Dylan paused, his tone turning sharp and deliberate. "You're not supposed to fall for her. Remember that."

I scoffed, leaning forward and resting my elbows on my knees.

"Who said anything about falling for her? It's just a kiss. It was part of the plan. You know, get close to her, earn her trust. That's all it was."

"Right," Dylan replied, skepticism heavy in his voice. "You sound awfully defensive for someone who's not catching feelings. Don't forget why you're doing this. You have a job to do. Celeste is not just some girl; she's a means to an end."

The words hit harder than I expected, even though I'd heard them before. I knew the drill: stick to the mission, stay detached. But the memory of the kiss lingered, uninvited, like a ghost I couldn't shake off. Her lips, soft and hesitant at first, then hungry and raw. That wasn't just a calculated move. It felt... real.

"I know what I'm doing," I lied, trying to push the thoughts away. "You don't need to micromanage me."

"Clearly, I do," Dylan shot back. "Because complicated is not the result we're aiming for. You're slipping, Micheal. Pull yourself together before this blows up in your face, therefore blowing up in my face. That's something I won't allow."

I clenched my jaw, staring at the shimmering water. His words stung, but he wasn't entirely wrong. This was supposed to be straightforward, get close to Celeste, find out what she knew, and report back. But straightforward went out the window the moment she looked at me with those fire-lit eyes that saw straight through the walls I thought were impenetrable.

"Dylan, I've got this," I said, my voice steadier now. "I'll keep her in check. Just give me some space to handle it my way."

There was a pause on the other end of the line.

"Fine," Dylan finally said. "But don't forget, we're running out of time. Keep your head in the game."

The line went dead, leaving me alone with my thoughts. I tossed the phone onto the bench beside me and ran a hand through my hair, frustration bubbling under my skin.

I needed to get with the program, and I had to get Celeste on the same page. Or at least try to get her to trust me. After a while of sitting, I stood up and decided to walk along the trail.

I got lost in my thoughts, tuning out the world surrounding me. I stuffed my hands into my pockets, the cool crisp air biting at my skin as I walked. The rhythmic crunch of gravel beneath my shoes was the only sound grounding me.

How was I going to confront her now? Should I make my way toward Nari's apartment? Track her down and try to speak to her? I obviously couldn't force her into giving me a minute of her time. That wouldn't help the situation at hand.

The question I should be asking myself is how am I going to get information out of her? How was I going to ask her? Or where could I find answers? Where did she keep them?

Lost in thought, I almost didn't notice the soft echo of footsteps behind me. They were faint, blending into the ambient noise of the city, but as I kept walking, it became harder to ignore. A sinking feeling crept into my gut, and my muscles tensed.

I realized I wasn't imagining it. Someone was following me. I stopped abruptly, the quiet hum of the river the only thing breaking the silence. The sound of footsteps halted just a fraction too late.

In a flash, I turned on my heel, grabbed the shadow trailing me, and slammed them hard on the ground. The impact reverberated, drawing a sharp grunt from the figure beneath me. Pinning them down with my knee, I grabbed their collar and leaned in close, my voice low and dangerous.

"Who the hell are you?" I growled, my grip tightening. "Why are you following me?"

The person squirmed beneath me, their hands shooting up in surrender. Now that I could see them clearly in the faint light, I noticed he was older than I expected—a guy in his late twenties or early thirties, wide-eyed and huffing.

"Micheal," he let out a strained voice. Hearing my name from his mouth only triggers me to press harder, pinning him more firmly against the ground.

"Don't make me ask again! Who the hell sent you?! How do you know my name?!" I barked, my gaze unfaltering.

He winced under the pressure, his breaths coming out in short gasps, but his eyes never left mine. "No one," he croaked, his voice cracking with the effort.

"No one sent me."

"Wrong answer," I growled, shoving him harder against the cold pavement. "Try again."

"I'm not your enemy," he stammered, his voice shaky but steady enough to make me hesitate. I wasn't buying it. Not yet.

"I need more than that or this will go very badly for you," I threatened him harder.

He winced but held his ground, staring back at me with a mix of fear and determination. The silence stretched between us, heavy and charged, until finally, he spoke, his voice quieter now.

"I'm your brother."

CHAPTER 27
MICHEAL

"I'M YOUR BROTHER." HIS WORDS STRUCK ME LIKE A BOLT OF lightning. I took a moment to take it all in and fully understand them. I looked at how similar his features were to mine; he had dark hair and striking green eyes. Before I threw him on the ground, I noticed how he was a tad bit taller than me.

"Brother?" I echoed, disbelief dripping from my tone. "I don't have a brother."

"You do," he said firmly, though his voice trembled. "Our mother, Evelyn–"

"Don't," I snapped, cutting him off as anger flared in my chest. The mention of her was enough to set me off. "You don't get to bring her into this. Not here. Not now."

"I'm not lying," he said, his voice quieter but no less determined. "There's so much you don't know. Let me explain. Please."

I stared at him, my grip loosening slightly as the weight of his words settled in. His face, his tone, the desperation in his eyes, all felt too real. But how could this be true?

"How much are they paying you to do this little act, huh? You think I'm fucking stupid?!" I yelled, quickly losing my patience. I didn't have time for this; whoever set this up was in for a real treat.

"Why would I be fucking lying? You're stubborn as shit!" he yelled back; he was also losing his patience. "If someone sent me, how would I know things only you would know?" he asked, dangling it as bait.

"Yeah? What do you know?" I quickly chuckled in anger, appalled at how dedicated he was to this role. But you know what? Fine, I'll take the bait.

"Our mother used to sing us a special song at night," he said, his voice steady, as if each word had been rehearsed. "Lyrics she wrote and never shared with anyone else."

His words ignited something buried deep, a memory I hadn't dared revisit. I narrowed my eyes, refusing to give him an inch.

"Really? That's not exactly unique. A lot of mothers do that," I countered sharply. "So, tell me—do you know the lyrics, or are you bluffing?"

For a moment, he held my gaze, unwavering. Then, with a quiet confidence, he began,

"Little boy, strong and scared,
Will you grow to fight with honor and care?
Will you bring victory, hold honor in your place,
Will you hesitate, or find courage in the race?"

My heart slammed in my chest as the words washed over me. Her voice—it was there, alive in every syllable. I could hear her, feel her, as if she were right beside me.

"Start talking," I demanded, my voice dropping into a cold, steady tone. My grip loosened slightly, but I didn't let him go. Not yet.

"I've been waiting for you to return. I tried to get a hold of you before you left, but it's not exactly easy to get in touch with a Zhang, is it?" he said. "I was oblivious to the fact that I had a brother like you. But when I found out, I knew that I needed to track you down."

"Why? For what reason? What could you want from me?" I asked, remembering the night my mother left. "My mother left me behind to run off and have another family, *another son.*" The words tasted bitter on my tongue. The truth was finally coming out to light.

"You don't know," he chuckled, like he was holding this big missing piece of the story. His chuckle vibrated throughout my body, igniting a storm of irritation that tightened my chest and set my nerves on edge.

"Know what? She left and never came back for me. A deadbeat mother. No excuse will ever justify that," I said, suddenly feeling the urge to cry. I released my hold on his collar and stepped back, trying to get my emotions in line.

"Don't speak about her like that," he spat. "Don't speak when you don't have all the parts of the story. Of course the fucking Zhangs would cover up the true reason." He stood up from the ground, dusting off dirt from his pants.

"She told my father the day she left that she never loved me. My father and I had spent that entire night sobbing on the floor. Do you have any idea how horrible that felt? Especially as a kid? I want to know nothing about that woman."

"She had a reason, Micheal!"

"Oh yeah? Enlighten me? What reason could possibly justify her actions?" I asked, trying to dial down the anxiety I felt. My hands slightly shook with how badly I wanted to know.

"She was forced to leave!" he bellowed.

"Cut the bull, she wasn't forced to leave. She walked out the door with her own free will! Nobody held her at gunpoint." I blurted out, tired of a stranger making excuses for the woman that gave birth to me. Fuck him, he knew nothing.

"Yeah, well, they might as well have," he replied, his nostrils flaring slightly as he fought to contain his anger. His jaw clenched, the tension in his voice barely concealed beneath a thin veneer of control. "The infamous Zhangs, one of the richest, most powerful families in all of Asia. Tell me—are you even aware that your family controls the majority of the medical field here? Or are you just as blind to their reach as you are to the damage they've caused?"

His words struck like a whip, sharp and deliberate. He leaned forward, his dark eyes boring into mine, filled with a mix of fury and disbelief.

"Do you even understand what that means? Your family held the keys to *my* survival. And they used it—*used her*—to keep their empire spotless. She didn't just leave you, Micheal. She made a deal with the devil to save me."

"What the hell is that supposed to mean?" I asked, slowly losing it.

"I had cancer, Micheal," he confessed, his voice dropping to a raw, vulnerable tone. His earlier anger seemed to waver, replaced by something deeper: pain, regret, maybe even guilt. "When I was a kid, I was dying. And your family knew it. They saw a sick boy with no money, no future, and a mother desperate enough to do anything to save him."

The words hit me like a punch to the gut, but he wasn't finished.

"They gave her a choice. She could stay with you and watch me die, or she could leave everything behind—her son, her life—and save me. In return, your family promised to provide the best treatment money could buy, and they did. They cured me. But only under one condition: she could never go back. Never see you again. Never even contact you."

My stomach twisted as he spoke, the weight of his revelation settling over me like a heavy blanket.

"That's insane," I muttered, shaking my head in disbelief. "Why the hell would they even care about keeping her away from me?"

He gave a humorless laugh, shaking his head.

"Because a woman leaving her old life for money looks

bad for the Zhangs, doesn't it? They couldn't risk the scandal. A single mother abandoning her child? That's a story they could bury. But if she ever tried to reconnect with you, their reputation would be on the line. So they made sure she stayed away."

I could feel my fists clenching at my sides, my nails digging into my palms. My head was spinning, anger and grief clashing in a chaotic storm inside me.

"She could have told me," I said, my voice trembling. "She could have found a way–"

"She couldn't!" he snapped, his voice rising again. "Don't you get it? She wanted to, but she couldn't. She spent every day praying you'd understand, that one day, maybe, when you were old enough, you'd find out the truth. But she didn't have time, Micheal. She–" His voice broke, and he took a shaky breath. "She died before she could."

Those last words slammed into me, knocking the wind out of my lungs. My vision blurred, and for a moment, I thought I might collapse under the weight of it all.

She's... gone?" I whispered, the word barely escaping my lips.

"She's gone," he confirmed, his voice quieter now, heavy with the grief we both shared. "She never stopped loving you, no matter what you think. You were her missing piece, Micheal. The one thing she could never stop longing for. I couldn't fill that spot up myself, no matter how hard I tried. Half of her heart belonged to me, and the other to you."

I staggered back a step, my mind reeling. The anger I'd carried for so long was crumbling, replaced by a grief I wasn't ready to face.

"Why now?" I asked quietly, trying to keep in the tears that threatened to escape. "Why come find me and tell me all of this now?"

He exhaled sharply, his gaze shifting away for a moment.

"I had to make sure they wouldn't trace anything back to me. Or my family."

"Your family?" I asked, my chest tightening at the thought. Was he talking about my mother's side, the part of her life I never knew?

His eyes met mine, steady and unwavering.

"Our family," he corrected gently. The weight of those words pressed against me, unfamiliar and foreign. "They're in Busan. We all live there. I took the train here to find you."

I studied his face, searching for something, any hint of deceit, but there was none. His features were open, earnest, and tinged with exhaustion. He looked around then, his eyes scanning the crowded streets of Seoul, as if seeing the city for the first time or perhaps checking for watchful eyes.

"Busan," I repeated softly, the name feeling strange on my tongue. It wasn't a place I'd ever thought to connect with *my family*. "So, she... she built a life there? With you?"

He nodded. "She did what she could. It wasn't perfect. Hell, it was hard most of the time. But we survived, Micheal. And every step of the way, she carried the guilt of leaving you. It haunted her. I think that's why she never really told me everything—just enough to know she'd lost something, someone, she couldn't get back."

I looked down, the flood of emotions making it hard to breathe. Anger. Sadness. Confusion. A strange, aching curiosity.

"Why tell me about them now, though?" I asked, my voice barely above a whisper. "What do you want from me?"

"I want you to know the truth," he said simply. "Not for me, not even for her—but for you. You've been carrying this weight your whole life, haven't you? The anger, the resentment, the questions with no answers. You deserve to know the truth. And... you deserve to know them."

"Them," I echoed hollowly. My chest tightened as the idea

sank in. A family I didn't know existed. A connection to a part of my mother's life I'd never been part of.

"They're waiting," he added softly. "If you're ready. If not, I'll go back and leave you to decide. But they want to meet you, Micheal. Even if you're not sure how you feel, they want to know you."

I swallowed hard, unsure of what to say. The streetlights around us flickered on, casting long shadows across the pavement. My hands curled into fists at my sides, and I looked away, my thoughts racing. Could I face them? Did I want to? Could I forgive her for the life she built without me?

"How am I supposed to just *trust* what you're telling me? How do I know it's not a lie or a trick to get me down there?"

"Why don't you ask the people you call family," he suggested, looking down at his watch and reaching for his pockets. "There's a train leaving for Busan tomorrow morning. I got two tickets for us, but I think I'll just get one for tonight since I accomplished what I need to. Here, they're yours. Use them however you'd like." He handed me two KTX high-speed bullet train tickets. The ticket was a smooth, semi gloss paper with a pastel green shade that contrasted well with the details and text on it.

Scanning the ticket, it says it departs from Seoul at 9:48 AM and is expected to arrive at Busan at 12:38 PM. Train number is 507, car number 2, and seats 2C, 3C. I looked up from the ticket to my brother's face.

"I'll think about it," I finally spoke, looking back down at the tickets.

"My numbers written on the back of ticket 2C, give me a call if you find yourself on the train." He shrugged with a small grin on his face, a small facial expression, and yet it reminded me of the time my mother used to smile at me. The resemblance was there.

Maybe, just maybe, he was telling me the truth.

"Min Ho," he added as I read the name above the phone number. "That's my name." I nodded as I watched him give me a small smile and walk away. The strange twist in my chest didn't go away. It was as if a part of me was desperate to believe him.

The thought twisted inside me, sharp and relentless. I'd spent years running in circles, trapped in a cycle of hurt and confusion. But now, there was something different. Something that felt like the edge of a revelation, just within reach.

I tucked the tickets into my pocket, my fingers brushing the ink on the back as if it could offer some kind of comfort. I could feel the weight of the truth they might hold. But I wasn't ready for it yet. Not now. I needed answers first.

And no matter what happens tonight, I *will* get them.

CHAPTER 28
CELESTE

"Morning," Nari spoke softly, handing me a warm cup of coffee as she entered the guest room. Last night I returned home with Nari. I wanted to avoid running into Micheal in the morning so my best option was staying with Nari for now. "Quite the event last night, don't you think?" She asked, reminding me of everything that had happened the night before. I groaned at the memory of kissing Micheal and actually enjoying it. I liked it a bit too much, and that concerned me.

I wasn't ready to find out what the kiss meant for us now. This wasn't at all what I had planned when the girls and I decided to call this trip a 'goodbye Micheal' trip. Now, it was looking more like a 'Welcome Micheal' trip.

So much has happened this past week and a half. It's Thursday, and our flight back to New York was in four days—Monday night—and I was about to leave with even more luggage than I had brought with me.

Mentally, that is.

I sighed, gripping the warm mug in my hands.

"Don't remind me," I yawned.

"I know you probably won't want to talk about it right now,

but eventually you'll have to confront him," she said as she sat on the edge of the bed.

"Eventually," I muttered, staring into the swirling steam rising from my mug. The rich aroma of the coffee wasn't enough to distract me from the gnawing thoughts in my head.

"I mean, you kissed him," Nari continued with a teasing glint in her eye. "That's kind of a big deal, don't you think?"

"It was just the heat of the moment," I shot back, a little too quickly. "Probably the alcohol in the soju, the music, and..." I trailed off, feeling my cheeks warm. Who was I kidding? That kiss wasn't just an accident; it had felt real, like something I'd been avoiding for far too long.

Nari tilted her head, studying me like I was a puzzle she was piecing together.

"Hmm. Sure, blame the ambiance. But you might want to figure out how you really feel before this trip is over, or you'll leave with even more unresolved baggage."

I groaned again, letting my head fall back against the pillow. The thought of facing Micheal after that kiss made my stomach flip in a way I wasn't ready to admit to anyone, not even myself.

"I'll handle it... eventually," I muttered. "But first, I need more coffee and zero judgment."

Nari chuckled, standing up and stretching.

"Fine, no judgment—for now. But don't wait too long. You can only avoid him for so many breakfasts."

I glanced at the guest bed's ridiculously pristine décor, plush white linens, fluffy pillows that seemed untouched, and a throw blanket folded to perfection. It was almost comical how every single one of the Zhangs' homes seemed to have these magazine-worthy guest rooms. As if their lives were effortlessly in order while mine was spiraling into chaos.

"I know, I know. I'm glad I met you; I don't know what I'd do if you weren't here," I confessed.

Nari turned back, her expression softening.

"You'd figure it out," she said with a small smile. "But I'm glad I'm here too. Someone's gotta keep you from overthinking yourself into oblivion. Plus, the guest room so desperately needed a guest," she chuckled.

I gave her a weak smile in return, the warmth of her presence cutting through some of the uncertainty swirling inside me.

"I just... I don't know what to say to him," I admitted. "Last night was a lot. Too much... and now it's like the second I see him, I'm not sure if I'll want to run away or—"

"Run *toward* him?" Nari interjected with a knowing raise of her brow.

"Ugh, stop." I groaned, setting my coffee down on the nightstand and burying my face in my hands. "This was supposed to be a clean break. A goodbye. Now it's all messy and complicated, and I have no idea how to deal with it."

"Maybe it doesn't have to be messy," Nari suggested gently. "Maybe it's just... different from what you planned. That doesn't mean it's bad."

I peeked at her through my fingers. "I hate how you make sense."

She grinned, unrepentant. "It's a gift. Now come on, let's eat something before we leave. How about a pastry with coffee?"

"Sure, but why are we leaving so soon?" I repeated, looking at her with narrowed eyes.

"My uncle just called, he said Micheal wanted us to come over for a family lunch. I don't know what's weirder, that Micheal planned this, or that Micheal planned this. He hates family gatherings. I mean, you witnessed it," she explained as she stood from the edge of the bed.

"Really?" I asked, totally surprised by the news.

"Yes, you might want to brace yourself. He's definitely waiting for you."

"Yeah," I quietly muttered, my stomach twisted at the thought.

"I left an outfit ready for you in the closet. You can't possibly go back wearing this," she said as she pulled the dress from the straps. "I mean, don't get me wrong—this would absolutely turn heads, but our grandmother would probably faint, and we'd never hear the end of it."

I couldn't help but smirk at her exaggeration.

She walked to the closet and pulled out a neatly hung outfit: a soft knit sweater and a pair of tailored jeans, simple but classy.

"This…" she declared, "… says 'I'm here for family lunch, not to disrupt the peace.'"

I eyed the outfit on the hanger, nodding slowly.

"It's perfect," I admitted. "Thanks for saving me from potential humiliation."

"It's what I do," Nari said with a wink as she laid the outfit on the bed. "Now, get dressed and let's go."

"I thought we were having a pastry with coffee," I said, not knowing the time.

"It's noon; lunch will be in two hours." Nari said, giving me one last encouraging smile before disappearing into the hallway, leaving me alone with my thoughts and my mug of half-finished coffee.

I sighed, staring out the window at the sunlight streaming through the curtains. The idea of a family lunch, planned by Micheal of all people, was enough to throw me off completely. Micheal, who usually avoided gatherings like the plague? The same Micheal who, during the last family event, had spent the evening hiding on the rooftop?

I shook my head, trying to make sense of it all. The kiss, this sudden lunch invitation: it was like I'd stepped into some alternate universe where nothing followed the rules I thought I understood.

Setting my mug down, I swung my legs over the side of the bed and ran my fingers through my hair. Nari was right. If Micheal had gone through the effort of arranging something he normally despised, it wasn't just casual. He had something to say or something he wanted... and it likely involved me.

The thought sent a nervous buzz through me. I didn't even know what I'd say when I saw him. Would he act like nothing had happened? Would he bring it up?

I groaned, burying my face in my hands for a moment.

Why couldn't life just follow the script I'd written for it?

But deep down, I knew that script was flawed from the start. If I really wanted closure or clarity, I'd have to step out of my comfort zone and meet Micheal where he was: family lunch, awkwardness and all.

With a deep breath, I stood, got dressed, and headed downstairs.

An hour later, we found ourselves at the entrance of Mr. Zhang's penthouse. We made our way to the elevator and prepared ourselves for whatever was waiting for us when we showed up. I couldn't help but feel like something was off, like this wasn't going to be what I was expecting.

The elevator doors slid open with a mechanical *ding*. The silence in the hallway was unnerving, broken only by the faint hum of the air conditioning. My grip tightened on the strap of my bag, the weight of unease pressing down harder with every step we took toward the door.

"Ready?" I asked, more to myself than to Nari.

"It'll be fine," she responded as she stepped out of the elevator. She walked through the halls, her soft clink of her heels on the floor filling the silence. I quietly, but hesitantly followed behind her as she maneuvered herself through the house.

I heard a faint chatter at the end of the hall, and I was sure that we were only seconds away from arriving. I started feeling sick to my stomach; my nerves not allowing me to think or even function properly.

Don't overthink it.

The faint chatter grew louder as we approached the end of the hall, muffled but undeniably present. My heart thudded in my chest, each beat amplifying the uneasy rhythm in my head.

Nari glanced over her shoulder, her expression unreadable but calm. My hands trembled slightly as I adjusted the strap of my bag again, trying to ground myself. The voice in my head repeated like a mantra:

Don't overthink it. Don't overthink it.

The murmur of conversation died the moment we stepped into the room. A dozen pairs of eyes turned toward us, assessing, calculating. The atmosphere was thick—too many undercurrents for me to grasp all at once.

Nari didn't miss a beat. She stepped forward with that same poised confidence, the click of her heels on the tile cutting through the silence like a metronome. She pulled out a chair and sat gracefully.

"We've arrived; I apologize for the late appearance. I had to get a few of my ducks in order, but all is good now," she spoke.

"Good," a deep voice broke the silence. I didn't have to look up to know it belonged to the man at the head of the table—Mr. Zhang. He exuded the same quiet power I'd felt in the home's design, like he didn't need to say much for people to understand he was in control. "We can begin."

I quickly scanned over the room, searching for any signs of Micheal. But I didn't see him, he wasn't here yet. I wondered where he was and why he wasn't the first to be here; this was all part of his idea to begin with.

As I stood at the door frame, a hand slightly brushed mine at my side. I quickly glanced behind me to find Micheal behind me. He placed a hand on my waist and pulled me back from view.

"Micheal," I said, searching his face for any signs of his plan.

"Are your bags packed?" he whispered as he leaned in, tucking a strand of hair behind my ear. The gesture is small, but big enough to make me feel on edge.

I nodded, giving him a confused look, right as I'm about to open my mouth to ask; he answered.

"I'll explain it later, okay? Just—" He takes a breath, looking down at the floor. "Be ready for my signal; grab your bags and wait downstairs for me. Okay?"

"Okay," I quietly agreed, deciding to trust him and not ask any further questions. His eyes slightly widened as he waited for any questions or arguments. He seemed surprised that I went along with what he said.

To be fair, I hadn't a clue why I decided to blindly follow him. But a part of me could feel the desperation on his side; he wasn't telling me anything right this second for a reason, and I needed to wait.

"I'm sorry for what you're about to see. If you want to go downstairs and wait for me there, you can." I shook my head frantically.

"No. I'll stay here and wait for the signal." I grabbed his hand and squeezed it, as I could see his nerves showing. "It'll be okay," I comforted him, without knowing what was going on.

He nodded and released his hold on me, walking into the room. I followed behind him to see what was going to happen next.

"About time; we were waiting for the host to make his appearance. Now, what's this all about?" Micheal's dad said, standing up from his seat. Everyone looked back and forth between the both of them. Something definitely felt off.

"I didn't want to accuse any of you without hearing your side," Micheal began by saying. "Let's make this quick and simple. I ask the questions and you answer without bullshitting me." Tiny gasps filled the room with Micheal's words.

The tension in the room thickened as Micheal's voice cut through the air. He stood tall, his presence commanding, though I could see the faint twitch in his jaw that showed his nerves. His father's sharp gaze bore into him, a mixture of skepticism and authority.

"What's going on here, Micheal?" one of the men at the table asked, his voice tight, a hint of unease creeping in. Micheal ignored him, his focus unyielding as he turned to his father. "This all started because someone here decided they could act without consequences. I don't care who you think you are or why you thought it was okay to do. Today, the truth comes out."

I felt like an outsider looking in on a chess game where I didn't know the rules, yet every move seemed to matter. Micheal's words echoed in my mind: *Be ready for my signal.* My pulse raced as I tried to decipher what that signal might be and why he seemed so desperate for me to trust him.

"First question," Micheal continued, his voice cutting through the thick silence. "Who's brilliant plan was to send her away?"

"Pardon?" his father asked.

"My mother. I want the truth and I want it now." The room seemed to freeze, the weight of Micheal's question hanging in the air like a storm cloud about to burst. His father's smirk faltered for a fraction of a second, replaced by something colder, more calculating. The others at the table exchanged uneasy glances, some shifting uncomfortably in their seats, while others sat stone-still, their expressions carefully neutral.

"Micheal," his father said slowly, his tone measured, "You're digging up matters that are better left buried. Your mother made her choices–"

"*Don't.*" Micheal's voice was sharp, slicing through his father's excuse like a blade. "Don't twist this. I know she didn't choose to leave. I want to know who decided it for her." His hands rested on the back of the chair in front of him, knuckles white with tension. "Who gave the order?" The sheer determination in Micheal's voice sent a ripple of unease through the room. He wasn't going to back down.

"Micheal," a woman at the far end of the table finally spoke, her tone soft but tinged with warning, "This isn't the time or place—"

"Oh, this is exactly the time and the place," Micheal snapped, his piercing gaze locking onto her. "You've all had your time to play games, to lie and manipulate. But not anymore."

His father sighed heavily, the sound deliberate.

"Son," he said, rising from his seat, "You're letting your emotions cloud your judgment. This is why you're not ready to take the reins. You're still too... naïve."

Micheal took a step forward, his posture rigid. "Call me naïve all you want. Just answer the question. Who decided to take her away? Was it you?"

The room held its collective breath as his father met his gaze, unflinching.

"Don't be fucking ridiculous; I loved her!" he yelled.

"Then who was it?!" Micheal yelled back, the volume of his voice could shatter glass.

"Your grandfather," he admitted, ashamed of his words. "At the time, I didn't understand why he did it. But soon I realized that everything he has done had been for this family, for our survival. You wouldn't understand–"

"Try me." Micheal's tone was venomous now, his composure beginning to crack under the weight of his anger. "Because from where I'm standing, all I see is a bunch of cowards hiding behind excuses."

A flicker of guilt or anger crossed his father's face, but it was gone just as quickly.

"Be careful, Micheal," he warned, his voice low and dangerous. "I'm still the man of this house and I will not be disrespected."

Micheal squared his shoulders, his determination unwavering.

"Disrespected? You think for one second that I still have respect for you?" He spoke the words like they were bitter on his tongue. He glanced around the room, addressing everyone now. "If no one speaks up, I'll assume you're all complicit, and believe me, I'll deal with every last one of you."

The room erupted in a low murmur, tension bubbling over as Micheal's words struck nerves. I could feel the air crackling with anticipation, the stakes rising with every passing second. My fingers itched to move, to act, but I waited, heart pounding, for Micheal's signal, whatever it might be.

"You know what? I think I've heard enough. I want nothing to do with this family." Micheal's voice rang out, resolute and dark.

He turned, his eyes locking onto mine. At that moment, I saw the weight of years of frustration, anger, and betrayal etched into his face. He looked like a man who had carried a burden for too long and was finally ready to let it go, no matter the consequences.

"Let's go," he said, his tone softer now, but still firm.

My heart raced as I nodded, already moving toward him without hesitation. The room buzzed with disbelief, whispers escalating into arguments behind us. Micheal's father's voice boomed over the others.

"Micheal! Don't you dare walk away!" he barked, his tone filled with both fury and desperation. Micheal didn't stop. His hand found mine, gripping it tightly as he led me toward the door. His stride was purposeful, each step defying the hold his family had tried to maintain on him for so long.

"Micheal!" his father roared again, but this time, there was no response.

As we reached the hallway, our bags were ready by the elevator. Someone placed them out, ready for us to grab and leave.

"Are you okay?" I asked, glancing at him as we hurried toward the elevator.

"Not yet," he admitted, his jaw clenched. "But I will be."

The elevator doors opened, and we stepped inside. Micheal hit the button for the ground floor, his hand still gripping mine as if afraid to let go. As the doors slid closed, sealing us away from the chaos above, I couldn't help but feel like we were stepping into something entirely new, uncertain but free.

"Thank you," he said quietly, his voice carrying a mix of gratitude and vulnerability.

"For what?" I asked, my voice barely above a whisper.

"For trusting me," he replied, his eyes meeting mine. "Even when I didn't deserve it."

I squeezed his hand, offering him a small, reassuring smile. "You'll be okay," I said. "We'll be okay."

CHAPTER 29
CELESTE

We got into a car and drove far away from the Zhang home. I hadn't spoken until it was out of sight. Micheal gripped the wheel like his life depended on it, his knuckles turning white as he clenched the stick. I laid my hand over his and gave him a reassuring smile. I didn't fully understand what had happened, but I know it pained him in ways I couldn't imagine.

"Where are we going?" I softly asked, not wanting to hurry her or pressure him for an answer.

"A hotel to stay the night," he finally spoke, breaking the silence. "Look, what happened back there–"

"Was horrible." I finished for him. "I don't expect you to explain everything right this second. Let's just get to the room and get settled," I said, looking out the window and taking in the views of this breathtaking city.

"Okay," he spoke gently, slightly loosening his grip on the wheel.

I wonder how he must feel now, how hard it must have been to confront his own family. He cut them off from fully explaining everything the moment he understood that they were responsible for his mother leaving him. I don't think he was ready to hear the full details or the full reason for their actions. Everyone has their reasons for doing the things they do, but most of those reasons will never justify the action that was done. Sometimes, the damage is too far beyond repair.

At the end of the day, they are his family and he'll return to them when he's ready to forgive them. I hope he will in the future, for it would only ruin and hurt him in the end.

Micheal parked the car in front of a modest hotel, its warm lights spilling onto the street like a silent invitation. He exhaled sharply, as though the weight of the last few hours had begun lifting off his shoulders.

"Stay here," he said softly, cutting the engine and reaching for the door handle.

"I can help," I offered, already unbuckling my seatbelt. He turned to me, his expression unreadable, but the faint shadow of exhaustion tugged at his eyes.

"I know you can. But for tonight, just let me handle this, okay?" I nodded, sitting back in my seat as he disappeared into the hotel lobby.

The air inside the car was still and heavy, carrying the residue of unspoken words. My eyes drifted out the window as I patiently waited for Micheal to come back.

Minutes later, Micheal returned with a keycard in his hand and a masked smile.

"We're on the third floor," he said, opening the passenger door for me.

The lobby was quiet, almost too quiet. The kind of silence that made me feel like even my footsteps were an intrusion. We took the elevator up, neither of us saying a word, the soft hum of the machinery the only sound between us.

When we reached the room, Micheal unlocked the door and pushed it open. The room was simple but clean, with a small desk, a neatly made bed, a couch, and a window that overlooked the city.

"You take the bed," he said, setting the keycard on the desk.

I shook my head. "Micheal, we can share—"

"I'll take the couch," he interrupted, his tone final but not unkind.

As he set his bag down and took a seat on the couch, I watched him for a moment. His shoulders sagged, his head tilted down as he stared at his hands. I wanted to say something, to comfort him, but I knew he needed to process this on his own.

Instead, I walked to the window and pulled the curtains open, letting the city lights spill into the room.

"It's beautiful out there," I said softly, hoping to lighten the mood even just a little.

He looked up, his eyes meeting mine for a brief moment, before shifting back to his hands.

"Yeah," he murmured, but his tone suggested he wasn't seeing the view at all.

I sighed inwardly, turning back to the window.

It's not the time to pressure him, let it go.

Micheal sat on the couch, staring at the floor like it held the answers to his inner turmoil. The silence between us stretched, but I could feel the tension in the air shifting. Something in him was about to break.

"Celeste," he said suddenly, his voice low and uneven.

I turned from the window, leaning against the sill as I faced him.

"Yea?"

He rubbed his hands together, the movement restless, his knuckles still pale from the earlier drive.

"I owe you an explanation. About what happened back there. About my family."

"You don't have to—" I started, but he cut me off with a slight shake of his head.

"I do," he insisted. He let out a breath that seemed to carry the weight of years. "You probably gathered what the conflict was about... Remember the story I told you, about my mother leaving us?" he asked, waiting for me to acknowledge that I remembered.

I nodded, waiting for him to explain further.

"Well, I found out she had a reason to. The people I've been calling family for years forced her to leave, and they hid the fact that I had a brother, too."

He paused, his jaw tightening as he glanced at me, searching my face for judgment. When none came, he exhaled and went on.

"Blaming my mother... I was a fucking moron. I never bothered to understand why she did what she did, and I just accepted the simple explanation that she didn't want me. It feels ridiculous, all the time I wasted, never trying to figure it out for myself."

His voice dropped, his gaze distant.

"My brother came to find me earlier this morning. It was because of him that I found out. He told me... he told me my mother passed away."

"Micheal," I whispered, my heart aching at the pain etched into every word he spoke. Shock quickly entered my system as I heard him say that he had a brother; that's huge news.

"I couldn't believe it. All those years I wished the worst for my mother, thinking that she couldn't care less. But that whole time, she was just as heartbroken and empty as I was. I could've looked for her; I should've tried harder. I shouldn't have just accepted it because that was the story they told me." He looked up at me then, his eyes heavy with emotion. "But finding this out after all these years... it still hurts. I wanted to believe that they had nothing to do with this, but I'd be fooling myself. I mean, you saw how obvious it was."

I walked over to him, sitting down on the couch beside him.

"I can't possibly imagine what you're feeling; I'm so sorry." A tear shed from his eyes, and he quickly turned his face away from me, hiding his emotions. I grabbed his chin and turned it back towards me. "There's nothing wrong with feeling, Micheal. It makes you human. It shows how much heart you have."

"Men crying isn't really our strongest look," he muttered, his voice thick with emotion. A weak attempt to hide the vulnerability threatening to show.

"No, I think tears are beautiful. Most people think they're awful, dreadful, and weak, but I don't. Tears, they're the only thing that can cleanse and heal the soul. It's why I find them so powerful."

He met my gaze, something softer breaking through the storm in his eyes.

"You're amazing, you know that? I don't know how you always say the right thing, but you do. You make me feel... seen."

"I–" I tried to reason with him, correct him. But he didn't allow me to.

"You're so incredibly strong and beautiful. I've never met anyone like you," he continued. My breath caught as his voice dropped even lower. "You're bold, unique, and intense in a way that fucking terrifies me. I don't know when it started, but I'm falling for you, Celeste. Slowly, but I can't stop it. You're–"

Before he could finish, I leaned forward, cutting him off with a kiss. It was gentle at first, a question more than an answer, but when he responded, his hand brushing my cheek, the other sliding to the small of my back, it became something deeper.

When we finally pulled apart, he gave me a small look of surprise and confusion? I hesitated and could not believe the stupid stunt I'd just pulled. What was I thinking?

As I'm about to stand from the couch and walk out the room, he grabbed me by my wrist and pulled me back down.

"What are you doing?" I asked softly, my heart racing.

"Don't go," he begged, his voice warm.

"I'm sor–" Micheal crashed his lips against mine, even more desperate than I had. He pulled back for a second, our problems slowly fading as his hand lingered on my cheek, his thumb brushing against my skin in a way that sent a shiver down my spine. His gaze held mine, intense and unguarded, and I could see everything he wasn't saying in his eyes, the longing, the vulnerability, the hunger.

I closed the gap again, pressing my lips to his, and this time there was no hesitation, no holding back. The kiss deepened, turning urgent and heated as his hand slid from my cheek to tangle in my hair, pulling me closer.

I moved into him, feeling his warmth against me as his other arm wrapped around my waist, steadying me as if he couldn't bear to let me go. My fingers found their way to his shirt, gripping the fabric as his lips moved against mine with a passion that left me breathless.

The tension in the room shifted, electric and undeniable. Micheal leaned back slightly, pulling me with him until I was straddling his lap, my knees pressing into the couch on either side of him. His lips left mine, trailing down to my jaw, then lower to the sensitive skin on my neck. I gasped softly, my head tilting back as my hands slid up to his shoulders, holding onto him like an anchor in the storm he was stirring inside me.

"Celeste," he murmured against my skin, his voice rough and unsteady, sending a thrill through me. His hands roamed my back, firm yet gentle, as though he was memorizing every inch of me.

I cupped his face, guiding his lips back to mine, pouring everything I felt into the kiss, my desire, my reassurance, my unspoken promise that he wasn't alone. His grip tightened around me, his movements more insistent, as if he needed me as much as I needed him in that moment.

When we finally broke apart, both of us breathing hard,

Micheal rested his forehead against mine, his eyes closed as a faint smile curved his lips.

"You're going to ruin me, Celeste," he said softly, his voice tinged with awe and something deeper.

I smiled, brushing a strand of hair from his face. "Maybe. But only if you let me."

His laugh was quiet but genuine, his hands still resting on my waist as he pulled me closer. "I think I already have."

His hands traveled up my thigh, slow and deliberate, his touch sending a shiver through me. The warmth of his palms against my skin was both grounding and electrifying all at once. His eyes locked onto mine, searching for any hesitation, any sign to stop, but I met his gaze with unwavering confidence.

"Micheal," I whispered, my voice barely audible, but the way he responded, his grip tightening slightly, his lips curving into the faintest smile, showed he heard me loud and clear.

He leaned in again, capturing my lips with his, the kiss deepening with an intensity that left no room for doubt.

His fingers traced small, gentle patterns against my thigh, his touch reverent, as though he were committing every moment, every sensation, to memory.

I slid my hands up his chest, feeling the taut muscles beneath the thin fabric of his shirt. My fingers brushed over his shoulders and found their way into his hair, tugging lightly as he groaned softly against my lips. The sound sent a thrill through me, and I pressed closer, letting myself melt into him.

His hands moved again, one traveling to the small of my back, pulling me flush against him, while the other cradled my face with a tenderness that contrasted the heat building between us.

"Fuck," he murmured against my lips, his breath hot and uneven. "I don't think you even realize what you're doing to me."

I smiled, brushing my lips against his neck before pulling

back just enough to meet his gaze. "Maybe I do," I teased, my voice soft but laced with certainty.

His eyes darkened; his grip on my thigh tightened, drawing a soft, involuntary moan from my lips. The sound seemed to ignite something in him, a shift that turned his gaze molten with desire.

Without hesitation, his hands moved to the hem of the sweatshirt I wore, his fingers brushing my skin as he tugged it upward. The fabric slid off me in a single fluid motion, and the intensity in his eyes as he took me in made my breath hitch.

"God, Celeste," he murmured, his voice low and rough. I hadn't worn a bra underneath; I was completely bare to him, no longer hiding from him. His hands trailed up to my breasts and softly cupped them. "You're perfect." He took one of my breasts in his mouth, sucking and licking.

His tongue sent instant shocks of pleasure through my body, and I began to grind on his lap. His erection in his pants sent me off the rails, and all I wanted was to get rid of the fabric that was keeping us apart.

He frantically unbuttoned my jeans, lifting me like I was weightless, taking them off and leaving me in my underwear. I'm about to slide out of my underwear until he stopped me, picking me up from the floor and throwing me over his shoulder.

"Keep them on," he said, walking over to the bed and dropping me on the edge. His body laid over mine, our bodies squished together, chest to chest, his lips leaving feather-like touches on my collarbone.

Micheal reached down to the hem of my underwear and dragged a finger to my clit, over the fabric of my panties.

I whimpered; the touch was painful but addicting.

"Hey," I whispered, arching my back as he pressed down a sensitive spot. He'd only touched my clit, and he already had me withering and running away from his touch.

"Celeste..." Micheal groaned in a gentle whisper as he

pulled me back down beneath him. He began to rub in a circular motion.

I gasped, surprised at the sudden action. He chuckled as he examined my face, fully focused on me. Everything was about me. I felt extremely exposed to him, as if I could no longer hide how I was really feeling. How he was making me feel.

"Should I stop?" he asked, clearly enjoying the control he had over me at this moment.

"I'd fucking hate you if you stop now," I managed to say. I was desperate to get away from his touch, but I felt like I would be close to dying if he stopped touching me. "I mean it," I hummed, everything thought in my mind turning hazy.

"That would be up to you, Celeste." he slipped his hand inside my panties, a finger sliding inside me. I struggled to keep my moans in and buried my face into his right shoulder.

He moved back, not allowing me to hide my face. I let out a loud groan in frustration.

"You never hated me, did you?" he asked, his eyes sparkling with the idea of me feeling the same for him.

"I did, I still do," I struggled to say through moans and grunts. My chest rose and fell as I hopelessly begged for more air. My body felt like it would overheat itself if I didn't find my climax soon.

"Yeah?" he asked, tilting his head with a boyish smirk. "Is that right?"

"Mhm," I muttered, trying to keep my breathing in check. He slipped his finger in and out, every time picking up the pace.

My moans filled the room as he finger fucked me like a maniac. My right hand gripped the hand he used to pleasure me and my other grabbed his free hand and placed it over my breast and squeezed. He allowed me to move his hand anywhere I wanted. His eyes rolled back for a quick moment, releasing a loud groan.

"Yes," I moaned, as I could feel myself closer to my

release. It wasn't until he heard my moan that he suddenly removed his hand. Robbing me of my climax that I urgently needed.

"What? no…" I whined as he leaned back and stood over my body. He looked down at me as he grinned proudly, sucking my juices off of his fingers, savoring the taste of me.

"Mmm, I didn't think I could ever be obsessed with the taste of someone. Yet here I am," he confessed with any care in the world.

"Are you fucking serious?" I asked, appalled that he would stop out of nowhere.

"I want to hear you say it," he said as he stared at me with all the control in the world. "I want to hear you say you want me."

"Yeah, and I want to fly," I sarcastically replied, spread out on the bed, aching for his touch, addicted to feel the warmth his body gave me.

"Hmm," he hummed, taking a few steps back until his back hit the wall. He stared at me with hunger; he wanted me as much as I wanted him. He was holding back with all his might, and I could tell if I made the right move, he would give in.

I laid back on the bed, took off my panties and bared myself to him completely, spreading my legs for him. His breathing hiked as he stared at me.

My hand trailed down to my chest, then down to my stomach until I reached my pussy. I began to play with myself, since he wasn't going to finish the job himself.

"I get it; you probably don't know how to make a woman cum," I said, looking into his eyes.

He let out a laugh and shook his head.

"Yeah, that's definitely it," he responded, pulling his shirt over his head. "But please, by all means," he added with a small nod.

I continued to rub and play with myself, my head falling back as I reached a spot that felt sensitive to me. I wasn't able to give myself the full satisfaction he could, but he didn't know that.

He growled as I moved faster. I allowed my body to take over, forgetting any small thoughts that would make me stop. I looked back at him only to find him staring with hunger in his eyes; he bit his lips like he was trying to hold back a little longer.

The feeling of being seen this way felt far too intimate. I couldn't help but feel more aroused, more on edge that I was the very reason that he had a hard time containing himself.

But I had to give it to him; he was doing better than I thought. However, I was going to take it up a notch.

I got off the bed and walked up to him, standing a few inches away from him. I brought my finger to my mouth and sucked, tasting myself. Humming in satisfaction, I brought my finger inches away from his mouth.

"Want a taste?" I teased, my heart beating frantically against my chest.

"You're good," he chuckled as he shook his head. I leaned in and kissed his chest. He sighed deeply before grabbing me from the waist and turning me around. Now my back was hitting the wall as he trapped me in. "I wanted to hear you say it, but I want to see something else more."

"See what?" I asked, breath catching in my throat, my body already reacting to the way he looked at me. Anticipation curled low in my belly, and when his fingers found the sensitive spot between my thighs, I gasped.

He knew exactly where to touch, slow at first, teasing, then deliberate, circling my clit with just the right pressure. My legs trembled as the tension built fast, sharp and sweet. I clenched around nothing, hips rolling into his hand, shameless in how badly I needed more.

"Right there," he murmured, lips brushing my ear as I broke apart in his arms.

The orgasm hit me in waves, pulsing through my body until my forehead was damp with sweat and my lungs burned with the need to breathe. He held me up, his hands strong and steady, grounding me as I came down from the high, my heartbeat echoing in my ears.

"Exactly this," he answered my question as he placed a kiss at my temple.

My hands traveled down to the hem of his jeans, and I gently tugged on the buckle. His breathing hiked again as I gently palmed his erection. I looked into his eyes, waiting for him to tell me what he wanted.

"I can–"

"Don't worry about me; I'm satisfied with just pleasuring you tonight." I looked into his eyes, confused. "You can do whatever you want to me next time, alright? But you need rest." He softly ran a hand through my hair, a gesture filled with adoration.

His arms, strong and sure, lifted me effortlessly from the floor, cradling me against his chest as if I were the most fragile thing in the world. The warmth of his body enveloped me as he brought me back to the bed, the soft sheets meeting my skin like a gentle caress.

As he set me down, his fingers brushed my cheek, a quiet promise in the tender look he gave me. Without a word, he reached for his belt, unfastening it with slow, deliberate movements before slipping out of his pants. The soft rustle of fabric filled the quiet space between us. He climbed into bed beside me, the weight of his body settling close. His hands found the blanket, pulling it over us, drawing me closer as he melted into the warmth of the sheets, his body fitting perfectly against mine.

The scent of his skin, the warmth of his breath, and the steady thrum of his heart beneath my ear filled me with a sense of belonging. I could feel every beat, every movement of his chest as he held me close, and for the first time, everything outside of this moment felt distant, unimportant. His touch was both a question and an answer, and I found myself lost in the intimacy of it, each second stretching into eternity as we melted into one another. He still wore nothing but his boxers, the soft fabric brushing against my skin as he held me, a reminder of how little we needed to be fully connected, how effortless this felt.

CHAPTER 30
MICHEAL

The following morning, I woke up with Celeste in my arms. She was buried underneath the blanket, which barely clung to her, leaving me to wrap myself around her from behind. The sun shone in our room, and I used my back as a human shield to hide her from the light that threatened to take this moment away from me.

The warmth of her body pressed against mine was a comfort I didn't deserve. I watched her body slightly move as she took small breaths, and I allowed myself to believe this was real. But the illusion didn't last. Dread clawed its way into my chest, sharp and unforgiving, as reality intruded. I was tricking her, playing her. The words echoed in my mind like a curse, and yet... none of it felt fake. It all felt terrifyingly real.

The doubts that harassed my mind distracted me.

What will she do when she finds out? Would she leave and never speak to me again? How was I supposed to face the guilt gnawing at me, consuming me piece by piece?

I tightened my hold on her as if that alone could stop the inevitable, as if I could freeze this moment in time and keep the truth at bay forever. But the questions wouldn't stop. What would I do when that time came? When I had no choice but to see the hurt in her eyes and know I was the one who put it there?

Slowly, I loosened my hold around her, moving carefully inch by inch to avoid waking her. Her soft breaths remained the same, her peaceful face half-hidden by the blanket. I lingered for a moment, mentally taking a picture of her like this to keep in my mind forever.

Sliding out of bed, I planted my feet on the ground as quietly as possible. The coolness of the floor grounded me as I stood, looking back at her once more. She slightly shifted, gripping the blanket closer to her chest, and I paused, holding my breath until she stilled again.

Searching for my shirt and pants, I found them thrown over the couch. I quietly stepped over to the couch and grabbed them, putting them back on.

I grabbed my shoes that were in a corner and made my way toward the door, tip-toeing as I tried to avoid any sounds that could wake her. I gently opened the door, not wanting the door to creak. Once I had half of my body out the door, I heard the little voice in my head speak.

You're leaving the room because you can't handle the emotions you're feeling.

My hand gripped the edge of the door as if holding on to something tangible might steady me. I turned my head slightly, stealing one more glance at her. She hadn't moved, still buried beneath the blanket, her breathing soft and even.

My chest aches painfully. The voice wasn't wrong. I wasn't leaving because I needed coffee or because I wanted to give her space. I was leaving because staying here, feeling her warmth, hearing the quiet rhythm of her breathing, now learning how much I cared for her despite the lies, was too much.

Coward.

I exhaled slowly, the weight of my guilt pressing down on

me. How long could I keep this up? How long before the truth unraveled and tore us apart?

Carefully, I shut the door and walked toward the closest elevator. I pressed the button and waited for the doors to open. Once they did, I got in and slipped on my shoes. Tying my shoes, I had one thing on my mind. Celeste.

With her asleep in the room, and the memory of her warmth lingering on my skin, none of it felt easy. My winning Celeste was like winning the lottery.

It was simple; guys like me didn't randomly win the lottery. Not without a catch.

I have her where she is now because of this job that I'm regretting more and more every day. I couldn't back out of it now; a part of me still wanted the money because of survival instincts.

I grew up surrounded by wealth, raised in a world where luxury was as natural as breathing. But by nineteen, it was all gone—lost because I made a choice to walk away. Leaving didn't mean I stopped craving it. That lifestyle still lingered, like a hunger I couldn't fully extinguish.

Like they say, freedom comes at a cost. And for me, that cost was steep.

This job, this lie, it was my way of clawing back what I'd lost my own way. It was my way of earning something for myself, and yet, the closer I got to the payout, the more it felt like I was losing something far more important.

The elevator dinged open as I reached the lobby. The smell of coffee wafted through the air as I headed toward the mini cafe they had.

The barista, a guy maybe a few years younger than me, glanced up as I approached. His tired eyes took in the way I stood there for a second, like I was carrying something heavy, before he said, "Morning. What can I get you?"

I didn't hesitate. "Two double shots, black."

"Coming right up." He moved to the espresso machine without a second thought, the sound of grinding beans filling the small space.

Glancing out at the lobby, I watched people walk in and out through the doors. The barista set the cups down in front of me, his hands moving quickly.

"Two doubles," he said with a quick smile. "It's a lot of caffeine for a guy who looks like he needs sleep."

"Only one is for me, but thanks," I gave him a half-smile.

He didn't ask any further questions, just nodded and went back to his work as I turned, walked back toward the elevator, and went back to the third floor.

I stepped back into the room, juggling two cups of coffee, the carton wrapping around the cup getting hotter by the second. Celeste was already awake, sitting up in bed with the sheets tangled around her, scrolling through her phone. Her hair was a mess, her lips pressed into a thin line like he was trying not to acknowledge me.

But her eyes flicked up the moment the door clicked shut behind me.

"Thought you'd skipped town," she said, her voice dry but not entirely devoid of heat.

I raised an eyebrow, setting the coffee on the table with exaggerated care.

"Funny. I thought *you* might do the same."

Her jaw tightened, her phone slipping from her hand onto the bed. She didn't deny it.

It had been reckless. A stupid, impulsive decision fueled by adrenaline and weeks of biting remarks, close calls, and unspoken tension. Last night, we crossed a line. This morning, it felt like she went back to pretending the line didn't exist.

"I don't run," she said finally, her tone clipped. "Not from you."

The words hung between us, heavy and sharp.

"I'd say otherwise after what happened last night." I tore my gaze from hers and busied myself with removing the tops and adding sugar to the coffee.

"Here." I handed the coffee to her. "I added sugar; I thought you'd find it too bitter. Thoughtful of me, right?"

Celeste snorted, grabbing the cup and taking a sip.

"Don't act like this is some grand gesture. It's coffee, not a diamond ring."

"I didn't say this was a grand gesture," I said, sitting on the edge of the bed, crossing my arms.

Her eyes narrowed, but there was a flicker of disappointment before she buried it beneath a layer of cool indifference. We sat there in silence; the air charged with everything we weren't saying.

Finally, I walked over to where our bags sat on the floor, pulled out the envelope that held the tickets to our train this morning, and softly threw it on the bed in front of her.

"What's this?" she asked, her voice skeptical.

"Tickets," I said simply. "Train to Busan. Leaves in an hour."

Her eyebrows shot up, and for the first time that morning, I saw her genuinely caught off guard.

"Busan? What's in Busan?"

"My family from my mother's side," I said, trying to keep my voice steady. "I think it's better if we leave Seoul and Busan is only four hours away. Plus, it's got nice beaches."

She looked at me, then at the envelope, then back again. Her lips parted, like she was going to argue, but she stopped herself.

"How long do you plan on staying there? Our flight to New York leaves in three days."

"It's Friday, and our flight leaves Monday night. Think of this as a weekend getaway; we'll be right back for our flight." I hoped that she'd agree without any arguments. I sat still, breathing steadily as I waited for her answer.

Instead, she set the coffee down on the table and swung her

legs off the bed, standing up with a slow, deliberate grace. She stepped closer, too close, her eyes locking onto mine with the kind of intensity that made it impossible to look away.

"You want me to come with you? Don't you think that's too… personal?" she asked, her voice low, dangerous.

"It is," I answered, my heart hammering in my chest. "But I'd rather not go alone."

She attentively searched my eyes for any doubt, but as she saw that there was none, she nodded.

"Okay," she murmured. "I'll accompany you, but just…"

"Just?" I asked, leaning in, wanting her to finish the sentence truthfully.

She shook her head deliberately, looking down at her cup of coffee.

"Nothing." She brought the cup back to her lips and took a sip. "One hour. We need to start getting ready if we want to make it in time."

Placing her drink back on the table beside her, she walked toward her luggage for fresh clothes.

"I'll be ready in fifteen," she said, walking past me toward the bathroom. "The ride better be good; if it's terrible, you're paying for my therapy later."

I chuckled as I watched her open the bathroom door.

"Deal." The door clicked shut behind her, leaving me standing there with the coffee cooling in my hand and my pulse racing like I'd just run a marathon.

The train station was busy when we arrived, people hurrying, their footsteps echoing in the cavernous space, the sharp clang of metal against metal in the background. The neon signs above the tracks flickered with departure times, the momentary flashes of red and green adding to the sense of urgency. Celeste was silent as we made our way toward the platform, her posture stiff, her eyes scanning everything and nothing at once.

We scanned our tickets at the gate, the electronic beep signaling our entry. The train was waiting for us, sleek and cold, a line of steel cutting through the station. We made our way down the platform, the sound of the train's engine rumbling in the distance.

As we climbed aboard, I felt her hesitation, felt the way she lingered behind me for just a second too long before following me into the car. The seats were already half-occupied, but there was an empty pair near the back, far enough from the crowds to give us a little space. I took a seat by the window and set my bag down beside me. Celeste followed suit, sitting across from me, her eyes already drifting to the window, watching the blur of the station fade into the distance as the train started to move.

"How long is the ride?" she asked, her stomach loudly growling over the sound of the train's engine.

"Three hours," I answered, placing my hands on the table between us. "You're hungry," I commented, sure that I was right.

"You don't say! How could you possibly know that?" she asked, irritated by the obvious.

"My intuition is far too great for this world," I responded with a smug smirk on my face. She rolled her eyes and leaned further back in her seat.

"You want a special treat for that?" she added quietly, full of sarcasm as she looked out the window. The train began to move faster with each passing second.

"What kind of treat are we talking about?" I asked, knowing that it'll only fuel the small fire she has deep within. She sighed heavily, ignoring my question entirely.

"Fine, I get it. No treats for me," I said, feigning disappointment. I leaned back in my seat too, crossing my arms with a dramatic sigh of my own.

The tension hung in the air for a moment, punctuated only by the rhythmic clatter of the train on the tracks. Outside, the countryside blurred into streaks of green and gold, the late afternoon sunlight casting long shadows across the fields.

"I did bring breakfast," I offered after a pause, my tone more sincere this time. "It might not be a gourmet meal, but it's better than sitting here pretending you're not starving."

She glanced at me sideways, her expression softening just a little.

"What are you talking about?"

Her eyebrows lifted in surprise as I began pulling items out of my bag. First, a neatly wrapped sandwich. Then four oranges, kimbap, pre-packed rice rolls with tuna and bulgogi filling, rice cakes, banana milk, and finally, a thermos filled with sweetened coffee.

"Where were you hiding all of this?" she asked, her tone caught between amusement and genuine curiosity.

"In my magical bag of wonders," I replied with a grin, holding up the thermos like it was a prized trophy.

"You're ridiculous," she said, though the corners of her mouth twitched as if fighting back a smile.

"Ridiculous or thoughtful?" I countered, unscrewing the thermos lid to reveal coffee, still steaming faintly.

She eyed the spread before us as I placed everything on the small table between our seats. Her sarcastic facade cracked for a moment, revealing a glimmer of appreciation.

"Well, what are you waiting for?" I asked, gesturing toward the food. "Your stomach's been trying to start a rebellion. This is a peace offering."

She rolled her eyes but reached for the sandwich, anyway.

"Fine. But only because my options are this or passing out."

"Fair enough," I said, taking a sip of coffee.

For a few moments, we ate in comfortable silence, the earlier tension replaced by a shared sense of calm. The rhythmic clatter of the train provided a soothing backdrop, and the warmth of the coffee was a welcome comfort against the cool, rushing air.

"This isn't bad," she admitted around a bite of the sandwich. She puts it down and reaches for a kimbap and takes another small bite. "This isn't bad either," she murmured.

"It pains me to think you even thought it would be bad. I'm appalled, really," I replied with a dramatic hand on my chest. "I deserve much more credit than that." I reached for the orange. "I'm amazing,"

She snorted at my comment. "Alright, now you're just getting cocky," she chuckled as she grabbed a bottle of banana milk. "You could've bought orange juice; I don't drink this," she said as she pointed at the bottle in her hand.

"Sweetie, I didn't bring that for you," I answered, snatching the banana milk from her hold. "If you want orange juice, I can squeeze some for you. Nice and fresh." Her eyes narrowed.

"Cute but–"

"What? You don't think I can?" I asked, my eyes widened at the hint of challenge. She shook her head as she continued eating bits of everything. "Alright, care for a little bet?"

"I learned long ago that making bets with you is like making a deal with the devil. Look at where it got me."

"In South Korea, on a train to Busan, one of the most beautiful sights of the country. I'd say it's pretty good," I added with a smile, now holding two oranges over my eyes.

"I know better not to make the same mistake twice,"

"Avoiding mistakes is overrated; let's spice things up." I tried convincing her, hoping she'd take the bait.

"What were you thinking?" Her curiosity got the best of her and I was so grateful for it. The hairs on my arms spiked up with excitement and anticipation. What should I bet? It has to be something good.

I pause, looking at the pictures on the brochures next to our seats, a picture of the beach house in Busan;, it looked just like the one I rented for these two days we were visiting. In the picture it was nighttime, the moon shining over the waters, the entire property screamed privacy, and a crazy thought came to my mind.

"If I squeeze a perfect glass of orange juice with these oranges only using my mouth, no hands or any objects, you'll go skinny dipping in the ocean at night." She lets out a hoarse laugh.

"If you don't?"

"Then I'll pause my relentless self-praise for a whole day," I declared, flashing her a grin that I knew would irritate her just enough to make her consider the bet.

She rolled her eyes, the corners of her mouth twitching in a struggle not to smile.

"That's hardly a punishment for you. You'd just find another way to be insufferable."

"Fine," I said, holding up an orange for emphasis. "If I fail, I'll go skinny dipping."

"And...?" she asked, waiting for more. I snickered at her seriousness.

"I'll do anything you say for the next two days. Whatever it is, I'll do it with no complaints, no shortcuts. Your wish will be my command, my lady," I added, taking a playful bow in my seat.

Her eyebrows shot up. "You? Do exactly as I say without any restraints? That's a gamble in itself."

I laughed. "You wound me. But yes, I'm confident I can do that. So, deal?"

She hesitated for a moment; her gaze flicking to the oranges in my hands, then back to my face.

"Alright," she said, finally relenting. "But don't say I didn't warn you when you regret this."

"Oh, I never regret a challenge," I replied with mock bravado, setting the oranges on the table.

She leaned back, arms crossed, clearly ready to watch me make a fool of myself.

"This should be good."

Taking a deep breath, I picked up the first orange with my teeth and bit into the peel. The tangy citrus burst onto my tongue, and I grimaced slightly but pressed on, determined not to let her see me falter. With exaggerated effort, I began squeezing the juice out by biting down and twisting the orange as best I could.

She was already laughing, her head tilted back as the ridiculousness of the situation unfolded.

"This is the most absurd thing I've ever seen," she managed between laughs.

"Don't distract the artist," I mumbled around the orange.

By the time I was halfway through the second orange, the small cup I'd grabbed from my bag was filling—though not nearly fast enough. Juice was dripping down my chin, and I could feel her gaze growing more smug by the second.

"Looks like someone's losing our bet," she teased.

I finished the last orange, panting slightly as I leaned back and wiped my face. Holding up the modestly filled cup of juice, I declared, "It's done. Behold: my masterpiece."

She inspected the cup, biting her lip as she fought to keep a straight face.

"Alright, I'll admit it—you got farther than I thought. But..." she smirked, "... that's definitely not a 'perfect glass.'"

"It's more than half-way filled though." I pointed at the cup for her to look at the evidence of my hard work. "Come on, give me some credit here. That's a lot of juice for no hands!"

She arched an eyebrow; her smirk growing wider.

"Oh, I'll give you credit—for creativity and determination. But a deal's a deal, and that's not a full glass."

I groaned dramatically, setting the cup down on the table.

"You're ruthless, you know that? No mercy."

"Rules are rules," she said, leaning back in her seat with an air of victory. "Don't forget, you're the one who suggested the bet."

I stared at her for a moment, then gestured to the cup.

"Fine. But I'll say this: I've given it my all, and that alone deserves a renegotiation."

She pretended to think it over, tapping her chin with exaggerated deliberation.

"Hmm... that sounds oddly familiar," she said, bringing me to the night she tried to renegotiate our seven dates; I obviously didn't agree or make it easy on her. Therefore, I already knew her answer.

"Alright, I got the hint. You won the bet fair and square," I gave in, knowing that it was the only way to play fair.

"I thought so," she said with a triumphant grin, leaning forward to take another sip of her coffee.

I leaned back in my seat, crossing my arms with a dramatic sigh.

"You're enjoying this way too much."

"Oh, absolutely," she admitted with no hesitation, popping another piece of kimbap into her mouth. "It's not every day I get to watch you lose so spectacularly."

"I wouldn't call it *spectacular*," I grumbled, though the twitch of a smile tugged at my lips. "It was a noble effort."

"Noble? Sure," she teased. "Messy, ridiculous, and maybe a little gross—but yeah, let's call it noble."

I grabbed an orange peel and held it up like a trophy.

"Mock me all you want, but this? This was the stuff of legends. Someday, people will tell stories about my heroic attempt to win a bet against impossible odds."

She laughed, a genuine, belly-deep laugh that made the whole embarrassing ordeal worth it.

"You're so full of it," she said, shaking her head.

"You love it," I shot back without missing a beat.

She froze for half a second, her expression softening before she quickly masked it with her usual sarcasm.

"Don't push your luck, juice boy. You still owe me a late-night swim, and I'm holding you to it."

"Don't worry, I know how much you're looking forward to it, and I'll make that swim *memorable*. Maybe I'll bring the rest of these oranges for ambiance." I teased her, successfully making her turn the little shade of pink.

As we sat there, the bet officially settled, I realized I didn't mind losing, not when it meant moments like this.

CHAPTER 31
CELESTE

I felt nice to win a bet against Micheal, I so desperately wanted him to know how it felt to lose. But I've got to say, it was the most ridiculous bet I've ever made with anyone. The image of Micheal trying to drain the juice from the oranges with his mouth was almost too good to be true. I wish I had taken a photograph. I would've shown it to the editor of *The New York Times* and begged for them to add it in their *'Lifestyle'* section titled *'How to make all natural orange juice in a matter of seconds!'*

The train ride went by quickly after that; those three hours felt like thirty minutes, at the most. Once the train came to a stop, we grabbed our bags and joined the slow shuffle of passengers disembarking. The platform was crowded, the air thick with the sounds of voices, luggage wheels, and distant announcements.

I stuck close to Micheal, his usual playfulness replaced by a quiet attentiveness. He constantly searched through the crowd, searching for someone.

"You okay?" I asked softly, my eyes scanning his face. Playtime was over; I knew that the moment his face transformed into what seemed like a sick blend of anticipation and nausea.

"Yeah," Micheal said, his voice clipped, though his hand unconsciously tightened around the strap of his bag. "Just... trying to spot him."

I nodded, staying close as we moved through the throng of travelers. The atmosphere around us felt charged, like the moments just before a storm. For once, I didn't try to make a joke or lighten the mood. I knew better.

Finally, Micheal stopped, his gaze locking on someone ahead. A man stood a little off to the side, leaning against a pillar. He was tall, broad-shouldered, with a face that bore a striking resemblance to Micheal's, though it was older and marked with subtle lines of experience. His hair was a little longer, a little wilder, but his eyes were a shade of bright green, sharp and unreadable.

Micheal took a breath, his chest rising and falling as if he were steadying himself for something monumental.

"That's him," he murmured.

"Your brother?" I asked, though I already knew the answer.

"Yeah."

Before I could say anything else, Micheal's brother had spotted us. His face broke into a wide grin, the kind that didn't quite reach his eyes but still carried warmth. He straightened, stepping toward us with an easy confidence that Micheal seemed to lack in that moment.

"So you decided to get on the train after all," he said, his voice deep and steady.

Micheal nodded, shifting his bag on his shoulder. "Yeah. It would be a waste not to use the tickets."

His smile grew wider, like it was the best sentence he's ever heard.

"Well, I'm glad you didn't let them go to waste. Welcome to

Busan." His gaze flicked to me, his smile softening just a bit. "You must be...?" he said, extending a hand.

"Celeste," I replied, shaking his hand firmly. "The emotional support companion." His grip was solid, his palm warm. He let out a light chuckle, a sound similar to Micheal's, but it didn't have the same effect on me. It didn't leave me feeling warm or fuzzy within.

"It's nice to meet you Celeste, I'm glad you could join Micheal on this trip. I'm Min Ho," Min Ho said, releasing my hand and turning back to Micheal. "You look...tired. Nervous."

Micheal let out a short laugh, the sound tinged with nervousness.

"Yeah, well, it's the first time I'm meeting everyone."

"Trust me, everyone's nervous to meet you too. The good kind, that is," Min Ho agreed, the weight of his words hanging in the air.

For a moment, they just stood there, two brothers connected yet separated by years of silence, not knowing the other existed. I felt like an intruder, but didn't dare step away.

Min Ho broke the tension first, clapping Micheal on the shoulder.

"Come on, let's get out of here. The car's parked nearby."

Micheal nodded, and we followed Min Ho through the crowd. As we walked, I stayed close to Micheal, his tension palpable. Min Ho led the way with an ease that suggested he was used to taking charge, his presence both commanding and reassuring.

As we reached the car, Min Ho opened the trunk and helped with our bags.

"The house isn't far," he said, glancing at Micheal. "It'll be a quick ride."

Micheal nodded, taking my luggage from my hand and handing it to Min Ho.

"Good to know."

Min Ho gave him a knowing look, closing the trunk and then slid into the driver's seat. I climbed into the back with Micheal, my shoulder brushing against his as the car rumbled to life.

The ride was quiet at first, the hum of the engine and the distant sound of seagulls filling the space. I glanced at Micheal, his jaw tight, his eyes fixed on the horizon.

I broke the silence eventually, my tone casual, not wanting to disturb the silence too abruptly.

"So, how long have you been living in Busan?" I asked, slowly starting the conversation.

"Uh, my whole life. But I lived in Japan temporarily for school. I got a full ride to study there," he answered, giving me the green flag to continue talking.

"That's nice; what did you study?"

"Biochemistry," he answered, shocking the both of us.

Micheal seemed as surprised as I did, turning his full attention to the conversation.

"Wow, I didn't picture you as the biochemist; that's really interesting." Min Ho chuckled as he looked at us in the rear mirror.

"Yeah, I loved it. It allowed me to create a business that provided for my family. Nothing crazy, but enough for them to be comfortable."

"You created something for yourself. That's cool; I respect that," Micheal added.

Min Ho glanced at Micheal through the rearview mirror, a small, knowing smile on his face.

"I bet it's more than just 'something,' though, isn't it? Don't sell me short, Zhang."

I caught the faintest flicker of pride in Min Ho's tone, and it was clear there was a deeper bond between the two men that seemed to be grounded in years of mutual respect and admiration, even though they only recently met.

Micheal nodded, his brows raising slightly.

"Seriously, that's incredible. An entire business? Biochemistry? What kind of work do you do?"

Min Ho's hands gripped the steering wheel a little tighter as he navigated a turn, but his voice was relaxed when he answered.

"I develop eco-friendly chemical solutions. Mostly things like biodegradable packaging and sustainable farming materials. It's not flashy, but it's meaningful work."

"That's not just meaningful; that's important," I said, genuinely impressed.

Micheal tilted his head, a teasing smile forming on his lips.

"Here I thought you were a surfer or something. You're out here saving the planet."

Min Ho laughed, shaking his head.

"Trust me, I'm not that noble. I just saw a problem and thought I could help. If I could do something that helps the planet and my family, it's qualified as a win in my book."

"You know," Micheal said, leaning back a little, "I'm kind of jealous. You've got your purpose all figured out. I'm still out here winging it."

"You'll figure it out," Min Ho replied firmly. "Besides, winging it isn't so bad. Some of the best discoveries happen when you're just going with the flow."

I could see Micheal mull over those words, his fingers tapping absently on the seat. The tension in his shoulders seemed to ease slightly, the weight of the day not completely gone but manageable now.

The rest of the ride was a mix of light conversation and comfortable silence. Min Ho pointed out local spots as we passed them, a market here, a café there. The kind of places that made the city feel alive and connected.

When we pulled up to a small modest house, with a stunning view and access to the ocean. Min Ho killed the engine and turned in his seat to face us.

"This is where you'll be staying. It's better than any Airbnb, so cancel the place you intended to stay in and stay here," he said, looking directly at Micheal. "You're family now. Don't forget that."

Micheal's mouth quivered into a small smile.

"You own properties like these just for fun?"

Min Ho shook his head, his gaze steady. "No, I got it for friends and family when they come to visit. Plus, it's close to the house. Go on, drop your bags and we'll continue on."

"Stay here," Micheal said with a wholesome smile. "I'll drop our bags inside." Min Ho threw the keys to Micheal, which he caught without looking, and got out of the car.

Min Ho watched him take the bags out of the trunk and make his way to the house entrance.

"He'll fit right in," he said.

"He will," I agreed, looking out the window as I waited for him to come back.

Two minutes later, he jumped back into the car and leaned back into his seat. Min Ho drove off, making a few turns until he reached a small, gravel-lined driveway, stopping in front of a modest beach house. The structure was cozy and weathered, with whitewashed walls and teal shutters that had seen better days. A wide porch wrapped around the front, and from where I stood, I could see the ocean stretching out behind the house, its waves glittering in the golden light of early evening.

"You weren't lying; it is incredibly close," Micheal said, opening the door once Min Ho parked.

"That's exactly why I said it." Min Ho lead us to the entrance; the blue door had a sign that said '어서 온나!' I looked at the symbols, unable to read them.

"It says: Come on in!" Min Ho said, noticing my confusion.

Micheal's throat bobbed as he swallowed, his voice low when he finally responded. "I'm not sure what to say to them. I don't know how to respond to them."

Min Ho covered the doorknob with his hand. "Begin by saying 'hi.' The rest will follow."

I reached out and squeezed Micheal's hand after he nodded. His fingers clenched around mine without a glance, a wordless acknowledgement that I was here and that there was nowhere else I would rather be.

"Take a breath. They're going to love you," I whispered to him as Min Ho opened the door; the warmth and rich scent of home enveloped us.

The house felt lived in, cozy, and full of memories, with a faint trace of something sweet wafting from the kitchen. Micheal stood a little straighter, his eyes scanning the small, cluttered entryway, while I stood behind him, offering silent support.

Min Ho led the way to the kitchen, the sound of voices filtering through the house. Before we reached the kitchen, a woman in her late sixties walked out into the hall. Her face lit up when she saw us, her smile wide and genuine.

"Micheal," she said, her voice trembling with emotion.

"Hi," Micheal said awkwardly, raising a hand in a half-wave.

The woman pulled him into a tight hug before he could say anything else.

"I can't believe you're here," she whispered, holding him like she'd never let go.

"That's Aunt Clara," Min Ho said quietly to me.

"Got it," I whispered back, watching as Clara stepped back, her eyes shimmering with tears.

She released Micheal from her strong hold and placed both of her hands on his face.

"My god," she said in a soft whisper, slight tears glossing her eyes. "Your energy; it feels just like hers."

"It's nice to meet you..." Micheal spoke, not knowing who the woman was.

"Aunt Clara. I'm your mom's sister," she explained with the sweetest smile that radiated warmth. She looked over at me and gave me a welcoming bow. "It's great to have you here dear, thank you for accompanying Micheal," she said, placing a hand on my shoulder. "Come, come," she said, ushering us in the kitchen.

As we entered the kitchen, the aromatic scent of delicious, mouth watering food mingled with the hum of conversation. The scent of home-cooked delicacies filled the room: soy sauce, shimmering vegetables, and seasoned meats. The kitchen was small but cozy, with a large table lowered down on the floor with round plush pillows surrounding it, placed right in the center that seemed to be the most important spot of the house.

A man in his early sixties, likely an uncle, was standing near the stove, cutting vegetables with a sharp knife. He turned around as aunt Clara called his name.

"Jae-hyun, our special guest is here," she said as she walked over to the fridge, taking out a glass jar of cold water.

His face lightened up, filled with excitement and curiosity.

"Micheal," he said, his voice deep with love. "I'm uncle Jae-hyun," he said, walking over to the both of us. "I can't believe the moment is finally here. We've been waiting for you."

"Really? Well, I'm glad to be here. I used to imagine a family just like this, and to know that it's real, is amazing," Micheal answered as he shook Jae-hyun's hand. "It's good to be home," he added, his voice more confident than it was before we walked in.

Suddenly, the soft patter of small, hurried footsteps echoed against the wooden floor. Two little kids burst into the kitchen, still wet and laughing in their swimsuits. They probably came in from the beach that happened to be their backyard.

"Hene, Juno, we have company," Clara said, with a gentle nudge, pointing toward Micheal.

Hene, the older child who seemed to be around twelve, observed Micheal with a sassy face. Juno, the younger boy who seemed to oddly remind me of Min Ho, kept his gaze on the ground.

"Who are you supposed to be?" Hene asked with her arms crossed.

Yup, this one's definitely a sassy one.

Micheal looked at Clara with a confused expression, waiting for her to explain.

"Hene, this is your cousin Micheal, Aunt Evelyn's son," she said, as Hene kept her gaze on Micheal.

"But I only have Min Ho," Hene responded, looking back at Min Ho.

"Yes, and now you have Micheal. Say hi." She pushed the little girl closer to Micheal. I could tell Micheal was a bit taken back and hesitant as he made the smallest lean backwards. It was the first thing he's done that I was adorable. Watching him experience all of this made my heart churn.

I felt like I didn't deserve to witness it.

"So, I guess we're cousins," he shrugged, not knowing what to tell a twelve-year-old girl who kept giving him a blank expression.

Hene tilted her head, one eyebrow raising in skepticism.

"Guess so," she said finally, twirling a dripping strand of hair. "I'm Hene, in case it wasn't obvious." She had a pink barbie bathing suit, and a pair of pink goggles in her hands.

"I like that name; it's a good one," Micheal complimented, waiting for her to throw him a bone.

"I know it is," she responded like a little diva. I absolutely love her and I didn't even know her.

Micheal chuckled as she turned his attention to the little boy that still had his gaze on the floor. "...and you are?" Micheal asked softly.

Juno sighed softly, his little gasp far too innocent for this world.

"I'm Juno." He was the smallest human I'd ever seen; maybe

he was around six or seven? He wore an orange bathing suit with his goggles still on his head. "Are you supposed to be my uncle Micheal?" he asked.

Micheal's eyes widened when he heard the word 'Uncle' and he turned his attention over to Min Ho, who only smirked off in the corner.

"Uncle?" Micheal questioned as he looked back down at his now younger nephew.

"Yeah, I forgot to mention I'm a dad," he responded.

"You got a mystery wife to go along with your mystery kid?" Micheal asked as he observed the child who was now drinking a tall glass of iced water.

"I'm afraid not. I've taken the role of full time single dad. It's a good thing I own my own business, no? Time and schedule are flexible for him," he explained as he walked over to Micheal and kneeled in front of his son.

"Juno," Min Ho began by saying. "I'm happy to present to you my brother, Micheal, and yes, he is your uncle." Juno pouted ever so slightly, only looking at his dad and then slowly turning his gaze back to Micheal.

"Hi," Juno spoke gently. Micheal crouched down to Juno's level to match his eye line.

"Hi," Micheal responded with admiration in his voice. This was an overwhelming and new obstacle for him, but I could see he was quickly falling in love with his new family.

I couldn't help but feel jealous. I would give anything to have this, to find out that I had the perfect, most accepting family ever.

I feel like it would heal young Celeste in more ways than I could've imagined. Micheal seemed to catch on with how I was feeling, he walked over to me and pulled me in by my wrist. He dragged me to where interactions were taking place, right in the middle of this intimate, private family reunion.

"Hene, Juno, this is Celeste, my girlfriend," he said,

surprising everyone in the room with his choice of words, especially me. My heart shouldn't flutter, but of course, it's doing its own thing, completely unbothered by my common sense.

And why was I overthinking this? So what if he meant it or not? I can't allow myself to get excited or happy when it would potentially hurt me.

The two kids gave me a king greeting, a couple of soft "hi's" and an awkward bow. I greeted them back with a soft smile, not knowing the right words to say or what I should even do. Bow? Wave?

Yeah, I'm definitely overthinking it.

"Food's almost ready; go on and sit down," Clara said with a smile and a wink. "Please, get comfortable, feel at home."

The family dinner was a success, more than a success; Micheal had fit right in with everyone. There was laughter, shared stories, and endless dishes. By the time the sun had set and the conversations got more personal, I walked out onto the porch. I wanted to give them some privacy as I soaked up the views Busan had to offer. It was different from Seoul's busier city life. Here, it was peaceful and quiet; a place to catch your breath.

I hadn't realized how much time had passed when I heard Micheal come out. He walked up next to me, leaned against the porch railing, staring out at the ocean. His shoulders were relaxed, and his smile was soft in the golden light the sunset offered.

"Hey," he said, turning his body to mine. "How are you doing?" he asked, intensively looking at me.

"I'm great; it's beautiful here," I said, finally looking into his eyes. "You look like a man who's been properly adopted."

Micheal chuckled. "They're incredible, aren't they? I didn't think… I didn't know that this would feel so natural."

I leaned against the railing next to him, our arms almost brushing. "It does. I think they were waiting for you as much as you've been waiting for them."

He turned to look at me, his expression thoughtful. "Thanks for being here. For all of this."

"Of course," I responded, my voice light. "It's been... amazing to watch."

Micheal glanced down, his lips twitching into a lopsided grin. "So, want to get out of here for a bit? Explore the city with me?"

I arched an eyebrow. "Is that a date, or do you just need company?"

"Both," he replied with a wink. "Let's see what Busan has to offer on a Saturday night."

My smile grew bigger as I looked back into the house. "You want to leave now? At this moment?" I asked, looking back at him as if he were the most exciting person to come into my life.

"They'll still be here tomorrow; let's go explore," he said, grabbing my hand and leading me away from the porch.

"Okay," I breathed with a giddy smile spreading across my face. In that moment, as he held my hand in his, I realized I was utterly, completely fucked.

CHAPTER 32
MICHEAL

With Celeste's hand in mine, I led her away from the house and hailed a taxi, taking us to the closest local hangout spots. The drive was short, but it gave us a moment to settle into the rhythm of the night. Min Ho told me they had a good sushi place and a karaoke bar, which I thought would be interesting to bring her to. It was the least I could do since this was basically her vacation away from her regular, hectic life in New York, and she deserved it with how supportive she's been with all the obstacles that have been thrown at me. In a storm of chaos, she was my only anchor that held me down, the only person who didn't allow me to lose my shit. I'm where I am, feeling the way I am because of her.

That's something to reward, because having someone who'll stay by your side through the tough, most dramatic times of your life is rare, extraordinary even. I could speak from experience that life is so much worse when that person is missing.

I guided Celeste down the cobblestone street, our footsteps echoing softly in the cool evening air.

"Where are you taking me?" she asked, as she glanced around the buildings.

"You'll see," I said, walking slightly in front of her. "Trust me—it'll be worth it."

We rounded a corner, and the neon sign for 노래방; *'singing room'* blinked erratically above a narrow doorway. From inside, muffled music and bursts of laughter spilled out, inviting and chaotic.

"A karaoke bar?" Celeste raised an eyebrow.

"Not entirely," I answered, opening the door with a flourish. "These are karaoke rooms, so instead of regularly sharing your singing voice with a bunch of strangers, you share it with those of your choosing."

The muffled sounds of music and laughter seeped through the doors we passed, and I kept walking until I stopped in front of one labeled *Private Room 3*.

I pushed the door open, revealing a cozy space lit with dim, multicolored lights that pulsed softly. A plush semicircular couch surrounded a small coffee table littered with a laminated song list and a menu. The karaoke machine stood against the wall, flanked by speakers, with a small screen mounted above it displaying a standby menu.

"Ours for the next hour," I showcased the room with a dramatic sweep of my arm. "Brilliant, I know. I chose to bless you with my voice tonight."

Celeste rolled her eyes with a playful scoff. "This is what you had in mind for an adventure?" she asked, picking up the song list.

"You just don't get it; you've never had crazy memories in a karaoke room." I grabbed the mic from the table and snatched the list from her hands.

"You're serious," she spoke, sitting down nonetheless.

"Never been more serious in my life, now shush." I clicked the song of my choice on the remote and watched the screen come alive with the opening beats of *"Give Me Everything"* by

Pitbull. The pulsing rhythm filled the small room, and I grinned, holding the mic like a seasoned performer.

Celeste's eyes widened. "Oh, no. This is going to be terrible, isn't it?"

"Terribly entertaining," I corrected, pointing at her as the first lyrics appeared on the screen. But instead of singing, I turned the mic toward her. "You're up first."

She crossed her arms, shaking her head. "Not a chance. This is your brilliant idea—own it."

"No, no, no," I countered, waving the mic in her face. "This is a duet. I'll be Pitbull, and you'll be Ne-Yo. Consider it a warm-up for the main event—me."

"You are out of your mind. I will not," she refused. I winced, walking around the room with a depressed expression on my face.

"I get it; you're not used to fun, are you?" I began by saying. "Is holding a brush all you really like to do? I bet you have trouble getting out of your comfort zone while painting. You don't have any authentic experiences to pour onto that canvas."

Celeste sighed dramatically but grabbed the mic, rolling her eyes. She stood up and reluctantly began the opening verse, her voice surprisingly smooth as she navigated the lyrics.

When the chorus hit, I snatched the mic back and launched into my part with full, off-key abandon. *"Grab somebody sexy, tell 'em hey!"* I bellowed, throwing my free arm wide as if I were performing to a sold-out arena.

The falsetto attempt on "tonight" made Celeste double over in laughter. She clutched her stomach, her face lighting up in the glow of the pulsing lights.

"You're so bad it's almost impressive," she managed between gasps of laughter.

"Thank you, thank you," I said, completely missing the rhythm as I gestured wildly at her, attempting an awkward spin before continuing. My voice cracked on every other line, and I somehow turned Pitbull's confident swagger into a hilarious parody.

By the second verse, I abandoned any pretense of staying in sync with the song, opting instead to dance horribly around the small room. Celeste was crying with laughter, hugging a throw pillow for support.

"You're... oh my God, you're *so* bad!" she squeaked.

"Bad? I'm amazing!" I retorted, dramatically belting out, *"I might drink a little more than I should tonight!"* completely off-key. *"Give me EVERYTHING tonight!"*

When the song finally ended, I collapsed onto the couch, tossing the mic aside. Celeste flopped down beside me, wiping tears of laughter from her cheeks.

"That was... wow," she said, still catching her breath. "I don't think I've ever laughed so hard in my life."

"I told you I'd bless you with my voice," I said, smirking.

"That wasn't a blessing. That was a *curse*," she teased, her eyes sparkling.

I nudged her shoulder with mine. "Your turn now. That was supposed to be a duet, but I saved you from it."

"I was going to do it," she replied, looking over the song list.

"You wouldn't have done it justice like I did." She pointed at a song, grabbed the remote and searched up it.

"It's a tough act to follow, I'll admit." She leaned forward with determination. "Close your eyes; I don't want you to see my pick until I start." She covered my eyes with her right hand, slamming it on my face.

"Ouch," I chuckled, laying my hand over hers. "I would've done it without the need of the abuse; your wish is my command, remember?"

"I remember," she said before the chorus of the song 'Kill Shot' by Magdalena Bay came on the screen. The lights in the room flashed red as she sang the second chorus. *"If I wanna stay alive, you should never cross my mind,"* she sang, her voice low and hypnotic as she swayed with the beat. Her eyes never left mine, each word a deliberate challenge, her lips curling into a teasing smile as she moved closer, her energy magnetic.

"Oh God, can you make my heart stop? Hit me with your kill shot, baby," Her hips swayed from left to right with an insane amount of ease; it was hypnotizing.

She moved closer toward me, her movements grew bolder, teasing with every step. Her body, her voice, drew me in like a magnet. It was like a siren reeling in a sailor from sea; the sailor knew it wouldn't go well for him, but he still gave in.

Her hips moved with a slow, deliberate rhythm, her body a perfect reflection of the song's seductive pulse. I could feel the heat between us rise, thickening the air as she moved even closer, her breathless voice brushing my skin.

She reached out, her fingers grazing my chest lightly before she slid them down to rest on my thigh. I didn't know if the music was louder now or if my heartbeat had simply drowned out the world, the heat, the magnetic pull of something greater than us. One that neither of us could deny.

My jaw clenched as I tried to control myself, keeping my hands on my sides, my knuckles turning white as I gripped the edge of the couch for support. I wasn't going to make a move until she did.

She leaned in slowly, her presence intoxicating, overwhelming. Her head nestled gently in the crook of my neck, her breath brushing against my skin like the softest whisper. My whole body tensed, the heat of her so close to mine sending shivers down my spine. Goosebumps spread across my arms, unbidden and uncontrollable.

I shut my eyes tightly, as if that would lessen the intensity of her touch. It didn't. Every nerve in my body seemed to come alive, every sense heightened by her proximity. The scent of her hair, the warmth of her cheek against my shoulder, the way her breathing matched the rapid rhythm of my own: it was too much and not enough all at once.

My hands trembled as I fought the urge to reach for her. The pull was undeniable, a gravity that had been building for what felt like a lifetime, and yet, I stayed rooted, determined to let her set the pace, to let her choose this moment.

"Do you feel this too?" she asked quietly, the song still playing in the background. I slowly turned my head toward her, our noses inches away from one another. She sat down on my lap, resting her entire body on mine.

"How could I not?" I answered, nudging my head toward her. She leaned back as I desperately tried to reach her lips. I groaned as she left my lips lingering in the space between us, the ache of her teasing almost unbearable.

My head fell back against the couch, a mix of frustration and longing swirling inside me. She tilted her head, and a teasing smile tugged at the corners of her lips as she ate up my reaction.

She was enjoying this.

Her fingers traced delicate patterns on my chest, igniting a trail of fire wherever she touched.

"Though I'm doubting you feel it as intensely as I do," I muttered, my voice hoarse, my restraint hanging by a thread.

Her smile softened, the mischief in her eyes giving way to something deeper, something vulnerable. She leaned forward again, her hands sliding up to rest on either side of my face. The warmth of her palms anchored me, drawing me back to her as though nothing else in the world mattered.

Her forehead pressed gently to mine, and for a moment, neither of us moved. The song in the background shifted to a closing, filling the room with silence once again. The karaoke machine gave her the lowest score possible for quitting the song halfway through, and the TV declared she'd lost, but the way she had me wrapped around her finger said otherwise.

Her breath fanned across my lips, her proximity sending another shiver through me.

"It isn't just you," she whispered, her voice trembling slightly as though she were scared of her words. "I thought it was only me," she confessed, her voice slightly trembling.

"No," I said, my voice firm despite the storm inside me. "It's never just been only you."

Slowly, achingly, she closed the distance between us, her lips brushing against mine in a kiss that was both tentative and electric.

I grabbed her by her waist and positioned her under me, so quickly, it felt like a reflex. My nose caressed the side of her neck as I laid soft kissing trailing down to her chest. My hands gripped the fabric of her shirt, itching with the need to rip it open.

Suddenly, a few loud sounds of laughter broke the moment. Both she and I rapidly got up and separated. She sat on one side of the couch, and I the other, like a couple of teenagers that got caught by their parents checking up on them.

Both our chests heaved with unsteady breaths, the tension still thick in the air despite the abrupt interruption. I ran a hand through my hair, trying to compose myself. The sound of laughter drifted in from the halls, a cruel reminder of the world outside our little bubble.

I glanced at her from the corner of my eye. She was sitting rigidly, her cheeks flushed, and her gaze fixed firmly on the floor. Her fingers nervously toyed with the hem of her shirt, the same fabric my hands had been itching to tear away only moments ago.

"Guess we're not as alone as we thought," I said, my voice low and strained, attempting to break the silence.

She finally looked up at me, her lips twitching into a small, embarrassed smile.

"Yeah, not exactly ideal timing," she said, her voice soft, but the tension in her tone betrayed her.

I leaned back against the couch, exhaling a shaky breath as I tried to regain some semblance of control. My body still hummed with the ghost of her touch, and it took everything in me not to reach out to her again.

"We should head back to the house," she said as she stood up from the couch, fixing her hair.

"You sure? We've got about twenty more minutes left," I said, checking the time on my phone. She shook her head gently as she made her way toward the door.

"I think I've had enough karaoke for tonight. Especially from you," she snickered, remembering my attempt at being a pop star. She opened the door and looked back at me once more. "I'm going to use the bathroom. I'll meet you outside?" she asked, holding the door open long enough to hear my answer.

"Yeah, I'll be outside," I replied, getting up from my seat as well. She nodded and walked away; the door shut by itself, leaving me with nothing but my thoughts.

We made it to the house Min Ho lent us, and we stood at the door. I reached in my pocket for the house keys Min Ho gave me before we left. The sound of crashing waves from the ocean filled the silence that hung between us for the past hour.

Celeste hasn't spoken a word to me the entire way back; I think our moment back at the karaoke room was too intense for her. To be honest, it was too intense for me as well.

I, myself, couldn't wrap my head around the fact that I was supposed to fake what I feel for her. The one person I couldn't spend more than fifteen minutes with without wanting to kill her. I was supposed to see her as my biggest enemy, the person who held the key to all the answers I needed to succeed.

God, I hated the fact that it was her, and I mean, really hated it. I don't know how I got myself in this position. It only meant problems for me, and I was either going to lose my job or her. Before I brought her on his trip, I would've been able to choose to lose her with no hesitation.

I wouldn't even second guess myself with how sure I would've been with my answer. But now, if someone were to ask me to choose between losing her or my job, it would be far harder to answer. Harder and uncomfortable because I knew my answer would be different.

Once I got the door unlocked, Celeste pushed it open and walked inside, not giving me a second look. Her sandals clicked against the hardwood floor as I watched her disappear down the hallway toward one of the bedrooms.

I shut the door softly, walking down the same hall. The lights in the house remained turned off, the darkness soothing in a way I didn't expect. The silver glow of the moon streaming through the wide windows lit the space, its reflection dancing on the ocean waves just beyond the glass. Faintly, the sound of the surf crashing against the shore filled the silence, steady and unyielding, like it had been there for centuries.

When I reached her door, I paused. It wasn't fully closed, left ajar just enough that I could see the faint sliver of moonlight spilling into the hallway. My hand hovered above the door frame, unsure of whether to knock or push it open.

Inside, I could hear the faint rustle of fabric, the creak of the bed as she shifted her weight. I imagined her sitting there, bathed in moonlight, her arms wrapped around herself like she was holding something fragile together.

I leaned against the wall beside the door, letting my head fall back with a quiet thud. The cool wood pressed against my skull, grounding me as I tried to steady my thoughts.

I knew better than to bother her, but I couldn't go to bed knowing that she was in the next room. I didn't want tonight to end, and I didn't know when I would have another moment like this. But what would I say to her?

The sound of the waves outside grew louder, or maybe it was just in my head.

Finally, I pushed the door open a little further, the soft creak breaking the stillness.

She was sitting on the edge of the bed, her back to me, her silhouette framed by the moonlight. She didn't turn around, but I knew she heard me. The way her shoulders tensed slightly gave her away.

I stepped inside, the weight of the moment pressing down on me.

"Celeste," I said quietly, her name carrying more meaning than I could put into words.

She stayed silent, but she didn't tell me to leave either. That was enough to keep me moving forward, one cautious step at a time.

The moonlight illuminated her profile as I moved closer, casting her in silver and shadow. When I finally sat beside her, the mattress dipped slightly under my weight, but she still didn't look at me.

I stayed quiet, searching for the right words. I thought I'd be silent forever until she finally spoke for the both of us.

"I thought you were going skinny-dipping," she said, reminding me of our bet from the train ride. "It's time to pay the price," she turned her face to me, her eyes gleaming with mischief.

"You're right," I answered with a boyish grin I couldn't keep to myself. With a quick moment, I threw my shirt over my head with one arm. I placed my shirt next to her, and she raised an eyebrow, clearly caught off guard by how quickly I was playing along.

Her eyes scanned my face, traveling down to my torso. "You're really going through with this?" she asked, her voice laced with mock disbelief; her eyes betrayed a flicker of amusement.

I stood up from the bed, kicking off my shoes. "A bet's a bet, Celeste, and I don't back out of a promise."

"Really?" Her eyes widened as I unbuckled my belt, pulling it off.

"Are you going to come and collect my debt?" I shot her a wink, the moonlight catching her expression as she tried, unsuccessfully, to suppress a grin. I unbuttoned my pants and let them drop to the floor in one swift motion, kicking them aside with dramatic flair. "What's the matter, Celeste?" I teased, stepping backward toward the door that led to the beach. "Don't tell me you're getting shy now."

I walked toward the door leading to the beach. Her chuckle was light and soft, the kind of sound that made my chest tighten in the best way.

She followed me outside, standing at the center of the porch.

I paused in the sand, turning to look at her one last time. She was standing on the porch, bathed in silver light, her hair flowing in the wind, her arms crossed over her chest, pushing her breasts up.

"You're missing one more piece of clothing!" she yelled to me, her smile contagious.

For a moment, I was caught between wanting to go through with this ridiculous bet and the sudden realization that I didn't want to leave her there, even for a second.

"You coming?" I asked, my voice softer now, the teasing edge fading.

Her smile faltered, and hesitation flickered in her eyes, or maybe something deeper.

"Oh no, no, that wasn't part of the bet," she said after a moment, her tone steady.

I nodded, swallowing the faint disappointment that crept in.

"Suit yourself. You're missing out." I shrugged out of my underwear, fully naked.

Celeste let out a loud gasp as she stared. I couldn't help but chuckle softly, the sound of it mixing with the crashing waves, knowing full well what had gotten her attention.

"Nothing you haven't seen before, sweetheart," I teased, turning slightly to glance over my shoulder at her. The moonlight caught the glint in her eyes, making them shine with a mischievous spark. "Still not going to join me?" I asked one last time before I ran in the water.

She stood back, unable to speak.

"No?" I shouted, walking backward toward the water. "Okay…" I added as I jogged down to the shore. The sand was cool beneath my feet as I made my way toward the water, the moon casting a glittering path across the waves.

The water was cold, biting against my skin, but I didn't care. I let out a howl right before I dove beneath the waves, letting the chill clear my mind and reset the rhythm of my thoughts.

When I reached the surface, gasping for air, I turned back toward the house, and to my surprise, Celeste ran in the water without warning in her underwear. She let out a sharp scream as her body crashed against the cold water. My body shivered underneath the water, and I swam toward her, desperate to feel her warmth.

She dipped her head under the water and emerged with a defiant laugh, her wet hair clinging to her face and shoulders. The moonlight shimmered off the droplets on her skin, making her look even more untouchable, as though she were part of the night itself. She shook her head, sending water flying in all directions, her grin wide and triumphant.

"I wasn't going to miss out," she said, her voice light but full of fire. The defiance in her eyes matched the cool night air, but there was something heavier beneath it all, something I recognized all too well.

I couldn't help but laugh, the sound of it mingling with the waves crashing around us. "I was wrong about you Luci," I said, my heart pounding in my chest as I swam toward her. The cold of the water still bit at my skin, but it didn't matter now.

She took a step back, dipping under the surface again, and for a moment, I lost sight of her. My heart skipped a beat; but then she reappeared, emerging from the water with a playful glint in her eyes.

"You're not getting off that easy," she called, splashing water toward me with a mischievous grin.

I ducked just in time, the water splashing harmlessly past me. "You're the one who decided to join me, remember?" I teased, my body aching with the desire to get closer, to feel her warmth next to mine.

She narrowed her eyes, a playful challenge dancing in her gaze. Without another word, she swam deeper into the water, her body moving with effortless grace as if the ocean were an extension of herself. I followed her, the distance between us shrinking with each stroke.

As I reached her, I caught her waist with one arm, pulling her close. Her breath caught for a moment, the closeness of our bodies making the air between us heavy, charged with something unspoken.

"You're the one who extended the invitation," she whispered, her voice barely audible over the roar of the ocean, but I could hear the laughter in it, the joy that she couldn't quite contain. Her legs wrapped around my waist, touching me at my core. The fabric of her underwear was the only thing blocking us from each other.

"All I did was suggest it. I might be crazy for jumping in, but you're just as guilty for following me in," I replied, my voice low, teasing, but with a hint of something more. I gripped her ass and rocked my hips against her center. She let out a soft moan, and my dick got rock hard with the sound.

Her eyes flickered down to my lips, the distance between us closing until I could feel the heat radiating off her body, even in the cool water. The tension in the air was thick, the space between us crackling with anticipation.

"I think we're both a little crazy," she said, her voice barely a whisper now. I reached out, brushing my lips against hers in a kiss that was as urgent, the waves crashing around us as though the world itself was urging us to give in. She clung close to me, her hand running through my hair as I held her tight.

My right hand stayed on her waist and my left traveled up to her left breast and squeezed. She let out a gasp and placed her lips on my neck. My breath hiked up with every moment, and even though the water around us felt ice cold, my body felt like it was on fire.

"Micheal, please," she whined as she started grinding on my cock once again. My eyes rolled back with pleasure as she sucked on my skin. "I want it," she whispered in my ear. I growled, thrusting my bulge at her core; the need to remove the fabric was too powerful.

"Want what?" I asked, wanting to hear her fully beg for it.

"Exactly what you want," she replied, trying to lean back to tease me once again. I held on to her tightly, bringing her back to me.

"You're not doing this to me again," she said as I dragged the both of us out of the water. I carried her in my arms and planted her on the shore. The waves kissed our feet as I hovered over her. "If you start something, you're going to have to finish it," she added with a quiet hum, a mix of challenge and anticipation in her voice.

A slow smile crept across my face before I kissed the delicate curve of her collarbone. Her body shook beneath my touch and against the cold wind. I unclipped her bra, bearing her to me. Her nipples pointed hard with the chilly breeze; they were a soft shade of pink, begging for me to take them in my mouth. Gripping one, I leaned down and sucked on it, and softly tugged on it between my teeth.

Celeste let out a sharp breath, writhing underneath me. My tongue traveled down to her torso and stopped at the fabric of her panties. With a swift movement, I ripped them off her skin. Abruptly, her thighs closed shut.

I looked into her eyes as my hands rested on her knees.

"You lost the bet; this isn't supposed to be a reward," she stuttered, her body obviously wanting something different.

"Who said this was my reward?" I asked as I squeezed my hand between her thighs. "This is your reward for winning," I whispered as I pinched her clit. "For bravely jumping in the water with me." I moved my hand lower, pushing two fingers inside of her. "For being such…" I pushed my fingers knuckles deep inside her, her thighs fully open for me. "A good girl…" I rested my head on her shoulder. "*My* good girl." She squirmed, holding my hand with all of her might. "Open wider for me, baby," I said as her thighs welcomed me.

"Don't stop," she cried as she rode my hand.

"No?" I whispered as I reached a spot that had her arching her back. I stared at her with maniac starved eyes, knowing that this view was the only thing that had me completely obsessed.

I pumped my fingers rapidly. "Finally doing what I ask," I grinned proudly.

"I didn't willingly do anything you want," she spat back, fighting against her need as hard as she could. It's easily one of the most attractive things I've seen from her. "You're supposed to be listening to me," she reminded me.

"Alright, tell me what you want," I said, taking my fingers out of her. "Your wish is my command," I repeated.

"Fuck me," she said, stunning me to silence. My erection grew harder, and now it was far too painful to ignore. Pre-cum glistening at my tip, I'm unable to pass by it. She had no idea of the monster she released. I was hungry, starving for her, and she was laying there, willing to give herself to me.

"Celeste," I tried to warn her before I allowed myself to lose control and give her what she wanted and more.

"Fuck me, now," she demanded like a true boss. Who was I to not give her what she wanted?

Just like that, the monster that was chained up inside me was released. I grabbed her and instantly flipped her onto all fours. The view from behind, had me losing my shit, and with a quick movement, I thrusted deep inside her.

I paused as I fully sat inside her, needing to take a breath and keep my heart beat normal. She pushed back, needing more.

Fuck. She was going to be the end of me.

I pulled back and pushed myself in her again. I pumped in and out of her, faster and harder with every thrust. She laid on the shore, her hands gripping the sand with all her might. My head fell back as I continued fucking her with everything I had.

She let out a sharp gasp when I gripped her hips and tilted them higher, angling her perfectly. My thrusts hit deeper, and I didn't miss the way her body reacted—tensing, shaking, craving more.

"Right there," she panted, voice breaking with need. "Yes—don't stop…"

She squealed when I lifted her hips higher, giving me the perfect angle to hit the spot that had her trembling. One of my hands slid beneath her, finding her clit and circling it in time with my thrusts.

"Yes, just like that!" she screamed, pushing back into me, her body needy and eager, matching my rhythm with her own. I was barely holding on, watching her lose control—the way she gripped me, the slick sound of our bodies, the heat, everything.

"Fuck," I groaned, trying to hold on. "You feel so damn good… so tight… so wet…" My words came out broken, lost in the pace of our bodies moving together.

She was trembling now, head dropping as her hands gripped the sand. "I'm—oh my god, I'm so close—"

"I've got you," I said low against her ear, keeping the pressure just right. The way she pushed back into me, matching my urgency with her own, had me unraveling.

She cried out, her body shaking violently as her orgasm hit, clenching hard around me. Her head dropped forward, and she gasped, her body shuddering. Watching her lose control like that, because of us, wrecked me. I groaned, buried deep inside her, and let go, shuddering through my release as I held her close.

Shortly after, we laid beside each other, looking up at the star as the waves crashed at our feet. I wrapped my arms around her. Placing a kiss on her forehead and feeling the most dangerous words at the tip of my tongue.

Her eyes fluttered closed as she soaked in the moonlight and the gentle, salty breeze. She snuggled close to me, her head resting on my chest.

"I love you Luci." The words slipped out of my mouth. I laid next to her, unable to believe the words that came out of my mouth.

Her eyes opened, and she stared into my soul, making me wait for her answer. She placed a hand on the side of my face and planted a kiss on my lips.

"I love you too, Micheal."

Those words being said back to me gave me an immense wave of peace. I felt completely invincible to the world with her in my arms.

Because if she loved me back, nothing in the world could have the power to hurt me.

CHAPTER 33
MICHEAL

The light from the sun shone down on my face. I tossed around, feeling an extreme amount of pebbles exfoliate my skin. I gripped the blanket I had on my torso and tugged it over my head, wanting to hide from the light. My hand reached out for a warm figure, but as I reached out, I felt nothing, only sand.

I squinted my eyes open and realized she was gone. Celeste must have left earlier and left me this blanket. What time did she leave? With a loud sigh, I stood up and wrapped the blanket around my torso.

Glancing over at the house, I couldn't see any lights on, or any sign of life. I walked toward the porch and opened the door. The house was silent, but there was a strong scent of butter and cheese coming from the kitchen. I made my way toward the kitchen and found Celeste cooking something on the stove.

Her hair was wet, as if she had just gotten out of the shower, her curls slowly drying. She had on my shirt from yesterday when I left it on her bed.

She didn't notice me at first, so I leaned against the doorframe, watching her cook. The blanket was still wrapped tightly around me like a makeshift towel. I couldn't help but smile at the peaceful scene. Despite everything, this felt like the most normal thing in the world.

"You're up early," I said softly, announcing my presence. "I didn't feel you leave."

She turned, her eyes lighting up with a mixture of surprise and affection. "Good morning," she replied, wiping her hands on a dish towel. "I didn't want to wake you. You looked like you were enjoying your nap by the waves."

I walked over, leaning against the counter. "Would've been nice if you brought me in with you."

She shrugged, giving me a playful smile. "I didn't want to disturb your beauty sleep. Besides, I knew the sunrise was going to wake you eventually."

I watched as she carefully cut a quesadilla into perfect wedges. "Also, there's been a random number calling you all morning," she said, glancing at my phone set on the counter.

"Did you answer?" I asked, picking up my phone and seeing Dylan's number on my call log. My palms sweat and my heart rapidly beat in my chest as I waited for her response.

"No, I didn't know if you wanted me to answer or not," she said. "But Min Ho called, I answered," she admitted. "He invited us over for lunch to say goodbye to everyone."

I placed my phone down and walked around the counter until I reached her. I held her from behind, wrapping her in my arms. "How do you feel?" I asked her, pushing everything she had just told me to the side. All I wanted to know was how she was feeling.

She turned around, her chest facing mine. "I feel amazing," she answered softly, brushing her lips against mine.

"Me too," I confessed, kissing her.

"Mmm," she murmured against my lips, pulling back. "Eat, and shower. You're full of sand."

"Whatever you say, Luci," I gave her a peck on her forehead, grabbing the quesadilla and taking a bite.

We headed back to the house one last time before leaving for the train station. The late afternoon sun cast a golden hue over the small home, making it feel even warmer, more welcoming, like the home I was always supposed to have.

In the kitchen, Min Ho leaned over the counter while Celeste said her goodbyes to my aunt and uncle. It was just the two of us, a quiet moment before the inevitable goodbye.

"I'm glad you came down for the weekend," Min Ho said, his voice full of sincerity. "I couldn't have asked for anything more. Everything feels complete now."

"Not fully," I said, tilting my head, implying that he needed to find his person to feel fully complete.

"For now I am," he replied, knowing exactly what I was hinting at. "Maybe one day I'll be more open to that idea."

I let out a short laugh, shaking my head, but then, almost without thinking, the words slipped out. "Is it horrible that I don't want to see or talk to my father again?"

Min Ho's expression shifted, confusion flickering across his face.

I exhaled sharply. "Spending time with you guys, meeting the entire family—it was exactly what I've been craving for years, and knowing that he's the reason I was oblivious for so long…" I clenched my jaw, anger simmering beneath the surface. "It makes me want to hate him."

Min Ho's eyes softened as understanding settled in. "No, Micheal, it's not horrible to hate him for hiding such a big part of your life," he said, crossing his arms. "But it is horrible to hold on to that grudge forever. It'll only hurt you. So do yourself a favor—talk to him one last time before you go back to New York."

My eyes widened at his suggestion. "Are you nuts? Did you not hear a word I just said?"

"I did," he said evenly. "Which is exactly why I'm suggesting it." He placed a firm hand on my shoulder, offering silent support. "Hey, do it, don't do it—it's your choice. Just think about it."

I scoffed, shaking my head. "Maybe another time," I muttered, unwilling to even consider it. Maybe someday, if he changed, if he proved he deserved my trust again, I would let him back in. But for now, I had to protect my peace. I wouldn't let anyone make me feel stupid and used. Not him. Not anyone.

Min Ho nodded in understanding. "Do whatever's best for you." His lips curled into a small smile. "Have a safe trip back, and don't forget about us."

"Not a chance."

"One of these days, invite Juno and me. We'll hop on the first plane out."

"Of course. I was already planning to." I felt a wave of warmth at the thought. In such a short time, these people had become family. Real family. The kind that didn't feel like an obligation but a choice. "Celeste and I will be back soon," I added, because the idea of returning without her didn't feel right.

Min Ho grinned. "I know you will." He pulled me in for a hug, clapping my back. "Take care, little bro."

"You got it," I chuckled.

Before I could take another step, Aunt Clara pulled me into an even tighter embrace. "You take care of yourself, you hear?" she murmured against my shoulder. "You've got people who love you; don't ever forget that."

I swallowed hard and nodded. "I won't."

Uncle Jae-hyun shook my hand firmly before pulling me into a half-hug. "Don't be a stranger. This is your home now, too."

Min Ho nudged my shoulder. "You're more than welcome to crash at one of my properties."

I smirked. "I'll keep that in mind."

Juno had been clinging to Min Ho's leg, his small face

scrunched in concentration like he was deciding whether he was too old to ask to be picked up or not. But the moment I crouched down, he let go of his dad and launched himself at me, wrapping his little arms around my neck.

"Bye, Uncle Micheal," he mumbled.

I closed my eyes for a moment, hugging him a little tighter. "Bye, buddy. I'll see you soon."

Standing off to the side, Hene crossed her arms, studying me with a skeptical look. "You better actually come back," she huffed. "Not just say it."

I chuckled. "I will, and I expect to be interrogated the second I step foot back here."

"Oh, you will be," she smirked.

I laughed, shaking my head, but as I turned, I caught Celeste's gaze. She had been quietly watching the entire interaction, her eyes shining with warmth. Without a word, I reached for her hand, threading my fingers through hers.

She gave my hand a gentle squeeze, and together, we stepped out of the house, the warmth of family still lingering in my heart. For the first time in a long time, I felt full. Whole. And as we walked toward the future, I knew this wasn't goodbye. Not really.

CHAPTER 34
CELESTE / MICHEAL

CELESTE

"Okay, I'm going to need you to slow down and explain to us how this happened!" Katherine exclaimed. I had arrived from Korea to New York just this morning and had the girls waiting for me at my apartment. They surprised me with champagne, cookies, and a big banner that said 'Mission Accomplished!'

After seeing the banner, I didn't hesitate telling them what had changed between Micheal and I. After telling them everything that had happened in explicit detail, it's safe to say that I had never seen their jaws drop faster. Katherine had spat out her champagne, Elaina had choked on her cookie, and Valery had gone completely silent as her eyes almost popped out of her head through FaceTime.

"Oh. My. God." Valery was the first to break the silence, followed by Katherine's need to tell me to slow down and explain how this happened. I shrugged, pouring myself a glass.

"But you hated him before you got on the plane," Elaina said, fully shocked.

"I did," I explained. "But then I got to see a different side of Micheal."

"Define 'different,'" Elaina said, raising a brow. "Because last time we spoke about this, you made it very obvious that you wanted to rip his head off."

"You're not wrong." I raised my hands in surrender. "There was a moment in Korea where we had a real heart-to-heart. He suddenly became someone who understood what it felt like to feel alone; he became someone who experienced pain, hurt, and loss. He opened up to me and proved to me that the version of Micheal that I so much hated, wasn't him at all. And then things just... clicked."

"Clicked?" Valery's voice crackled over FaceTime. "There are different types of clicks...which one are you talking about?"

"I don't know how to explain it. We were forced to spend time together, and it just... felt right." I took a breath before continuing and thought about the next words I was going to say to them. "All the types you could think of," I answered truthfully, knowing that they would take it exactly how it was.

"Emotionally and...physically?" Katherine asked in a low voice as she grabbed onto a cushion from my couch.

I nodded, taking a sip of champagne as I heard their gasps fill the room.

"You naughty girl! I can't believe you!" Elaina prompted, leaning forward with an enormous smile plastered on her face. "Don't leave us hanging!"

"I..." I paused, considering my next words. "It was the best I ever had."

That sent Katherine into a fit of laughter, while Elaina gasped so loudly I thought she'd sucked all the air out of the room. Valery's jaw dropped again as she stammered, "How did it even get to that point?"

I couldn't help but smile as I recounted the moment. "It just happened. It wasn't planned or anything, but it was... unexpected and perfect."

"This was the most unexpected thing I thought you'd tell us today," Elaina said, finally leaning back in her chair. "I mean..." She pops a confetti popper. "Are we celebrating? What's the vibe here?"

"I-I'm not sure." I stared at the tiny pieces of confetti drifting down like awkward snowflakes. "He told me he loved me afterwards, but he hasn't really communicated to me what we really are, and I don't want to jinx it or get too excited."

"Fair." Elaina swept some confetti off the table. "Wait, did you just say he said he *loved* you?"

"Celeste, that's huge," Katherine interjected, slamming her hand on the table like it was the most enthralling thing she's heard all morning. "You realize you just turned this into a plot twist, right? Like, are we still supposed to eat after *that*?"

"Don't let it go to waste," I said, gesturing toward the snacks. "I promise, this isn't even the weirdest part."

Elaina froze mid-bite. "Wait—there's *more*?"

"Well," I hesitated, searching for the right words. Before I could feed them more details, my phone buzzed with an email notification. I glanced at it, my eyes widening as I read the words on the email.

"What is it?" Valery asked.

"Meredith wants me to come down to the Gallery; she says it's important." I gripped my phone as I felt a wave of anxiety wash over me.

Was this a good important or a bad important? If it's important, it's urgent. It has to be bad, right? Why else would she have contacted me today and not tomorrow, which is the day I returned to work?

Elaina raised an eyebrow, sensing the shift in my mood. "Is that a bad thing?"

I glanced at Elena and Katherine, trying to steady my breath.

"I don't know... It's just—why would Meredith be reaching out today, out of all days? It's not like her to send something urgent like this unless something went wrong. I just got back from my trip."

Valery dialed in, her voice soft but steady. "Maybe it's just something she needs your help on. Could be something simple."

I wasn't convinced. "Maybe. But with Meredith, nothing is ever simple. Nothing about this internship is simple."

Elaina set her fork down slowly, her expression shifting to one of concern. "What do you think?"

I hesitated. I had a feeling that it might be a situation with the days I've been absent. Though they had been excused, I still have a feeling that this had something to do with it. We were entering the beginning of June; this might be the time she will make some cuts. "I don't know." But I didn't want to admit it out loud yet; it would be so devastating if I was right.

I glanced at the phone again, the email still staring back at me.

Important. Come to the Gallery. That was all it said, but it felt like it held a thousand meanings.

"Well, go find out!" Katherine encouraged me. "I'm sure it'll be fine."

Right, or it could be the worst-case scenario.

I left the girls at the apartment and made my way toward the gallery. With each step, the weight of uncertainty pressed harder against my chest, my heart pounding faster than I could calm it. I tried to distract myself with shallow breaths, but the closer I got, the more the doubt and anxiety twisted inside me.

This always happened to me; I always pictured things turning out badly when, at most times, it turned out being the complete opposite. It was like this every test, every interview, every show or auction I did.

It wasn't like I was anxious to disappoint anyone; I had no one I wanted to win for. It had always been for me; which was why the losses felt much more personal and intense. The fear of failing was always there, tattooed in the back of my mind, even when everything was going smoothly.

By the time I reached the gallery, my palms were clammy, and my stomach felt sick. The glass doors loomed in front of me, with people standing and observing the art pieces hung on the wall. The place continued to be as busy and as elegant as I left it.

I took a deep breath and pushed the door open, preparing myself for whatever awaited me. The faint hum of voices and soft clinking of glasses from an ongoing exhibit buzzed in the background.

Meredith stood by a display in the back, her gaze fixed on something behind me, her expression a mix of focus and intrigue. She saw me before I could say anything, gave a small nod, and walked towards me.

"Celeste, I'm glad you could come in," she said as she motioned for me to follow her. "It's better if we go to my office to further speak about the reason I called you in early; it'll give us more privacy."

I swallowed hard as I followed her through the gallery. The soft hum of conversations and displays of contemporary art usually drew my focus, but I wasn't paying attention to the pieces. My focus was on her and what she wanted to tell me.

As we got to her office, she unlocked the door and opened it for me to enter. When I walked in, she shut the door and made her way to her chair. "Please, take a seat." She motioned toward the chair set in front of her desk.

I sat, crossing my legs to stop them from bouncing unconsciously.

"Now that it's just us, how was your trip?" she began by asking. I looked at her for a beat, confused if this was the reason she brought me in.

She wanted to know about my trip? No, don't be stupid, Celeste, she's obviously asking out of politeness.

"It was great," I responded with little detail. She nodded and placed both of her hands on the desk.

"That's great," she said with a shift of tone. "I imagine you're wondering why I asked you to come in."

"Honestly, yes," I admitted, sitting up straighter. My voice came out steadier than I felt.

She offered a small smile, but it didn't reach her eyes. "Are you aware that Oliver left us last week?" she asked, patiently waiting for my response.

"What? No, I didn't. He had told me he really liked this job."

"Yes, we thought so as well.. Anyway, since he left, and you two shared the internship until one of you proved your dedication and commitment to the role, his departure changes things," she continued, her voice calm but firm.

I blinked, struggling to process the news.

Oliver had left? I thought he was thriving here, always so confident and sure of himself. Did he leave because of me? Why would he give up something he wanted so badly?

"So, what does this mean?" I asked cautiously.

"Well, that's what I wanted to speak with you about... His departure changes things," she repeated.

"Okay..." I said slowly, trying to mask the swirl of emotions rising inside me. "Changes things how?"

She clasped her hands together on the desk, leaning back slightly. "With Oliver gone, the full internship position is now available, and we've decided to offer it to you."

My breathing hitched. The full position? Just like that?

"I... wow. I didn't expect this," I admitted, my words tumbling out.

"That's not all," she said, my gaze faltering because there was more. "I wanted to speak to you about an opportunity—one

I believe you'd be perfect for. We'd also like to offer you a promotion."

"A promotion?" I repeated, my voice barely above a whisper. The room seemed to still as the weight of her words settled over me. She had just given me great news; this was out of this world.

"Yes," she confirmed, leaning forward again. "Not only would you take on the full internship role, but we'd like to elevate your responsibilities beyond what's typical for an intern. You've shown exceptional potential while you have been here, and we believe you're ready for more."

"Meredith, I would be beyond honored to accept! But before I do, what kind of responsibilities would I be taking on?" I asked, still trying to process everything.

"You'd oversee the planning and execution of our upcoming exhibit—managing artist relations, coordinating logistics, and working closely with the marketing team to ensure its success. Essentially, you'd be acting as an associate coordinator for this project. It's a significant step up, but I'm confident you can handle it."

My hands slightly tremble on my thighs at how overwhelmed I felt with the news. This was the best news I could ask for, and I had never imagined them giving it to me so soon.

"I won't let you down, Meredith. Thank you so much for this!" I exclaimed in my chair, the excitement getting the best of me.

Her lips curved into a faint smile. "It's well-deserved, Celeste. You've shown dedication, creativity, and an ability to adapt under pressure—qualities we value highly. This project we have coming up, we're importing a new piece from Rome. It's the main piece of the entire exhibit—*The Kiss* by Gustav Klimt —It's important it goes smoothly if you want to keep this position."

"Of course," I agreed, ready to take on the responsibility. *The*

Kiss by Gustav Klimt was a classic, a gift from history, one of the most iconic artworks of the 20th century. I was so excited about helping plan this event, I was shaking. My mind was already racing with ideas: how to showcase such a masterpiece, how to ensure the event would be unforgettable.

"I'll make sure everything is perfect," I said, my voice calm despite the thrill coursing through me.

Meredith nodded, her expression serious. "I know you will. That's why we chose you, Celeste. But I won't sugarcoat it. This will be one of the most high-profile projects the gallery has taken on. There's no room for error. We'll be coordinating with art historians, conservators, and international logistics teams. I trust you to work alongside me."

"I understand; you will not be disappointed," I responded, wanting to prove that her confidence toward me felt amazing, and I was eager to live up to the expectations she had of me.

"Good. I'll forward you the details later today, including the timeline for the piece's arrival—which is two days from today—and the key players you'll be working with. The exhibit is scheduled to open this coming month, so we'll need to start preparations immediately." She stood, signaling the meeting's end.

"Got it," I said firmly. I felt like pinching myself to ensure that this was real.

"I'm excited to work with you on this. I know it will turn out great," she said, opening the door for me and handing out her palm for me to shake. I gripped her hand and gave it a firm shake, closing the deal.

"Thank you again." I walked out of her office and headed out of the gallery. Once I made it outside, a little further away from the doors, I jumped up hysterically, spinning in a circle as the adrenaline surged through me, and I shrieked out loud. I couldn't believe it. I got a promotion, and not only that, I was given the biggest opportunity of my life. The excitement bubbled over uncontrollably.

I stopped mid-spin, laughing breathlessly. *The Kiss.* I could barely wrap my mind around the fact that I would be involved in the exhibit of such an iconic piece. It felt surreal.

I pulled out my phone, hands still shaking, and dialed Micheal on my phone. The first person I wanted to share this news with was him; his face was the first one I pictured when I grabbed my phone.

The phone rang twice and went straight to the voice machine. *"It's Micheal Zhang; leave a message and I'll think about getting back to you."* I blinked, not expecting it to go straight to voicemail; I hadn't heard it until now.

Micheal was always quick to answer, but I guess he's probably busy right now. I smiled anyway, feeling the rush of adrenaline still coursing through my body. I took a breath as I heard the beep to record my message.

"Hi! It's me, Celeste. I just got the best news at work! Bring a bottle of wine and come by my apartment at… say eight? I can't wait to tell you everything. See you then!" I bit my lip as I hung up the phone.

Even though he didn't answer my call and I wasn't able to hear his voice right now, I knew Micheal would've been as happy as I am.

∼

MICHEAL

"What's up? What was so urgent that you needed me to come and see you in person?" I asked as I set my jacket and bike helmet on Adam's desk.

"First, get your shit off my desk. Second, I asked you to come because what we need to talk about is important," Adam answered as he stood up from his chair. "Before I start, how was your trip with Celeste?" I ignored his question for a second as I moved my things off his desk.

He's always so up tight...

"Great," I answered, not wanting to share too many details. I knew if I told him, he would not be happy with the truth. He specifically told me that getting with Celeste was not a good idea, and if I tell him I've fallen for her? I wouldn't hear the end of it.

"Right. We'll go further into that later. Sit, Aaron should be here any second," he said.

"Aaron? The Pearson brothers, together with it being planned? This must be very important," I said sarcastically, but Adam didn't budge. He stood still as he stared at the door. "Okay... what's this about?" Adam didn't look at me, he looked everywhere but at me. He was disappointed; I knew that look. But I didn't get why.

Within a few seconds, Aaron opened the door, walking in. "I had to reschedule two meetings this morning to be here. Let's start talking," he declared as he shut the door closed again and leaned against the wall, crossing his arms and watching from a distance.

"Okay, is this some kind of intervention? Is this about me going out with Celeste? Listen man, I–" As I was about to explain what my feelings for Celeste had turned into, Adam spoke over me.

"We know what you and Dylan Cruz are up to, and let me just say, this heist might sound nice and easy, but one of you will end up behind bars and I'd much rather it be Dylan than you."

I froze, my mouth half-open as Adam's words sunk in. How the hell did he even find out about Dylan and me?

Aaron raised an eyebrow, pushing off the wall to step closer. "What? Surprised we know? Since when did you become some kind of criminal mastermind? Did you really think we wouldn't find out?"

"I don't know what you're talking about," I shot back, trying to keep my voice steady even as my pulse pounded in my ears.

Adam crossed his arms, his eyes narrowing. "Don't play dumb, Micheal. I know you've been meeting with Dylan, planning something that involves a lot of money and a certain artwork. The question is: how deep are you in, and how do we pull you out before this goes sideways?"

"Hold on," I interrupted, trying to maintain control over this conversation, even though my mind was racing. "You're making it sound like I'm some kind of criminal. This isn't what you think it is."

Aaron scoffed, shaking his head. "Oh, it's not? So, you're not working with Dylan on a plan to swipe a multi-million dollar painting? Because that's exactly what Adam told me."

I shot a glare at Adam, who remained stoic, his arms crossed like a disappointed father. "You've been digging into my business? What the hell, Adam?"

"Don't turn this around on me," Adam snapped, his voice rising just enough to make me flinch. "I didn't dig into your business; I got a phone call regarding this situation you're now involved in. I'm not about to sit back and watch you ruin your life because you got in over your head with someone like Dylan Cruz."

"I'm not in over my head," I said, my voice tight with frustration. "You don't even know the full story. This isn't just about stealing a painting. There's more to it than that."

"Oh yeah? Please, enlighten us," Aaron said with a sarcastic grin. "Tell me how this is actually a good idea and not the worst decision you've ever made."

"It'll only be this once. I'll get paid fifty-four *million* dollars. This would be my money, and I can make an even bigger fortune with it. I'm tired of working my ass off only to get the bare minimum!" I yelled back, frustrated.

"It's dirty fucking money Micheal, how could you want that?" Adam asked with desperation in his voice.

"That dirty money will make me filthy rich! I'll never need to depend on anyone, not my boss, not my father, no one!" Aaron and Adam looked at each other, both unhappy with the words coming out of my mouth.

"Alright, look. Not only is it dirty money, but this is a suicide mission. There's no way you'll stay out of jail after it. I mean, *The Kiss*? Really? Why don't you pick a more popular painting, one they'll without a doubt notice is gone!" Aaron argued, marching closer to the desk and standing behind Adam.

"I'm not explaining the plan to you step by step, alright? Who the hell told you about this?" I asked, feeling an insane amount of hatred for the person who spoke of my personal business.

"Diego Ford," Adam answered truthfully. I stayed quiet; the name sounded oddly familiar. I heard of him, but from where? Wait, no, I got it. Diego Ford, owner of Avenue.

How the hell did he know about me?

"I think you'd like to know that Diego is in the same side business as Dylan. So much so that they are rivals and they are constantly fighting over clients and pieces. Diego was not happy to hear that he recruited another person in his group, which is why he reached out to us," Aaron explained. "You didn't think that Dylan was the only one planning to pull this off, did you?" he asked, making me feel like a stupid child.

"Of course I knew that. Do I look stupid?" I responded with anger bleeding through my voice. I was bluffing; it was obvious they knew more about this 'side business' than I did. I couldn't help but feel embarrassed that I didn't bother digging up my own information.

"We didn't bring you here to make you feel stupid Micheal; everyone has their reasons for making the wrong choices. What most people don't have is someone who cares for them and is willing to do anything to get them out of trouble," Adam said, his tone firm.

This was his way of looking out for me; it was tough love. Adam and Aaron aren't related to me, but they were my brothers. Which is why it pained me to turn my back on them. There was no way I was going to stop when I was so close to reaching my end goal.

"I understand why you both brought me here, and it means a lot to know that you both care this much for me. But... this is my choice, and I'm going to continue until I finish it," I said, standing up from my seat, grabbing my jacket and helmet from the couch. "I'm sorry," I added, heading toward the door.

"Micheal," Adam called after me, and I paused, my hand gripping the doorknob. "You don't want to go through with this. Once it's done, there's not much we can do to get you out of trouble." I could hear the pinch of pain in his voice, his fear of what would happen to me once I left this room.

"There are other ways you can make money, Mike; if you just give us a chance, we'll help you get there. With time," Aaron added.

I turned the doorknob, opened the door, and I turned my head back to them to give them a small smile. "I don't have time," I answered and walked out the door.

My walk down the hallway was silent, even though the building was booming with noise, everyone working in their own cubes and others inside glass meeting rooms. Each step I took that led closer to the elevator felt heavier. Almost as if I was walking through quicksand, and I yearned to turn back and allow them to help me.

But my pride, my ego, wouldn't allow me to just give in. I needed to do this for myself, even if it meant it would end badly for me.

Once I was out of the building, I took a deep breath and put on my jacket. My hands slightly shook as I zipped up the jacket, reaching my bike parked on the side of the street. The sun was out, but it offered little warmth against the storm swirling in my chest.

The streets were alive with the usual noise of the city—cars honking, people rushing past, their conversations blending into a dull hum. But my mind was elsewhere; I kept replaying Adam's words, Aaron's stance, the weight of their disappointment pressing against my ribs like a vise.

I reached for my phone, begging for a distraction, and turned on the screen. 'Missed call from Celeste' was the first thing I saw. I let out a breath of relief as I played her voicemail and placed the phone against my ear.

"Hi! It's me, Celeste. I just got the best news at work! Bring a bottle of wine and come by my apartment at... say eight? I can't wait to tell you everything. See you then!"

I slightly smiled as I listened to her voice, the only sound that calmed the storm of nerves swirling inside me. I talked to plenty of people in one day, but none of them compared to the smile she gave me in one second.

I checked the time; 12:00 pm. It was only noon, and she wanted me to meet her at eight. If it were up to me, I would go straight to her right now, but she's probably busy. I slipped the phone back into my pocket and sighed.

I swung a leg over my bike, hovered over the engine, and turned it on. The starting engine's hum vibrated through me. I missed riding; it had always been my escape.

Pulling into traffic, I drove off; the city blurred past me, buildings and people fading away as I focused on the road. Only a few hours until I saw Celeste; until then, I'd ride until I got tired of it.

CHAPTER 35
CELESTE

At exactly 7:59 p.m. I heard a knock at my door. After I finished lighting up the last candle in the living room, I ran to the door, hoping it would be Micheal. I opened the door and found Micheal leaning against the doorframe, holding a bouquet of purple roses and a bottle of red wine. His grin grew wider as he looked me up and down.

"I was going to wait for it to be eight, but I didn't want to wait another minute," he said, his voice warm and playful. He handed me the bouquet of roses, his fingers brushing mine briefly as he walked inside.

His eyes lingered on me, taking in my dress and the effort I'd put into setting the scene. "You're lucky I'm a nice host," I said as I snuck a sniff from the roses while he looked around the room. "I won't take any points off for that one minute."

"How generous of you." He glanced back at me with the most charming smile I've seen on his face. "So, what's the big news you wanted to tell me?" he asked as he rolled up his sleeves. He wore a black button up long sleeve shirt that fit skin tight, and a pair of black pants.

He walked into my kitchen, opened a drawer and found the

corkscrew without having to ask; it was as if he knew his way around here already. He opened the bottle of wine, made his way back out to the living room, and poured the drink into the glasses I had set up at the table.

"I got called in to come in today, and at first I thought it was going to be bad news..." I said, holding the cup up for him to fill. He nodded, listening. "But my manager, Meredith, offered me the full internship, along with a promotion!" I added excitedly.

Micheal looked up at me, his eyes gleamed with joy. "Are you serious?" he asked, smiling hard. I nodded quickly, biting my lip, trying to contain my excitement. "That's amazing!" he exclaimed, setting the bottle down on the table and wrapping his hands around my waist, pulling me in for a tight hug.

"I couldn't believe it at first. But that's not even the best part. I get to be in charge of this upcoming exhibit, where they're bringing in *The Kiss* by Gustav Klimt! Me! In charge of such an iconic piece!" His smile faltered for a moment, his arms slightly softened their grip. "What's wrong?" I asked as I felt the sudden mood change.

He shook his head, standing back. "I just... wow, *The Kiss*. That's such a big deal. It's fantastic," he said, grabbing his glass of wine and taking a big gulp.

I tilted my head, studying him closely. Something in his voice felt... off. I was expecting a bigger, happier response. "Micheal, what is it? You seem... weird."

He set his glass down and rubbed the back of his neck, a habit I recognized when he was nervous. "I *am* happy for you. Really. It's just..." he trailed off, looking anywhere but at me.

"Just what?" I pressed, crossing my arms, taking a step back to give him the space he obviously wanted.

"It's nothing," he said, his voice steadying. "You caught me off guard, that's all. I wasn't expecting *this* kind of news." He smiled and stepped closer toward me. I instantly took another step back to maintain the distance; he sighed heavily when I kept my distance.

I frowned. I wasn't expecting this from him tonight; we were supposed to be celebrating. "Caught you off guard? Why would my good news do that?"

He swallowed, which only frustrated me more. "Because... *The Kiss* is such a high-profile piece, and now you're tied to it. I guess I wasn't prepared for that."

I nodded, but I wasn't convinced of the reason for his reaction.

His expression softened, but I knew he could see I wasn't entirely convinced.

"Micheal, is there something you're not telling me?" Something inside me told me I should ask this question, maybe he was hiding something. He stood still, quiet, as if he was contemplating telling me. "Micheal?" I said slowly, my voice lower now.

Whatever he was thinking about, he pushed it to the side as his eyes met mine again. "No, there's nothing," he said with a faint smile. "I'm just proud of you, Celeste. You deserve this."

I stared at him for a moment and chose to believe him. Sighing, I stepped closer, my fingers brushing up his arm. "Alright. But if there *is* something, you know you can tell me, right?"

"I know," he murmured, his voice soft.

"There's nothing you can say that will change the way I feel about you." His breath caught for a moment, so subtle I almost missed it. He looked at me; his dark eyes were soft but shadowed with something I couldn't quite name.

"You mean that?" he asked, his voice barely above a whisper.

"Of course I do," I said firmly, stepping closer. "Why wouldn't I?"

Micheal's jaw tightened, and he let out a slow exhale. For a moment, I thought he might finally tell me. The air between us felt charged, heavy with the weight of unsaid words. When I thought he'd say something, he leaned in, his lips hovering above mine.

"I want to believe you," he murmured, his breath warm against my skin.

My heart pounded in my chest, each beat echoing the tension that filled the space between us.

"Then do," I whispered back, my voice steady but pleading.

Micheal hesitated, his hand trembling slightly as it cupped my cheek.

"You don't know everything about me," he said, the vulnerability in his tone cutting through the walls he'd so carefully built. "If you did, you might not say that."

I placed my hand over his, holding it against my cheek.

"Then tell me," I urged softly. "Let me in, Micheal. Whatever it is, we'll face it together."

"I wish it were that simple," he said, his voice breaking. "But I can't," he said, barely audible. "One day you'll know everything, and the only thing I ask of you is that you'll stay with me. Don't—" He took a deep breath before continuing. "Don't walk away from me."

"I won't," I assured him, wanting to comfort and protect him from his fears, his mistakes, and his demons. He nodded softly, with a broken smile on his face.

"Good. Just remember that for me, will you?"

"Okay," I whispered. Then he leaned forward, his movements slow. I tilted my head, meeting him halfway, and when our lips finally touched, the tension melted into something softer, something tender. His hand slid to the back of my neck, pulling me closer, and I felt his heart beating against mine, frantic and alive.

The kiss deepened, slow and purposeful, as though he was pouring everything he couldn't say into the connection between us. I trailed my hand up his chest, unbuttoning the top of his shirt.

He pulled me in by my waist, his hands slid down and rested at the sides of my hips, tracing a path that left a trail of heat in its wake. My breath hitched when his lips left mine, traveling to the corner of my mouth, then along my jaw. The soft graze of his teeth made my knees weak, and I clutched his shirt, pulling him closer.

"I love the way you taste," he murmured against my skin, the words raw and breathless, sending a shiver down my spine. "I love the way you smell, the way your skin feels against mine." His voice was a mix of adoration and need, and it made me feel weightless, untethered.

I opened my mouth to respond, but the words dissolved into a soft gasp as he found the sensitive spot just below my ear. He chuckled, low and deep, the sound reverberating through me like a secret meant only for us.

"There's nothing else that could ever beat this," he whispered, his lips brushing the shell of my ear. "Nothing." He licks my earlobe and travels down to my collarbone.

"Don't ever take this away from me. Not when I've fully understood what it means to have it." He tightened his grip on my hips, his fingers dug into my skin. "You're mine," he grunted, lifting me up on the dining table.

Tiny gasps escaped from my lips; his touch heightened every part of my body. "I'll admit, there's something undeniably addictive about crossing boundaries." The hairs on the back of my neck that stood on end, my nipples pierced through my dress, and beneath I was completely drenched. "But that was your plan all along, wasn't it?"

"Micheal…" I said in a low whisper.

"Do you like to see me like this?" he hummed under his breath, continuing to leave trails of wet kisses. I spread my legs, allowing him to stand between them and get closer. "Do you like seeing how badly I want you? How bad I need you?" A moan left my lips as he dragged my dress down to my waist, revealing my breasts.

"N-no...I–" I stuttered between breaths; he grazed my nipples with his tongue, slightly wetting them. He grabbed my hand and placed it over his warm and throbbing erection, his eyes filled with desire. I moaned at how large he was.

"Look at what you do to me," He groaned. "You think there's anything fair about this? I crave you every day, every hour, every minute and every second." I gazed into his eyes while unbuckling his pants. His eyes wouldn't leave mine; it was like a challenge between us, waiting for someone to look away first.

I got off the table and pulled his zipper down. I reached inside his drawls and pulled his thick, hard cock. Pre-cum glazed at his tip; I licked my lips, thinking of how warm it would taste on my tongue.

Grabbing his arm, I turned him around and pushed him back into the table. He leaned against the edge and continued to gaze into my eyes, not looking away for a second. I got down on my knees and took him in my mouth.

My tongue swirled around him as I took him deeper down my throat.

"Fuck Luci," he breathed heavily, brushing the stray strands of hair out of my face as he pushed my head down. His cock reached the back of my throat, and my eyes watered as I fought to keep him in my mouth longer. When we pulled my head away, I gasped for air, saliva rolling down my chin.

"You look so fucking pretty, taking my dick down your throat." I moaned loudly in response to his dirty words. I loved how he didn't need to disrespect me with the insults for it to sound sexy. He still made me feel respected, even though I was kneeling before him doing the most inappropriate things.

I sucked the tip of his cock as I jerked off the rest of his length. His breaths hiked up as I picked up the pace. He bobbed his head back, slightly scrunched his nose and bit his bottom lip as he thrusted into my mouth. He looked back down at me when I groaned around his cock.

"That's a good girl,"

His praise turned me on even more; I was practically dripping on the floor with how wet I was. Sucking Micheal's cock had to be my new favorite thing to do; I loved making him feel good. I loved knowing I had the power to make him weak, to give him this vast amount of pleasure. The way his eyelids fluttered shut when I sucked on his tip hard, the way his breaths came out huskier and heavy with every head bob, the way he licks and bites his lips when he's trying to stop himself from coming.

All of those things were stuff I craved and wanted to see.

He pulled back and grabbed his erection, smacking it against my right cheek. "You fucking love this cock, don't you?" he groaned, a huge smirk playing on his face.

"Mhm," I nodded, kissing his tip. He grabbed my arms and pulled me up with a growl, spinning me around and bending me over the table. I shrieked when he turned my back to him, lifting my dress up to my waist. He pulled my underwear to the side and smacked his erection against my ass.

"Do you want this?" he rasped, grinding his thick length against me. "Tell me."

"I—" I gasped, my breath shaky, body aching to be filled.

"Tell me how much you want me to fuck your sweet pussy," he whispered in my ear while smelling my hair.

"Yes," I huffed out. I felt like I was about to die if I didn't have him inside me within the next few seconds.

"Yes?..." He pushed, wanting me to say the full response.

"I want to feel your big cock deep inside your sweet pussy," I said, out of breath. He let out a heavy groan.

"Say that again," he demanded, looking at me with admiration in his eyes.

"What?" I responded, consumed by lust.

"This is *my* sweet pussy. I want to hear you say it again."

I swallowed hard, my body trembling under his touch, heat pooling low in my stomach. He wasn't just asking; he was claiming, commanding, and something about the way he looked at me, possessive yet reverent, made me want to give him exactly what he wanted.

"It's yours," I breathed, my voice unsteady but sure. "This is your sweet pussy."

A slow, satisfied smirk curved his lips. His grip tightened, fingers digging into my hips as if grounding himself in the moment.

"That's right, baby," he murmured, his voice dark with need. "I'm going to make sure you never forget it."

He thrusted into me with full force. The sounds of his thighs smacking against the back of mine filled the silence in the room. All I could hear in the haze of my thoughts were our gasps and our groans of pleasure.

"There's no one like you, Celeste," he groaned, his voice tight, reverent. "No one."

His rhythm became erratic, chasing that final high. My fingers clawed at the table's edge, my body trembling as the pressure inside me coiled impossibly tight.

"Micheal," I whimpered, voice catching as my climax barreled into me, a rush of heat and trembling spasms that took my breath away. My walls clenched around him, milking every inch of him as I came hard, seeing stars behind my fluttering lashes.

"Fuck—Celeste," he growled, grabbing my hips with bruising intensity. He pulled out quickly, panting, and stroked himself once—twice—before he came with a sharp gasp, hot spurts spilling across my lower back and ass. His free hand held me steady as he rode out the waves, breath shaking against my ear.

After a long moment, he let out a low, satisfied groan and

grabbed a napkin from the nearby counter, gently wiping me clean with slow, careful hands. The act, tender and wordless, made my heart thud harder than the orgasm.

He leaned in, pressing a kiss to the back of my shoulder, his fingers tracing lazy circles into my hip. He tucked his head gently against the curve of my neck and shoulder, his breath ragged but soft, a quiet laugh escaping his lips.

Our breaths tangled together, and his hands held me firmly in place as if I might slip away, grounding me in this moment that felt infinite. He tucked his head gently against the curve of my neck and shoulder, his breath ragged but soft, a quiet laugh escaping his lips.

"No one will ever come as close," he murmured, his voice husky and tender, a vow I could feel echoing in my chest.

This time, I believed it.

CHAPTER 36
MICHEAL

The shrill ring of the phone cut through the silence, waking me from sleep. I groggily reached for it, quick to silence it before it woke Celeste. The bright screen flashed Dylan's name on the caller ID. It was four in the morning; he shouldn't be calling me at this time unless something was wrong.

I glanced over at Celeste; she's sleeping peacefully, her face soft and serene in the faint moonlight spilling through the window. With slow and careful movements, I slipped out of bed, cringing as the floor creaked under my weight, and ducked into the hallway before answering.

"Dylan?" I whispered, my voice heavy with sleep and unease. "What is it?"

"Micheal," he said, his voice tight. "We've got a problem. A big one."

My stomach churned. Hearing those words come out of Dylan's mouth woke me up instantly. Those words... it meant something life-altering; I knew it would only dig me into a deeper hole than I was already in.

"What kind of problem?"

"*The Kiss*," he said, cutting straight to it. "Our client just changed the terms. They're threatening to pull out unless we deliver it sooner. Two days, tops."

I froze in place, understanding what those words meant for us, *for me*. The plan to swipe the painting was barely coming together as it was.

"Two days? That's impossible! They know this isn't a grocery store grab, right?"

"They don't care," Dylan snapped. "Either we get it done, or the deal's off. Micheal, if they walk, we're out millions—and possibly worse. These aren't people you want to disappoint."

I leaned against the wall, the weight of the situation settling on my shoulders. Stealing *The Kiss* had always been a long shot, a near-impossible task. Now, with this new deadline, it felt suicidal.

Then there was Celeste.

I closed my eyes, guilt gnawing at my chest. She trusted me—probably more than she should. She had no idea I was using her, and every passing day made it harder to imagine telling her the truth. At first, I didn't care because, quite frankly, I hated her. But that's not the case anymore.

Don't fall for her... Yeah, well, it's too late for that.

"Dylan," I said slowly, "I don't think I can go through with this."

"You don't have a choice," he shot back. "You're in too deep, Micheal. We both are. I won't lose this client because you can't pull off your part of the job. Get that information tonight."

I hung up without another word, my mind racing. Two days. That wasn't enough time to execute the plan, let alone figure out a way to come clean to Celeste.

I stepped out into the living room, thinking of how the hell I was going to get the information Dylan needed. Turning to the right, I saw Celeste's Macbook charging.

Don't do it. A voice instantly warned me. *You don't have a choice.* The opposing voice argued.

Stuck between two choices, I shook my head and walked toward the laptop. I opened it, expecting a lock screen with a password request, but to my disappointment, it was unlocked.

"Oh, Celeste," I whispered, guilt filling me. I was hoping she'd have a password, just so I wouldn't have access so easily. A part of me didn't want to go through her privacy, and I was desperate for a reason to stop me.

I clicked on a few files until I found a document labeled 'Laurosse Exhibit Overview.' My heart sank. She had everything here: floor plans, security schedules, where *The Kiss* would be displayed, the codes, and even information on the alarm systems. It was all here, handed to me on a silver platter.

I stared at the screen, my fingers hovering over the keypad. This was it; this was what I have been trying to get for the last few months. With this information, we could easily pull off the operation in two days.

But at what cost?

Celeste trusted me, and it was not easy for her to do so. Now, I betrayed that trust in the worst possible way. This could ruin her career. She was never supposed to be collateral damage in this scheme; she was just supposed to be a pawn in this game.

But she had become someone I deeply cared about. The only person, really.

My stomach churned as I scrolled through the document, scanning and memorizing the details as I read them. As I scrolled, I caught a glimpse of a photo pinned to the corner of the screen.

It was a photo of me, on our trip to Seoul, stuffing noodles in my mouth by the river. She had taken that photo without me knowing. I remember how we learned so much about each other that day, when I realized we were similar in terms of pain.

I sighed heavily, remembering the memory vividly.

I'm sorry.

That was the only phrase I kept repeating while I kept

reading the document. I shut the laptop closed the moment I finished reading the last sentence.

Quietly, before I did anything else, I walked back into the bedroom; the floor creaking once more. I carefully sat beside Celeste, my body weight sinking onto the mattress.

She stirred, her lashes fluttering as she looked up at me.

"Everything okay?" She murmured, her voice soft with sleep.

I forced a smile, tucking the blanket around her shoulder. "Yeah," I lied. "I need to leave to take care of a few things. We'll talk in the morning, okay? Go back to sleep." I kissed her forehead, allowing myself to enjoy these last few moments I had with her.

"Okay, I love you," she said quietly, faintly smiling, and closed her eyes again, falling fast asleep. Those words pierced through my heart; I didn't deserve to hear that from her now.

"I love you more," I whispered, hating myself more than ever. I rose from the bed and headed out.

Every step I took closer to the door was torture. If it had been up to me, I would've stayed by her side. But my guilt wouldn't allow me to get some rest, not when I was physically next to her.

Once I made it outside, I headed towards Dylan's to give him the information needed to finish this job once and for all.

"Micheal, this is Carter Blackwood; he'll be assisting us with swapping the painting. He has experience in this area." Dylan introduced me to another fellow billionaire—Carter Blackwood, CEO of Blackwood Enterprises, the biggest law firm in the country.

He was known as the best lawyer in New York, winning roughly 30,000 cases. I knew of him; his firm offered unparalleled legal expertise, handling everything from corporate mergers to high-profile criminal cases. He built his reputation on a mix of brilliance, ruthlessness, and a network of influential connections. They said that if Carter Blackwood took your case, you were guaranteed to win. But what most didn't know was that behind his polished exterior, Blackwood was as dangerous as he was brilliant.

Carter was like the modern day Batman, except he didn't have the suit, but he did have the Batmobile.

"Pleasure to meet you," he greeted me in a heavy British accent.

Of course, he was British.

"Likewise. So, what's the plan?" I got straight to the point. I wanted to be over this as quickly as possible. Dylan looked at Carter, who fixed his perfectly tailored suit.

"Well, Micheal," Carter said, his accent giving a heavy weight of authority, "the plan is rather straightforward, though the execution will require precision, which is why I'm here." I rolled my eyes.

Arrogant much?

"I've already analyzed the layout of the gallery and the information provided by you. Security systems are top of the line, but they're not inaccessible. We'll be going in after closing time, which will leave us to only have security guards to deal with. Dylan will handle the distraction—drawing attention to the front —while I'll take care of the disabling the cameras."

"Okay, and what do I do?" I asked, just wanting to hear my part.

"You'll be the one to make the actual swap." My jaw dropped to the floor. I chuckled, positive that he was joking. There was a sudden, uncomfortable, and serious silence. I blinked. *Me?* That wasn't exactly what I had envisioned. I thought I'd be the one in the getaway car or simply the one to watch from behind the scenes.

What in the actual fuck was this...?

"Hold on," I interrupted, glancing between the two of them. "Why am I the one swapping the painting?"

Dylan smirked, clearly enjoying my reaction. "Because you're the most inconspicuous of us," he said with a simple shrug. "No one's going to suspect the *rookie*."

Ouch. Rookie?

I nearly scoffed out loud. "I'm deeply hurt and offended by your words, Dylan. Ever heard of the phrase words will bring you down? Words will break my bones like rocks and stones?"

"The phrase is words will *never* hurt me, and you completely butchered it," Dylan shot back, grinning.

"Close enough," I muttered, waving him off. "My point still stands. I'm *offended*."

Carter raised an eyebrow, clearly unimpressed by our back and forth. "It's a simple exchange. We're not asking you to crawl through ventilation shafts or dodge lasers."

"Oh lucky me, I'd fail spectacularly at that," I muttered.

Dylan shook his head, slightly smirking, but Carter didn't even crack a smile. He leaned closer, lowering his voice as if sharing a secret.

"I'll ensure the timing is flawless. Trust the process, Micheal. I've done this before."

"Uh-huh, and what if something goes wrong?" I asked, folding my arms.

"You run," Carter said bluntly. "Fast."

"Right." Yeah, that wasn't exactly reassuring. "I just need to ask, why is someone like you doing this? What's in it for you?"

"I find it entertaining," Carter answered truthfully. "The payout is just a bit of pocket change."

I'm sorry, did he just call a few millions *a bit of pocket change*? Who the fuck says that? I'm baffled.

Dylan walked over to me, clapped a hand on my shoulder.

"Lighten up. Carter's the best in the business. What could possibly go wrong?"

I shot in a glare. "Yeah, *Batman* seems to know what he's doing. You're a lawyer; aren't you supposed to do right by the law?"

Carter smirked faintly this time—his first crack of humor—gestured toward a blueprint rolled out on the nearby table.

"As a lawyer, I know how to cover my tracks and resolve any issues if they ever arise. Now, shall we go over the details or do you have more questions for me?"

I sighed and leaned over the table, already regretting every life choice that had led me here.

CHAPTER 37

MICHEAL

"Can you hear me?" Carter asked through my earpiece as we got set up for the operation. His voice crackled slightly, sharp and precise, cutting through the quiet hum of the preparations.

"I wish I didn't," I muttered, adjusting the device to make sure it was snug in my ear.

"Great. Just remember, timing is everything," he said, his tone calm and collected. "Once we're in position, there will be no room for mistakes. Stick to the plan and we should be in and out before anyone realizes."

"Right," I replied, feeling a mix of nerves and adrenaline. I waited beside the vehicle Carter was in, waiting for him to give me the green flag to go.

"Are you ready for this?" Dylan asked as he stood nearby in his disguise.

"Let's just say I'll be glad when I have the money in my bank account." I said firmly, my knees slightly shaking, not knowing what to expect the moment I sneak into the gallery.

"Listen carefully Micheal," Carter's voice came through again, "Swap the painting swiftly, and most importantly, *do not* touch anything other than the painting. No doors, walls, glass, *nothing*. We want to avoid fingerprints."

I nodded, even though he couldn't see me. "Got it. No fingerprints."

Silence followed after my reply; my pulse quickened as the weight of what we were about to do settled in. Carter wasn't joking. The stakes were high; one wrong move and we'd be done for. I wiped my palms on my pants, trying to steady my nerves.

"Alright," Carter's voice returned, steady and commanding. "Dylan, you're up. Go in on my mark."

Dylan walked toward the entrance, wearing all black from head to toe.

"Mark," Carter ordered.

With that, Dylan walked over to the very front, pretending to look lost. A security guard instantly saw him and walked over.

"Sir, is there anything we can help you with?"

"Yes, I'm looking for Claire. She said she'd meet me here to speak about a potential piece I'd be interested in." The security guard looked lost, unsure of what to say.

"Sir, it's late, and no one informed me of this arrangement; I'm going to ask you to leave," he said, not moving from the doors.

"That's unfortunate; I'm sure a man like yourself honors his job very much. I imagine you want to keep it longer than today?" Dylan asked, knowing how to manipulate him. The security guard stiffened when Dylan threatened his job.

"I–" Dylan cut him off before he said anything else.

"Let's not make this difficult, yeah?" He gestured to the side to continue speaking. "She'll be upset, but I'm sure we can come to an agreement that won't put your job at risk. I'll let Claire know she has very loyal security working here; what's your name?"

"Donald Grant, sir," he responded, moving to the side, leaving the doors unattended.

"That's our opening," Carter said, his voice like steel. "Micheal, get moving."

My stomach churned, but I pushed off the wall and slipped into the restricted section of the gallery. Each step felt heavier and louder than the last as I moved down the hall. My ears listen for any footsteps or alarms.

The lights at night were dimmer, casting long shadows over each painting and the polished marble floors.

"Left corridor," Carter directed, reassuring me that I wasn't alone. "Camera three disabled. You're clear."

I glanced up at the now-dark camera lens and exhaled through my nose.

Not bad so far, keep going.

Reaching a room in the gallery, I eased the heavy wooden door open just enough to squish inside. My breath hiked as I entered. The painting—*The Kiss*—hung under a spotlight on the far wall, framed like a holy relic. It was exquisite, the burst of colors that contrasted with the gold perfectly. This was history, and I couldn't believe I was standing before it, front and center.

"Micheal, focus," Carter reminded me firmly, bringing me back into the game. "Timers running, do it now."

"Alright, I get it," I whispered, not liking the feeling of being pressured. I pulled the duplicate painting from the tube slung across my back. My hands were slow and steady as I unrolled it, though my heart rapidly pounded louder with each movement.

I reached for the painting, carefully looking at the security wires attaching it to the wall. I swallowed hard. "Um... you didn't mention there'd be laser sensors!" I whispered-shouted.

"Don't pay mind to that; they're only triggered if you lift the painting too fast," Carter explained calmly, as if it was common sense. "Ignore it. Slow and steady."

"Before any of this you said 'swap the painting swiftly!' Now you're saying slow and steady?" I argued, frustrated that I was the one stuck with this responsibility.

"Micheal, we don't have time. Swap it now," Carter hurried, only adding more to the anxiety I already had.

I crouched down, gripping the bottom edge of the frame. One inch at a time, I lifted, hyper-aware of the tiny *click* sounds as the wires loosened. My arms burned as I held with such careful tension.

Still moving, I held the fake painting up to the wall, aligning it perfectly with the empty brackets. Sweat beaded on my forehead as I eased it into place, praying the weight and feel were close enough to the real thing.

"Three... two..." Carter counted in my ear, only making it more nerve-wracking. Within a second, the final wire clicked into place. I froze. I waited. Nothing happened. No alarms, no flashing lights.

"I did it," I whispered, relief washing over me.

"Great work," Carter replied. "Just in time; now get out." I turned toward the door, but a faint creak in the hallway made me stop cold. Footsteps.

"Carter," I hissed, "We've got company."

"I see," he replied evenly. "There's another exit at the back of the room. Move quietly, and you'll be fine."

A narrow staff entrance concealed behind a partition caught my attention as I looked over my shoulder. I began walking toward it, being cautious to keep my footfall quiet, and my heart rate increased. I heard the main gallery door opening, and my palm was on the door handle as the footfall outside became more deliberate and louder.

"Micheal," Carter's voice dropped, low and urgent. "Move. Now."

I didn't need to be told twice. I slipped through the door and into the dark service hallway, the quiet *click* of it shutting behind me echoing like a gunshot, and I didn't stop to breathe, didn't dare look back. I just ran.

"There's going to be an exit door at the end of the hall; make a run for it." Carter's voice came through, calm as ever.

At the end of the hall, I saw the bright red exit sign Carter told me about and I ran to it like it was the last thing I'd do. There were exposed pipes along the ceiling and the smell of old paint that filled the air. I could barely hear the sound of my feet hitting the floor as I ran; my heart pounded in my chest.

My hands reached the door, and I shoved it open, sprinting out. The cool night air hit my lungs, and I felt instantly relieved to be outside, but it wasn't over yet.

"The getaway car is two buildings down, parked in an alley," Carter added.

"Got it," I muttered between sharp breaths, my lungs burning with each step. My thighs burned as I continued running; my body begged for a break, but I couldn't afford to risk it. The painting was still resting on my back, and I needed to get it out of sight.

"Micheal," Carter's voice crackled back in, "You're almost approaching the alley, make a sharp turn to your right in thirty seconds. Dylan's in position to pull you out, but you'll need to move quickly. You're on a two-minute window before the guards start searching outside."

"Two minutes?" I hissed. "Couldn't make it three?"

"No. Now move," he replied coolly.

Sprinting, I turned a corner and instantly saw a black Aston Martin v12 Zagato, its headlights dimmed, and Dylan leaning casually sitting in the driver's seat.

"Look who made it," Dylan called with a smirk as I bolted toward him. "You're lucky you have that painting behind your back or I would've already left you."

"I love how secure you make me feel," I answered as I jumped into the passenger seat, carefully placing the painting in front of me.

"We made it," I said into the earpiece, waiting for Carter to give us the okay.

Carter's voice cut in. "We're not clear yet."

I sat up, suddenly alert again. "What do you mean, we're not clear?"

"Exactly what I said," Carter replied, his tone calm but edged with steel. "We tripped a silent alarm. They're looking for us now."

"Perfect," I muttered, slumping back into the seat. "Absolutely perfect."

"Relax," Carter said, as Dylan steered around another corner at an alarming speed. "I've planned for this. Dylan will drive to an empty parking garage, where I'm already waiting for you guys. You'll ditch the car and get into mine."

Within the next few seconds, Dylan drove into a parking garage, swerving and moving up floors with extreme acceleration. I closed my eyes, rapidly saying a prayer in my mind until the car came to a stop. I opened my eyes and saw Dylan jump out of the car.

I quickly followed, getting out of the car and jumping into the backseat of a black Bentley Bentayga Speed.

The driver, Carter, of course, didn't say a word. The SUV surged forward with a growl of the engine, tires screeching faintly against the pavement as we sped out of the garage.

"What are you going to do with the car?" I asked as I looked back. The garage entrance shrank into the distance, but my mind stayed stuck on the loose end we'd left behind. "Seriously, Carter. That car—what if they find it?"

"They won't," he said, his voice annoyingly self-assured.

I frowned. "How can you be so sure?"

He smirked faintly, finally sparing me a glance through the rearview mirror. "Because I took care of it."

Within seconds, a sudden, fiery bloom lit up the rear

window. A thunderous *BOOM* followed, rattling the SUV as the black sedan we'd just abandoned erupted into a cloud of flame and smoke.

I whipped my head around to see the chaos. "What the hell?!" I yelled, Dylan slightly chuckled.

"Relax," he said, his hands steady on the wheel as he made a sharp turn, seamlessly merging into Manhattan's relentless traffic. "Better to get rid of it now than later in a police impound," Carter said, his hands gripping the wheel as he merged into Manhattan's traffic as if it were a normal Tuesday.

"Have you lost your *mind*?" I asked, still in half-shock at the sudden change of events. "You just blew up a car in the middle of Manhattan, Carter!"

He gave me a brief, almost amused glance. "Yet, here we are, driving away clean."

"But it was an *Aston Martin*." I added with a frown; silence followed not long after. I stared out the window, unable to grasp the reality of my life. This was straight out of an action movie, and I was one of the lead roles. How did I come out of this alive? I have not the slightest clue.

"I've got to say that was a smooth exit," Dylan remarked, breaking the silence. "You looked like a natural back there."

"A *natural*?" I shot him a glare, my chest still heaving. "I nearly had a heart attack, and nothing about my look says *smooth*."

"Oh, come on, you've got to admit. It was thrilling," Dylan said, smiling as he looked at the painting set beside me.

"*Thrilling*? More like nerve wracking. I was practically shitting bricks in there!" I spat out, looking at him incredulously.

Carter, focused on the road, spoke up again. "We're fine. If anyone asks, we're just three colleagues heading home from a long night at work."

I scoffed. "Sure, because we look *exactly* like a carpool crew."

"Micheal," Carter said, his voice clipped, "Sit back and relax, you just made fifty-four million dollars."

The words sank in, the realization that we actually pulled it off settling in. I had just swapped a painting worth millions of dollars, and it's sitting right next to me. We did it. I did it.

Holy shit.

CHAPTER 38
CELESTE

WHEN I ARRIVED AT LAUROSSE TO PREPARE THE ARRANGEMENTS for the exhibit, police cars and detectives surrounded the gallery. The gallery was normally quiet during the early hours of the morning, but it was now a blinding scene of flashing red and blue lights.

What happened here?

I walked toward the building, scanning the area for Meredith, but as I reached the entrance, an officer raised a hand to stop me.

"Ma'am, this is a restricted area," he said, his voice firm.

"I'm with the Gallery," I answered, pulling out my ID badge from my bag. "Celeste Castillo. I'm one of the staff in charge of coordinating the exhibit." He gave me an unimpressed look as he quickly glanced at the badge.

"Wait here," he ordered and walked toward another officer. I stood in the middle of the chaos, still oblivious to what was going on. Perhaps they were for *The Kiss* and needed extra security for its arrival. *If it's not that, what else could it be?*

A moment after, that same officer returned. "Come with me Miss Castillo." He gestured toward the entrance. I followed him inside the building, of the rooms were closed with a simple caution tape across each entryway.

"Could you tell me what's going on?" I asked, taking in the surrounding madness. The entire gallery was shut down; no one could go in, and no one could go out. I realized that when I saw our staff standing outside a room, their faces pale with worry. "Are they being questioned?" I asked another question, but he ignored that one, too.

"He'll answer your questions," he finally responded, pointing toward a tall man in a dark suit who was standing beside Meredith.

"Thanks," I said, continuing to make my way through the tense crowd. As I approached them, I noticed Meredith's uneasy expression. Whatever happened, it was serious. "Meredith, what's going on?" I asked, desperate to at least get some answers from her.

"Celeste, this is Detective Jason," she said, disappointment written all over her face.

"It's unfortunate we have to meet under these circumstances, Celeste," he began by saying; his tone is strictly professional. "We're investigating a theft reported late last night."

"A painting was stolen? Which one?" I asked, glancing at Meredith for a quick second.

Detective Jason exchanged a glance with Meredith before answering.

"*The Kiss.*"

My heart instantly dropped down to my feet. The words hit me like a bolt of lightning.

"That's impossible." I said, unable to wrap my mind around it. Everything went exceedingly smoothly, or so I thought.

The detective nodded at my response. "Meredith tells me you were one of the very few who knew the painting was being imported yesterday."

"Yes, that's correct."

"That's why we'll need to question you," Jason replied, his gaze steady. "Preliminary evidence suggests the painting was swapped with a counterfeit during or after closing."

"Swapped?" The room seemed to tilt slightly. "A fake? But how would anyone—" Stuff like this only happened in movies, it wasn't supposed to be happening in my life, or my career.

"Why don't we step into a room and further speak on this privately?" he interrupted, his voice firm but not unkind.

"I-sure," I stammered, my voice wavered.

"Let's go inside," he said, gesturing toward the door of an office.

I followed him down the halls. Looking around, I saw officers dusting for fingerprints, and more staff huddled in small groups, their faces twisted with concern. When we reached the main gallery, I froze.

The spotlight that had been trained on *The Kiss* now illuminated an exact copy. The gilded frame that had housed the masterpiece appeared to still be there, except it wasn't. How could they tell the difference?

"How could this happen?" I murmured quietly, more to myself than anyone else.

As we talked into the office, Detective Jason shut the door closed behind me. "Let's start with your statement."

I spent the next hour and a half recounting every bit of information I had about the exhibit and about the previous night. The final walkthrough, the locked doors, the double-checking of the security system, and the information that was transferred to me.

I stepped out of the office once we finally finished. The first person I saw was Meredith waiting for me outside. Her face was drawn and tense. "Celeste, a word."

The tone in her voice made my stomach roll with nausea. I followed her to a corner, where she stopped and turned to face me.

"I don't know how else to tell you this," she began, crossing her arms. "You were one of three people who knew *The Kiss* was being imported yesterday, along with all the information regarding security, alarms, locks and codes," she sighs heavily. "The owners of Laurosse feel that there is an extreme coincidence of how you align with the timeline. Whether this was intentional or because of negligence with the information, I have no choice but to let you go."

Her words served as a slap to my face. "What? No, Meredith, I had nothing to do with this. I did everything by the book; I kept the information confidential. This was not my doing; I absolutely had no part in it."

"I believe you, Celeste. But unfortunately, there's no way to prove if you're innocent or guilty. They just don't feel comfortable keeping you here. This is a disaster for the Gallery, and I was serious when I said there was no room for mistakes. This is a significant one, regardless if it was your doing or not."

Tears threatened to escape, but I looked up and blinked them back, refusing to cry in front of everyone. "This isn't fair. I didn't do anything."

"I'm so sorry, Celeste," she said, her tone holding sympathy as she rubbed my arm. "You'll receive an official notice by the end of the day. Please collect your things and leave immediately."

"Meredith, please," I pleaded, not wanting to leave the only job I loved. It was only the beginning of my career.

"You're fired," she said firmly and turned away from me.

I stood there, stunned, as she walked away. My chest felt tight; I felt like I couldn't breathe. My head spun in circles as I took in her last words to me. *You're fired.* Just like that, I had lost everything: the internship, my reputation, my future in the art world, all because of something I didn't even do.

CHAPTER 39
MICHEAL

I tossed and turned in my bed all night; I haven't been able to get some decent rest. The guilt of what I had done wouldn't allow me to. Sure, I felt a little guilt leading up to this, but actually completing the mission was mind numbing. I don't think there are enough words to explain the vast amount of guilt I'm currently feeling.

For hours I've laid in my bed, not having the energy to stand up to get a glass of water. At this point, I don't even think I deserve to see Celeste or hear her voice. She will be hit with the news this morning, and I was dreading the moment she'd tell me.

How would I manage to keep a straight face or keep my calm demeanor when I'm the one to blame for this? How was I going to keep lying to her? How would I even tell her the truth? Did I want to risk losing her? Would I be self-sabotaging the only good thing I had going for myself?

Regardless of having fifty-four million dollars in the bank, I didn't know what to do with myself. The money didn't give me the security I yearned for; it wasn't about that anymore. The security I was desperately looking for, I found in Celeste.

I've done some questionable things—I've lied, I've schemed, I've betrayed, and every single time, I would have cared less about how that person was affected. It was always a fair game when it came down to me, but as for the other person… let's just say they didn't pull a lucky card.

But this time, the guilt crawling at my insides and the fear that I'd irreparably hurt Celeste was too much to bear.

My phone buzzed beside me, breaking the rapid thoughts that had wrapped themselves around me all night. The name on the screen made my stomach drop. It was the person I'd been dreading hearing from, because I knew *exactly* what she was going to say.

I stared at it for a second, my heart pounding outside of my ribcage, before finally picking up.

"Hello?" I answered, my voice shaky despite my best effort to sound calm.

"Micheal," she choked out, her voice trembling with half sobs. "I…I got fired. They… they think I…" Her words were shaky, and she was unable to finish a sentence as she gasped for air, trying to pull herself together.

Her voice, her words… It was a knife piercing through my heart.

"*The Kiss*, it's gone and they think I had something to do with it. I didn't do it, I swear to you Micheal, I didn't." She sobs even harder now.

"They *what*?!" I knew she'd find out about the painting, but I never expected them to pin it on her and fire her. They had no fucking evidence; they can't fire her for something they can't prove she did. Who did those assholes think they were? I felt an unforgivable anger burn within me; I wanted to hurt the person responsible for hurting Celeste.

But then, I felt a lump rise in my throat. The knowledge that I was the reason behind it made my stomach churn. I was the one to blame for their choice of firing Celeste. She was the new girl, after all. God, how could I have been so fucking stupid?

"Celeste, listen to me. Come over. I'll leave the key under the mat. Just... just come over, okay? We'll figure this out."

"But–"

"Celeste," I interrupted, my voice firmer now, fueled with hatred. "Come over. Please."

There was a pause on her side, and for a moment, I thought she might hang up. But then she whispered, so quiet and so delicate, it shattered my damn heart to pieces.

"Okay. I'll be there soon."

The call ended, leaving me alone with my thoughts once again. I stared at the phone in my hand, tightly gripping it as I tried to think of a solution. She was never supposed to be the one they blame; she was never supposed to take on the consequences of my actions.

I'm a horrible person. I–

No. I had to do something. I had to fix this. The least my pathetic ass could do was get her out of this.

I grabbed my jacket and helmet and ran out the door, my mind made up. Dylan. He was going to be the one to help me. He had connections, the kind that could make things... disappear for a person, and he could easily pin this on anyone else.

If he wasn't willing to help, I was going to force him to..

The drive to Dylan's office was quick and filled with adrenaline, my knuckles white as I gripped the handle clutch. When I arrived, I didn't bother with the pleasantries. I stormed right past his secretary, who kept calling me back, and I bursted into his office, forcing his attention to me. I had expected him to be startled, but surprisingly, his eyes shifted to me with ease. A knowing look on his face, as if he predicted my visit.

"Micheal," he drawled, leaning back in his chair, putting away the papers that were laid out on his desk. "To what do I owe the pleasure?" I marched further into his office, throwing my helmet on the floor.

"They *fired* her," I said, my voice cold as ice.

He nodded with an unpleasant calmness and didn't say a word. I could read the words he wanted to say on his face— *How's this my problem?*

"They're pinning it on her. Fix it," I added, my voice demanding.

He raised an eyebrow, impressed with my boldness. I had never spoken or ordered anything from Dylan. I never crossed that line, but for Celeste, there wasn't a line I wouldn't cross.

"Fix it? Micheal, you know as well as I do that this isn't something I can just… fix. It's too fresh, too risky."

I strengthened my posture, my head held up. "That's where you're forgetting something, Dylan."

"What's that?" he asked, placing his hands firmly on his desk.

"If you don't," I began, slowly stepping closer, "I'll turn myself in," I said; a smirk tugs at the side of his mouth. He looked at me, searching for a sign that said I was bullshitting. When he didn't see that, he shook his head with a low chuckle.

"That would be your choice Micheal, I can't help you there." he shrugged. *Oh, he's going to love this part.*

"But that's not even the best part," I drawled, leaning down, slamming a hand on his desk. "I'll turn myself in, and *you*. Carter can have the luxury of staying out of this, unless you also choose to drag him down, too." His jaw ticks, his nose flaring with anger. "Hey, and who knows? We could be *roomies*. It wouldn't even feel like we're behind bars. Well, just as long as we don't look at them."

"I knew you were a comedian, but this? This is idiocy. You're playing with fire," he threatened, as he stood from his chair, slightly hovering over me.

"We've been playing with fire. But the real question is, are you willing to get burned?" Dylan's smirk faltered. He studied me for a long moment, his fingers drumming on the desk before tightly fisting his hand.

Finally, he sighed. "Fine. I'll take care of it; take your little girlfriend out of the picture."

"Perfect," I responded, unable to grasp how I got him to do what I wanted.

"But Micheal?" He added with venom in his voice. "The next time you try to blackmail me with this shit, I'll put *you* behind bars. Don't underestimate my power. I'll take everything away from you in a second. You're on your own after this."

I nodded, my jaw tight. "Just handle this. Now." I turned around, picked up my helmet, and headed toward the door.

"Micheal," Dylan called. I glanced back at him, waiting. "I need the last few pages of the painting report."

"I'll bring it next time. It's on my coffee tab—" I paused, remembering how I left all the pages of information I stole from Celeste's laptop scattered on my coffee table in the living room. Then I remembered I told Celeste to come over and let herself in. She's going to see it; she'll know what I did. "Fuck!" I yelled out and ran out the door.

Dylan called my name once again, certainly confused by my reaction. But I ignored him; I had to get to my apartment as fast as possible. I had to get there before Celeste did. If I didn't make it in time, I was beyond and utterly fucked.

No matter how fast I raced down the streets, I didn't make it in time. When I entered my apartment, there was no sign of Celeste. But I knew she was here because she stacked the pages neatly and left them sitting right in the middle of the coffee table.

Not a note was left behind, only the key I had left for her to use. I then had the strong, knowing feeling that I had lost her.

CHAPTER 40
CELESTE

I had told myself I wouldn't snoop. I'd come over, let myself in, and wait for him like he'd asked, like any normal girlfriend would. But when the first thing you see walking in is a mess of papers sprawled across the living room floor, with your name and your old gallery's logo staring right at you, curiosity isn't an option. It's instinct.

My chest tightened, the shock entered my system so suddenly, it knocked out the air out of my lungs. I stilled, picking up a page with shaky hands, reading it as if they might burst into flames. This couldn't be. He couldn't have been.

No, this had to be a mistake. But the longer I stared at the page, the more excuses I tried to come up for him, and the more none of them made sense. Not when I saw the evidence before me.

I sank to my knees, my arms trembling as I picked up another page. The words hit me like a slap: notes, details about my routine, my work, my life. I picked up another page and this time, the words on the page acted as the knife that plunged right in my heart and soul: information about *The Kiss*, timeline for its arrival, floor plans, security codes, everything Meredith had sent to me were in Micheal's hands.

But I didn't stop there. I picked up the next page and saw the contract he had signed to deliver this painting to Richardo Brock. The name sounded foreign to me; I didn't recognize the name, but that didn't matter. What mattered was the information I just read off these pages.

He swapped the paintings.

Forget the knife stabbed in my heart; these words ripped it out of my chest and sliced it in half. The realization and the knowledge of Micheal being someone completely different from what he's shown me had sickened me. My throat burned; I felt a sharp sting of betrayal.

I had just been fired from my dream job, ruining my reputation before I even had one in the art industry. *The Kiss* was stolen, and I was the number one suspect on their list, and my so-called boyfriend turned out to be a fucking spy and painting thief. He had used me, lied to me, and was letting *me* take the fall.

How…was this all happening to me? What the hell did I ever do to deserve this?

I wanted to scream at the top of my lungs; I wanted to cry. But mostly, I wanted to tear and burn every one of those damn pages and scatter the ashes all over his apartment. How could he do this to me? How could he use me, lie to me, and look at me like I was… God, I was an idiot.

How could I have been so stupid and naïve to just trust him? I knew it; I sensed this from the beginning. I hated him, yet I was foolish and reckless and fell for the enemy, anyway.

My fingers curled into a fist around the first page, crumbling it. Anger churned within me, tangling with the agonizing ache of heartbreak. I took a deep breath, trying to get my emotions in line before I destroyed everything in sight.

The saddest part of all of this was that my heart thought this was all a dream. None of this was real; it couldn't be. But the harsh reality in my mind knew better, especially with everything written out before me.

As much as my little heart wanted to protect me, there was no overlooking this. I had to leave before he came back; I couldn't give him the pleasure of seeing how much this had affected me.

So I wiped the one tear that had rolled down my face, stacked the papers neatly, left them on the table with his key on top, and walked out with the last bit of dignity I had left.

I held my head high and held it together and got onto the elevator. The moment the doors closed, I completely lost it. I leaned back on the wall and cried my eyes out until I heard the doors dinged open again.

The only place I wanted to be in a situation like this was the art studio. I entered the room and was hit with the strong scent of linseed oil and fresh paint. A familiar smell that made me feel right at home. It never failed to bring me comfort in moments of despair; that's why it's wired in my brain to get here.

Though, I haven't been at the studio for a while, not since I began my internship at Larousse. I missed it, and I wish I didn't have to come back feeling broken, in desperate need of repair.

I sat at my regular station, set up all my tools and began to paint. What was I painting? I had no idea; I was allowing the brush to move and fill the canvas with bold colors. The color I found myself deeply drawn to was dark violet; It symbolizes an anger that is restrained but seething beneath the surface. It's the type of anger that is persistent, a simmering rage that has built over time.

The shadows bled into the violet, swirling in a way that almost looked like a storm brewing in the distance. Maybe that's what this was: a storm I had kept bottled up for too long, finally demanding to be seen.

I might not express myself with words, but I sure as hell can explain and express myself in the language of colors. Most people forget that when they 'read' paintings, they often get the wrong message. There's a word, a syllable, a sentence with every color and how it's presented on the canvas.

The act of painting was enough to numb my mind for a bit. The studio was silent, except for the occasional creak of the floorboards beneath my weight and the soft swish of the bush on the canvas. I would've been blasting music instead, but I didn't bring my speaker. So, for now, I'd settle for silence.

But that's what I needed, to be here and away from everything. Away from him. Away from the chaos I had in my life. With every stroke, every paint splatter, I felt more relieved.

Then suddenly, a soft creak of the floorboard broke my trance, and I didn't need to look up to know who it was. The only person who used to join me on late painting nights.

"Celeste?" Oliver's voice broke the silence; his voice was careful. He hadn't seen me in weeks. "You're here."

I didn't respond right away. My hands moved unthinkingly, adding another brush of color to the canvas, pretending like I didn't feel the heavy weight of his eyes on me. I couldn't bring myself to speak to him, not now. Not with everything I was currently dealing with.

"I'd been hoping that you'd turn up one of these days," he said, stepping closer but not getting in my space, But I still didn't look at him. "I... I wanted to apologize... God, I wasn't a good friend to you. I was selfish and wanted you to only consider the way I was feeling, and I didn't consider how you might have felt throughout it all," he said, surprising me.

Yet, I still wouldn't meet his gaze. I didn't know what to say. "I care about you, and I want us to be friends, and we'll probably never be as close as we were, but you're an amazing person and you deserve better." I held my tears in, not wanting to cry in front of him. Hearing his apology was nice, but it wasn't great timing.

Not when I wanted to hear the apology from someone else.

I sniffled, giving myself away.

"C, are you okay? What happened?" He instantly caught on and the question hung in the air.

Obviously, I was nowhere near okay, but I didn't want to tell him that. I didn't want to tell him anything. He warned me about Micheal in the beginning, and I just couldn't bear to hear an 'I told you so' from him.

"I'm fine," I mumbled, my voice quieter than I intended. It wasn't a lie, exactly. I was *fine;* I just wasn't telling the whole truth.

He studied me from a distance, and I could tell he wasn't the slightest bit convinced. But he didn't push me for information, which I appreciated. Instead, he walked across the room, sat down at his own station, and picked up his brush, letting the silence envelop us once again.

My phone buzzed on the table, an incoming call from Micheal. The brush in my hand trembled as I stared at the screen, a mix of anger and fear surfacing. I didn't want to hear from him, not now.

Oliver noticed the change in my posture, how I looked at the phone like it was my doom. He was constantly switching his gaze from the canvas to me, but he stayed quiet and watched.

I quickly silenced the phone and pushed it to the far edge of the table. Out of sight, out of mind. My heart raced, and I just wanted to pretend it wasn't there for a little while longer.

I tried to lose myself in the process of painting again, but I couldn't. No matter how hard I tried to get back into it, I couldn't find that same flow. I couldn't think of anything else but Micheal.

What did he have to say to me? What was he going to say?

Was he going to apologize? Tell me the truth and beg for my forgiveness? Or was he calling to make sure I wouldn't go to the police? Was he going to manipulate me again?

I had so many questions that were racing through my mind and I wanted to put all of those to rest with one answer. But as much as I wanted that answer, it terrified me. I know it sounds crazy, but there's still room to hurt me again.

Even though I felt like there was nothing else that could make me feel worse, Micheal entered the chat. He had all the right cards, the right moves, and the right focus. What did I have? A broken heart yearning for it to be amended by the one responsible for its damage.

It was pretty clear who had the advantage in this game, and it was anything but fair. The best thing I could do now was ignore him. Ignore his texts, his calls, cut off all contact and pretend he never existed.

Micheal Zhang was dead to me.

CHAPTER 41
MICHEAL

Every single one of my calls had gone straight to voicemail, my text messages wouldn't deliver, and every place I thought she would be at, she wasn't. Celeste had disappeared from my life in a matter of six days. Six excruciating days.

She had become this figment of my imagination; the memories became dreams that felt too good to be true. I began questioning if she was even real, if everything we'd gone through was just my mind playing tricks on me because I was so lonely. If it were anyone else doing the ghosting, I wouldn't care. In fact, I'd be relieved because I didn't have to do the dirty work myself.

But Celeste doing this to me was making me physically ill. Every night I dreamt about her, and every morning I'd yearn for her to be next to me. I didn't know how to fix things; I didn't know how I'd get her to forgive me and take me back. What I did... It's unforgivable.

I couldn't see how she could ever look past it. I know if it were me in her position, I wouldn't think twice about the decision I'd make.

Suddenly, a thought came to mind. The only person who

could help me with this was Adam. He was the only string I had that tied me to her. As long as Adam was still with Katherine, she'd be at some reach.

Though I was dreading to see Adam. The last time I saw him was when he was trying to get me out of the mission. He and Aaron both tried their best that day, and I walked out without another thought. Would he even want to help me?

I sent him a text, telling him to meet me at the bar we always go to when we want to talk outside of his office—Scarlette Lounge. It always bothered him when we made surprise visits to his building; he'd much rather go to the bar for whatever reason. He'd kick everyone out of his office except Katherine.

I waited for his response, but didn't get one. Regardless, I got out of bed, got changed and went straight to the bar, hoping I'd see him there.

The drive to the bar was nerve-wracking. Would Adam show up? Would he hear me out, and laugh in my face for thinking I deserved his help? Every time I thought of turning my bike around, Celeste's face flashed through my mind. If I wanted her, I needed to set my pride aside. A man's biggest enemy is his pride and his ego. Without those things, we're weak. At least that's what we've been told our whole lives.

The question I needed to ask myself was, is she worth it? Is she worth setting all things aside? The answer was yes, and to be honest, I didn't understand how my answer had drastically changed from a no to a yes.

But when you love someone, you'll spend the rest of your life trying to understand it.

I snapped out of my thoughts the moment I realized I had arrived. I took off my helmet, parked my bike, and walked in. Adam was already sitting at the bar, texting on his phone, probably answering emails. I headed toward him and took a seat on the barstool next to him.

I knew he felt my presence, but he was silent at first, just leaned back, his arms crossed as if he was waiting for me to start the conversation. I swallowed hard, sensing the disappointment.

"Thanks for showing up," I said, tapping my fingers on the wooden bar top.

"So," he said finally, his voice as calm and measured as ever. "What do you want, Micheal? I saw the news; you've succeeded with your plan."

"I fucked up," I said through gritted teeth. I hated admitting it out loud to another person. Especially him, who would most likely say the lines 'I told you so'.

Swallow your pride. I thought in my mind.

"I need your help," I added, my voice quieter than I'd like.

He raised an eyebrow, a slight smirk tugging at the corner of his mouth. "Didn't think I'd hear that sentence anytime soon."

"Adam, I wouldn't be here if it weren't important," I said, meeting his gaze. The smirk fell off his face the moment he saw the desperation in my eyes. "It's about Celeste."

He sighed and leaned forward slightly, his eyes narrowing. "What about her?"

"This whole thing got blown out of proportion, and I didn't plan for it to be like this." I said, the words tasting bitter as I spoke them. "I haven't been able to reach her for days, and I know I messed up—badly—but I need to find her. I thought... no, I *know* you could help."

Adam studied the look on my face, leaning back again as he processed what I'd just said. His silence felt heavier than his words ever could.

"You've got some nerve asking me this after everything," he said finally. "Especially after how hard Aaron and I tried to convince you to not proceed with the mission. Did you honestly think she wouldn't be involved in this mess?"

The accusation hit me like a punch to the gut, but I didn't flinch. I deserved it.

"I know," I said, my voice harsher. "I know I don't deserve

her forgiveness, and I know I screwed everything up, but I love her, Adam, and I can't just let her go without trying to fix this."

For a moment, Adam said nothing. Then he shook his head, a mix of frustration and pity on his face.

"I don't know how you could fix this, Micheal," he began. "But a piece of advice from someone who had a similar experience in fucking up, you need to tell her how you feel. Not only tell her, but show her. Does that sound familiar?" he asked with a slight smirk on his face.

I remembered the day Adam had completely lost it because he had lost Katherine. I told him to tell her and show her that he loved her, and he did. Now they're living like the perfect couple, and it was fucking annoying as shit.

"But that's just it—I don't have a plan. I don't even know where to start, and I can't even find her or contact her. I wouldn't be able to make this happen without your help."

Adam's expression shifted from a casual vibe to a slightly nervous one. "Alright, look. I wasn't going to tell you this yet, or tell anyone for that matter, but... Katherine and I are hosting a get together on the Fourth of July."

"That's five days from now," I said, hating the idea of having to wait another week.

"Will you let me finish?" he responded, reaching for something in his pocket. "It's going to be at the Central Park Conservatory Garden and right before the fireworks, I'm proposing to her," he admitted, setting a red ring box on the table in front of me.

I blinked, caught completely off guard. I stared at the red Cartier box, and I grabbed it, opening the lid. Inside was a diamond Cartier Destinée solitaire. "Holy shit, this must've cost a fortune. This is fucking insane, man!" I exclaimed, still in disbelief. Adam Pearson, engaged. That's something I didn't see coming for ages.

Adam grinned, his dimples making an appearance. "Yeah. I

got the ring, and I've been planning this for months. She loves fireworks, and I figured it'd be the perfect setting for it. But the reason I'm telling you this is because Katherine's inviting Celeste to the party."

I sat up straighter, my heart skipping a beat from hearing her name come out of someone else's mouth other than my own. "She'll be there for sure?"

Adam nodded, grabbing the red ring box and putting it in his jacket again. "Yes, she'll be there. This is your chance; you'll show up and make your case. But—" He pointed a finger at me. "You have to be genuine. No games, no lies, no beating around the bush. Just you, straight to the point, raw and honest. Otherwise, don't bother showing up."

"Do you think she'll listen to what I have to say?" I asked, needing validation.

Adam shrugged. "If she's smart, she won't let you come within a foot of her. But if she's as much of a sucker for you as you are for her, she'll give you a few seconds. All I know is that if you really care about her, you owe it to yourself to try."

I nodded, slightly smiling at the thought of her loving me. I hope she still did, deep down. "Thank you."

Adam stood, tossing some cash on the table for his untouched drink. "Don't thank me yet," he said. "If you mess up my proposal night because of your drama, I'll break every bone in your body. That's the price to be paid, so don't fuck it up."

I chuckled, shaking my head; the first real chuckle I had in days. "I won't."

"Good. Because you deserve to be happy, regardless of how bad you've fucked up." He squeezed my shoulder before walking out of the bar, leaving me alone with my thoughts.

CHAPTER 42
CELESTE

Fourth of July rolled around and Katherine was hosting an event at the Central Park Conservatory Garden. Adam had rented a private section—The French Garden—which had intricately trimmed boxwood hedges, vibrant seasonal flowers, and one of the most charming fountains. It was a hidden gem in New York City, with a cast iron Vanderbilt gate at the entrance.

As for my outfit, I decided to wear a navy blue dress with small sparkling stones. The front details are embroidery in gold tones, depicting a celestial theme and there's a radiant sun design near the bust area. The dress was form fitting and had a short slit on one side. I absolutely love this dress and found it perfect for the occasion. I also decided to wear my hair naturally and let my curls out.

For my plus one, I invited Oliver. I had a feeling Adam would be inviting Micheal, and I did not want to show up alone. Maybe if he saw I was with someone else, he would leave me alone. He wouldn't even try to speak to me.

At least I don't think so...

When we arrived, Oliver offered his arm like a true gentleman, and he led me through the Vanderbilt Gate. Inside, the

French Garden was astonishing. It was even better than the photos I saw online. The leaves and grass were bright green, and the scent of fresh roses mingled with the faint trace of the fountain's mist.

The first person I saw coming in was Katherine. She was glowing in a pastel pink dress, moving along the crowd of guests with a champagne glass in hand. Her smile was bright, she was absolutely glowing with happiness.

I continued to look around the garden, my eyes scanning the entire area until they found Adam near the fountain, looking polished as ever in a tailored black suit. His eyes narrowed with a small smirk when he saw me. He instantly stepped to the side to reveal Micheal in a black tailored tux as well.

There he was, standing in a relaxed posture. He stood at Adam's side, speaking to a small group of men with that effortless charm I found so magnetic. My heart did its stupid little jump, the one I've been trying to stop since... well, since him.

My hand grips Oliver's arm tightly. Oliver winced at my harsh action. I rapidly removed my arm and apologized. "I'm sorry, I–"

"I know why I'm here. It's for him, isn't it?" he leaned in closer, slightly pointing at Micheal's direction.

I felt embarrassed that he caught on so quickly; it meant I didn't hide my emotions as well as I thought I was. I nodded, looking down at the grass.

He grabbed my hand and wrapped it around his arm again. "Hey, it's okay. I'll do whatever you need me to. After all, that's what friends are for, right?" he asked, making me feel more at ease now that he knows his reason for being here.

"Right," I smiled.

Suddenly, I felt a pair of eyes on me. I looked over at the fountain and found Micheal staring at me with his jaw clenched. His hands were stuffed in his pockets, his posture was even straighter than before. I instantly looked away from his gaze; I couldn't take it for much longer without feeling so many things.

"Katherine's coming over," Oliver said, nodding in her direction. Sure enough, Katherine walked up to us with a welcoming smile.

"You're here! Just in time," she exclaimed, pulling me in for a tight hug. Her eyes moved to Oliver, and she placed her hand on his shoulder. "You brought Oliver as your plus one," she said, looking mildly disappointed.

"Yes, I did; It was time for Oliver to come to one of our get-togethers." Katherine nodded, welcoming Oliver.

"Well, it's nice to see you again. I haven't seen you since Celeste's graduation. How have you been?" she asked, making conversation.

"I've been great, I actually..." Oliver's words faded slowly as I felt my body's temperature suddenly drop. I felt the same pair of eyes on me—heavier this time. When I glanced toward the fountain again, Micheal was no longer with the group. He was standing right behind us.

I silently gasped under my breath, shocked at how close he was. Up close, he was even more striking, his tux tailored to perfection. His jaw was still tight, but his expression softened just slightly.

"Katherine," he said smoothly, his voice effortlessly commanding. Then his eyes flicked to me. "Luci."

My breath caught for a moment, and I hated myself for the warmth that spread through me at his words. "Micheal," I said, keeping my tone neutral. "I didn't expect to see you here." I lied.

His lips twitched into a small, knowing smile. "You should've."

Oliver cleared his throat, stepping closer to my side. "I like the suit."

Micheal's eyes shifted to Oliver, his expression unreadable. "... and you are?"

"Oliver," he said, extending a hand with a friendly smile. "A friend."

Micheal hesitated for a fraction of a second before shaking Oliver's hand. "Micheal." His tone was polite, but there was an edge to it.

"What are you doing here?" I whispered to him, a slight aggression in my voice.

"To celebrate the Fourth of July," he said, leaning in closer. "Same as you." His gaze softened for a quick second, his eyes scanning every inch of my body. "You look breathtaking," he admits, his voice low. So low, only I could hear his comment.

"I know," I responded with an attitude. I flicked my gaze over his suit, hating how good it made him look. Why did I still have this intense gravitational pull towards him? I didn't know who to be angrier at... him or myself.

I stopped the moment I saw a familiar grin playing on his face. I looked at Oliver and placed my head on his shoulder. "Let's go see the rest of the flowers; I heard there's a trail that goes around the entire garden," I said, opening my eyes wider, my words a cry for help.

Oliver's eyes narrowed until he understood what I was trying to say. "Ah, yes. Let's go see." He grabbed two glasses of champagne from a server who walked past us. "Katherine, it was great to see you again." He handed me one and removed me from the conversation.

"Likewise," she responds, looking uncomfortable for Micheal.

Without looking back, Oliver and I headed deeper into the garden. We ended up finding a quiet bench in the garden beside some orange tulips. "So, you want to tell me what happened between you two?" Oliver asked as we sat down.

I sighed heavily, trying to enjoy the last bit of sunlight before the sun completely went down. It would start getting dark soon, and we'd have to go back out for the firework show. My fingers toyed with the stem of the champagne glass. I wasn't sure I was ready to bring up that conversation just yet. "Not really," I responded, taking a sip from my glass.

"You know, if I didn't know any better, I'd say Micheal's package comes with drama. That man looked ready to stake a claim on you," he said, chuckling.

I rolled my eyes, refusing to acknowledge the rapid beat of my heart. I could feel the heat rising to my cheeks. "Yeah, well, let's not waste our breath on him. He's… repugnant. Utterly unbearable."

"Right," Oliver nodded, leaning back with a conspiratorial air. "He must really bother you, huh?"

"Yes," I whispered, not fully telling the truth. Well, it wasn't exactly a lie; he bothered me. But not in the way I was telling Oliver, and I think he knew that as well. He raised a brow, giving me a look that screamed '*Yeah, right.*'

"Are you sure about that? Because for someone so 'repugnant,' he seems to have you a little… flustered."

I scoffed, clutching my champagne glass tighter. "Flustered? Please. Try irritated beyond belief."

He looked down at the floor, a grin growing on his lips. "Irritated, huh? Is that what we're calling it these days?"

I playfully punched his arm, getting a small wince out of him. "You're supposed to be helping me by distracting me, not psychoanalyzing my feelings for Micheal. There's nothing now."

He rubbed a hand over the nonexistent injury. "Fine, Fine. No psychoanalyzing. No feelings. But just to better your understanding of the word 'repugnant', it doesn't usually come with flushed cheeks and lingering glances."

"I did not–" I argued, but the look he gave me stopped me from trying to deny it. "Fine. Lesson noted."

"Great. Now that we have that out of the way, what do you suggest we do now?" he asked.

"Enjoy the evening. The sun's going down faster than I thought it would," I answered, looking up at the soft orange and pink hues streaking across the sky.

Oliver followed my gaze and nodded. He leaned in a bit closer. "Not a bad plan. So, what's next? A nice stroll or—"

Before he could finish his sentence, a sudden blast of cold water hit me square on the side of my shoulder.

"WHAT THE–" I shirked, jumping up from the bench. Oliver stood up, drenched in cold water from head to toe. A few droplets landed on my skin, but Oliver… he looked like he took a dip in the fountain.

We both looked at each other, confused. Then we looked above us in disbelief.

Above us, a narrow bridge stretched across the garden, lined with ivy and soft lanterns. And standing right at the center of it —one arm lazily holding a drink, the other gripping a garden hose—was Micheal.

His expression was maddeningly relaxed as he took a slow sip, meeting our eyes with amused nonchalance.

"Oh no," I muttered under my breath.

Without urgency, Micheal began to descend the winding stone stairs that curled down from the bridge into the garden. Each step was deliberate, like he was walking into a scene he'd planned in his head a hundred times. He didn't break eye contact with Oliver the entire way.

Then, as he reached the last step, he gave the nozzle a gentle squeeze—drenching Oliver even further.

"Huh," he said, raising his brows slightly. "Thought the safety guard was on." His tone was light, but the glint in his eyes was anything but innocent.

Oliver wiped the dripping water from his face with a hand, blinking through the shock. "What the hell, man? What's your problem?"

Micheal shrugged, slow and dramatic, followed by a heavy,

theatrical sigh. "Thought you might want to cool down," he said, his smirk widening. "You looked... a little heated there."

Oliver looked beyond upset, and I didn't blame him. I could feel the anger bubbling up in me, too. He glanced at me, shivering slightly. "I think I'm gonna head home and change. I've got another tux."

"Of course you do," Micheal muttered under his breath, just loud enough to be heard.

"Excuse me," Oliver said, and walked off without looking back.

"Are you serious right now?" I scoffed, my hands balling into fists, slightly trembling with anger.

Micheal carelessly dropped the hose on the floor, the last few droplets of water being soaked up by the grass. "Completely."

I shook my head in disbelief. "I hate you," I admitted in a low voice, crossing my arms.

He walked towards me, getting alarmingly close. His smirk transformed into something more dangerous, tempting. I knew that smirk, and nothing good or smart came out of it.

"Yeah, you keep saying that... but that's not what you were saying before," he paused, his voice dropping to a tantalizing whisper. "Matter of fact... you were begging for me."

My cheeks turned bright red at what he was hinting at. I glared at him, my heart racing as every nerve in my body screamed at me to run or stay.

"Go to hell, Micheal," I whispered, unable to speak louder. I turned on my heel to leave, but before I could take more than a step, his hand caught my wrist, pulling me back just enough for me to feel his breath against my ear.

"Too late," he murmured. "I've already been there..." he traced his lips down my throat, his touch was feather light. "...and it's nowhere near as interesting as this."

I yanked my hand away, refusing to give him the satisfaction of a response. But as I walked off to get back to the party, he followed me behind me, tracking me down. I couldn't stop the shiver running down my spine, the goosebumps running up my arms. It seemed like no matter how hard I tried, Micheal had a hold on me I couldn't shake.

I turned to argue with him further, only for him to pin me against a wall filled with vines and flowers. His face inches away from mine, his hot breath caresses me. "Did you honestly think I'd let you go that easily?"

"What more do you want from me, Micheal? You got everything you needed." The words spilled out of my mouth like venom.

"I want you," he admitted.

"That's too bad," I whispered, my voice trembling with a mix of anger and lust. I couldn't decide if I wanted to slap him or kiss him. "Because I don't want you," I lied.

His hands trail up my thighs and up my back. "See, your mouth is saying one thing, but your body…" His fingers trace down my shoulders. "Your body is saying something completely different." He softly kisses my ear, heat spreading everywhere in my body. "You know what it's saying?"

"What?" I asked, out of breath, lifting my right leg for him to hold. His other hand gripped the outside of my thigh.

"It's saying, touch me…" I let out a breathy chuckle that was quickly replaced by a gasp when he softly bit my neck. "…love me… take me."

"You're so full of yourself," I managed to say, though my voice lacked its regular spike. My body kept betraying me, leaning into the warmth of his touch, like it had a mind of its own.

Micheal smirked against my neck. "Perhaps. But I'm not wrong, am I?"

I wanted to argue, to push him away and prove him wrong. But his hands held me firmly, and his lips found the sensitive spot just below my ear. I bit down on my lip to stifle a moan.

"You're unbearable," I hissed, my words becoming weaker.

"Yet you can't stay away," he whispered.

"It's getting dark; everyone will start to look for us," I said, hoping he would take the bait, but he didn't. "Don't," I added, though it was more of a plea than a command. My hands moved to his chest, but instead of pushing him away, they lingered, feeling the warmth of his skin through the fabric of his shirt.

"Don't what?" he teased, pressing closer, his body flush against mine. "This?" He trailed a line of kisses along my collarbone.

I swallowed hard, my breath ragged. "Micheal, we can't do this."

He pulled back just enough to look into my eyes, his gaze intense and unrelenting. "Why not? Tell me you don't want this —tell me you don't want me—and I'll stop."

His words hung in the air, daring me to say what he knew I couldn't. My silence was all the answer he needed.

Micheal's lips curved into a slow, knowing smile. "That's what I thought."

Before I could respond, his lips were on mine, and any thought I had disappeared into the electric heat of his kiss. Suddenly, the crackle and boom of fireworks shattered the charged silence, their light casting flickering colors across the garden. Startled, I broke the kiss, looking up at the sky, where the night was lit up with vibrant explosions.

Micheal chuckled softly, brushing a strand of hair from my face. "Seems the universe approves," he murmured, his lips grazing mine.

My pulse was still racing. "Or maybe it's a sign to stop."

Micheal's eyes searched mine, intense and unwavering. Then, with a teasing bite to my bottom lip, he murmured low and dangerous, "If it is… I'm sure as hell ignoring it."

Before I could speak, his lips crashed into mine again, desperate, wild, and full of hunger. The distant fireworks cracked through the sky, but their rhythm couldn't compete with the sparks erupting inside me. This time, I didn't hold back. I gave in, melting into him, wrapping my arms around his neck, and pulling him closer, deeper. I wanted all of him.

He pulled away, barely, his breath ragged and warm against my lips. His eyes were heavy with need. "Take off your panties," he whispered, "and ride me."

I froze, wide-eyed. "What?"

His voice deepened, gravel scraping silk. "Do it. Or I will—and I won't be gentle. I've waited too long for this."

There was no denying the heat rushing through me, the way he looked at me like I was the only thing keeping him tethered to the earth. Wordlessly, I reached under my dress, slid my panties down, and kicked them off into the night. His eyes followed the movement like a hunter watching prey. Then he lowered himself to the grass, pants undone, waiting for me.

I stepped over him, straddling him slowly, deliberately, as his hands slid up my thighs. The second I sank down onto him, a sharp and unrestrained moan escaped my lips. He filled me completely, and I saw stars. My hands gripped his shoulders, and I began to move, rolling my hips as heat coiled low in my stomach.

"God, you're so wet for me," he groaned, his voice a hypnotic murmur. "You feel like heaven," he said in a breathy sigh. Why, why must he have such an alluring voice? I'd never heard anything like it. It was like his voice had a special power; it was inhuman. He voiced a command, and it came true. I don't think he'd ever had a person say no to him, and I doubt anyone fought as hard as I did, or tried to.

Damn him.

I lifted up, only to pound back down onto him. The sound of the fireworks mirroring the movements of our bodies. His hands gripped my hips, guiding me with an unrelenting command that matched the determination in his eyes.

"Damn you," I muttered, betraying the battle in my mind that I had already lost.

A slow, wicked smile curved his lips. "Say it again," he murmured, his voice thick with satisfaction.

I bit my lip, refusing. That only spurred him on; he lifted his hips and thrust into me hard. A cry tore from my throat.

"Say it," he growled.

"Damn you!" I gasped just as he reached up and pinched my nipple, sending another shockwave through me.

"Oh, Celeste," he grunted. Then, in a blur, he shifted, laying me down in the grass and entering me again. He hooked my thigh over his arm, thrusting into me with slow, relentless precision.

"Yes," I breathed, every word heavy with need.

He pressed his lips to my ear. "I'm gonna treat you right," he whispered, his rhythm never faltering. "If you let me. You'll never feel hurt again, not from me. I swear it."

My heart clenched. Pleasure tangled with emotion until I couldn't tell where one ended and the other began.

"All I want to give you is happiness. And pleasure. Every day. Seven days a week," he said, kissing my neck, my shoulder, my heart. I was too far gone to respond, except with moans and trembling limbs. "I love you," he said, just as my body shattered around him, waves of pleasure rolling through me like a tidal wave.

The last firework exploded in the sky as I held on to his neck tightly and rode out my climax. The pleasure, the emotions, it was all like a big explosion. He soon followed after and dropped his head on the crook of my shoulder.

A tear drops escapes from my eye as I take in his words. I loved him, but he hurt me. I wasn't ready to put it behind me yet. It was all too fresh and it couldn't possibly be fixed with sex and an apology.

He lifted his head to kiss my temple, and he noticed me

crying and quickly held my face. "Baby, please don't cry. I'm sorry, I love you. I'm so fucking sorry," he said, resting his head on mine. "I won't ever hurt you again."

"That's right, you won't," I said softly, pushing him off me and standing up from the floor.

"Luci..." he pleaded, his voice breaking as I fixed my dress. I avoided looking him in the eyes because I knew I wouldn't be strong enough to walk away.

"I love you." I swallowed hard, more tears running down my face. "But love isn't enough to erase the hurt you caused. It's not enough to fix what's broken."

He rapidly stood up, pulling his pants up. "Then tell me what to do. How do I make it right? I'll do anything—just—don't walk away from me. From us."

"I can't, not now," I said and ran out of the garden. I kept running with my heels in my hands until I reached the main garden, where there was a celebration going on, trying to make my exit, but Elaina saw me.

"Celeste!" she called out. I turned around, slowly and painfully. I didn't want them to see me like this, and I prayed my makeup was still intact As I walked towards her. "Is that grass in your hair?" she asked, taking it out.

"Uh.. yeah. I fell asleep in the garden and got woken up by the fireworks. What happened while I was gone?" I asked, hoping my excuse was convincing enough.

"You missed something huge," she answered.

"What do you mean?" as Elaina was about to answer me, Katherine ran to us.

"Celeste, where were you?" she exclaimed with the biggest smile possible.

"That's not important... but—" I choked up on my words as I saw the breathtaking diamond ring sparking under the soft glow of the garden lights. Katherine raised her hand, giving me a better look.

"He proposed during the fireworks. It was all so beautiful. Celeste—you should have seen it!" she exclaimed, her voice filled with excitement and happiness.

"Wha–" I stuttered, standing before her in complete shock. "Oh, my god! That's incredible," I smiled, genuinely happy for her. I hugged her tightly, putting aside my emotions, so I didn't spoil her moment.

"I know! It's crazy; I never thought it would happen," she admitted.

"You deserve it, now go find your fiance and celebrate with him!" I said, pushing her back into the crowd to find him. As I scanned the room, I saw Adam standing right at the center, gazing at Katherine like she was everything.

Elaina studied me as I watched Katherine stumble into Adam's arms. "Celeste, are you alright?" Elaina asked, noticing my mood change.

"I just need some air, and preferably a nice shower," I said, gripping my heels even tighter in my hands. I glanced at the exit, anxious to leave before Micheal came out looking for me.

"Okay, go," she nodded, giving me the validation I needed before leaving. The only thing that stopped me was Katherine and celebrating with her and for her. But every time I looked at her, she looked insanely happy with Adam, laughing and gazing at him with tremendous admiration. I felt truly happy for her, for them.

"Alright, bye," I said, waving goodbye to Elaina and walking out the Vanderbilt gates. I looked back once more at the garden before I left and saw Micheal scanning the crowd, surely searching for me. My heart dropped as I watched him, but quickly left before he saw me at the exit.

I left without looking back.

CHAPTER 43
CELESTE

It's been a week since the Fourth of July incident and Katherine and Adam's proposal. To catch up on things, Katherine has been the happiest she's been in forever. She's practically been glowing and staring at her ring like it was her *precious*.

Me, on the other hand? I've been doing the most overthinking.

Overthinking about Micheal. About our encounter. That wasn't at all how it was supposed to go; I couldn't believe I allowed it to happen. It's like I had no boundaries when he was close enough, and what I hated the most is how much I craved it, how much I needed it.

It's beyond infuriating knowing that the memory of him lingers in my mind. It's like instead of lining rent free in my mind, he's taken up permanent residence, completely owning the main parts of my brain. Restocking the space with memories I couldn't shake. For the past few days, I've replayed our exchange in the garden at least a thousand times now.

Well, to be fair, a thousand times would be an understatement; it was probably more.

I wanted to hate him the same way I did the first time I met him. I wanted to feel the same way I did before this whole mess started; life was much simpler before. But every time I tried to get back to how I was... my heart and mind betrayed me. I had no control over what I felt and apparently looking at the way I reacted on the Fourth of July; I didn't have control over my own body.

To make matters worse, I haven't heard from Micheal. I thought he might try reaching out after that night to convince me to give him another chance. But nothing. It was both a relief and an aggravation. To be honest, I didn't know what I was expecting. Closure? Another excuse to see him again? Another excuse to stand closer to him and feel everything he makes me feel?

I sighed, throwing myself on the couch. Katherine and Elaina, oblivious to my inner turmoil, were moving around the apartment like ants on caffeine, chatting away about venues and color schemes for the wedding.

"What do you think, C?" Elaina asked, holding out a cup of coffee to me.

"Think about what?" I asked, completely lost. I've been absent for most of their conversation. The sound of the rainstorm outside my window calmed my thoughts.

"Are you even listening?" Katherine asked, giving me a pointed look. I instantly felt bad for getting lost in the thoughts in my own mind.

"Of course," I lied, forcing a smile. "Something about the color white and pinches of pink?"

Elaina and Katherine looked at each other, then back at me with narrowed eyes. "You've been... distracted lately. Something on your mind?" Elaina sits down next to me, waiting for my answer.

"Yeah... just work stuff." I said, brushing off the truth like it was nothing. I'd hoped they'd both accept my lie and wouldn't push.

"But you don't work right now," Elaina responded, hitting an extremely sensitive spot. That's right, I didn't have work. Much less a career, a reputation, or a name.

I nodded, feeling ashamed. "Yeah, that's exactly what I'm thinking of. Where should I apply to work?" I added, hoping I saved myself from an awkward conversation.

But Katherine being Katherine, always asked the questions that hit too close to home. "Is this about Micheal?" I gulped, the mention of his name sending an electric jolt through me. I sat up straight, brushing my shoulders back.

"Micheal? No, what on earth would provoke you to ask that?" I chuckled awkwardly. "What does anything have to do with him?"

"Mhm," she hummed with a knowing smile. "Maybe because you both practically set the entire garden on fire with the tension between you both. I mean, here I thought the fireworks would do that, but no, you both took care of that."

"Set on fire? Tension? There was no such thing," I said quickly, maybe too quickly. It definitely gave me away. "It was… it was nothing," I tried denying once more, my voice lacking conviction.

"You ran out the event with grass in your hair, your makeup smudged, and your heels in your hand. I bet you lost more than just jewelry in that secret garden, huh?" Elaina interjected, making me red in the process.

"No!" I exclaimed, knowing that I'd been caught. "It's not what you think."

Katherine chuckled and shrugged alongside Elaina. "Alright, if you say so," she said lightly, but the tone in her voice suggested she thought otherwise. "...and," Katherine added, looking over at Elaina for validation, when she nodded in response, Katherine turned back to me and continued her sentence. "There's a gallery opening right in the middle of the upper east side. Maybe they're accepting some applications for internships. Want to go see?" she asked in a tone she usually uses when she's hiding the full truth.

"There is?" I asked, suspiciously.

Elaina nodded. "Yeah, you should check it out; it's breathtaking. Even if they're not hiring or taking applications."

"Sure, when?" Katherine bit her bottom lip, another sign that she's nervous or hiding something.

"Now. Right now," she responded, getting up from the couch.

"Now?!" I exclaimed, completely confused by the timing. We were in the middle of planning her wedding and she wants to stop all of that right now and go to an art gallery that hasn't even opened yet? What is this girl planning?

"Yup! Let's go before it starts raining again," Elaina said. I looked out the window and saw that the rain had stopped, but it wouldn't stop for long.

"Okay, this is crazy." I stood up from the couch, both Elaina and Katherine putting on their raincoats. They stood at the door, waiting for me to join them. "You know what? Yeah, fuck it, let's go." I shook any extra thoughts in my mind and grabbed my jacket and joined them.

We finally made it to the empty gallery after fifteen minutes of going on subways and walking. The gallery was under construction; plain white walls, dust, and plastic sheets were taped to the floors and to various entryways to close off areas. The air smelled of fresh paint and sawdust, the space echoed with the soft hums of our voices.

The open floor plan gave way to massive windows that framed the city skyline like a masterpiece itself. I'd never seen anything like it; it truly was breathtaking. We stepped further inside, my eyes wandering everywhere. "This place…" I said softly, taking it all in.

"Amazing, isn't it?" Katherine said, smiling like her entire plan was going by smoothly.

"See? Told you it was worth seeing." Elaina nudged me.

But something didn't feel right, though. The way they were watching me from a distance, exchanging secretive glances and smiles. My suspicions grew bigger, but I couldn't put my finger on it. I was too distracted by the beauty of this gallery. It was exactly how I pictured my own in my dreams. It was simply love at first sight.

I turned back to them, and as I'm about to ask what's really going on, a familiar voice cut through the silence.

"Luci."

My heart stopped, and my body froze in place. Slowly, I turned to see Micheal stepping out from behind one of the unfinished walls. He dressed casually as always, a dark shirt and dark jeans, his hair perfectly styled in messy waves that made him look effortlessly perfect.

I immediately shot Katherine and Elaina a sharp look that said, 'I'm going to kill you.' "You two planned this, didn't you?" I asked, trying to keep my voice calm. Katherine nodded slowly as Elaina pointed a finger at Katherine, looking elsewhere. Katherine gasped when she saw, slapping Elaina's hand away.

Katherine glanced back at me, grabbing Elaina by her right arm. "We're guilty, but we did it out of a good place! We're just going to leave you both to talk," she said, with Elaina giving me a thumbs up.

Before I could protest, they slipped out of the gallery, leaving me to fend for myself in front of Micheal.

CHAPTER 44
MICHEAL

I stood there, watching Celeste eye her friends as they left the gallery. She stared at the door her friends exited from for a few seconds more before turning back to me. Her eyes look anywhere but at me. I waited silently with my hands in my pockets to stop them from shaking, feeling all the nerves coiling in my stomach.

"What is all this?" she jumped straight to the point, skipping small talk. She crossed my arms, waiting for my answer.

I slightly smirked at her choice of tone and took a step forward; my eyes scanning her face. She looked perfect; I missed looking at that face. "It's a gallery."

"Yes, I can see that," she shot back, her tone sharper this time. "But you know that's not what I meant. Why am I here?"

I looked around the space, searching for my next choice of words. "Do you like it?" I asked, completely ignoring her question. She took a deep sigh before answering.

"It's beautiful," she responded. My heart skipped a beat; I felt instantly relieved that she liked the space.

"Good," I said with a soft smile. "Because it's yours,." I admitted, and she stood still.

I had bought this gallery for her as a gesture of love and an apology. I didn't expect this to fix everything, but I had hoped it would be a start. Her eyes widened, and for what seemed to be the longest time, she was at a loss for words.

She blinked, certain she heard the wrong thing. "What did you just say?"

I shrugged, feigning nonchalance, though my pulse was racing. "This gallery," I said, looking around the space, "I bought it. For you. It's yours; you can do whatever you want with it."

Her gaze darted around the space, taking in the raw potential the gallery held. Her breath hitched for a moment as she understood what I meant. "You–"

"Remember that time we played pool? You lost, and I won? Your bet was that if I lost, I had to pay off all your student loans? Well, that's covered as well," he said, interrupting me.

She let out a nervous chuckle, completely in disbelief. "Ok, wait a second. Just rewind, just so I understand what's happening. You bought me my dream gallery and you're giving it to me? On top of that, you paid off all my student loans?"

I nodded, a smirk growing bigger on my face.

"Why... what? Why would you do that?" she asked.

I stepped close, my voice honest. "Because I know how much this means to you. This is your dream—to run your own gallery to showcase your work alongside other artists. I wanted to give you the chance to make that dream a reality."

She shook my head, clearly overwhelmed. "This is insane. You can't just... I can't take this."

"Yes, you can." I ran his hand up her shoulder as she looked around the space once more before meeting my gaze.

"What's in it for you?" she asked, taking a step back.

"Nothing," I said gently. "You don't have to accept it if you don't want it. But please just... take it. Make it yours. Turn it into everything you've ever dreamed of."

"You're crazy," she whispered under her breath. She turned

her face to the side, blinking rapidly. When she finally met my gaze again, her eyes shimmered with unshed tears. "I—" She didn't even bother finishing her sentence.

She ran out the door and straight into the rain, not caring if she got wet or not. With little thought, I ran after her.

"Celeste!" I called after her, my voice cutting through the heavy patter of the rainstorm. She wouldn't stop; she kept walking further and further away. Her arms wrapped around her tightly as she continued, her steps quick.

The downpour soaked through my clothes and hair instantly; the cold sting of rain was nothing compared to my desperation for her.

When I finally reached her, I grabbed her wrist and forced her to turn and look at me. "Will you just stop for one second?" I urged, my voice filled with emotion.

She roughly pulled her arm away from my hold and shot me a glare mixed with anger and vulnerability. "Why? God! I feel like I just keep asking you the same damn question! What do you want from me?!" she claimed, her voice slightly trembling.

Water dripped down my face, my soaked shirt clinging to my skin. Stepping closer to her, I slammed my chest against hers, ignoring the rain pouring down on us. "I feel like I'm telling you the same damn answer! I want you!" I exclaimed back. "Am I so nuts to say that I missed you like crazy? I mean, I'm practically going insane here!"

"No, I don't think it's nuts. I think it's ridiculous. You missed me? You used me, lied to me, and manipulated me into falling for you. All while it was just a game to you," she spat the words out, trying to wrench herself free from my hold, but I only held her tighter.

"You think it was just a game to me? That none of it was real?" I argued, my voice cracking.

She let out a sharp, humorless laugh. "Are you seriously asking me that? Micheal, you *stole* from me! You destroyed everything I worked for, everything I was! Do you have any idea what you took from me?"

Her voice broke at the end, and the sound of it gutted me. She wasn't just angry—she was broken. I felt it in the way she trembled, in the way her chest rose and fell as if she were struggling to breathe past the weight of it all.

"I lost my dream job. My entire career—ruined. The people I respected, the connections I spent years building, gone. I was supposed to make something of myself, and now? I'm nothing but a joke. A cautionary tale about the stupid girl who trusted the wrong man." She shook her head, rain soaking her hair and clinging to her face. "So tell me, Micheal. *Why?* Why did you do it?"

I swallowed hard. My throat was dry, but I owed her the truth.

"I never meant to hurt you," I said, my voice barely above a whisper. "I took the job before I even knew you existed. It was supposed to be simple—get close, get information, swap the painting. But then you happened, and everything changed."

Her eyes burned into mine, a mixture of betrayal and disbelief. "That's not good enough."

"I know," I admitted. "I know it's not. But I swear to you, Celeste, somewhere along the way, I stopped caring about the painting. I stopped caring about the money. All I cared about was *you*."

Her breath hitched, but the fire in her gaze didn't waver.

I exhaled sharply, gripping her hands as I sank to my knees before her. "I love you," I murmured, rain dripping from my hair, my clothes soaked through. "I know I don't deserve you, and I know I ruined everything. But I swear to you, Celeste, I never wanted to hurt you."

She stood there, staring down at me, her hands still in mine. For the first time, she didn't pull away.

"Please," I begged, my pride burning along every syllable

leaving my lips. She glanced down at me, through her eyes, I saw the gates to her soul, and for a split second, she scraped those gates open, allowing me to feel and see her weaknesses, her fears. In that exact moment, I understood what love was.

Love... it's when pride burns to ashes and dust. It's when you could give less of a fuck of what others thought of you; what matters is how that one person saw you, and how desperately you'd be willing to change that perspective for the better.

"Get up," she stuttered, shivering as she stood above me.

"I'll do anything and everything," I responded hopelessly. "I'm just a man, but I'd give you the world if you asked for it. I don't know how I'd get it, but I know I wouldn't stop until you held it in your hands." I said, my throat was clogged with emotions, whipping the rain droplets off my face.

Before she could open her mouth to respond, I continued. "You want to burn it? I'll pass you the match and stand by your side to watch the ashes fall at your feet. You want to drown it? I'll give you every source of water I can find; even my sweat and tears are yours. You want to destroy it? I'll hand you the weapon of your choice, even if it means that I'd get destroyed along with it too. I'd accept it, if it meant I'd be with you."

Her eyes clouded with tears once again, and she glanced up at the sky, allowing the rain droplets to mix with her tears. "Why are you making this so complicated? This should all be easier, simpler."

"You and I were never simple to begin with." I stood up, searching her eyes for the answers I so badly wanted to find.

"We weren't," she agreed, her voice small and fragile.

"But why would you ever want to be simple? It's a synonym for the word boring, plain, and bland. You and I are splattered paint on a blank canvas, we're the mess in the masterpiece. The chaos that ties it all together." Then, when I thought I wouldn't get her attention, she tilted her head to the side and gazed into my eyes.

"Yeah, but it sounds too messy, even for us. That chaos will probably never settle; we're likely destined to burn each other out."

I stepped closer, not wanting to be an inch apart from her. "You're probably right." I said. She frowned at my words, confused and disappointed. "But let me tell you something," I said, holding her face in both my hands. "Even if we do burn out, I'd much rather burn brightly with you than slowly fade on my own." She lets out a heavy breath she'd been holding in this entire time. "Wouldn't you say the same?" I asked, my body shaking in the cold.

Her lips parted, but no words came out. Instead, her fingers lightly brushed against my shirt as though testing whether I was really standing in front of her, whether this was real.

I held my breath, waiting for her answer.

Her eyes flickered to my eyes and lips, her breath slow and heavy. My pulse quickened as I stood still, allowing her to make the move. For a moment, we stared into each other's souls, appreciating the quiet storm of each other's emotions.

Then, ever so slowly, she reached up, her hands slightly trembling as they brushed against my wet face and hair. I waited, hoping, wishing she'd do something.

Suddenly, without a word, she leaned into me, her lips pressed gently against mine. I let out the breath I was holding, beyond relieved. Her kiss felt like home and even though I was standing in the middle of the cold rain, I felt warm and safe.

"I'll take the gallery if you work with me," she murmured against my lips.

I nodded, "Anything you wish."

"Then yes, I'd say the same," she smiled, kissing me again. I wrapped my arms tightly around her, and just like that, I felt alive again.

CHAPTER 45
MICHEAL

For years, I wondered what my purpose was. I struggled through life, searching for something I didn't quite understand. That was until I met Celeste; she swirled into my life as an unbearable person and shaped my life into what it is. She became my favorite person, and suddenly, I wasn't just searching anymore—I was living, and for the first time, I could see a future I was excited for.

"Let's move the name a bit more to the left," Celeste voiced, tilting her head as she directed the handyman fixing the letters atop the gallery's entrance. She stepped back, admiring the sleek black font.

The name, "Lucí" was bold, standing out against the cream-colored wall.

"Perfect," she assured the handyman, allowing him to climb down the stairs.

"Luci—like the light?" the handyman asked as he looked up at the name. Celeste smiled as she switched her gaze to me.

"Yes, Luci—like the light," I responded, holding Celeste's right hand. She tugged my arm and pulled me inside, urging me to continue working.

We're preparing the gallery for the opening next weekend, and behind the scenes, I was pulling some strings with Dylan, who worked with me as an art provider. He would push new artists into our arms and in return we would give him a piece of the pie: ten percent annually for his contributions.

The good news was that the gallery was quickly coming together. Faster than we'd imagined and just the way we wanted. The ceilings featured a geometric grid pattern with ceiling lights, adding dimension to the space. The wooden floorings added warmth to the modern, minimalist space we were creating, balancing the color scheme.

We had placed modular white partition walls to display the art. Panels that allowed flexibility in curating exhibitions, making the artwork stand out more. The tone space, gray ceiling, white walls, and wooden floor served as a subtle canvas for the dynamic artwork we would soon bring in.

As an opening gift to Celeste, I had our first piece imported from Seoul. I had tracked down Kim Whan-Ki's 여름태양 *Summer Sun 14-III-72;* Which is a known beautiful piece that combines traditional Korean aesthetics with modern abstract. There's a combination of yellow, red, brown, and orange. It's meant to be vibrant, sun-like hues. Looking at it brought a sense of light and warmth. It was one of my favorite pieces and I'd hoped she felt the same way about it as well.

I hung it on the first panel and stood back to admire it. Celeste walked over, her gaze fixed on the vivid colors contrasted against the minimalist panel. She stared at the painting in awe, her eyes softening as a small smile appeared on her face. "It's beautiful," she said, her voice warm. "How did you get a hold of it?"

I shrugged. "A friend of a friend back home," I responded, turning my gaze on her. I had gotten it from a friend of Nari's; she had plenty of connections to the art world in Korea as much as she did in nightlife.

Celeste sighed and turned her body to face me. "So far, you're an even better business partner than I thought you'd be," she said, running her hands up my arms.

"Is that supposed to mean that you thought I'd be a horrible one?" I asked, arching a brow at her as I wrapped my arms around her waist.

"Well... I didn't exactly say that..." she responded, slightly leaning back.

My lips thinned, feeling the tiniest bit offended. "So, you *did* think I'd be a disaster?"

Celeste chuckled, her eyes sparkling with mischief. "Not a disaster, just..." she paused, trying to find the right words

"Just?..." I pressed, eager to hear what she would say.

"A procrastinator," she voiced, my eyes widened.

"Procrastinator," I repeated, my tone playful. "Remind me who brought in this spectacular piece and negotiated the deal with Dylan again?"

"Okay, fair," she admitted, tilting her head. "You've proved me wrong, big time."

"Indefinitely," I said, leaning closer. "I must say, your expectations for me were quite low. I can't help but feel offended, and I deeply believe you owe me an apology for doubting me."

"Oh, do I?" she teased, her voice dropping to a soft, sultry note.

"You do," I murmured, my gaze fixed on hers. "I think I know how you can make it up to me."

Her lips curved into a sly smile, and she stepped out of my arms, turning toward the wall where we'd hung *Summer Sun*. "Well, if I do owe you this apology, it'll have to be after we finish working. We've got plenty to do."

I groaned, running a hand through my hair. "Didn't your parents teach you that the best apologies are the ones done in the moment?"

"Nope, I'm Latin," she responded over her shoulder, glancing back at me with a wink.

"What's that supposed to mean?" I asked, chuckling as I followed behind her. She continued to walk, paying no mind to me.

∼

Around midnight, we had left the gallery fixed and spotless. Every inch of the space was ready to become the new home to some of the greatest pieces in New York. Celeste and I stood side by side, overlooking the place with a shared sense of accomplishment.

"Now that all our 'work' is done. I should now be receiving this apology from you," I voiced quietly, softly filling the silence.

"Don't you mean to *hear* my apology? It's something vocal Micheal," she corrects me with sass.

I let out a half chuckle, shaking my head slightly. "Oh no, Luci," I said, using her nickname, my voice dipping lower. "You made me wait. You're going to make me *feel* this apology."

Her brows narrowed as she tried to understand what I was hinting at. I knew she wouldn't have the slightest clue about the apology I had in mind.

"Wait here," I said, my voice soft but commanding. I hurried to the back, where I had left a blank canvas and an open purple paint bucket. With one hand, I held the canvas and with the other, I carried the paint. I headed back outside and placed the things on top of a plastic sheet.

Celeste only seemed more confused, her eyes narrowed in a playful suspicion. "You want me to paint something for you?" she asked, tilting her head as she walked towards the canvas.

"Not exactly," I replied, a small smile tugging at my lips. "*I'm* painting today." I reached for her hand, pulling her gently closer to the setup. "I don't have a paintbrush. So…" My eyes held hers as I let the words hang in the air, teasing her curiosity. "You're going to be my tool for this piece. Yes?"

Her eyes widened slightly, her expression a mix of amusement and disbelief. "Okay…" she replied, drawing out the word cautiously. "What exactly do you mean by that?"

"Step onto the plastic," I instructed, choosing to let her question hang in the air. I guided her into position in front of the canvas. She hesitated for only a moment before following my lead, the soft crunch of the plastic beneath her heels the only sound between us.

"Take off your shoes," I said gently, my tone leaving no room for argument. She complied, kicking off her glossy black heels and leaving them to the side. I knelt down briefly, picking them up and placing them neatly out of the way.

"Micheal," she said, her voice carrying a hint of a warning. "What are you planning to do?"

"Do you trust me?" I asked, standing and brushing my hands off my pants.

She sighed, rolling her eyes but smiling. "Yes…"

My voice dropped slightly, its tone calm but commanding. "Now," I began, letting the word linger between us, "take off your dress and lay on your back on top of the canvas." I gestured toward the blank white space behind her.

With a slight pause, she unzipped her dress from the side and shrugged out of it. Underneath she had a delicate lace bralette with a black lace panty. I smirked at what she chose to wear underneath her dress when we were supposedly working all day today.

Her smile matched mine as she turned slowly, and did what I asked.. I stepped closer, positioning her body precisely where I wanted her. "Perfect," I murmured, my voice barely above a whisper.

Before she could say another word, I reached into my back

pocket and pulled out a black silk blindfold. Her eyes widened as she caught sight of it. "Micheal," she voiced, a nervous laugh bubbling from her lips. "What—?"

"Shh." I placed a finger to her lips, silencing her. "You trust me, don't you?"

Her breath hitched, and she nodded as I slid the blindfold over her eyes, tying it securely at the back of her head. "This is a new level of apology," she said, her voice softer now, carrying an edge of vulnerability and humor.

I leaned in close, my lips brushing the shell of her ear. "Best apology ever," I whispered.

I reached for her wrists, carefully bringing her hands to the top of her head. "Hold still," I said as I wrapped a rubber band around them, not tight, just enough to keep her hands in place.

"Is that a rubber band?" she chuckled, struggling to pull her wrists apart.

"Shh," I responded, suppressing a grin as she giggled under her breath.

Stepping back, I took in the sight of her—blindfolded, restrained, laying on top of the blank canvas like a living masterpiece waiting to be created.

"Okay…" I said, dipping my fingers into the purple paint. "This might feel weird at first," I warned as I hovered over her.

At first, her body stiffened as she anxiously waited for me to begin. I watched her back arch as the cool paint touched her skin. Her breath hitched at the sensation, her back pressed against the canvas again. I couldn't help but watch her with admiration, surrendering herself completely to me.

I dipped my finger into the bucket of paint again and brought my finger to her chest. "Don't move," I said as I kissed her chin as I traced the first letter, M. Then the next letter, I, dragging my finger between her breasts. N, the next letter traced on her abdomen.

My breath was ragged as I wrote the last letter, E, right under her navel. I looked at the word MINE vertically down her body.

When I reached for more paint, the paint tilted over. Not only on her, but on the canvas behind her. She shrieked, giggling at my mistake. I placed my lips at the crook of her neck and laughed along with her.

"Now this..." I whispered in her ear as I traced my paint covered hand up the side of her waist. "This is *art*," I breathed, my voice thick with praise. I couldn't help it—my hand ran over her body, tracing and memorizing every curve and every inch of her skin. "A masterpiece that only *I* get to admire." I lost myself in the feeling of her beneath me, and it wasn't the paint. It was the trust, the love, and power I felt in this moment.

"Do you want to see how beautiful the painting is?" I forced myself to stand over her and acknowledge the painting from further away. In that moment, I realized that between us, I was no longer the one in control of pulling the strings. I was now completely tied up in everything that had to do with her. I could feel it in the weak spot in my knees that had never existed before. It was exhilarating, almost dizzying, as if my body knew how I felt way before I did.

Her chest rose and fell under the cold and without hesitation, I fell to the floor, slowly and deliberately. I traced my lips up the length of her glossy legs, between her thighs, until I reached the place where she held all the power.

"There's only one thing left to do," I murmured, my voice rough with desire as I pressed a lingering kiss to the inside of her thigh.

"W-what?" she stuttered, a shiver running through her as I began my slow ascent.

"I need to sign my art." My lips trailed upward, grazing over the soft skin of her stomach before I made my way to her ribs, then her collarbone. "I want to leave my mark here..." I pressed a kiss to her shoulder, then another, slower this time. "...and here…" My mouth moved down the column of her throat. "Everywhere."

Her body levitates, trying to move away from me. I pulled her back down, waiting for her answer. When she doesn't say anything, I move up, my chest now resting against hers. "What about me?"

"Hmm?" I hummed as I continued to kiss my way up her body again.

"Don't I get to sign something as well? I have just as many rights to this painting as you do," she responded.

"You can sign it; we both can. It'll be ours forever."

"Untie me," she whispered, bringing her tied hands between us.

"Why would I do that?" I asked, curious of her response.

She leaned closer, managing to whisper right into my ear regardless of being blindfolded. "I need to make sure my signature comes out perfect," she said, her breath hot against my skin, making my cock pulse. I instantly felt goosebumps and with one quick bite, I broke the rubber band.

She wrapped her legs around my waist and her arms around my neck. I unzipped my jeans and pulled my throbbing cock out. Within seconds, I was inside her. Her gasps and moans mingled with mine as we moved together in a rhythm that felt natural, familiar. Our connection was undeniable and our souls tangled together in ways that could leave someone breathless.

In that moment, there was only the wright of her hand in mine, the warmth of her skin against mine and the paint that traced our every movement.

I wanted nothing more than to be here, with her now and forever. For she was the only thing in my life that made sense.

CHAPTER 46
CELESTE

It was opening day for our gallery, and we had invited every single one of our friends to celebrate. Katherine showed up with Adam and Aaron; their voices filled the room as they conversed with familiar faces. As for Elaina, she had texted earlier to say she was running late. "I'm bringing a surprise," she'd written cryptically, leaving me curious and a little impatient.

Micheal had his half-brother Min Ho flown in along with his young son, Juno. They walked toward me, and I couldn't help but smile. Min Ho and Juno wore a matching grey turtleneck; it was the cutest thing I'd ever seen.

"Juno, say hi to Celeste," Min Ho encouraged, his voice gentle and full of patience.

Juno gripped Min Ho's hand as he slightly moved closer, shy and nervous. "Hi," he mumbled, his face facing the ground.

"Hi Juno!" I said, crouching to meet his eyes. "I love your sweater; it's very stylish," I complimented. He slightly tilted his head up, looking into my eyes. A small smirk appeared on his lips, his face lighting up with the smallest effort.

"Thanks, dad picked it!" he exclaimed, his finger digging into his neck. He was so proud to be matching with his dad.

"He must always be happy to match with you." I said, smiling up at Min Ho. He chuckled low, slowly shaking his head.

"Hardly. Juno fought me on these matching turtlenecks for thirty minutes." Juno looked up at his father, scrunching his nose.

"Did not!" Juno protested, tugging down Min Ho's arm.

Micheal came into the conversation, resting his hand on my lower back. "Well, those thirty minutes of war definitely paid off. You look good, buddy," he said, ruffling Juno's hair.

"Thanks, Celeste said so too," he replied, his cheeks a bit flushed. *So adorable*, I felt like pinching his cheeks.

"Yup. Now, why don't you explore all the new paintings we have with your dad? You let me know what you think about the place, okay?" I smiled, rubbing Juno's arm.

"Okay!" He exclaimed, pulling Min Ho's arm and directing him to another part of the gallery. Min Ho ran behind him, following him.

Across the room, I spotted Dylan lingering near one of the displays. Micheal had told me everything about him, including that he got him to provide these abstract high listed pieces for the gallery. He raised his glass when Micheal caught his gaze.

We walked over to him at the same time Katherine did, along with Adam and Aaron. "Dylan is it?" Katherine asked, placing her hand out for him to shake. "This is Adam and Aaron, they've been dying to meet who helped Micheal find the abstract pieces."

"Uh yes, he's been brilliant," Micheal added, announcing our presence in the conversation.

"Helping isn't the word I would use," Dylan finally responded, locking eyes with Adam. "I'd say I mostly supervised and gave orders."

"I'm sure you do plenty of that," Aaron grinned, his voice tight with tension.

Dylan chuckled, his eyes flicking between the Pearson brothers. "You could say that."

Just as I turned to check my phone for Elaina's message, the door opened. Everyone's eyes darted toward the door, and Elaina walked in with a tall brunette. "Sorry I'm late!" Elaina said, a little breathless. "But I come bearing your surprise!" She pointed toward the woman.

I let out a loud gasp when I recognized her. "Valery!" I exclaimed, stunned.

Her smile was radiant despite the slight exhaustion in her features. "I'm back," she said simply, opening her arms for a hug.

"Oh, my god!" I exclaimed, pulling her into a tight embrace. Katherine ran behind me and wrapped her arms around our hug.

"How could you not tell us anything?!" Katherine said, just as shocked as I was.

"That's the point of a surprise," she teased. "You know I always love a good surprise."

Once we finished our hug, we stepped back, wanting to hear everything. "How long are you back for?" I asked.

She shrugged effortlessly. "I finished culinary school in Barcelona; I'm here to stay."

"Seriously?" Katherine shirked. "It's going to be just like old times!"

Valery chuckled, nodding her head slowly. No matter how long she's been gone for, she always maintained her elegant demeanor. Her British accent is as polished as ever. God, I missed her; our group will feel complete.

"You look amazing," I said, stepping back to take her in.

"Thank you," she replied, though the faint circles under her eyes told a more nuanced story. "I'm extremely exhausted—but I'm happy to be reunited with my girls."

"So, what do you think?" I said, spinning around, showcasing my gallery.

She let out a small gasp, taking it all in. "Oh, it's breathtaking. I'm so happy I could be here to support you. I've already missed so much—including Katherine's engagement! Which, by the way—"

"Is a story for another time," Katherine interrupted, joining us with a playful grin. "Over some much needed wine."

Valery laughed, shaking her head. "Fine, but you *are* telling me everything later."

"Well," I said, turning back to the room, "let me introduce you to everyone!" When I turned back, the only person missing was Dylan—he left without a word. He must have had an important meeting or something.

I shrugged off the thought and continued to introduce everyone else. Valery finally met Micheal and gave me her famous 'I approve' smiles and continued speaking with the other guests.

As I got lost in a conversation between Adam and Valery, Micheal grabbed my hand and pulled me away. "I'm just going to borrow my girl for a second," he said with a mischievous smile, giving both of them a nod before whisking me away.

"What are you doing?" I whispered, my heart beating faster than normal as he took me to another room in the gallery.

"Ready for one more surprise?" he asked, his voice low.

"Depends what the surprise is," I teased, gripping his hand harder. The anticipation and excitement in his voice were contagious; I suddenly couldn't wait to see what the surprise was.

Though he didn't answer, he only let go of my hand and stood behind me as we stood in front of a familiar canvas. The moment I got a clear look at the canvas, I realized it was the one we'd made together with the title—*I Purple You*—underneath it.

"*I Purple You?*" I asked, my voice soft with awe. A smile tugged at my lips as my gaze roamed the canvas. Then I saw it.

Right in the middle, scribbled in deep violet, were the words: *she and I are splattered paint on a blank canvas.*

Something about it made my eyes sting.

He nodded, stepping closer to me, my back to his chest. "Did you know the phrase 'I purple you' is actually a saying? It means I will trust and love you forever. The color purple is also the last color in the rainbow, meaning our love is never ending. It's infinite."

I shut my eyes as I savored the words coming out of his lips. He wrapped his arms around me, his mouth to my ear. "It belongs here. I want everyone to see it, for it to see us, and only we know the true meaning behind it."

I reached out to touch the edge of the painting, my fingers hovering above the vibrant purples. The chaotic strokes were so raw and perfectly imperfect, like us.

"I love it." I said, my voice soft and full of emotion as I turned to him.

"I love you," he said, his hands sliding down my waist, holding me closer.

"You know, I've got to say. This game between us ended way differently than I expected." he chuckled; his lips brushed mine in a kiss, slow and full of meaning, as if we had all the time in the world.

When we finally broke the kiss, he rested his forehead against mine. "We'll just have to call it fair game," he murmured, his voice sending a shiver down my spine.

"It's a fair game," I echoed, my voice barely above a whisper. As I looked at him, this painting, and the gallery we now called ours, I realized we came a long way. He wasn't perfect, I wasn't perfect, but the ending we created for ourselves was.

We'd call it fair game. We both played to win, but we ended up with more than we could have imagined. And I realized our game was worth playing.

EPILOGUE
MICHEAL

FIVE MONTHS LATER...

"Care to play another round with me?" I asked Celeste as she stood across the pool table with a cue stick. She shrugged lazily, looking unbelievably stunning. We'd just left an art event at Luci gallery; I still wore my suit, and she still wore her black silk dress.

"Are you sure you want to give me this chance for revenge?" She grinned, her eyes sparkling with mischief.

I raised a brow, leaning closer against the table, setting my cue down with a deliberate slowness. "I wouldn't start with the big talk; allow me to remind you who won last time." Her brows narrowed, gripping on her cue stick harder now.

I thought she'd snap back with some sarcastic remark, but she smiled, the challenge in her eyes stronger than ever. "Alright," she began by saying as she slowly walked toward me. "Show me your tricks," she said; I could feel the fire within her tone.

"Why would I do that?" I asked, standing still.

Her smile deepened, and she leaned in just a fraction, her

chest inches away from mine. Her breath warm against my ear as she whispered, "You're scared I might beat you this time."

I couldn't suppress the smile that grew on my lips and the slight thrill that shot through me. "Scared?" I repeated it like it was a joke. "I thought you wanted revenge, not a handout."

"Handouts? I wouldn't call it that. Unless you got these tricks from someone else," she replied, her voice low. "If that's the case…"

I positioned myself behind her, cutting the rest of her sentence off. Reaching down to hold her hand, my chest resting against her back, I lowered my head, my breath now caressing her ear. "Fine, if you want me to teach you…" I gripped her hand around the cue stick. "It's going to require a more hands-on lesson."

My hand enveloped hers, and she followed my back-and-forth motion of the cue stick. "Your moves should always be calculated beforehand," I spoke as she shivered against me. "The way you'd do that is moving the cue about four times before stopping at the point closest to the ball."

She freezes, calculating her current position. "You got it?" I asked, looking at her side profile. She nodded, waiting for my next instruction. "Keep your eyes on the ball. One, two, three—" She hits the ball right into the hole.

"Not bad, but it's not really a trick," she replied as I moved back. I leaned against the pool table, turning to look at her.

"It's a lesson, not a trick," I answered, stuffing my hands in my pockets. She stood in front of me and placed a hand on my chest. Suddenly, she pushed me back onto the pool table. My back slams on the table, slightly moving some balls.

"Look what you did; the ball is so far away from the hole now," she announced, leaning on me. With her cue, she moved my tie to the side.

"Is this how you repay your teacher? This is highly inappropriate, Ms. Castillo," I said as I gazed up at her. Her small smirk fired something within me. She dragged the cut stick down to my zipper and back up to my tie. "It seems like you're enjoying this," I added as I leaned on my elbows.

"Just a tiny bit," she admitted, smiling wider. I leaned up closer to her.

"If you wanted to learn a trick that badly, all you had to do was ask nicely." I wrapped my hand around her waist as I held myself up with my other hand. "I know a teaching technique that might work for you."

Holding onto her tightly, I switched positions with her. Instead of me laying beneath her, now she laid beneath me, her back against the pool table. I grabbed her cue stick and stood between her legs. "Pay attention," I said as I leaned down. "I'll only show you once."

Setting the cue stick on top of her, holding her in place, I aimed at the ball closest to the hole. Her breath hiked as her face got closer to mine.

I could feel the heat in the room rising as I positioned myself carefully, And I tried my best to focus on the game when I had her on the table writhing. I had to keep control, even if everything within me screamed 'fuck it'.

Celeste's chest heaved heavily as I moved my cue stick back four times. "Focus, Celeste," I murmured, a quiet command more for myself than it was for her. My hand gripped the cue stick hard, slightly pulling back.

She held her breath beneath me, her eyes never leaving mine. "Ready?" I asked her, my voice hushed in a whisper as I steadied my shot. Her lips parted, not a word leaving her lips, instead she gave a small nod.

Then, without hesitation, I made the shot, and the ball sank into the hole. I lifted myself off her slowly, my breath heavier than before. "There's your trick," I said, my voice rough.

"Want to see mine?" she asked, her smile still there but softer. I nodded, my body still trapping her on the table. "If I make this, I get to do whatever I want to you." She lifted her head, grabbed an eight ball with her hand and looked back at me. With a swift movement, she threw the ball in the hole with her hands. "Tada," she said quietly.

I chuckled low, leaning back down. She wrapped her arms around my neck and pulled me down for a kiss. "That's cheating," I murmured against her lips.

"Shh," she replied as she ran her hand through my hair. "It's in the hole, is it not?" she whispered.

I smiled, feeling her warmth press against me. "Okay, you win," I whispered back, my fingers trailing down her spine. "I'm all yours."

AFTERWORD

Thank you for reading *Call It Fair Game*! If you enjoyed reading this book, I would greatly appreciate it if you could leave a review on the platform(s) of your choice.

Reviews are good feedback for authors, and every one is appreciated!

With Love,

Amber

ACKNOWLEDGMENTS

First and foremost, thank you to every reader who picked up *Call It Hope*, the first book in the *Call It* series—and to those joining the journey with this second story, welcome. Whether you're returning or just discovering my work, your support means everything to me.

Writing this book has been both a blessing and a privilege. Knowing that these stories are reaching hearts and finding homes among readers continues to inspire me every day.

Celeste and Micheal's story was such a fun, emotional, and romantic journey to write. The enemies-to-lovers trope has always held a special place in my heart, and bringing my own version of it to life has been an unforgettable honor.

To Sarah, my incredible editor—thank you for believing in me. Your sharp eye, patience, and unwavering dedication have helped shape this series into something I'm deeply proud of.

To Julie at Books and Moods—your breathtaking cover art has brought these characters to life in a way words alone never could. Thank you for lending your magic to my stories.

To my family: thank you for being my steady foundation of love and encouragement.

To my amazing sisters—Genesis, Jazmin, Michelle, and Nicole: your strength, heart, and complexity live in every female character I write. You inspire me more than you know.

To my sweet nephew, Miles—the newest joy in our family and the inspiration behind the character of Juno—your auntie loves you more than words can say.

And finally, to every single person who has supported this journey—whether with kind words, a shared post, or simply by turning a page—thank you. Your love, encouragement, and belief in me mean the world.

ABOUT THE AUTHOR

Amber Lee developed a strong passion for reading and writing from a young age. She loves to write contemporary romances with plenty of steam, angst, and swoon. When Amber Lee isn't writing, she can most likely be found reading them, binge-watching dramas paired with sushi, or trying to learn a new language. An introvert by heart and an extrovert by mind, she dreams of traveling the world to learn about various cultures she can add to her stories.

*You can find her online at amberleewriter.com
and on social media @amberleewriter*

www.ingramcontent.com/pod-product-compliance
Lightning Source LLC
LaVergne TN
LVHW091654070526
838199LV00050B/2170